THE HEAT OF THE DAY

Elizabeth Bowen was born in Dublin in 1899, the only child of an Irish lawyer and land-owner. She travelled a great deal, dividing most of her time between London and Bowen's Court, the family house in County Cork which she inherited. Her first book, a collection of shorts stories, *Encounters*, was published in 1923. *The Hotel* (1926) was her first novel. She was awarded the CBE in 1948, and received honorary degrees from Trinity College, Dublin in 1949, and from Oxford University in 1956. The Royal Society of Literature made her a Companion of Literature in 1965.

Elizabeth Bowen died in 1973.

ALSO BY ELIZABETH BOWEN

ELIZABETH BOWEN

The Heat of the Day

WITH AN INTRODUCTION BY

Roy Foster

VINTAGE

TO
CHARLES RITCHIE

Published by Vintage 1998

22

Copyright © Elizabeth Bowen 1948
Copyright © renewed by Spencer Curtis and
Graham Angus Watson 1976
Introduction Copyright © Roy Foster 1998

First published in Great Britain by Jonathan Cape 1949

First published in the United States of America by
Alfred A. Knopf, Inc., 1948

Vintage
Random House, 20 Vauxhall Bridge Road,
London SW1V 2SA

www.vintage-classics.info

Addresses for companies within The Random House Group Limited
can be found at: www.randomhouse.co.uk/offices.htm

The Random House Group Limited Reg. No. 954009

A CIP catalogue record for this book
is available from the British Library

ISBN 9780099276463

Penguin Random House is committed to a sustainable future for
our business, our readers and our planet. This book is made from
Forest Stewardship Council® certified paper.

Typeset in India by Thomson Digital Pvt Ltd, Noida, Delhi
Printed and bound in Great Britain by Clays Ltd, St Ives plc

INTRODUCTION
Roy Foster

Famously, this is a novel about the war, spying and London: precise in place and time, it starts on 'the first Sunday of September 1942' and ends almost exactly two years later. The events of the war punctuate the narrative, marking time for the high points of the story. Stella meets her lover Robert during the fall of France; she hears of the victory at El Alamein during her pivotal visit to Ireland; the climax of her involvement with Robert coincides with the North African landings; Louie's child is born during the Normandy invasion. London is the theatre of action – 'that particular psychic London' of wartime – but the world war is all around. At the same time it is a novel about allegiance on a wider scale, into which Ireland oddly but logically comes. It is no accident that Bowen describes those left in blackout London as a 'garrison society', since that is the very phrase often used to describe her own Ascendancy caste in Ireland. And it is also, in its way, a ghost story.

The Heat of the Day brought Bowen success beyond her other novels, but it was not written easily – perhaps because so much of it came out of intense personal experience. She began it while the bombs were still falling in 1944, sending the completed chapters out of London for safe keeping; her letters record worries about how to introduce 'point-blank melodrama' (a new departure for her) and lurches into humour. The novel was not ready for publication until 1949, when it received tremendous acclaim, restoring the strange atmospheric glamour of an era which already seemed mythological. For her, it recalled a period when she felt, sensed, experienced life more powerfully than she had ever known: not only through her work as an ARP warden and her missions to Ireland for Churchill's government, but through her deep wartime love-affair with a young Canadian diplomat, Charles Ritchie. Stella and Robert share the same ages (and age difference) as Bowen and Ritchie, the Regent's Park location is that of her own house (where she resolutely stayed until bombed out in 1944 – the last to leave 'her' side of the Park) and she dedicated the novel to him. The supercharged intensity of the prose recreates the closeness and strangeness of wartime alliances, the scent of charred wood and the tinkle of glass being swept up on the morning after an air-raid, the enforced new habit of walking everywhere, the chancy excitement of living lives of 'canvas-like impermanence'.

'The war hasn't started anything that wasn't there anyway,' somebody remarks: but it acts as a forcing-house: 'thinning the membrane between the this and the that'. At once ominous and liberating, the conditions of wartime London provided ideal Bowen terrain. Her fiction had already shown a preoccupation with the fracture of things below a surface just beginning to crack, the progress of slippage and collapse, the psychology of hurt and betrayal; the subsidence of houses is a recurring image. In an astonishing short story from the war, 'Mysterious Kōr', she envisages night-time London, with its canyon-like streets and surreal gaps, as the moonlit ruined city in Rider Haggard's *She* – one of the books which had lit her imagination as a child, and remained a talisman.

In the London which Stella slips through with Robert or with Harrison, his nemesis and doppelganger, the blackout creates cinematic effects, and the sense of a sinister enemy hovering overhead calls authenticity itself into question: the language is accordingly tense, nervy, jumpy.

'She came to a stop; he pushed against a door showing a dimmed sign, OPEN. Inside, light came up stone stairs which he took her down; at the foot he held open another door and she walked ahead of him into a bar or grill which had no air of having existed before tonight. She stared first at a row of back-views of eaters perched, packed elbow-to-elbow, along a counter. A zip fastener all the way down one back made one woman seem to have a tin spine. A dye-green lettuce leaf had fallen on to the mottled rubber floor; a man in a pin-stripe suit was enough in profile to show a smudge of face powder on one shoulder. A dog sitting scratching itself under one bar stool slowly, with each methodical convulsion, worked its collar round so that the brass studs which had been under its ear vanished one by one, being replaced in view by a brass nameplate she could just not read. Wherever she turned her eyes detail took on an uncanny salience – she marked the taut grimace with which a man carrying two full glasses to a table kept a cigarette down to its last inch between his lips. Not a person did not betray, by one or another glaring peculiarity, the fact of being human: her intimidating sensation of being crowded must have been due to this, for there were not so very many people here. The phenomenon was the lighting, more powerful even than could be accounted for by the bald white globes screwed aching to the low white ceiling – there survived in here not one shadow: every one had been ferreted out and killed.'

As the brittle stucco houses of London shudder, crack or simply disappear, the apparently undisturbed world outside the beleaguered capital takes on a new symbolic importance. The visits to 'Holme Dene', the Surrey lair of Robert's appalling mother, supply much more than a change of mood. The house itself, part of a monster 'hatch-out' over southern England in the Edwardian era, is a 'man-eater': permanently for sale, rigorously inauthentic in every detail, its unnecessary steps, turnings, alcoves and inglenooks may have bred a traitor. 'Wisteria Lodge', where Anglo-Irish Cousin Nettie has taken refuge with other mentally confused gentlefolk, is equally symbolic: a glossy and *gemütlich* haven for people who are 'not all there', and whose slightly sinister owners refuse to describe it as what it is. But the house which symbolises continuance and integrity is Mount Morris: the Irish demesne which Stella's son inherits, and which she visits in a key section of the book. 'Standing outside the war, it appeared also to be standing outside the present.' But it does not; in fact (neutral though Ireland is), this decayed house represents the possibilities of the future, and the world that is being fought for.

It is no accident that it is located in Ireland, nor that its description recalls Bowen's own home in Cork, Bowen's Court. During the war, she travelled to Ireland and sent back confidential reports to Whitehall on Irish attitudes, Irish morale and Irish politics. These included a strong defence of Irish neutrality (which Cousin Francis, in the novel, similarly

4

defends to uncomprehending English relations). Mount Morris's steward, Donovan, leaves no doubt about his commitment to the war effort: like the London girls Connie and Louie (based on the people Bowen met at her ARP Post), he represents something that is being fought for. Significantly, the surge of energy which the war precipitated in Bowen's writing had already produced her emotionally charged family history, *Bowen's Court*, and a memoir of her Irish childhood, *Seven Winters* (both published in 1942). Here, she faced up to the history of dispossession and antagonism which lay behind seventeenth-century 'planter' families like hers, but stressed the need both for her kind to see themselves as Irish, and for an independent Ireland to accept them as part of its complex historical inheritance. Similarly, in her contemporary articles for the Irish literary journal *The Bell*, and many of her classic wartime short stories, she interrogated questions of belonging, allegiance, and Irishness. *The Heat of the Day* explores this territory too.

Form as well as content required the breaking down of barriers: again in a very Irish manner, Bowen uses language as a strategy to maximise mobility and evasiveness. The shifting world of London at war is replicated in her shifts of tone: idiom invades the opulence of the narrative, conversations are risky, inverted, interrogative. Careless Talk Costs Lives. At the same time the novel sustains a beautiful symmetry – as in the two simultaneous nighttime encounters at its climax, with Harrison, Stella and Louie in the black-out bar, and Robert, his mother and sister in Holme Dene. It is full of doublings: Stella and Louie, for all their differences, are twinned, as Harrison points out; Harrison himself and his quarry Robert even turn out to share a name. Neither 'belongs'; both are in a sense spies. Harrison gapes at Stella's ostensibly elegant life 'like a German in Paris' – and this means an invader, not a tourist. Stella herself, with her supposedly semi-scandalous past, her transient life, her slight vagueness, her speculative intelligence, her furnished flats that do not quite 'reflect' her, is one of Bowen's most memorable heroines. When Roderick remarks that his mother has always 'done what she's liked', Donovan, again, states the essentials: 'I should say she's always done what she could. Whatever she went through, she's very gentle.' But she is also, in a phrase carefully repeated, 'a soul astray'.

That is what war does to people, and what they try to resist. Above all this is a novel about the ties that bind people to each other – tested, sharpened and strengthened through the shared experience of civilians under attack. Over and over again, the images of people being close to each other persists: on streets, in shelters, at concerts in the park. Louie, flailing around London 'looking for someone to imitate', is also looking for people to be with; the idea recurs of people permeating each other. And this is where the ghosts come in, for not all these people are alive.

'Most of all the dead, from mortuaries, from under cataracts of rubble, made their anonymous presence – not as today's dead but as yesterday's living – felt through London. Uncounted, they continued to move in shoals through the city day, pervading everything to be seen or heard or felt with their torn-off senses, drawing on this tomorrow they had expected – for death

6

cannot be so sudden as all that. Absent from the routine which had been life, they stamped upon that routine their absence – not knowing who the dead were you could not know which might be the staircase somebody for the first time was not mounting this morning, or at which street corner the newsvendor missed a face, or which trains and buses in the homegoing rush were this evening lighter by a single passenger . . . The wall between the living and the dead thinned. In that September transparency people became transparent, only to be located by the just darker flicker of their hearts. Strangers saying 'Good night, good luck', to each other at street corners, as the sky first blanched then faded with evening, each hoped not to die that night, still more not to die unknown.'

Harrison is himself like a ghost, who appears, disappears, can sleep anywhere or nowhere, has no continuous being ('Is he anybody?' Robert asks). Even the car hired on the fateful night Stella comes back from Ireland is haunted. Bowen's wartime short stories, like 'The Demon Lover' or 'The Happy Autumn Fields', return again and again to supernatural themes, and *The Heat of the Day* similarly evokes the uncanny: it is a world possessed, where the dead go on recharging the atmosphere with their 'torn-off senses'. Bowen herself described the way that war dissolved psychic as well as social frontiers: 'I felt one with, and just like, everyone else. Sometimes I hardly knew where I stopped and somebody else began . . . Walls went down; and we felt, if not knew, each other. We all lived in a state of lucid abnormality.'

The Heat of the Day, as the title implies, powerfully evokes the union and alliance of battle – without sentimentality or self-congratulation. Only in the rapid last pages, where time is suddenly opened out like a fan and the struggle for Europe pushed to its conclusion, are the words 'us' and 'we' insistently used for the Allied war effort. By then, the larger issues are triumphantly clear. Bowen herself, years afterwards, reflected on her wartime short stories in a judgement which also encapsulates the achievement of this novel: 'Every writer during this time was aware of the personal cry of the individual. And he was aware of the passionate attachment of men and women to every object or image or place or love or fragment of memory with which his or her destiny seemed to be identified, and by which the destiny seemed to be assured . . . Through the particular, in wartime, I felt the high-voltage current of the general pass'.

1

That Sunday, from six o'clock in the evening, it was a Viennese orchestra that played. The season was late for an outdoor concert; already leaves were drifting on to the grass stage – here and there one turned over, crepitating as though in the act of dying, and during the music some more fell.

The open-air theatre, shelving below the level of the surrounding lawns, was walled by thickets and a few high trees; along the top ran a wattle fence with gates. Now the two gates stood open. The rows of chairs down the slope, facing the orchestra, still only filled up slowly. From here, from where it was being played at the base of this muffled hollow, the music could not travel far through the park – but hints of it that did escape were disturbing: from the mound, from the rose gardens, from the walks round the lakes people were being slowly drawn to the theatre by the sensation that they were missing something. Many of them paused in the gateways doubtfully – all they had left behind was in sunshine, while this hollow which was the source of music was found to be also the source of dusk. War had made them idolize day and summer; night and autumn were enemies. And, at the start of the concert, this tarnished bosky theatre, in which no plays had been acted for some time, held a feeling of sequestration, of emptiness the music had not had time to fill. It was not completely in shadow – here and there blades of sunset

9

crossed it, firing branches through which they travelled, and lay along ranks of chairs and faces and hands. Gnats quivered, cigarette smoke dissolved. But the light was so low, so theatrical, and so yellow that it was evident it would soon be gone. The incoming tide was evening. Glass-clear darkness, in which each leaf was defined, already formed in the thicket behind the orchestra and was the other element of the stage.

The Sunday had been brilliant, without a stain of cloud. Now, the burning turquoise sky of the afternoon began to gain in transparency as it lost colour: from above the trees round the theatre there stole away not only colour but time. Music – the waltzes, the marches, the gay overtures – now began to command this hourless place. The people lost their look of uncertainty. The heroic marches made them lift up their heads; recollections of opera moulded their faces into unconscious smiles, and during the waltzes women's eyes glittered with delicious tears about nothing. First note by note, drop by drop, then steadily, the music entered senses, nerves, and fancies that had been parched. What first was a mirage strengthened into a universe for the shabby Londoners and the exiled foreigners sitting in this worn glade in the middle of Regent's Park. This Sunday on which the sun set was the first Sunday of September 1942.

Pairs of lovers, fatigued by their day alone with each other, were glad to enter this element not themselves: when their looks once more met it was with refreshed love. Mothers tired by being mothers forgot their children as their children forgot them – one held her baby as though it had been a doll. Married couples who had sat down in apathetic closeness to one another could be seen to begin to draw a little apart, each recapturing some virginal inner dream. Such elderly people as had not been driven home by the disappearance of sun from the last chair fearlessly exposed their years to the dusk, in a lassitude they could have shown at no other time.

These were the English. As for the foreigners, some were so intimate with the music that you could feel them anticipate every note; some sat with eyes closed: others, as though aroused by some unbearable movement inside the breast, glanced behind them or quickly up at the sky. Incredulity, as when waking up from a deep sleep, appeared once or twice in faces. But in most of them, as they continued to sit and listen, stoicism only intensified.

A proportion of the listeners were solitary; and, of the solitary, those who came every Sunday, by habit, could be told from those who had come this Sunday by chance. Surprise at having stumbled upon the music was written on the faces of first-timers. For many, chiefly, the concert was the solution of where to be: one felt eased by this place where something was going on. To be sitting packed among other people was better than walking about alone. At the last moment, this crowned the day with meaning. For there had been moments, heightening towards the end, when the Sunday's beauty – for those with no ambition to cherish, no friend to turn to, no love to contemplate – drove its lack of meaning into the heart.

There were those who had followed the others into the theatre automatically, and who asked nothing now they had sat down. You could observe one or two who remained locked in some unhealing obsession – for instance, an Englishman in civilian clothes who had placed himself towards the outside end of a row, half-way up the slope from the orchestra. On his left a Czech soldier, on his right a bareheaded woman wrapped in a coat, each was spaced out from him by a vacant chair. This man's excessive stillness gave the effect not of abandon but of cryptic behaviour. He sat body bent forward, feet planted apart on the grass floor, elbows lodged on his knees, insistently thrusting the fist of his right hand against and into the open palm of his left. His hat was pulled forward over his eyes. The concentration with which he frowned at his hands showed the music to be no more than a running accompaniment to his fixed thought. Unmistakably he was waiting for something here: he would not change his position or go away until whatever it was had resolved itself. Sound, however, had become a necessary circumstance: having begun to think in it he could not think without it – whenever a number ended in a ripple of clapping he looked sharply up, with an air of outrage and dislocation, as though the lawn had shifted under his feet. He would turn his frown sharply on the conductor – who, facing round at the audience, bowing, let his baton slowly fall to rest at his side – as though to say: 'What are you doing? Go *on*.' Then, in the early minutes of every interval, he would cast about at his neighbours a baited look, as though blaming everyone else there.

That recurrent look of his at first directly encountered no other eye. None the less it had begun to be noted, to be wondered at, then to be lain in wait for – it was at last to be trapped. His right-hand neighbour opened her mouth abruptly.

'That was number seven they've just played.'

He at once looked, distasteful, the other way.

'Like to look at my programme?'

'N'thanks,' he said. Being accosted jerked him near enough to the surface to make him remember he had forgotten to smoke. He felt for his packet of cigarettes, lit one,

12

let the match drop between his knees, then shifted one foot to stamp it out. All was done without looking her way again.

In a voice quick with injury she continued: 'All right, I just thought you might want to know.'

He replied by a pull on his cigarette and a prolonged gaze away past the Czech soldier. Behind the thicket, at the far end of the row, the last silent crackle of sunset was going on.

'I was not just speaking to you – if that's what you thought.'

'Did I?'

'Oh, you did! – now I'm sorry I spoke.'

'Right: then suppose we leave it at that.'

She watched him glance at his wrist watch, meanwhile feeling him calculate whether to move or not. But the orchestra, by coming to the alert, beginning to turn over their sheets of music, looked like beginning to play again – this hope of an end of further annoyance made him turn to look at the speaker, for the first time. He more than looked, he continued to look, he stared at this person, so disingenuous, of a so impassioning wish to be in the right. So strong had become his habit of mind that he saw no behaviour as being apart from motive, and any motive as worth examining twice. His and her eyes met with what was already familiarity; her pertinacity and his rudeness having created a sort of bond between them and brought them to the point of a small scene.

He confronted a woman of about twenty-seven, with the roughened hair and still slightly upward expression of someone who has been lying flat on the grass. Her full, just not protuberant eyes looked pale in a face roughly burned by summer; into them the top light of the roofless theatre struck. Forehead, nose, cheekbones added no more than width. Her mouth was the only other feature not to dismiss; it was big; it was caked round the edges, the edges only, with what was left of lipstick inside which clumsy falsified outline the lips turned outwards, exposed themselves – full, intimate, woundably thin-skinned, tenderly brown-pink as the underside of a new mushroom and like the eyes once more, of a paleness in her sun-coarsened face. It was the lips which struck him and could have moved him, only that they did not. Halted and voluble, this could but be a mouth that blurted rather than spoke, a mouth incontinent and at the same time artless.

She were an imitation camel-hair coat; the chill of dusk had made her turn up the collar and wrap the fullness over her crossed knees. One hand was lost in a pocket; the other, holding the programme by one of its corners across her lap, had a knocked knuckle; also from time to time the pads of the thumb and forefinger rasped on the yellow paper. Brown and white shoes, not bad, had been walked and worn out of shape; veins appeared in the naked arch of her foot, and the profuse softness of hair on her bare legs showed these to have been never pumiced or shaved. About her way of sitting, about as much of her body as her way of sitting could let be seen, there was a sort of clumsy not quite graceless pre-adolescent strength. The effect of her was, at the first glance, that of a predominating number of London girls of this summer when the idealization of Russia was at its height – that of a flying try at the Soviet comrade type. Or at least, this seemed the effect she hoped to convey. But with her this had not been successful, or gone far enough – otherwise why, in the look that met his, should the attempted frankness be so uncertain; and why should colour appear, uneasily burning, under the sunburn of her cheeks? Somewhere hardiness

14

failed her. She had committed herself, by speaking, then by speaking again to him, to the being of something she never was: what crisis of egotism or loneliness had been reached by her in the musical fading light? Egotism could be the more likely; it had been her self not her sex that she had wished to assert.

Their look at each other, across the chair between them, took a second or two. She, during it, faced a man of round thirty-eight-or-nine, in a grey suit, striped shirt, dark-blue tie, and brown soft hat. His unconsciousness, which had been what had mainly drawn her, was now, like the frown with which he had sat through the music, gone; it was succeeded by a sort of narrow, somewhat routine, alertness she did not like. His 'interestingness' – had that been a lie of his profile? No, not quite: now that she had him full-face a quite other curious trait appeared – one of his eyes either was or behaved as being just perceptibly higher than the other. This lag or inequality in his vision gave her the feeling of being looked at twice – being viewed then checked over again in the same moment. His forehead stayed in the hiding, his eyebrows deep in the shadow of his pulled-down hat; his nose was bony; he wore a close-clipped little that-was-that moustache. The set of his lips – from between which he had with less than civil reluctance withdrawn the cigarette – bespoke the intention of adding nothing should he happen to have to speak again. This was a face with a gate behind it – a face that, in this photographic half-light, looked indoor and weathered at the same time; a face, if not without meaning, totally and forbiddingly without mood . . . It could not be enough to say she was discountenanced; her eyes dropped, looking their last at those stained two of his fingers, holding the cigarette.

'We haven't met before?' he finally said, with the air of having at any rate thought this over.

'How do you mean, met?'

'We don't, I mean, know each other?'

'I don't know you,' said she. 'I don't even know who you are.'

'Then that settles that.' (All the same, he seemed not quite certain.)

'Why,' she added, 'are you anyone special?'

'Ha-ha, no. No, I'm sorry to say I'm not.'

'I do know one thing; I know I've never seen you about this park.'

'No, you wouldn't have.'

'You mean you don't ever come here? Of course, I should know you now. I don't ever forget a face: do you?'

'I could,' he said, after thought.

'That must come from you thinking so hard, you hardly notice. All this band and you hardly noticed a note?'

'So, you thought I must want to know what the music was?'

Lest this be too subtle, his tone was unkind enough to drive at least his will to unkindness home – it did: she withdrew from the pocket her other hand in order to, self-protectively, fold her arms. She could be felt to falter behind the barricade; and the programme, let go of by her as though incriminated, fluttered to the ground. She nudged her chin sideways into her turned-up collar, then could but complain: 'You keep wanting to catch me out!'

'You?' he threw back, with a nervy bitten-off yawn, one eye on the orchestra – what *was* holding them up?

'Because *I* can't help what it sounds like; I speak the truth every time. Because I –'

16

'– Oh, pipe down.' He gave a jerk of the head. 'They're off!'

They were: having hung for just that instant more suspended the music now broke with a light crash. The audience let out a breath and settled into its attitudes on the chairs. Evening had gained on the theatre even in that meantime; a more perceptible smell of it stole from under the thickets, rose from the trodden grass. Cigarettes would soon be seen to glow. On the stage, the musicians' grouped, black, seated bodies had fastened to them the faces and hands of ghosts. They were to continue to play till the clock in the distance struck – but for how long, How much longer, it was being wondered in the emptying ranks of chairs, would they be able to see their score?

Louie Lewis – whose name, that evening, was to remain unasked – unfolded her arms to rewrap herself in her coat. She could not, she could never, leave it at that – accordingly, leaning over the empty place, she glumly said, *sotto voce*: 'Going to think some more?'

She had made that impossible. Had she not borne in on him, in her moron way, the absurdities to which thinking in public could expose one, the absurdity with which one exposed oneself? She had given him, the watcher, the enormity of the sense of having been watched. New, only he knew how new, to emotional thought, he now saw, at this first of his lapses, the whole of its danger – it made you *act* the thinker. He could, now, do no better than travesty, repeat in order to judge exactly how much it showed, his originally unconscious trick of the hands; he recalled this trick in his father, not before in himself – but it must have been waiting for him. Yes, he had had recourse to it, fallen to it, this evening out of some unprecedented need for emphasis in the body. Yes, he had been forced to it by the course of what in the strict sense had not *been* thought at all. The futility of the heated inner speed, the alternate racing to nowhere and coming to dead stops, made him guy himself. Never yet had he not got *somewhere*. By casting about – but then hitherto this had always been done calmly – he had never yet not come on a policy which both satisfied him and in the end worked. There never had yet not been a way through, a way round or, in default of all else, a way out But in this case he was thinking about a woman.

She had asked him to go away and stay away: that was the best he could do – she said, last time. What did she expect him to do? She expected him to do whatever he did do: she had no idea what he did, but surely he did do something? – why not get on with that? She had finished up with: 'I'm sorry, but it just is that you don't attract me. Why should we go on wasting each other's time? . . . There's something about you, or isn't something about you. I don't know what.'

He was not, however, through.

He was once again, this evening, on his way to her flat. He proposed, in fact, to be back with her as the clocks struck eight. Up his sleeve he had something – only, the question was, in exactly what manner to bring it out? He had hoped, by sitting down at the concert, to have arrived at the answer before they met.

It seemed to Louie that there was overmuch music at this concert. There was nothing for her but to drop back again into the stupor in which she had been sitting before her notice lit on the thinking man. The quality of the stupor was not much altered – content at having forced him to notice her, she did not look back over their conversation or ask herself what it had come to or where she stood. Unlike him, she did not look at things in the light of their getting or failing to get her somewhere; her object was to feel that she, Louie, *was,* and in the main she did not look back too willingly at what might have been said or done by her in pursuit of that. She had her misgivings; though always, she hoped, no cause for them. She had never had any censor inside herself, and now Tom her husband was gone – he was in the Army – she had no way of knowing if she were queer or not. Possibly she addressed herself to unknown people in the hope of perceiving what *they* thought – she had perceived just enough queerness in this last man to make her fancy he might not be a good judge. She often was disconcerted, but never for long enough to have to ask herself why this happened. Left to herself, thrown back on herself in London, she looked about her in vain for someone to imitate; she was ready, nay, eager to attach herself to anyone who could seem to be following any one course with certainty.

Tom, by this time, had been drafted abroad; more or less she understood him to be in India. In his letters home he expressed the hope that she was getting on well and being a good girl; to this she never had any notion how to reply, so did not. She maintained what had been their married home, a double first-floor room in one of those little houses in Chilcombe Street, and worked every day at the factory in another, not too far distant part of London. In order to continue to meet the rent at Chilcombe Street, she drew, with Tom's consent, on the sum of money which had come to her from her parents, both of whom had been killed by a bomb. She had been the only child of their late marriage; they had been people who, having done well with their little business, or shop, at Ashford, found themselves in a position to sell it and retire; accordingly, when Louie was ten years old, there had been a removal to Seale-on-Sea, where the family had already spent happy holidays. It was at Seale, in the little villa they had so much enjoyed, that the elderly couple had been wiped out during the Battle of Britain. Louie, having been married by Tom early in 1939, was then in London. The marriage had been a surprise to everyone, most of all herself – actually, the goodness of her home and the solidity in every sense of her people had been reassuring: she had been a far from bad match – as for her as a wife, it only could be supposed that Tom, himself solid, a serious and progressing young electrician, had a soft spot for comics. They had happened to meet when he was at Seale on holiday – *how* it should have arrived that she caught his fancy he had not explained to her, and she had never asked. Child of Kent, she had been to London only a few times on a day-ticket before Tom brought her there as a bride. She now, that is to say within these last years, never left London, having been left with no place to go to.

She was lucky, she understood by reason, in being left with Chilcombe Street: few wives of men called up remained placed as they were before. But the idea of Chilcombe Street's being home, which at the best of times had resided in Tom only, had been taken away by him to India. For her part, as things were now, she was glad to get out of it every morning: she neglected the rooms – front and back, opening on one another through an arch across which Tom had fixed a curtain – the Turkey-patterned lino lost its gloss and she went out leaving the big bed slatternly; in revenge, perhaps, for its being so cold all night. Her return from the factory every evening had in one or another manner to be survived – all the fine evenings of this summer there had been the solution of a walk in the park; when it rained, she either sat in a movie or else lay on her bed in a series of heavy dozes alongside the hollow left by Tom's body. In this state, drugged by the rainy dusk, she almost always returned with sensual closeness to seaside childhood; once more she felt her heels in the pudding-softness of the hot tarred esplanade or her bare arm up to the elbow in rain-wet tamarisk. She smelt the shingle and heard it being sucked by the sea.

Louie had, with regard to time, an infant lack of stereoscopic vision; she saw then and now on the same plane; they were the same. To her everything seemed to be going on at once; so that she deferred, when she did, in a trouble of half-belief to either the calendar or the clock. At present, though bodily seated on a chair on a darkening slope listening to music, she was in effect again in the park rose garden, where she had been walking that afternoon. Great globular roses, today at the height of their second blooming, burned more as the sun descended, dazzling the lake. Lagging along the turf between the beds, Louie repeatedly stooped to touch petals, her raspy finger-tips being every time entered by their smoothness. She above all desired to snap two or three of the roses from their stems – had she been alone she would have taken the risk, but she dared not because of her Air Force friend. She had found all men to be one way funny like Tom – no sooner were their lips unstuck from your own than they began again to utter morality.

To divert his attention she had once, even, tried staring up alarmedly at the sky. '*Look* – that balloon there's come all untied!'

21

But his glance had been too brief. 'They don't,' he said to her, tolerant.

'Oh, they do!'

He only resettled his guiding thumb more firmly inside her elbow.

'My husband saw one do,' she improvised. 'He told me.'

'I shouldn't wonder he told you a lot of things.'

The sneer at Tom turned her scarlet – she veered away from roses, rebelliously stiffening her muscles inside the airman's hold. He and she returned to the slope of mound under the ilex where they had already been lying most of the afternoon: here once more she spread her coat out, and he, somewhat absently, set to tickling her behind the ear with a blade of grass. Round them the lawns were dotted with other couples imploring with their extended bodies the yellow last of the sun. To this spot, to which Tom had been so much attached, a sort of piety made her bring any other man: she had thus the sense of living their Sundays for him. She stared up into the tree.

'Not ticklish?' said the airman, dissatisfied.

'What, aren't I?'

'You ought to know,' he said, throwing the grass away. 'Don't you know anything?' He heaved over on to his back, dropping one hand over his eyes; and she, having for the moment forgotten what he looked like, turned round to wonder what was under the hand. Something more began to invade his manner – he began: 'Where was it you said you lived?'

'Why, I never did say.'

'Still, you must live somewhere. You ought to have a nice place, a nice girl like you.'

'Oh, I have,' she said with enthusiasm.

'You have?' He shifted his hand and rolled round his head in order to look at her with increasing interest. 'Still, lonely, all on your own.'

With resentment she thought of the unpicked roses: *so*, why ever should he? 'I'm not,' she promptly said. 'I live with my auntie. She lives with me.'

'Look,' said the reddening airman, 'what's this all of a sudden about having an auntie?'

'An invalid,' threw in Louie even more rapidly. 'Poor thing. Never goes out.'

The airman looked at her harder. 'Come on,' he said, 'we'll drop in and meet the old cup o' tea – Well?'

Louie, sitting up, removed a twig from her hair. 'You have no right to speak of my aunt like that,' she said. (Nor of Tom, either, she added in her own mind.)

'You've never got an aunt any more than I have,' said the airman, stern with sexual anger.

'How was I to know,' she replied, 'you had never got an aunt?'

'You make me sick,' he said, getting up. 'Starting off by saying you were lonely. Wasting my afternoon.' He stood up, pulled at his tunic, slapped at his pockets, finally stooped to brush shreds of moss from his trousers. 'You ought to be ashamed with your husband fighting.'

'Oh dear,' said Louie, disheartened, 'whatever is the matter?'

'Time,' he said aloofly, 'I was getting along.'

'Still, it's been nice,' she ventured, lying there sadly, receiving the last blast of disparagement from his back view as he marched away. However, that was that, and she was now more than even with him about the roses and his mocking of Tom. When she was not disobliging, and she was not always, everything still somehow ended in her being told off – with a resignation no sigh could express she reached out for a new blade of grass and experimentally tickled her own ear, but was still not ticklish. Saddest of all, she found herself without any real desire to return to the roses; she stayed where she was, on the suddenly hard, chill and unloving breast of the lawn, till she saw people moving towards the concert, whereupon she got up and moved after them.

There is a freedom about an outdoor concert: you come or go at will – there is easy passage between the rows of chairs and your step muted by the grass disturbs no one. However, either the punctiliousness of a stranger or the superstition that rules any movement to do with love made the thinker wait where he was for the coming interval. Nothing more now than suffering the music, he sat on tensely, eye fixed on his watch. The music ceased: he shot up, stood, looked round at the thinned-out clapping, then, in the hurry of flight, made his way out past the Czech soldier, along the row of chairs, up the middle gangway. So far, so good.

He paused for less than a second to get his bearings at the theatre gate – whereupon, up came Louie, breathless from her run. 'I've had enough, too,' she said. She swung into step with him like an old companion. 'Looks quite ghosty,' she said of the reach of lawns. 'That must be mist off from the lake.'

'Good night, then,' he said prematurely – for fifty yards more they had to share the path.

'I'm going back home,' she volunteered, 'now, I think.'

'Much the best thing you can do.'

'You mean, the evenings are drawing in?'

They were – the weeping trees, one by one, shivered slenderly in a tide of ground-mist; away on the mound each ilex stained with a little night of its own the after-death shining of the day. Ahead stood, still open, Queen Mary's gate, high gilded plaque and garlands having not yet forgotten their all-day glittering in the sun.

'Are you?' said Louie suddenly.

'What?' he said with a start. 'Going home? No. I've got a date – thanks.'

She took this with unconcern; if anything, she sent him a puzzled look as though wondering how such a thing could be. He quickened his step, she hers. Paths parted, *they* did not – she continued manfully at his side. Riled to a point, he turned on her, saying harshly: 'What I meant was, I'd *go* home, if I were you. You know, you'll land up in trouble one of these days. Tacking on like this. There are funny people about.'

'You mean, *you* might be funny, for all I know?'

'Which *is* your way?' he demanded, stopping dead in his tracks. 'Which? – either,' she said in a struck, preoccupied tone. They were by this time outside the lovely gate; they went legging it down the short serpentine road that, with trees, railings, and air of a private avenue, runs downhill from the Inner into the Outer Circle. Ahead one had still an illusion of wooded distance, out of whose blue and bronzy ethereality rose the tops of Regency terraces – these, in their semi-ruin, just less pale than the sky. They were shells: the indifference of their black vacant windows fell on the scene, the movement, the park, the evening they overlooked but did not seem to behold. Inconceivably, London was behind them. This moment of walking to meet the houses seemed to have its place in no given hour of time – though across it, in contradiction, St Marylebone clock began striking eight. During the first stroke Louie and her companion, apart, and on his side hostile in thought, experienced a fusion of the nerves. He stepped off the kerb, crossing the road obliquely; she followed. 'I don't know your name,' she said.

'No. Why should you?'

She seemed nonplussed. 'Oh, I don't know. I only thought . . .'

'Well, I can't help that. That's eight o'clock.'

'Oh,' cried Louie reproachfully, 'your date!'

The end of the road was definitive: she for the last time turned, looked, with her big lips parted, then was with start-ling completeness gone. He stood in a sort of aftermath of suspicion, not yet sure she might not have picked his pocket, then walked the other way.

2

Stella Rodney stood at a window of her flat, playing with the blind-cord. She made a loop, through which she looked at the street, or coiled the cord round a finger, then swung the finger, making the acorn tap on the pane. The harsh black-out blind, its roller hidden under the pretty pelmet, was pulled some way down, throwing a nightlike shadow across this end of the ceiling; the blind of the other window was, on the other hand, right up. She did not correct the irregularity, perhaps because the effect of it, *méchant*, slipshod, was in some way part of her mood.

Nothing is more demoralizing than waiting about for someone one does not want to see. She mimed by this idiotic play at the window the disarray into which the prospect of Harrison had thrown her – she was too uneasy, felt too much reduced by the whole affair, was too angry to wish to collect herself. From the first he had shown her his imperviousness to everything she felt – would she be able to show him the indignity, if for himself only, of this impervious return? He was forcing his way back.

It was some minutes since she had heard eight strike: she wondered why, since he had got to come, he had not come – she did not yet dare to hope he might not be coming. He was as a rule punctual, wheeling in on the quiver of the appointed hour as though attached to the very works of the clock.

27

Eight had been his choice, and seemed a stupid one unless he intended to take her out to dinner – his not having said so had given her no chance of saying she would on no account dine with him. But it had seemed pointless to quibble as to the hour when he had gained his main point, was coming, and on his own terms. Indeed, she determined not to quarrel again till she had found out, as she should at once this evening, why he was taking this new tone of the person in power. On the telephone, the exaggerated quietness of his voice hinted at some undefined threat – she was at a disadvantage through having avoided knowing him; she had no way of knowing, now it had come to this, how valid a threat of his could be, or what its nature. Having gained his point he was already – which made her ponder – being a little lax in being a little late. As one does when thinking about an enemy, she endowed him with subtleties which, in his case, on second thoughts, were unlikely.

Up to the last half-hour she had at least felt defiant. In so far as she had set the scene at all, everything had been arranged to show that she did not care – either for him, which he should know already, or as to anything more he might have to say. To show the careless negligence of her way of living, she had left the street door unlatched and the door of her flat, at the head of the stairs, ajar: thus it was left to him to make his own way in, unmet half way, without even that little taste of imperiousness to be got from the ringing of a bell, and with the best face he could. This fairly old house in Weymouth Street, of which her flat took up the top floor, was otherwise in professional – doctors' and dentists' – occupation and was accordingly empty at week-ends: below her now were nothing but empty rooms; the caretakers living in the basement almost always went out on Sunday evenings. Silence mounted the stairs, to enter her flat through the door ajar; silence came through the windows from the deserted street. In fact, the scene at this day and hour could not have been more perfectly set for violence – but that was not on the cards. She had recognized in him, from the first, the quietness of a person perpetually held back from some extreme: it had not, however, been till this morning, on the telephone, that the quietness became an extreme itself.

Now the clock had struck, no step could not be his. She did hear a step, and unwound the cord from her finger, on which it left a red spiral weal.

Stella Rodney had taken this flat furnished, having given up the last of her own houses and stored her furniture when the war began. There had been an interlude, up to the late autumn of 1940, in which she had lived in London lodgings. Here in Weymouth Street she had the irritation of being surrounded by somebody else's irreproachable taste: the flat, redecorated in the last year of peace, still marked the point at which fashion in the matter had stood still – to those who were not to know this room was not her own it expressed her unexceptionably but wrongly. Sensitive whitish walls registered every change in the mood of the London weather; a complete and no doubt valuable set of dark glass pictures of Regency goddesses hung round them. The feather-etched chintz encasing armchairs and sofa advertised its original delicacy by being these days always a little soiled: about on the low tables stood high alabaster lamps with pale veined shades. Between the windows, a fragile escritoire had been topped by her, earlier in this week, with a bowl of roses – today, the petals began to fall. Some books of her own were wedged among those not hers in the shelves in the arched recesses. There were two or three *gros point* stools: and against the end wall, just inside the door, was a second, more formal sofa – brocade-covered, heaped at each end with cushions, and long enough for a person, even of some stature, to be able to lie on it full length.

Propped on the chimneypiece above the built-in electric fire were two photographs, not framed yet – the younger of the two men was Roderick, Stella's twenty-year-old son. Over the photographs hung a mirror – into which, on hearing Harrison's footsteps actually upon the stairs, she looked; not at herself but with the idea of studying, at just one more remove from reality, the door of this room opening behind her, as it must. But no, not yet: he was still knocking into something, putting down his hat, out there in the tiny hall. This gave her a moment in which to reconsider – she swung round again, after all, to face him – stood stock still, arms folded, fingers spread over the sleeves of her dark dress. There came to be something dynamic, as he entered, about her refusal to move at all.

She had one of those charming faces which, according to the angle from which you see them, look either melancholy or impertinent. Her eyes were grey; her trick of narrowing them made her seem to reflect, the greater part of the time, in the dusk of her second thoughts. With that mood, that touch of *arrière-pensée*, went an uncertain, speaking set of the lips. Her complexion, naturally pale, fine, soft, appeared through a pale, fine, soft bloom of make-up. She was young-looking – most because of the impression she gave of still being on happy sensuous terms with life. Nature had kindly given her one white dash, lock or wing in otherwise tawny hair; and that white wing, springing back from her forehead, looked in the desired sense artificial – other women asked her where she had had it done; she had become accustomed to being glanced at. That, but only that, about her was striking: her looks, after the initial glance, could grow on you; if you continued to know her, could seem even more to be growing *for* you. Her clothes fitted her body, her body her self, with a general air of attractiveness and ease.

Younger by a year or two than the century, she had grown up just after the First World War with the generation which, as a generation, was to come to be made to feel it had muffed the catch. The times, she had in her youth been told on all sides, were without precedent – but then, so was her own experience: she had not lived before. The early failure of her early marriage had not encouraged her; still she sought equanimity; she wore a sort of hardiness as a poor resource. Her parents were dead; her two brothers had been killed fighting in Flanders while she was still at school. Since her divorce, ironically rendered almost at once unnecessary by her husband's death, she had been left with her son and a life to make for them both: left as they both were, money had been a difficulty, if not a pressing one, Roderick, at school when this war began, was now in the Army – to her, the opportunity to make or break, to free herself of her house, to come to London to work had been not ungrateful. In the years between the wars she had travelled, had for intervals lived abroad; she now qualified by knowing two or three languages, two or three countries, well – having had some idea what she might most usefully do she had, still better, known whom to ask to support her application to do it. She had in her background relations, connexions, and at least former friends. She was now therefore employed, in an organization better called Y.X.D., in secret, exacting, not unimportant work, to which the European position since 1940 gave ever-increasing point. The habit of guardedness was growing on her, as on many other people, reinforcing what was in her an existing bent: she never had asked much, from dislike of being in turn asked. Or, could that have been circumstance? – for by temperament she was communicative and fluctuating. Generous and spirited to a fault, not unfeeling, she was not wholly admirable; but who is?

She now stood watching Harrison make his entrance.

'Good evening?' he said.

'Good evening.'

'I'm a few minutes late. I was listening to that band in the park.'

This was, for some reason, startling. She said: 'Oh, were you?'

Harrison turned back to close the door behind him, but paused to ask: 'Not expecting anyone else?'

'No.'

'Good. By the way, I found your downstairs door on the latch. That in order?'

'Quite. I left it open for you.'

'Thanks,' he said, as though touched. 'So I shut it – that was in order, too?'

She waited for him to come to the end of this in a silence which could not have been more unhelpful. He, having settled with the door, looked at the carpet, at the distances of carpet between them, as though thinking out a succession of moves in chess. Under a slight, if anything humble, frown, his downcast eyes zigzagged from chair to table, from table to stool; step by step he came forward behind his look. He paused by a cigarette box, and, reminded by this, brought his own cigarettes out. 'Mind if I smoke?'

'Do.'

'You won't?'

'No – Then you could have come earlier?'

'Well, I could, as it happened, as things panned out; but I took it that, as we had said eight, before that might not be convenient to you.'

'It has not been convenient that you should come at all.'

Harrison, looking about him for somewhere to drop his match, said: 'Ha-ha – you know, you're the frankest person I know! – *Should* I have found you, say, at around seven?'

'Yes. And I should have been glad to get this over.'

He looked straight at her; this time just failing to utter that maddening little self-contained concise laugh. 'Well . . .' he began, then stopped – one might have thought, helplessly.

She went on: 'What else can you suppose? After what I said to you last time – detestable things I should not have been forced to say – only you could have insisted on coming back!'

He said. 'You talk as if there were rules. All I know is, there's something like nothing else between you and me, even if you don't know it. I'm seldom wrong – and anyhow,' he wound up, 'you told me this was O.K. You said eight o'clock.'

It was her turn to say: 'Well . . .' Tightening her spread-out fingers above her elbows, she looked away from him at the windows across the street. Oblongs of mauve-brown dusk were by this time framed in the white curtains. To point out that he had forced this meeting by an implied threat would be to admit that in her life *any* threat could have force or context at all. She said: 'You had something to tell me?'

33

'I said I wanted a talk – Look, is that an ash tray there?' One hand held cautiously cupwise under his cigarette, he advanced, gained the hearthrug, knocked off the head of ash into a tray on the chimneypiece near her shoulder. 'Pretty,' he said softly. 'All your things are so pretty.'

'What is?' she said sharply.

'Even this ash tray.' He was touching around the rim of it with the tip of a finger; it was an ordinary little enamel-flowered one, from any Chinese shop.

'It's not mine,' she flickered. 'Nothing in this flat is.'

There were, naturally, any number of other ash trays about the room: she put the stratagem in its place by ignoring it. He had brought himself face to face with the mirror and photographs; she went on looking out of the window – only, her stillness and heedlessness became more rigid and arti-ficial. He did something quite unexpected – turned and switched on a lamp.

'You don't mind?'

Mind? On the contrary, this released her; this could make it imperative to black-out the windows. Moving from one to the other, tugging cords, settling folds into place, she tried not to show how welcome the release was. She switched on another lamp, then looked round: he was fixedly staring at the photographs. 'Splendid,' he said. 'I wanted to see these better.'

'You've seen them before.'

'They did always interest me. One of them's very like.'

'Roderick's?'

'Can't say: never met the original – No, I meant the other.'

Stella, turning to the desk, pulled a drawer open, took one of her own cigarettes: she remained with her back to him,

34

slow over the business of lighting it – long enough to at last be able to say with enough indifference: 'Oh, you know him?'

'I know *of* him – know him by sight. I don't say we ever have what you might call met – he might not know me. An attractive chap – at least, so I always think.'

'Do you?' She sat down on the stool by the escritoire, propping her elbow among the letters on the pulled-out flap. Glancing at the letters obliquely, idly, she went on, as idly: 'Oh, you've seen him around?'

That's about it. On his own sometimes, sometimes around with you. To be frank, I'd seen you with him before you and I met.'

'Had you?' she uninvitingly said.

'Yes, So the first time you let me drop in to this delightful flat, I was not altogether surprised when I spotted this. I was on the point of saying, "By Jove, yes; we both know him!"'

'So why didn't you?'

'You see, one never knows – you might have thought me a bit pushing. Also it's a habit of mine to keep my thoughts to myself.'

'I see. But did that amount to a thought? So many people do know each other.'

'Absolutely, yes. But depends who the people are.'

His uneven eyes met hers, across the hoops of lamplight, the more intently for showing no change of expression. 'Anything is a thought when one person is you,' he said. 'Girl I met asked me only this afternoon if I ever forgot a face: I said, sometimes. I was about right, I think – never a face that interests me. *There,*' he said, eyeing the photograph, 'is one case in point.'

'Indeed? Robert Kelway ought to be flattered.'

Harrison uttered a deprecating laugh. He then said: 'Ever mentioned my name?'

'You mean, has he mentioned your name to me?'

'No; have you mentioned my name to him?'

'I've no idea; I may have; really I don't remember.' She paused and ground out her cigarette. 'Look here,' she said, 'you asked yourself here this evening – it would not be too much to say that you forced your way in – because, you said, it was urgent that you should tell me something. Just exactly what have you come to say?'

'As a matter of fact, that is what I've been getting round to. Now we've got there, I hardly know how to put it.'

She, on her side, could not have sat looking blanker. It was a trick of Harrison's to drop rather than raise his voice for emphasis: he thus now said ultra-softly: 'You should be a bit more careful whom you know.'

'In general?' Stella returned, in a tone which by contrast was high and cool.

He had, as though under instruction, kept his eyes on the photograph. 'Actually, I did rather mean in particular.'

'But I am. For instance, I did not want to know you.'

He took two or three more pulls on his cigarette – perhaps to steady himself, perhaps not – before, still frowning with concentration, unloading more ash on the Chinese tray. His mind was, where she was concerned, a jar of opaquely clouded water, in which, for all she knew, the strangest fish might be circling, staring, turning to turn away. She glanced at her wrist watch, glanced again at her letters, felt gooseflesh, bit off a nervous yawn.

'That's not so much what I mean,' he went on, 'about taking care. Care should come in more where there's someone

36

you do like knowing – with me, as you say, so far that does not apply. Good: that's that – for the moment. You shy off me because I am not your sort; you can't get me taped because you feel something's missing. I agree: there is – if you cared, I could tell you what. No, I'll tell you – vanity. That's been left out of my composition. You turn round one fine day, for instance, and tell me you can't abide me – after which that, you think, is the end of that.'

'Yes, I do. I imagine most people would.'

'Most people you know might. To me, that is simply one more thing that you say.'

'I can't help that,' said Stella, 'it's what I mean. You imagine everyone puts on acts?'

'You think *I* put acts on?'

'I haven't even thought. I do not care what you do.'

'Neither do I,' said Harrison promptly, pleased. 'I don't care what I do. That's where it comes in – no vanity!'

'I should have said, no feeling,' she abstractedly said. (She was thinking, was that to be, after all, all? Had he hinted and threatened his way in, his way back, for nothing more than one final bid at self-salesmanship, one last attempt to 'interest' her? But then – this was itself a point – how had he known she had melodramatic fears? How had he guessed her to be a woman with whom the unspecified threat would work?)

'Yes, it's that,' she went on. 'You can't understand feeling.'

'I don't understand fine feelings – if that's what you mean. Fine feelings, you've got to have time to have: I haven't – I only have time to have what you have without having time, if you follow me? You and the types you go with, if I may say so, still seem to fancy love makes the world go round. For me it's a bit of a spanner in the works.' He directed a look past

37

her, at some shadow behind her head. 'You like to trust the people you like to know?'

'I suppose so. Why?'

'As to one of them, I could tell you a thing or two that might surprise you.'

'Why, what are you then – a private detective?' She laughed, genuinely and without a touch of hysteria. 'To be fair,' she said, 'before we go any further I ought to tell you, I do often wonder whether you are quite ordinary in the head. That's to say, I still wonder – you know what I took for granted you were, originally.'

'Frankness again, ha-ha,' said Harrison. 'Yes, what a day that was. However, we cleared up *that* misunderstanding.'

'I'm not so sure.'

'What, though, makes you wonder specially now?'

'I don't know. I suppose, in some way, the war.'

'Oh, you mean the war? Yes, it's funny about the war – the way everybody's on one side or the other. Look, I insist on your smoking one of my cigarettes!'

He came across to her with his case open: it was as hypnotizing as being offered a cigarette across a consulting-room desk or a lawyer's table, and with just that rebellious subservience she had to take one. He returned the case to his pocket, then struck a match – but he fumbled over the business; the flame shook and she drew unkindly back to stare at the shaking hand. He observed it also: 'Yes, funny, you know,' he said, 'this has never happened. Must be being here with you, all on our own like this, if we *are* doing nothing better than splitting words – Look here, if it's your nature that's up against me, *be* up against me; it's your nature I want – you as you are.'

'Exactly what do you want?'

'You to give me a break. Me to come here, be here, in and out of here, on and off – at the same time, always. To be in your life, as they call it – your life, just as it is. Except –' He stopped, to mark the crux of the matter, command himself and, from then on, alter his tone. He returned to the fireplace, picked up the photograph, turned it face to the wall. 'Except,' he said, 'less of that. In fact, none at all of that. No more of that.'

She could not believe he was saying what he could be heard to say, so looked at him in hardly more than surprise. Evidently he thought she was acting blank. 'Don't let's waste time,' he said. '*I* know how it is. I've checked up on that affair.'

She said, indifferently: 'I imagine most people know.'

'Most people don't know the half – in fact, no one does. Certainly not you.'

'What don't I know?'

'What I know.'

'You want me to ask what that is?'

'Better not, I think. Better just take the hint.'

'Or you would not,' she said, 'would you, call this an attempt at blackmail?'

He looked at her out of the corner of one eye.

Whereupon she flamed up. 'You're suggesting,' she asked, white with tension and rage, 'that I should break off one friendship, begin another – with you? And I'm to do both at once, in a minute, now, with no more questions than at a government order, less trouble than I should have these days in changing my grocer, less fuss than I should make about changing my hat? Nothing, you take it, could be simpler – what *I* call feeling does not enter at all. Even so, with what may no more than look like feeling, one has got, I'm afraid, to waste just a little time. That you do not expect to waste time you make quite clear. You keep hinting at something, *something*, that should cut out all that. It may, of course, be simply that you see yourself, as you manifestly do, as a quite exceptional man. But no, no – you mean to convey that there's something more. What, then? – then what? I should like to know what you mean. I should like to know what you think you have up your sleeve. You mean, I am to do as you say – *"or else"*, "otherwise" . . .? Well, otherwise what?'

'It's funny,' said Harrison, 'when you begin "you mean", you remind me of a girl I met in the park. I would say, for instance, "How blue the sky is," whereupon she'd say, "You mean, the sky's blue?"'

'I cannot wonder at her; quite ordinary things you say have a way of sounding, somehow, preposterous. But in this case you are saying something preposterous – or trying to. You must be clearer, though, if you're trying to frighten me.'

'I'm afraid, you know, I have somehow done that already. You sounded rattled when we talked on the phone.'

'You ring up like the Gestapo,' she said with a laugh or yawn.

'That would be just the impression I'd hate to give you – Then, you haven't a thing in the world to be frightened of?'

'Who would dare say that these days?' She, sitting bolt upright, paused, moulding the stuff of her dress over one knee. 'Obviously,' she went on, 'only a fool would say so at any time at all. Who has not got fears? However, one learns to say, "Such things do not happen."'

'Ah, but they do.'

She raised her eyes. He said: 'Only look around you.'

'Yes, the war. I had been thinking of life in general.'

'What's the difference? War, if you come to think of it, hasn't started anything that wasn't there already – what it does is, put the other lot of us in the right. You, I mean to say, have got along on the assumption that things don't happen; I, on the other hand, have taken it that things happen rather than not. Therefore, what you see now is what I've seen all along. I wouldn't say that puts me at an advantage, but I can't help feeling "This is where I come in."'

'In other words, this is a crooks' war?'

'I shouldn't call it that. It's a war, of course; but for me the principal thing is that it's a time when I'm not a crook. For me there've been not-so-good times when I did seem to be a bit out in my calculations, so you must see how where I'm concerned things have taken a better turn; everything about adds up to what I made it.'

'What you wanted to tell me, then, was about yourself?'

Harrison apparently could not blush, but in a flash his face took on the expression that in other faces goes with a change of colour, a chagrined rise of blood. 'In fact, not. – Sorry,' he shortly said. 'As a rule myself's not one of my topics; it only ever could be if it ever interested you – which *could*, you know, happen,' he added, frowning again. 'Is it so odd I should want a place of my own?'

'What seems to me most odd is the way you expect to make one.'

He, as though directed by some involuntary thought of hers, turned to stare at the back of the reversed photograph. 'You'd feel bad about him, sore about him?' he said. 'In that case, I ought to tell you – worse could happen to him than saying good-bye to you.'

41

'Oh, I expect so,' said Stella with her most idle air. She soon, however, dropped into staring at him with an accumulation of weariness, distaste, mistrust, boredom, most of all the strain of her own sustained ungentleness and forced irony. Hesitating, he touched his moustache – as though it concealed a spring which could make his mouth fly open on something final. She was looked at narrowly.

'A lot could happen to him,' he said. She made no observation. He went on: 'At any moment – which would be too bad, eh? As against which, it might not. If you and I could arrange things, things might be arranged.'

'I don't follow you.'

'The fact is, our friend's been playing the fool. *Is* playing the fool, I should say, for all he's worth.'

She said sharply: 'Is he in a mess about money?'

'Not so simple as that. You may find this far from being a pretty story. Want it?'

'Just as you like.'

Harrison cleared his throat. 'For reasons you'll see,' he said, 'I can't tell you the whole thing. In fact, if we'd got the whole thing he would not still be where he is – however, there still is something we're working on. He's, as you know, at the War Office – that's probably all you do know: we've no reason to think that in any social relations he's not been ordinarily discreet. *You* may have some rough idea what he's doing, but I should doubt that he's ever given you more. Unfortunately he's giving considerably more in another direction. We've traced a leak – shortly, the gist of the stuff he handles is getting through to the enemy. For a good bit of time this has been suspected; now it's established, known.'

'This is silly,' she interjected.

'Now the point is, he's being given rope. The open point is, just how much more rope we can afford to pay out to him? There's one argument for leaving him where he is, up to what he's up to, till we've got his contacts; there's one very big thing we're after compared to which your friend's small fry. He's watched – as a matter of fact, I'm watching him. He repays watching – as I told you, I've got to like the chap: I'd be in a way sorry to have things happen to him. But they might, I must tell you frankly – because here, you see, we come to the other argument, in favour of pulling him in right now. He's not doing half he hopes, but he's doing *some* damage. In that case, we'd put ourselves back as to the other thing. However, some do say, pull him in double quick, stop *that* rot, cut our losses . . . For my own part, I'm keeping an open mind.'

'And this open mind of yours, is it so important?'

He said modestly: 'Well, you might say it is. Just as things are now, I could tip the scales either way. The thing could just turn on the stuff on him I send up. As to that, if you follow me, I do use my judgement. I *could* use my judgement a bit more . . . I am, for instance, holding quite a bit of stuff on him that I haven't turned in yet. It ought to go in – I can't quite make my mind up. Perhaps you could help me to?'

She looked at him and began to laugh.

'I *could* leave things over,' he went on, with the air of one intensely pursuing an inner argument, 'for quite a time. In that case who knows what might not have happened – this whole show might be over; he might for some reason think better of it and drop this little game of his of his own accord; he might just somehow be lucky. There's no saying. Anyhow, it's a hope – if he *could* be kept out of trouble a bit longer.

43

And when I say that rather depends on me, what I feel is, it rather depends on you.'

'Yes, I quite see.'

He said with relief: 'You do?'

'Perfectly. I'm to form a disagreeable association in order that a man be left free to go on selling his country.'

'That's putting it a bit crudely,' Harrison said, downcast.

'It might matter more how one put it if we'd been for a moment talking about the same man. Evidently I have been right – you *are* crazy. When did you think this up?'

He said dubiously: 'It doesn't make sense to you?'

'I'm afraid not.'

'Now, why?'

'Well, first and last, I suppose, because you don't make sense: you never have. Quite apart from Robert and everything in the world that I know of him, there are people one simply does not believe, and you are one of them.'

'Well, I don't know . . .' he said.

'What don't you know?'

'Quite how to make you see. I can't give you any proof – I'm in deep enough, already, having said what I have.'

'Exactly – yes!' she exclaimed. 'That would be another thing, if one needed anything more. If this story were for one instant true, if you for one instant were what you hint you are, would you tell *me*, me of all people, knowing I'd go with the whole thing straight to Robert? Of course I'll tell him anyhow, simply as something comic. What else would you expect?'

She threw the words in his face, which reacted as though to a light if insulting buffet from a balloon – it remained stony, certain, and, in a way to detest but not to discount,

44

mature. He said: 'Expect? I'd have expected the sort of person you are to have a better head. Warn him? That would be a pity – but not for me. Once known to have been put wise, he's no more use to us, so then he *does* get pulled in. No, speaking as the chap's friend I should certainly not do that.'

'So, I take this from you, ask no more questions, break with Robert?'

'That would be best for him.'

'Yes, but wait a minute – "known to have been put wise"? Who is to know – still more, how would anyone know?'

'I should have thought that stuck out a mile. You expect him to laugh this off, or, should we say,' he said with an almost delicate air, 'kiss it off, when and if you bring the matter up. To make your mind nice and easy and as you were. And so, no doubt, if he's half the chap we both think he is, he would. But don't forget he'd have more than you on his mind. Having got the gist, been given the gist by you, of your and my little talk this evening, would you really expect him not to alter his course a bit – if it were only in one or two small particulars? His timetable would alter, and his beat – that could not not happen; it would be bound to. One or two of his haunts would miss his familiar face; he'd start cooling off one or two of his buddies, and so on. Not to veer a bit, it might be ever so slightly, would take more nerve than a man humanly has. I've never yet known a man not change his behaviour once he's known he's watched: it's exactly changes like that that are being watched for. No, he'd let us know in an instant that he'd been tipped the wink: in which case, what? He'd be pulled in before anyone coud say knife, before *he* could tip the wink any further . . . I should not say anything to him if I were you.'

'Well thank you. But what would there be to stop me saying to him, "Go on just as you're going, but be careful. Be most careful to go on just as you've been going on"?'

'Nothing, nothing at all,' said Harrison promptly. He shrugged his shoulders. 'In that case, you're taking a chance on how well you know him. *I* speak, of course, merely as an outsider. It's clear to me he's got quite his share of nerve – but this would take more; it would take tiptop acting. How much of an actor would you, now, take him to be?'

She flinched, oddly. 'Actor? How should I of all people know? He has never had any reason to act, with me.'

'No,' he said thoughtfully. 'No, I suppose not.'

'No.'

'I should say, if a chap *were* able to act in love, he'd be enough of an actor to get away with anything.'

'I – I suppose so,' she said, turning away her head.

Harrison, having waited, all the more quickly said: 'We can leave it, he's no sort of an actor.'

It was just not a question. Nothing could be more telling than this show of his of compunction, muffled compunction, at having touched her on what could conceivably be the raw. By, next, renewing an awkward silence he made apparent to her what she had made apparent to him – that, out of the whole of a conversation abhorrent and shocking to her from the very start, it took one remark to get her under the skin. Lips compressed, as though he had taken refuge in silent humming, Harrison meanwhile looked round the room which should so well know the person under discussion. He looked, in fact, everywhere but at Stella. Finally he said:

'As to all that, though, I'm naturally off my ground. All I mean is, I should feel bad if I let you ruin the chap. A

46

chap is quite often ruined, I shouldn't wonder, by someone's expecting too much of him. Of course, I can't make you take my advice – I quite see that my position in the whole matter may seem a bit funny. I more or less come and say to you, "Better liquidate Robert." But that means just as a friend, be it understood. Otherwise, I haven't a thing against him. You say, no, he can't act up. Ought you, then, to take such a cracking risk?'

'Risk of telling him what you've told me? Perhaps not,' she said, so amenably that he looked at her with suspicion. He was right, she had not been listening – or not completely. Thinking off at a tangent, she had arrived at a point which, it really seemed, made it unnecessary to listen to Harrison any longer or ever again. Her eyes now sought and insisted on meeting his with a quite new dark and embattled glitter. 'Your position funny? But you've been so kind – you've thought of me, Robert, everyone but yourself: surely now it's time we thought about you. Are you not the one who's taking rather a risk – if you *are* really what you imply you are? For all I know, you may be – indeed, why not? You're not to be accounted for in any other way: I cannot believe you spend your whole day sitting in the park; you never have volunteered any information as to what you do do; these days it is inevitable that everybody should be doing something, and that in most cases one doesn't ask what. Let's certainly take it, then, that you are a counter-spy, which I understand to be some sort of spy twice over, and that you're officially employed. In that case, if I may ask, what *are* you doing? Employed and accredited as you are, you go out of your way to tell me – remember, I never asked – that you are on to, or working around the edge of, something exceedingly dangerous to this country and our conduct of war. You've traced, or are tracing, a leakage of information in which x number of people may be involved. If that *is* true, it's vital – and if it's vital surely the pre-essential should be absolute secrecy, silence? But, oh no. You brag – no, let's put it calmly and say you talk – to me about your power to tip scales. Assuming you have that power, you wouldn't, I take it, have it without having been given immense responsibility. You may even, as you hint, be a key man. Very well, then – what? Your behaviour staggers me. Is this country really so badly served? What do you do? – You ask yourself to this flat and turn in, attempt to trade in, this information with a view to getting a woman you think you want. You attempt to use what you know to implement blackmail. You propose that by becoming your mistress I buy out a man, in whom I have an interest, who is by your showing dangerous to the country. That is what you are proposing – stop me if I am wrong . . . Very well. You've bludgeoned me with your perpetual "we" – your "we" is my "they": what view would *"they"* take of that? Is there any reason why I should not report you – your attempts to make use, for amorous reasons, of official secrets at a most crucial time? I cannot say I am pleased to be the woman you want – but what's a good deal more the point is, I am not the right woman to try this on with. If I should in my turn decide to turn something, in, I shouldn't fail to see that it went to the right quarter. I am not a woman who does not know where to go. You would be sorry, you say, if I sunk Robert. How would it be if I sank you?'

Harrison, throughout this, had not shifted from Stella's face a look of patience and admiration. When she stopped,

48

he returned to himself with a slight start. 'Absolutely,' he agreed. 'You would certainly have me there.'

She sat more upright than ever, pressing together in her lap hands which, she found, trembled.

'Or, I should say, could have me? (You've got a first-rate head: that's one thing I like.) But for one thing, that is.'

'Oh. What?'

He said warmly: 'All you said sounded fine – you'd do right as you say, to go straight ahead. But there's this. – Do you imagine I am the only one who's got your friend taped? In that case I should have made myself plainer; I must say I thought I had. No, to put me out wouldn't close the case against him: in point of fact it would have the reverse effect. You're not only the most charming woman, if I may say so; you're also officially known to have quite a heart. That is – how should I put it? – where our friend's concerned. Your interest in Robert has, with everything else concerning him, been of some interest elsewhere for quite a time now – yes, I may say I was pretty well up to date with that particular story before I met you. You say you'd know where to go, and I've no doubt you would – but do you imagine that by the time you got there anyone there would imagine you'd gone *straight* there? If you hadn't gone round by Robert's to drop the word to him, it would none the less be assumed you had – a woman's always a woman, and so on. The gaff would be taken as blown; the game would be taken as up. Oh yes, you'd be seen to the door with handshakings and many sincere thanks – but I'm prepared to say, practically before you were into your taxi, the word would go out and your friend Robert would be where a number of people (I don't say I) are of the opinion we rightly ought to have popped him a good long time ago. Phut, you must surely see, would have gone the only possible argument for leaving him any longer on the loose. I go – he goes. However, of course that is up to you.'

'I should have done my duty.'

'Ah – to the country?' said he, jumping to the point with surprising ease. 'Exactly – how right your are. And it seems,' he added, 'so right *for* you to be right that I almost wonder we haven't got round to that before. Naturally, if you're thinking about the country we shall have to go back and run through this whole matter over again; I mean to say, it puts everything in a somewhat different light. So if that's what is on your mind –'

'– Well, it's not. If it were,' she said, 'do you suppose I'd submit my conscience to you?'

As to this, he seemed to have no opinion; or, at any rate, showed no great concern. Having looked suspiciously at her clock, he confirmed what it said by reference to his wrist watch. 'I'd no idea, do you know, it was getting so late!'

'Hadn't you?'

It might have been midnight – might have even been the most extinct and hallucinatory of the small hours. She had by now passed through every zone of fatigue into its inner vacuum, and had forgotten hunger. She wanted nothing, nothing but that he should not be any longer there. Her fingers, having exhausted any capacity to tremble, any to further feel the touch of each other, lay in an inanimate tangle in her lap. Her spine by now ached from having sat so long on the backless stool; her head was empty.

'Anything else?' he said. 'Because, if not –'

'How am I to know you are not bluffing? – In fact, I know you are.'

50

He stood, frowned, tatted at his moustache. 'Yes, that's the devil, of course,' he feelingly said. 'I don't quite see how you *are* to check up – on me, that is – without bringing down the roof. You can't be too careful.'

'Still, I still think there's someone who can confirm that you're a fake.'

'Trouble is, everyone's so damned cagey.'

'But I know a lot of people!' she said, with the first touch of hysteria.

Harrison shrugged his shoulders. 'That's, again, always up to you. Go ahead.'

To release any kind of feeling could be to release it all. Stella rose, went to the chimneypiece, and, impassively reaching across Harrison, turned round Robert's photograph once more to face the room. 'And another time,' she said, 'leave my things alone!' She then turned full on him, from less than a yard away: they were eye to eye in the intimacy of her extreme anger. There is actually little difference as to colour in the moment before the blow and the moment before the kiss: the negligible space between her and him was now charged, full force, with the intensity of their two beings. Something speechless, tenacious, unlovable – himself – was during that instant exposed in Harrison's eyes: it was a crisis – the first this evening, not the first she had known – of his emotional idiocy, and it was as unnerving as might be a brain-storm in someone without a brain.

The moment broke: he did not attempt to touch her. Having shaken a loose sleeve back, she supported an elbow against the chimneypiece, a side of her face against the palm of a hand, and continued to study him, though vacantly. He, having come to one of those pauses in his fidgety smoking, slowly slid his hands down into his pockets. 'And as far as we're concerned,' he said, 'think it over.'

'I'd never love you.'

'I never have been loved.'

'Do you wonder!'

'The thing would be, we'd get to know each other.'

'You're not still expecting me to do what you say?'

He said softly: 'That would be what I'd like.'

'Not again see Robert?'

That took him back. 'Or – might not that seem a bit suspicious? I should have suggested, more, as things are, ease out.'

'Just like that. I see – Do you know much about love?'

'I've watched quite a lot of it.'

'How much time do you give me?'

'Listen,' he said, 'I hate you to put it that way.'

'A month?'

'Good enough. If it suited you, I might drop in from time to time?'

'To see how everything's going?'

'In case you *had* made your mind up.'

'And meanwhile, nothing will happen?'

'I think one may pretty safely say pretty likely not. – And now –'

'Now what?'

'You don't think, a spot of dinner?'

'No thank you,' she said in a final tone.

His face fell. 'Oh but, I say, I say – I'd got a table for us. What's the matter? You're not upset? Can't you eat, aren't you hungry?'

'Simply, I'm staying in.'

'Oh, that's it, is it – you're staying in? Staying in, who for?'

He heard the telephone before she did, being one of those people who receive that vibration just before the ring; he had jerked his head in the direction of the dividing door before she was aware of the telephone in there in her bedroom. The same possibility made them exchange a glance – as though already there were complicity. She stood where she was, head down, while the telephone continued its double-ringing – to which Harrison, for his part, listened closely as though trying to familiarize himself with a code.

'Look, take it, why don't you?' he said at last.

She made a sweeping turn and went through to the other room, contemptuously leaving the door open behind her. Behind the mirror the curtains were still undrawn; there was an ashy glimmer of window – she went round the foot of the bed to sit at the pillow end, her back to the scene she had left behind. In the dark she took up the receiver with the unfumbling sureness of one who habitually answers a telephone at any, even the deepest, hour of the night. Her hand would have reached its mark before her eyes opened; before her brain stirred her ear would be ready, so that the first word she heard, even the first she spoke, would be misted over by some unfinished dream. This mechanical reflex of hers to a mechanical thing suggested to Harrison, standing there aware in the other room, the first idea he had had of poetry – her life. Enflamed by the picture he could not see, he could but think, 'So *that's* what it can be like!' Meanwhile, feet planted apart in the lamplit drawing-room, he looked about him like a German in Paris.

'Hullo?' she said – to be checked: whoever it was had failed to press Button A. Then – 'Oh – *you* – oh, darling! . . . You are, are you? For how long? . . . However, that's better than nothing. But why didn't you tell me? Have you had any dinner? . . . Yes, I'm afraid that might be best: I don't think I've got anything in the flat. How I wish you'd told me . . . And directly after that you'll come straight here? . . . Of course; naturally; don't be so idiotic . . . Yes, there is just at the moment, but there soon won't be . . . No, no one you know . . . Soon, then – as soon as ever you can!'

She hung up, but remained to black-out her bedroom. And in the series of rushes with which she made the curtains run on the rail could be heard release, a lightening, a lark-like soaring up of her mood. She lit up the dressing-table, hummed a tune, tranquilly touched her hair. Harrison could not but be drawn to the doorway, in which he remained standing – he searched, with his eyes, the room, the built-in cupboards, the satin low bed, her face reflected in the dazzling mirror. He said: 'Well, that was that. You always sound so surprised?'

'Only when I am,' she replied, turning. 'That was my son, on leave.'

'Oho.'

'He's just got to London. He's at the station. He's on his way round here.'

54

3

Roderick never came to the flat without giving warning.

When, at a quarter to ten that night, Stella heard the bell of the street door, she was in the act of pulling blankets out of a cupboard. Had her parting with Harrison been of a different kind she would have called after him, as he went downstairs: 'Please leave that door on the latch again, for Roderick!' As things were, she had had the irritation of hearing Harrison pause outside, to make sure the door *was* shut, before making off down Weymouth Street. He had gone — but he had brought life to one of those passes when nothing is simple, not even opening a door. She dropped the armful of blankets, intended for her son's night on the sofa, when Roderick rang.

In any case, she would have gone to meet him on the stairs.

It was a time of opening street doors conspiratorially: light must not escape on to steps. Roderick, considerably broadened by his equipment — 'Everything,' he had once said, 'but a mousetrap, and not impossibly that,' — inched in round the door his mother held. They embraced; with, on her part, an exclamation, for the happiness of reunion is surprising. Half-way up the stairs he said: 'You are out of breath!'

'I must be getting fat.'

'I hope not,' Roderick said gravely.

55

'Go ahead,' she said at the top, stopping to turn off the landing light – through the door she watched Roderick, in the square yard of vestibule, bend his cropped head as he unslung his equipment. Clumsily, he unyoked himself from what was to her an anonymous tangle of webbing and knocking things, and in so doing showed an animal patience. He stacked up some of the stuff, kicked the rest out of view, and plonked down his tin hat on the small marble table. There was now so little space left that he had to move on before she could enter the flat. So in the front room he waited, vaguely staring around him at lit white lamps and their reflections in dark glass pictures. This did not look like home; but it looked like something – possibly a story.

She came in and said: 'Roderick, you did get something to eat? I began to worry after you'd telephoned, because lately almost all places are shut on Sunday.'

'Fred knew of a pub that has pork pies.'

'Fred came up with you?'

'Yes. He's gone to his married sister's at Wood Lane.'

'I thought if I made some coffee?'

'Or you wouldn't,' Roderick ventured, 'have any cake?'

'Absolutely none. If only, darling, you'd tell me the day before!'

'Everything depends on so much else – Can I have a bath?'

'Yes, go on; while I make the coffee.'

Roderick left the bathroom door ajar; steam came curling into the kitchen where Stella was: meanwhile, the percolator began to bubble. Later he called out: 'Would there be a dressing-gown?' so she unhooked Robert's dressing-gown from her hanging-place and tossed it to Roderick through

56

the walls of steam. As a family she and he liked their coffee strong; she was therefore still standing over the percolator when her son came out of the bath and propped himself in the door. This kitchen was, by agents' definition, a kitchenette; between the electric stove, the sink, the refrigerator, there was room for one slender person to stand and turn; all other fitments had been constructed to hang above or fit underneath each other. Roderick admired the scene in which he could play no part – this glazed, surgical-looking cabinet was the first kitchen in which he had seen his mother at work. Reaching up for the cups she said: 'Are you really dry?'

'I am drying off.'

'You are looking more like yourself.'

'More like myself, am I looking?' asked Roderick, with interest and curiosity. He attempted to remember what she must mean. He looked reflectively down at Robert's mottled silk dressing-gown with the froggings, even tweaked, with a frown, at one end of the cord he had knotted tightly about his middle. Not unnaturally, the dressing-gown gave no clue: it hung in Byzantine folds about the concavities of his frame, except where it stuck in patches to the damp of his skin – for his mother's suspicion was right; he was imperfectly dry. 'Would there be a pair of my pyjamas anywhere round?' he said. 'If not, it naturally doesn't matter.'

'Why, yes; there should be – surely you left some here?'

Stella's work at any time in her kitchen was not badly done but erratic, punctuated by thoughts. Tonight she accomplished things rapidly in the wrong order – she had reached round for china, rattled about for spoons, chipped at last week's sugar crusted around the bowl before she remembered that one must have the tray, still on its bracket over Roderick's head. Yet all her movements seemed to him charmed and deft as, shifting his weight from one bare foot to the other, he re-propped himself against the frame of the door. In repose at last, he stood as she often stood. It was to be seen how, each time he came back like this, he was at the beginning physically at a loss; until, by an imitation of her attitudes he supplied himself with some way to behave, look, stand – even, you might say, *be*. His body could at least copy, if not at once regain, unsoldierly looseness and spontaneity. And he traced his way back by these attitudes, one by one, as though each could act as a clue or signpost to the Roderick his mother remembered, the Roderick he could feel her hoping to see. He searched in Stella for some identity left by him in her keeping. It was a search undertaken principally for her sake: only she made him conscious of loss or change. It was his unconscious purpose to underline everything he and she had in common. And this worked each time: each time she was reassured. While she and Roderick stayed so closely alike, it seemed less likely that he would, after all, shift away to somewhere outside her ken – whatever happened, whatever was done to him. For what nagged at her, what flickered into her look each time she confronted the soldier in battle-dress, was the fear that the Army was out to obliterate Roderick. In the course of a process, a being processed, she could do nothing to stop, her son might possibly disappear. There must still be so many months before he saw action: she did not envisage or dread his death. She dreaded dissolution inside his life, dissolution never to be repaired.

Months in the Army had made Roderick notice what he had taken for granted when he was more at home – the particular climate in which his mother dwelled. Of this, the temperature and the pressure were gauged by no other person, unless Robert. To re-enter this climate, to be affected by it, could have been enervating, if one had not loved her. He was prepared to suppose that to be a soldier in training made one's thoughts desultory, one's feeling torpid – but of what else, what more, what better was he capable really, left to himself? Since he was seventeen, war had laid a negative finger on alternatives; he had expected, neutrally, to become a soldier; he was a soldier now. To his year at Oxford there had been denied meaning – any meaning it could have been disastrous to have caught. Now, his ineptness to play any other part would have more distressed him had there been any other part to play. Everybody was undergoing the same thing. The alternatives shadowed in Stella's mind only troubled him in so far as they troubled her: he could see, not feel, war's cruelty to a world to which he had so far given no hostage; with which, warned, he had never engaged himself.

What did more nearly trouble him, this evening, was the probable disappearance of his pyjamas – those only things of his own in his mother's flat. He had been thinking of them on the journey up, and had even spoken of them to Fred. Everything else of his had gone into store, to limbo, when Stella gave up their house.

As against this, Roderick now owned property he had never seen. Last May, he had inherited from a cousin of his father's a house in the south of Ireland, Mount Morris, with which went about three hundred acres of land. Probate, likely to be retarded by the complication of Mount Morris's being where it was, had not yet been obtained: legally, the estate was still in the course of becoming his. Personally, he had entered into possession the day the effect of the will was made known to him – the bequest was as unexpected as the testator's death. Up to that date, all Roderick had known of the house was that his parents spent their honeymoon there: arguably, Mount Morris was inauspicious; for the marriage, of which he was the only child, had broken before he was three years old. His father's and mother's divorce and his father's death had come so close together that only by a process of reasoning (necessary to go through over again each time he bent his mind to the matter) could the son be clear which had happened first. Cousin Francis Morris, of Mount Morris, had played no subsequent part in the life that Roderick and his mother shared.

Possessorship of Mount Morris affected Roderick strongly. It established for him, and was adding to day by day, what might be called a historic future. The house came out to meet his growing capacity for attachment; all the more, perhaps, in that by geographically standing outside war it appeared also to be standing outside the present. The house, non-human, became the hub of his imaginary life, of fancies, fantasies only so to be called because circumstance outlawed them from reality. Submerged, soporific, and powerful, these fancies made for his acquiescence to the immediate day. Whether he sought them out or they him; whether they nourished him or he them, could not be said. They did not amount to desires, being without object; nor to hallucinations, for they neither deceived him nor set up tension. Now he was in the Army, they filled those pockets of vacuum underlying routine. They were at their most vivid, most satisfying, in the bodily coma before sleep; but through the day they diversified those long docile will-less waits for his turn for something further to happen, fatigues, inspections, or simply hanging about.

He got known as one of the dreamy ones who get by somehow. He was most nearly bestirred when he had to regret his mother's regretting the Army for him. Each time, at the first glance, her eyes cried out: 'What are they doing to you?' She saw how exposed, naïve, and comically childishly slender his neck looked rearing out of the bulky battle-dress collar; she saw the grain of his skin harshening over face-bones not much less fine than hers. Through his hair now stiff to the roots from cropping she perceived the bony planes of his skull. His eyes, like hers, were set in their sockets in a striking rather than lifelike way; they looked – in the surround of what he now was and wore – anachronistic. These days he held himself, almost pigeon-breastedly, as though aspiring to fill out the bulky concavities of the khaki. He did not succeed: so unamenable was his over-growing thinness, so straggling and light his frame that, once he shed the ballast of his equipment, only his great boots seemed to be weighting him to the ground. Had he looked more like a soldier, any kind of soldier, she might have taken it more calmly – she could have felt the authority of a real change.

As it was, the anomaly of her son's looks made Stella no longer know where she was with him: she could not believe he knew where he was himself. She had, for instance, not once actually asked whether Roderick liked being in the Army . . . He was therefore relieved to learn he was looking more like himself, even in another man's dressing-gown. In a minute she passed him the tray of cups and said: 'Will you take this into the other room?'

'Where shall I put it?'

'Anywhere you like.'

'Yes, Mother, yes,' said Roderick patiently, 'but there must be some place where it always goes?'

'Anywhere,' she repeated, not understanding.

He sighed. In this flat, rooms had no names; there being only two, whichever you were not in was 'the other room'. Proceeding into what *he* saw as the drawing-room, Roderick, grasping the tray, stood looking round again. Somewhere between these chairs and tables must run the spoor of habit, could one but pick it up. He could not envisage his mother as so completely alone as one would be without any customs. Fred and his other friends were all for the authoritarianism of home life; the last thing they wished was Liberty Hall. Roderick, for the moment, was confounded by there being no one right place to put down a tray – he examined, like a detective, the armchairs, to see which showed signs of being most often sat in, the ash trays to see which had been in most recent use. The stub-heaped little Chinese one on the chimneypiece was a puzzle – why should anyone *stand* to smoke for so long?

He gave up, placed the tray on the floor and himself on the edge of the sofa which was to be his bed. Picking up and nursing one bare foot, in the posture of the boy with the thorn, he examined one toe-joint closely. 'I say,' he shouted, 'I've got a corn!'

'Got what?'

'Oh, nothing,' he said, already bored. He swung his legs up on the sofa, tested it out for length, refolded the dressing-gown round his body, built himself up an elbow rest of brocade cushions and tossed a couple more of them over his feet. 'What are you doing?' he shouted. 'I've more or less gone to bed.'

His mother came in with the coffee, looked about for the tray, exclaimed, 'Really, darling!' and moved it on to a stool. She towed the stool into position beside the sofa. 'I wish,' she remarked, 'I had something for you to eat.' Sitting down beside his feet at the foot of the sofa, she removed the cushions in order to tuck them into the small of her back. Her attention was caught – 'Why, Roderick, that's not a *corn?*' she said, staring.

'That's what I've been telling you.'

'If your feet are cold, I can get the blankets.'

'You're mixing up corns with frostbite – don't go away again!' He added: 'Now we're in the same boat.'

'What? – how?' she said, starting.

This is like being opposite one another in a boat on a river.'

'*Have* we ever been in a boat on a river – have we?'

'Is there a boat for the river at Mount Morris?'

'I only remember the river: it was in autumn.'

'All the same, you think there might be a boat? By now it may need tarring or caulking – you don't think someone should see to that? Perhaps next time you're writing to the lawyers . . .'

'No,' she said firmly, 'that really will have to wait. We are not even certain there is a boat. – Suppose this coffee keeps you awake?'

'Nothing could,' declared Roderick, blowing politely into his little cup. – 'I only hope to stay awake long enough. There is so much I want to know – For instance, what has been happening?'

She ran a finger swiftly along the streak in her hair. 'Why should anything happen?'

He looked at her in not unnatural surprise. 'I only meant,' he explained, 'since you last wrote.' He broke off, eyes fixed on the tray. 'Mother, I thought you told me –'

'– What? –'

'– Told me there was nothing to eat. In that case, what are these three biscuits for?'

'Oh, you, naturally. But I'm afraid they're musty.'

Roderick tried, ate them, then picked crumbs from his chest. 'Who was it who was here whom I didn't know?'

'When?'

'Just now, this evening, when I rang up. You answered in your company voice; I could hear that. Have you made any interesting new friends?'

'No; it was only a man called Harrison.'

'The man who was at the funeral – What had he come about?'

'He just came to see me.'

'But I thought you said he was a commercial traveller?'

'I only said I rather got that impression.'

'Anyway, as it's Sunday probably he'd be taking the day off. If he's not a commercial traveller, what does he do?'

'Roderick, what about your commission?'

Roderick rearranged the cushion under his elbow. 'What do you mean?' he said.

'You haven't heard anything?'

'I should be very much surprised if I ever did: why should I? I should be surprised enough if I ever got a stripe – Fred, you know, got his a month ago. I see how you feel; I am very, very sorry I'm not more like your brothers, Mother, but there it is. I'll really try and exert myself if you'd rather, but I don't think the Army's quite what it was in your day – everything

64

now depends on so much else. I must say, I should like to be known as "the Captain" when I settle at Mount Morris; but I suppose quite a lot of water will have to flow under the bridge before then.'

'I wonder about your commission. I was saying to Robert –'

'Oh yes, how *is* Robert? I hope, well?'

'Very. This week-end he's at his mother's.'

'Like I am,' said Roderick genially. However, the idea of the elder man made him look anxiously down the length of his own person in Robert's dressing-gown – he had a notion he might have spilled some coffee, but was relieved to find it had no more than left a runnel on his bare chest. He wondered what had made his mother ask, and ask so abruptly, about his commission – a subject she as a rule approached in only the most roundabout way, or hinted at. It had been clear from her manner that she did feel strongly, but about something else: the commission, this time, had been made to act either as a diversion or an unconscious revenge – the saying of something to irk or nettle him because he had, somehow, irked or nettled her. In which case, what? Raising eyes which held, where she was concerned, the brooding intuitiveness of a young animal rather than intelligent speculation Roderick gazed at Stella – who slightly changed her position at the end of the sofa he had called their boat.

The reality of the fancy was better than the unreality of the room. In a boat you were happy to be suspended in nothing but light, air, water, opposite another face. On a sofa you could be surrounded by what was lacking. Though this particular sofa backed on a wall and stood on a carpet, it was without environment; it might have been some derelict piece of furniture exposed on a pavement after an air raid or washed up by a flood on some unknown shore. His return to his mother cried out for something better – as a meeting, this had to struggle for nature, the nature it should have had; no benevolence came to it from surrounding things. It is the music of the familiar that is awaited, on such an occasion, with most hope; love dreads being isolated, being left to speak in a void – at the beginning it would often rather listen than speak. Even lovers can feel this – how many passions have not been daunted by the hotel room? – and between son and mother the absence of every inanimate thing they had had in common set up an undue strain. Perhaps his fidgeting with the cushions was an attempt to acclimatize at least those. Stella and Roderick both, in their different ways, felt this evening to be beyond the powers of living they now had. They could have wished to live it as it could have been lived.

Both felt the greatness inherent in being human and in their being mother and son. His homecoming should have been one more chapter added to an august book, a book on a subject greater than themselves: nothing failed, to make it so, but their vision. It may still have been such a chapter in the vision of God. Where they were concerned, the ban, the check, the caution as to all spending and most of all the expenditure of feeling restricted them. Wariness had driven away poetry: from hesitating to feel came the moment when you no longer could. Was this war's doing? By every day, every night, existence was being further drained – you, yourself, made conscious of what was happening only by some moment, some meeting such as tonight's.

Stella and Roderick were too intimate not each to extend to the other that sense of instinctive loss, and their intimacy made them too honest to play a scene. Their trouble, had it been theirs only, could have been written off as minor – the romantic dismay of two natures romantically akin. But it was more than that; it was a sign, in them, of an impoverishment of the world. There was not much left for either of them to say, and in this room in which they sat nothing spoke, either – a mysterious flutter, like that of a fire burning, which used to emanate from the minutes seemed to be at a stop. The actual fire's electric elements, vertical hot set lips, grinned away at the empty end of the room. At half-shadow level, some way above the lamplight, the photographs were two dark unliving squares. Outside the curtain-masked windows, down there in the street running into streets, the silence was black-out registered by the hearing.

It was imperfect silence, mere resistance to sound – as though the inner tension of London were being struck and struck on without breaking. Heard or unheard, the city at war ticked over – if from this quarter, from these immediate streets, the suction of cars in private movement was gone, there was all the time a jarring at the periphery, an unintermittent pumping of vital traffic through arterial streets into arterial roads. Nor was that quite all: once or twice across the foreground of hearing a taxi careered as though under fire.

The room lacked one more thing: apprehension of time. Inside it the senses were cut off from hour and season; nothing spoke but the clock. The day had gone from the moment Stella had drawn down the fitted blinds and drawn across them the deadening curtains: now nothing took its place. Every crack was stopped; not a mote of darkness could enter – the room, sealed up in its artificial light, remained exaggerated and cerebral.

In spite of this, something happened – petals detached themselves from a rose in the bowl on the escritoire, to fall, one by one, on to Stella's letters on the pulled-out flap. Roderick watched them; she turned her head to see what he was looking at and watched also. Then she said: 'That reminds me – three more letters from Cousin Frankie's lawyers came this week; I must show them to you. I answered them all in one.'

'It is awful for you me being a minor,' said Roderick. 'However, time will cure that. Have we come yet,' he inquired rearing up on the sofa, 'to anything crucial that can be really signed? I suppose so far there's been no way of knowing when I *do* enter into possession?'

'At this rate, one would imagine when you're about eighty.'

'Fred's sure the whole thing ought to be simpler. – You haven't been in all day writing letters on my account?'

'No, no; I wrote several others – I wrote a long one to you. The only annoying thing is, not knowing you would be coming up I took today as my day off; I shall have to work tomorrow. What shall you do?'

'Oh well, it can't be helped. And it does seem more natural your being at home on Sunday. – So you were writing away when poor Mr. Harrison came?'

'Why "poor"?'

'Well, for one thing you don't seem to have given him much to drink; or at any rate I don't see any glasses. Don't you like him, or is he a teetotaller?'

'No.'

'And yet,' said Roderick, glancing thoughtfully in the direction of the ash tray on the chimneypiece, 'he stayed on and on. He must be fascinated by you, Mother.'

Stella put down her coffee cup, left the sofa and, saying something about the Mount Morris letters, went to the escritoire. It was imperative that she should overcome, with the unconscious aid of Roderick's presence, her aversion from that part of the room where, forced to listen to Harrison, she had been forced to sit. Even the papers, letters, among which she had rested her elbow, listening to him, seemed to be contaminated; she shrank, even, from phrases in purple type on which, in the course of the listening, her eyes had from time to time lit. She could, further, fancy the papers were disarranged, not quite as she had left them that afternoon – Harrison *had*, no doubt, glanced through them quickly while she was at the telephone. She wanted to burn the lot – sorry for the petals of the roses for having fallen here at the end of their lovely life, she brushed the petals from the flap of the desk with a violence which was enough to make others fall.

'Still, I may see you some time tomorrow evening?' she heard Roderick say.

Roderick's being for one more night in London would, of course, mean her putting off Robert. She perceived, if there had not been Roderick, she might have been casting about her for some other excuse. Before they did meet again she would have to think – and to think seemed of all things beyond her power. She was not, therefore, then, in effect, again to see Robert until she *had* thought? In that case, she might never see him again.

'Came all the way across London, I shouldn't wonder?' pursued Roderick, recrossing his feet in the place where Stella had sat. 'I should have said he'd have had a thirst.'

'Who, Harrison? No, he'd been listening to the band in the park.'

'Oh, is that what people here still do on Sunday evenings?' asked Roderick, willing to document himself as to civilian life. 'But I suppose there'll be a stop to that: winter'll be coming on.'

'Yes, winter will be,' she said, vaguely thumbing the letter she ought to show him. 'It will be coming on.'

'Those in fact must be nearly the last roses,' he pointed out, looking, with the elegiac pleasure possible at twenty, at the desk, 'Mother, I don't think you ought to knock them about like that.'

'It's nothing more than September,' she sharply said – 'Here, do you want to read this?'

He reached across for the lawyer's letter, but only went on to say: 'Then he's musical?'

'For Heaven's *sake*, Roderick – on and on about Harrison! What's the matter with you? Can't you see how he bores me?'

'Then why do you have him in the flat?'

'You know how people come in.'

'I know they keep coming into houses; I didn't think they kept coming into flats. That was the point of a flat, you once said.'

She sat down again on the sofa, angrily took a cushion back and, unconsciously holding it against her like a shield, said: 'You're not growing up to be a bully, are you?'

He seldom was, and was not this time, put out. 'But I always have taken an interest in you, Mother. Once I knew most of your friends, or at least about them. I sometimes wonder where some of them are.'

'Then you would put them all in the past tense?'

'Oh no,' said Roderick, once again surprised, 'I dare say it's I who am in the past tense.' Forthwith he began to arrange himself for sleep, lay flat, arms folded loosely across his chest; his mouth hung slightly open after a yawn as he dropped his head back to stare up into the ceiling's inverted depths. 'Did you say there were blankets . . .?'

She stared at him, repeating: 'I am so sorry about tomorrow.'

'I shall sleep, you see,' said he, with his air of total detachment.

'But not all tomorrow – how can you?'

'You've no idea how I can.'

'But it seems such waste.'

'Waste of what?'

She did not seem sure. 'Waste . . .,' she said again, for an instant closing her eyes. She bestirred herself and said: 'What about your friends? David, for instance, came running across the street the other day to ask where you were: and I saw Hattie on the top of a bus looking so nice.'

'I have nothing against either David or Hattie,' said Roderick tranquilly, 'except that I haven't a word to say to them.'

'They might not expect that.'

'Why shouldn't they? They ought to. Fred does.'

'Oh, very well,' said his mother – 'In case you do wake up, have you got any money?'

'Well, that is a point,' he conceded, knitting his brows. 'I mean, it could be a point in case of – that is, I mean to say if possibly –' He showed, for the first time this evening, signs of some inhibition, 'But no,' he went on, 'I don't imagine, on second thoughts, that you would ever *be* free for dinner tomorrow evening? . . . If you had been, you and I might have gone off somewhere and had a slight blowout.'

'Roderick, there's nothing I'd like more.' The answer, at any time natural, was in this instance intimidatingly true. It was dream-like – how long would it last, in fact? – this

71

throwing of desire into reverse. 'I can count,' she said, 'on your being awake by then?'

'Yes – Well,' he said, sighing, 'that will be very nice. In that case, I should be glad if we could arrange a loan.'

It had been clear, since Roderick was a child, that friendship with him would have to be one-sided. Not minding if he saw a person or not had been as far, apparently, as he would ever go; though he showed a well-mannered pleasure, wrongly read as response, in efforts to entertain or attach him. Stella had seen, if never taken to heart, the folly of hopeful comment on interests he did seem inclined to form. If he was what Harrison claimed to be, without vanity, that only made him more passive in his relations with people. If his willingness to be told a quite new story wore the deceptive guise of a new friendship, the deceived one, rather than Roderick, was to blame. He coupled a liking for, a curiosity as to, what was going on with a reluctance that it should involve him – more, a positive disbelief that it ever could. In general, he was in favour of what was happening, but preferred what *had* happened as being more complete: so far, his heart had never moved from its place, for it had felt no pull from a moving thing. His attention, as an entirety, was yet perhaps to be daunting, to be reckoned with: up to now it had never been wholly given. His motives were too direct to be called ulterior; he liked going out to tea with families who had a brook through their garden, hypothetical snakes in their uncut grass, collections of any kind in cabinets, a haunted room, a model railway, a funny uncle, a desk with a secret drawer. He attached himself to the children of such families in a flattering, obstinate, reserved way – you still could not, somehow, accuse him of cupboard love.

Stella could not fairly reproach in Roderick anything that savoured of only-childishness: was it not she who had left him an only child? In, *as* a child, preferring objects or myths to people he probably had resembled most other children: her unformed worry began when he failed to grow out of this. Having once seemed old, he now seemed young for his age. Her anxiety mingled with self-reproach – how if he came to set too much store by a world of which she, both as herself and as an instrument of her century, had deprived him? He would have esteemed, for instance, organic family life; she had not only lost his father for him but estranged herself (and him with her) from all his father's relations. She could perceive, too, that Roderick was ready to entertain a high, if abstract, idea of society – when he had been a baby she had amused him by opening and shutting a painted fan, and of that *beau monde* of figures, grouped and placed and linked by gestures or garlands, he never had, she suspected, lost interior sight. The fan on its fragile ivory spokes now remained closed: she felt him most happy when they could recreate its illusion in their talk.

Yes, what he liked about people was the order in which they could be arranged. Such idealization of pattern, these days, also alarmed his mother. She had supposed for some time that adolescence might make him more difficult but less odd – it had not yet done so when he went into the Army. Before that, she had watched him being confronted by people not only patternlessly doing what they liked but, still more preposterous from his point of view, expecting to be liked for their own sakes . . . Since she felt, or believed she felt, that Roderick ought to change, how foolish to dread lest the Army change him!

'Well, it's your leave, darling,' she said. 'Do as you like.'

Roderick was loath to remind his mother that she had so far done nothing about the blankets – however, nature spoke for him: he sneezed twice. At this she started up. He unfolded his arms in order to delve about, underneath himself in the cushions, then down the cracks of the sofa, for a handkerchief. Nothing, however, came of this – 'Wait,' he said, 'or possibly in this pocket?' He dived his hand into the slippery pocket of the dressing-gown; in which, audibly, it came upon at least *something*. Stella and he both heard the tired crackle of paper – paper long ago folded, pulped by age in its folds, limp from being in silk near a body's warmth. The sound from that pocket of Robert's made Stella start: her eyes, with an uncontrollable vehemence, interrogated her son's. 'Correspondence?' Roderick vaguely said: he fished out the paper, lay holding and staring at it, noncommittally twiddled it round and round.

'It's not yours,' she sharply said. 'Put it back.'

'Or had you better take charge of it? It might fall out again.'

'It didn't *fall* out this time,' she could not help remarking.

'However, it always might; and you never know.'

She said 'What on earth do you mean?'

'Well, you never know, you know, who might pick up what. And isn't what Robert's at quite important?'

She over-easily smiled, took the paper from him, made ready to tear it up. 'Hi!' he expostulated. 'It isn't yours, either.'

'It can't be anything much.'

'Still,' he said gravely, 'it was found worth keeping.'

'So are old bus tickets and empty match-books and receipts for things at two-and-eleven-three, and envelopes telegrams have arrived in.'

'I am sure, though, you ought to have a look at it.'

'Are you?' said she derisively, holding the twice-folded paper, dingy along its edges, pincer-nipped between her fingers and thumbs. She was aware of Roderick's eyes upon her in a suspended, dispassionate curiosity. Up to now, with that evasiveness a division between any two loves makes natural, she never had come to the point of asking herself what Roderick thought, or did not think, of herself and Robert. It could be possible that Roderick had succeeded in thinking nothing. If so, here was a crisis for them both. Like an ignorant looker-on at some famous game, trying to grasp the score and get the hang of the rules, he was watching to see what she would now do – expecting, evidently, to learn how far the prerogative of love went. He was waiting to see if this paper from Robert's pocket did count, was to be counted, as also hers. What a blunder, this bringing things to a head by this insane show of tearing the paper up. All the proprieties, everything sweet and lasting between herself and Roderick seemed to be caught up into this moment – in which she could hardly spare *them* a thought.

This was dynamite, between her fingers and thumbs. That she was terrified of the paper – she wondered, could Roderick see that, too? This secretively-folded grey-blue half-sheet became the corpus of suspicion – guilt, hers, baseness, hers. What did she feel to be possible? – and, how could she?

Smiling, as though Roderick were some atrocious contemporary, she remarked: 'It always could be a letter from a woman.'

He said naïvely: 'Oh, I shouldn't think so, should you? – No, more likely notes on some conversation.'

'But why should anybody make notes on a conversation?'

75

'Why, but really, Mother,' he exclaimed, heaving himself up on the sofa for greater emphasis, 'conversations are the leading thing in this war! Even I know that. Everything you and I have to do is the result of something that's been said. How far do you think we'd get without conversations? And can you really suppose that someone where Robert is doesn't have conversations *about* conversations, even if he doesn't have conversations himself?'

'Very well, very well, very well; I dare say he does.'

'And in that case,' said Roderick, lying back mollified, 'he might be expected to jot down points.'

She, however, went on staring at nothing, till she suddenly asked: 'Do *you* believe what you're told?'

'Depends on what I'm told, and who tells me.'

'Naturally. But, in general?'

'Well, I am not told much. In fact, as Fred says, it comes to seem fishy when one *is* told anything. Go by what you find out for yourself, he says. If a thing's true, you find it sticks out a mile once you come to look. Whereas if anybody goes out of his way to tell you something, Fred says you can take it he's got an axe to grind.'

'If what you were told were about someone you knew?'

'In that case, how could I be told anything? If I properly knew the person I'd already know the thing – I should imagine. If I knew what I was told was true, it would not be news to me. If it both was news to me and then did turn out to be true, I suppose I should take it that after all I never had properly known the person.'

'It all sounds so simple.'

'Well, so it should; it is.' He qualified this, however, by uncertainly, broodingly, looking at Stella's face. 'It would be

76

no good,' he warned her, 'coming to me for answers about anything complicated – I don't know anyone well except you and Fred.'

'Perhaps Fred might know what to do with a piece of paper?'

'Might it not just be best if I simply put it back again where it came from?' Roderick, having cleared his nose by an exhaustive, racking, prolonged sniff, added: 'All I was doing was looking for a handkerchief. No luck, however. – Could I have one of yours? Not one of those better ones with the monograms.'

She nodded. Rapidly she had unfolded the sheet of paper: now she was glancing through what was written on it in a semi-abstracted, calm, quite businesslike way. 'Nothing at all,' she said, 'as we might have known.' Idly, she tore it across once, still more idly tore it across again, then stood up to brush the pieces from her dress to the floor.

'We shall need the waste-paper basket,' Roderick said.

But she had walked away, humming, to come back with blankets and a handkerchief: she rugged up Roderick for the night while he blew his nose. By the time St Marylebone clock struck twelve the sofa had become a solitary bed. Through the dividing door between this and the other room he, still just on the surface, still just afloat, heard his mother moving dilatorily about, heard her pearl necklace being trickled on to the glass-topped table, on to which tops dropped from little bottles and pots. She kicked off her shoes, hung up her dress with a clatter of hangers along a rod. Soon he did not distinguish between what he heard and what he dreamed he heard; she might or might not have said quietly, 'Roderick?' – something, however, made him open his eyes. She had left a lamp alight on the stool beside him: the watery circle on the ceiling seemed for the moment to swell or tremble – so earthquake stories begin; but this could be only London giving one of her sleepy galvanic shudders, of which an echo ran through his relaxed limbs.

The lamp's dazzling shade was on a level with his eyes: beyond it the tide of his own sleep submerged and blurred what was in the room. He had only to put out a hand to put out the lamp, but for some time he continued to lie and stare at it with the beatific helplessnes of a drugged person – till at last, with a sigh like an exclamation, he heaved himself over, face inwards to the back of the sofa. He fell asleep with his forehead butted into the tense brocade.

In the other room, the telephone was given time to ring only one note. Stella answered it in a hurried low voice. 'Back?' she said . . . 'Listen, I can't talk now. Roderick's here, asleep – I think . . . I did not know myself: he came up this evening . . . Forty-eight hours.'

Roderick had rightly pigeon-holed Harrison as the man at the funeral – Cousin Francis Morris's. It had been on that occasion, four months ago, that Stella had for the first time met him. None of the little family party of mourners knew him, or had any idea who he was or how he came to be there – the funeral was meant to be strictly private. Wearing a dark suit, the intruder had occupied a pew to himself, some way down the church, some way back from the last of the rows of relatives. Afterwards, as the party straggled away from the graveside, out through the lych-gate and down the village street, he was found to have attached himself to its tail end. Stella's first view of him, glancing back, had been of someone stepping cranelike over the graves. During the procession to the hotel, at which a buffet lunch was to be served in a private room, the idea sprang up, to be discussed in murmurs, that he must have taken the funeral to be that of someone other than Francis Morris. The idea of his performing a pious duty under a wrong impression became embarrassing: no one cared to address him.

Stella had on the whole been grateful for the diversion Harrison's presence caused. For her, the day had not been an easy one; it involved, as well as the train journey to this old-world nucleus of a new dormitory town, the presenting of some sort of face to her once relations-in-law. She had not seen any of them, they had not seen her, since the disastrous end of her short marriage; they had every reason to feel coolly towards her, and today, in the main, gave evidence that they did.

She had nearly not come to the funeral at all: for her the good-bye she had spoken to Cousin Francis on the steps of his Irish house, at the end of her honeymoon, could be most happily left as the final one. The news of his death had done little more than stir up unwelcome memories – her melancholy, rather guilty regard for him had for a long time been of the kind one has for the dead. His actual death returned him to life again – his glass-grey eyes careering round their sockets, his kind wild smile and ragged pepper-and-salt moustache. His gestures, the intonations of his voice gained a renewed sharpness from the fact that they now would be made no more, heard no more. She had lost touch with the living Francis Morris completely: she had not even known him to be in England till she heard of his dying suddenly in this place.

She had come to the funeral because the lawyer's letter, notifying her of the arrangements made, had been in its final paragraph so worded as to suggest that she *should* be there, with her son. She had been surprised, as things were, at the invitation. But she had also come because she recalled Cousin Francis as being, like other Irishmen, himself an unfailing, feeling funeral-goer: three times, during their stay with him, had he set out, top-hatted, black as a crow all over, to travel unnumbered miles. The unfairness, not of his dying but of his dying as and where he had, touched and wounded her. War made the return of his body to Ireland impracticable: at home, his funeral following would have been a mile long – he was a respected landlord. As it was, death had surprised him in this neighbourless place: he had, even, few relatives left living in any part of England. After his seizure and death in the span of minutes, his lawyers – or, rather, the London representative of his Dublin lawyers – had been telephoned for and had taken charge, making the few sombre, meagre arrangements for what should have been Cousin Francis's greatest sociable day. There was no chief mourner; no one figure stood out from the indefinite level of cousinship; an awkward lack of priority made itself felt more and more among those present. There was wanting not only a head but a core of grief. They let themselves be shepherded by the lawyer.

Cousin Francis's death from a heart-attack at Wistaria Lodge could hardly have given more trouble: everything had had to be hushed up. It could have endangered the equilibrium of Dr and Mrs Tringsby's six tranquil uncertified mental patients, of whom Nettie Morris, the dead man's wife, was one. The whole frightful occurrence had confirmed the Tringsbys' prejudice against visitors: aided by the war, they had for some years succeeded in staving off Cousin Francis. They had felt he would prove upsetting – and so he had. Happily, the thing had been swiftly dealt with while the dear people were induced to keep to their rooms – the first to escape was fended off from the drawing-room by being told someone had gone to Heaven. Cousin Nettie, busy with arts and crafts, expected nothing, guessed nothing, was told nothing. She had not only forgotten Cousin Francis was coming, she happened to be enjoying one of those happy spells in which she was unaware that she had a husband at all.

Cousin Nettie was very well where she was. Heaven had intervened on her behalf, for she could not have set eyes on her husband's face without dreading that he had come to take her away. This would have returned to its full force her dread of having to cross the sea. Having been left undisturbed at Wistaria Lodge for years, she was now, the Tringsbys were certain, much more herself. She had possibly never been as happy as she now was; in the prospect of Cousin Francis's visit her good friends foresaw the undoing of their work. The elderly man's pigheadedness in the whole matter was more inexplicable – now that they thought it over – than, even, his collapse: the post-mortem had revealed cause for the second; nothing rationalized the first. Up to a month or two ago he had been the ideal patient's husband – elsewhere, quiescent, steadily (through his solicitors) paying up. *No* visit, in the Tringsbys' opinion, could be expected to go off completely well: Cousin Francis's missed by a hair's breadth being a total fiasco for Wistaria Lodge. Death came on him, however, in the drawing-room, before he set foot on the stairs to poor Nettie's room.

The taxi bespoken by Cousin Francis to drive him back again to the station had arrived on the tail of the ambulance coming for his body: both were greeted by music from gramophones wafted out of the windows of the patients' rooms. This month, the flower which gave the house its named bloomed in mauve trickles down the cream stucco front. Late afternoon sun struck on the blue curtains drawn hastily across the drawing-room windows. It irritated Dr Tringsby, who in these days had difficulty in arranging motor-car outings for his patients, to see the taxi going to waste. When Cousin Francis had at last been removed, the Tringsbys sat down and looked at each other; and this signalized the dawn of a mood in which they saw no reason to do anything more. They had already telephoned to the dead man's lawyer, with whom they had always been in touch, it being he who made all arrangements for Cousin Nettie, and paid, as meticulously as he scrutinized, their account. He thought highly of them and they thought highly of him. The lawyer could be relied on to see their point, which was that the funeral could not, under any conditions, be expected to take place 'from' Wistaria Lodge. Next day, Mrs Tringsby so far rallied herself as to telephone to the florist's for a beautiful wreath – which Cousin Nettie must send but not be allowed to see. Mrs Tringsby inscribed the card with:

From his loving wife
Till the day break and the shadows flee away

It was she who suggested that the Station Hotel might be persuaded to run a light buffet lunch.

Unexpectedly – and, it was felt, nicely – Mrs Tringsby turned up at the funeral: more, she brought with her the two steadiest of the patients, to swell the mourners' mournfully thin ranks. These two were told nothing more than that this was the funeral of a gentleman who had died: they enjoyed themselves quietly and asked no questions.

Cousin Francis's visit to Wistaria Lodge had been a matter of honour, not merely of obstination. His real object in making the journey to England had been to offer that country his services in the war – his own country's abstention had been a severe blow, but he had never sat down under a blow yet. Bound to Mount Morris both by passion and duty, he had waited two and a half years for Eire to reverse her decision: hopes of German invasion had for part of that time sustained him – he had dug tanktraps in the Mount Morris avenues – but as those hopes petered out he resolved to act. It appeared that he might have waited just too long, for by now the regulations affecting an Eire subject's travel to England had been forbiddingly tightened up. Having tried everything, everyone, in an increasing frenzy, Cousin Francis found he could only obtain an exit permit on 'compassionate' grounds – the pretext of a visit to his afflicted wife. The repugnance to him, and the pointlessness, of the visit he must therefore endeavour to overlook. Though annoyed by the tone of the Tringsbys' letters, he could not at heart have agreed with them more profoundly that Nettie was better left alone. But not having, in the course of his sixty-five years, ever obtained anything under false pretences, he could not, as he saw things, omit Wistaria Lodge. An Irish gentlemen's honour is a hard master – he decided to swallow the pill at once, polish Nettie off, then have his time his own. So – having spent one day in his London hotel, writing letters to influential people he thought he knew and people he knew who he thought might be influential, and having kept one appointment – he caught the train into the Home Counties next morning. To be out of town for some hours, at this juncture, should just give the letters time to mature. Of course, if anyone were to telephone it would be a pity: he charged the hotel to tell them he would be back by eight.

The recipients of his letters learned from *The Times* announcement that they had been spared the embarrassment of replying. The insertion of the word 'suddenly' in the notice and the suppression of the locale of the death, gave rise in some quarters to the notion that Cousin Francis had been killed by a bomb. This, in a month when enemy action was not severe, seemed particularly tough on the poor old chap who had so lately quitted his own safe shores. Otherwise, for the death, under any circumstances, of an obscure and elderly Irish landowner there could not be much emotion to spare. It was recollected, with a final breath of relief, that the widow was in no state to receive letters. Most grateful of all was the intimation that the funeral was to be strictly private.

Stella had been among the few to be notified as to time and place. The lawyer's letter, redirected from her pre-war address, only arrived on the eve of the day itself – she had made this her justification for not so much as trying to contact Roderick. She did not see how he could get leave at such short notice, for the funeral of a first cousin once-removed. It was difficult enough to get leave herself. All the same, she ought – as she recollected only when she was half-way there in the train – to have let Roderick know Cousin Francis *was* dead: he was a name at least, and her son set store by names – though Roderick's only connexion with Cousin Francis was that of having been conceived under his roof. To face the truth of the matter, she did not want Roderick with her on this occasion – did not want him to see her being cold-shouldered, even possibly cut; nor did she want him eyed in a solicitous manner, as being a bad mother's fatherless son. The world in which one could still be seen as *déclassée* was on the whole ignored by her, but not yet quite.

Alone, she could hope to keep cool and wear a face. As the train slowed down for the station, she hastily glanced at herself in her handbag mirror, trying on an expression of imperviousness – even, should it be necessary, of effrontery. The London black suit she wore, though severe and matt, somehow failed altogether to look like mourning. No other mourner seemed, after all, to have been in the train with her: all others must have allowed the margin necessary for being in good time. She lost her way between the station and the church, made her entrance only just not late, and, as she clicked up the aisle on her high heels, felt treacherous colour flaming up her cheeks. Several heads half-turned and at the half-turn paused. She carried a bunch of tulips and white lilac, but was too shy to place this on the exposed coffin, adorned only, so far, by Cousin Nettie's wreath.

Delinquent in being known to be who she was, she could not fail to recognize Harrison as a fellow-delinquent in being not known to be anyone. How right she had been, she thought, to keep Roderick out of this.

It was not till she learned what was in the will that she saw she had been, on the contrary, very wrong. It was Roderick who ought to have headed the wavering procession out of the church; it was Roderick who should have stationed himself at the raw lip of the lonely grave, coming as near as he could to the sonless man who by naming him heir had sought him out as a son. Cousin Francis left Mount Morris and the land to Roderick – 'in the hope', it was written, 'that he may care in his own way to carry on the old tradition'. Such capital as had not been placed in trust to provide for the widow during her lifetime went direct to Roderick; the rest would come to him later. There was not very much.

It was not, of course, till they had reached the hotel that she was taken aside to be told this. Until then, the lawyer was occupied in moving sheepdog-like, in his shadowy role of host, up and down the little straggle of mourners, improvising a murmured remark for each. The gathering, one learned, was by no means over; for ever-severer cuts in the train service so worked out that nobody could depart, on the up or down line, for something under two hours more. It was therefore necessary to acclimatize the sad visitors, and at least to coax them to linger over their buffet lunch. There was, frankly, not much here to view and admire, except the church – of which, by this time, they had had enough. So, at least, said the lawyer – Mrs Tringsby, more locally proud, pointed out landmarks along the street.

The main street was by now empty: today nothing more would happen. Before noon the housewives had swarmed, so completely, whitely, stripping the shops that one might ask oneself why these remained open. A scale or two adhered to the fishmonger's marble slab; the pastrycook's glass shelves showed a range of interesting crumbs; the fruiterer filled a longstanding void with fans of cardboard bananas and a 'Dig for Victory' placard; the greengrocer's crates had been emptied of all but earth by those who had somehow failed to dig hard enough. The butcher flaunted unknown joints of purplish meat in the confidence that these could not be bought; the dairy restricted itself to a china cow; the grocer, with costless courage, kept intact his stocks of dummy cartons and tins. In the confectioner's windows the ribbons bleached on dummy boxes of chocolate among flyblown cut-outs of pre-war blondes. Newsagents without newspapers gave out in angry red chalk that they had no matches either. Pasted inside a telephone booth, a notice asked one to telephone less.

The sun did not shine; and, as in May so often, there was something uneasy about the lowered sky and ink-blue fumy darkness across the distance. The leaves of the pollarded trees along the pavement burned an unnatural green. One seemed

87

to have left the churchyard with its alert headstones for a scene of less future, order, and animation. Thankful, at any rate, that they did not live here, the mourners glanced at their dark reflections in the darkling windows as they streamed past the shops: in the hush, an express train not stopping here could be heard roaring away down the main line.

'We are actually full of soldiers,' said Mrs Tringsby, piloting the party across the trafficless street. They are always an interest; my dear people love them. But I suppose they are all at their dinner now.'

Stella, not yet aware of her standing as heir's mother, was glad when her turn for a word from the lawyer came. She was ready for company; it was by the merest chance that she had not been left to walk quite alone – one of the Tringsby patients had drawn alongside, but he skipped on and off the pavement and did not speak. Trying to fight off the influence of the street and day and still more of the memory of the grave – on which, it seemed to her, they had so shame-facedly, hurriedly turned their backs – she supported herself by thinking about Robert. When the lawyer bowed at her elbow and said how much he regretted Roderick's having been unable to come, she explained for the second time that he was in the Army. The lawyer accepted this with an incredulous second bow, and said he would ask for a word with her later on. She at once looked deeply apprehensive: he, as though to dispel something, cleared his throat and asked if *she* had any idea who the stranger might be.

'Not the slightest,' said she, having looked behind her. 'Hasn't anyone else?'

'Apparently not. And he does not correspond with anyone on my list.'

'Oh dear,' said Stella vaguely. 'So what do you think he's up to? Perhaps he simply saw the thing in *The Times.*'

'But I did not put place or time of the funeral in *The Times;* in accord with general feeling that it should be strictly private.'

'But, good heavens,' cried Stella, '*whose* general feeling? Anybody would think Cousin Francis had been hanged! I cannot feel he'd have liked things hole-in-a-corner. I should have liked to have given him a send-off.'

'All this has been very trying for Dr and Mrs Tringsby.'

'But really much more trying for Cousin Francis!'

The lawyer, who had compressed his lips, unparted them to begin, 'But, my dear lady . . .' paused, sized up Stella, began again.

'I allow for feeling,' he said. 'I am not without feeling. At the same time, placed as I have been, and in the absence of any expressed wish of any near relation of Mr Morris's, I could not have felt myself justified in ignoring the interests of Dr and Mrs Tringsby. The charge of uncertified patients, such as they undertake, is at all times a delicate matter. I am satisfied that their conduct of Wistaria Lodge is above reproach. I have been, therefore, at pains to safeguard the establishment against further disturbance and, still more, publicity of an unwelcome kind.'

'Oh.'

Oppressed by so much explanation, Stella glanced away from the lawyer towards her other companion – the hatless Tringsby patient not unlike Mr Dick. Something struck her – 'Of course,' she suggested, 'your stranger you cannot place may be one more of the Wistaria Lodge party?'

'Oh?' . . . said the lawyer, 'ah . . .' He moved on ahead at once to check up the matter with Mrs Tringsby. As he failed to return to put Stella right, she continued to think of Harrison as a Tringsby patient: she continued to look at him in that light when, at the hotel, he came up with a cup of coffee. Some ideas, like dandelions in lawns, strike tenaciously: you may pull off the top but the root remains, drives down suckers and may even sprout again. Her uncontrovertible sense of Harrison's queerness dated, she saw ever afterwards, from that day of the funeral. His stops in talking, apparently due to some inner cramp; the exaggerated quietness of his movements, as though their importance must be at all costs hidden; his ununified way of regarding you simultaneously out of each eye – these, in the months that followed, were to keep on alimenting her first idea. He had followed the funeral like a shark a ship. 'Originally,' she was to tell him from time to time, 'I took for granted you were a lunatic; and I am still not so certain that I was wrong.'

No sooner had the procession reached the hotel than Stella was prised apart from it by the lawyer. In default of any other place where they could be private, he took her to a recess under the stairs: surrounded by hanging macintoshes, he made known to her the effect of Cousin Francis's will, and placed in her hands the envelope of the typescript copy. Askance, she asked: 'But aren't you going to read it aloud to everyone?' 'I shall be ready to do so, in response to any expressed wish. As you and I know, it effects no one else here. It is, as you say, a pity your son could not be present. As against which, his being still a minor and your being his guardian makes the legacy, for the time being, equally your concern.'

'Yes, of course, I see.'

Agitated, not knowing what she felt and wondering what Roderick would feel, she rejoined the party in the private room upstairs. Looking round at the others with a new eye, she supposed that, if they knew what was in the will, they would look with a new eye at her. Not one of these faces stood out clearly; the interior, with its maroon walls, was, like the day outdoors, overcast. The windows wore wire gauze half-blinds; through one window a chestnut threw its viridian reflection, balancing waxy flowers, into a tarnished mirror across the room. And this tall wide mirror, relic of some vanished ballroom, reflected also Roderick's father's people, sombrely milling around the buffet. Mrs Tringsby, annoyed by the misunderstanding about Harrison – who did not look to her, she had told the lawyer, at all the type of person she would have had in her house – had placed her two real dear people side by side on a bench, at the greatest possible distance from the intruder: circulating, herself, amongst the rest of the party, she plied back from time to time to the bench with more sandwiches, and could be heard to hope that they were enjoying themselves.

No sooner was Stella inside the room than Harrison came up with the cup of coffee. 'Or if you'd rather,' he said, 'I see there's some so-called port.'

This looks very nice,' she said, accepting the coffee, neutrally smiling.

'Or one could always nip down and see what they've got in the bar?'

'No, thank you; this really looks very nice.' She attempted to move away, but he headed her off again with a plate of sandwiches. 'Not much of a send-off, this,' he said, 'for the poor old boy. What a place to snuff out in, when everything's said and done!'

'Wistaria Lodge?'

'Well, I mean to say – in a nut-house! If he had even been having a bit of fun . . .'

She frowned, bit into a sandwich, and revised, at least for the moment, her idea. So, one was once more back where one started – nowhere. She said: 'Oh, you knew him, then?'

'Why not?' said he, eyeing her in a moody but somehow rallying way. 'What else would make one show up at a show like this?'

'I don't know, really.'

'You probably can't place me?'

'I don't know that I've tried – I had not seen Cousin Francis for such a long time that I have no idea whom he might not know.'

'Frankly, no more had I,' said Harrison promptly. 'At this side of the water, that's to say. You rather cut out Ireland? I knew him there. What an old place that was of his – right off the beaten track! And what a reception one got there – quite Oriental! Yes, dear old Frankie and I had great get-togethers. You'd be surprised how often I heard your name – I do rightly take it you're Mrs Rodney?'

'Yes,' she said, far from pleased. She looked round the room, hoping for some way out. She resignedly added: 'You come from Ireland?'

'I go there.'

'Fishing?'

'Alas, no time.'

She had rather thought not. She passed on to her second idea – which was also, in its own way, to strike down a root – that he must be a travelling salesman, gentleman-type. She could picture him punting up in a small car and broaching country house steps, to assure the owner he had a fine old place here. Cousin Francis had always looked kindly on new inventions, though with a final reluctance to take advantage of them. With regard to heating, lighting, and plumbing he was happy to keep Mount Morris in, almost, its original state; and his farm was fun and his land worked with few aids unknown in his grandfather's day – none the less, systems, outfits, fit-ups, gadgets and all forms of mechanized labour-savers entranced him; he wrote for booklets containing further particulars of almost every device he saw advertised. He had flirted, to within danger of breach of promise, with an air-conditioning plant, a room-to-room telephone, an electric dish-washer, and a fireproof roof. Any salesman would find him as easy to 'interest' as he would prove impossible to pin down. He could be written off as a famous waster of time.

'Yes, remarkably fine old place he had there, too,' said he, with an apparent clairvoyance which made her start. 'And now, I seem to remember, that's to go to your son?'

Too much annoyed by his manner to be surprised at his knowledge, she said, 'I believe so, yes,' and glanced round the room again. She told herself, it was like her to have attached this person: from every point of view this was the last straw. She caught, and held for a moment, the solicitous eye of a Colonel Pole. Meanwhile, Harrison uttered – for the first time, where she was concerned – his laugh. 'You wonder a bit,' he said, 'at my spotting you? As one's not, as a rule, introduced at a show like this, one puts two and two together – *My* name, by the way, is Harrison – Frankly, there's no one else here who very well could be you – I having, as you might say, so oft heard your praises sung.'

She exclaimed – to herself, aloud, overlooking him – 'If I'd ever known he remembered me, still was fond of me, liked to talk about me! I could have so often so easily gone to see him – or else sent him Roderick, if he'd wanted that!'

'Yes,' agreed Harrison smugly, 'rather a pity, really. One so often thinks of a thing too late.'

Tears filled her eyes; from that moment she hated him.

He went on: 'Now, when I saw old Frankie in London the other day –'

'You saw him? This time – since he came over?'

'Mm-mm. Why not?'

'You ran into him?'

'Far from it – we'd got a date. That was when he came to mention he was due down here, this place, next day, to look up the poor old girl. We left it I was to give him a ring again first thing next morning when he'd got back to London. When I did ring, the fat was in the fire. The hotel had just been notified he'd popped off. And more, his lawyers had taken over, and on their instructions they'd locked his room up; which was the devil, he having some stuff of mine. Of course I went round, but the management were not playing. So I then thought, well, the remaining thing one can do is to stand by the poor old boy through the final round. Next, of course, the question arose – but *where?* To cut short a longish story, I put two and two together. Knowing there'd been a run on London burying-space, and that one would think twice these days about shipping a stiff to Ireland, I considered here a good bet, which it proved. I may say, I went to the trouble of checking up.'

'You certainly went to a good deal of trouble.'

'Then again, why not, after all?' he said. 'An old friend.'

She just was beginning to wonder why the reply did not, somehow, either rebuke or convince her, when Colonel Pole approached with a glass of port. Colonel Pole, with whom her refugee glance had found its mark, had for some time now been wishing to cross the gulf dividing this lady from the rest of the party; now that his wife Maud had fallen into conversation with Mrs Tringsby, he seized the opportunity of doing so. With a courteous determined movement of the shoulder he drove a wedge between Stella and Harrison: the latter immediately turned away. Colonel Pole said he supposed she did not remember him?

'Of course I remember you!' Stella said. 'Do you still breed those lovely Samoyed puppies?'

'Hitler has put the lid on that, for the time being. You would not care for some port? . . . I'm afraid you're right.' Colonel Pole shook his head. 'Frankie himself,' he said, 'would have done us very much better. Making allowance for everything, I cannot feel this solicitor fellow has done his best – at the same time, he strikes me as taking a bit too much on himself. Bit of a bee in his bonnet about these Tringsbys – makes one fancy he must have put money into their place? And he does not seem clear who is here today and who isn't – for instance, your son is not with us, I understand?'

'No. He – he couldn't get leave in time.'

'Very gallant, of you, coming down on your own like this.' Colonel Pole, looking cautiously after Harrison, added: 'Or is that a friend of yours?'

'No.'

'I somehow thought not,' he exclaimed – the more warmly because Maud had taken the other view. 'I should not be surprised to hear that you've no idea who he is – any more, that's to say, than the rest of us have.'

'He says his name is Harrison.'

'That does not tell one much.'

She agreed. Colonel Pole went on: 'He's not been annoying you?'

'Not exactly.'

'He did not happen to say what he thinks he is doing here?'

'He knew Cousin Francis in Ireland.'

'Ireland? Things may not be what they were in that unfortunate country, but you won't get me to believe that chap is an Irishman! So what was he up to there, I should like to know?'

'I don't think he said.'

'Up to some kind of hanky-panky, I should not wonder.'

'Apparently Cousin Francis knew all about him.'

'It was characteristic of Frankie,' said Colonel Pole, 'not to spot hanky-panky when he saw it. Up to a point he'd listen to any story; he was as innocent as a babe unborn. At the same time, he'd got a memory like a sieve – he had no doubt completely forgotten he ever met this fellow.'

'I don't think he can have,' said Stella mildly. 'They met by appointment in London only the other day.'

'What, not *this* time?' said Colonel Pole, changing colour.

'That is what Mr Harrison told me. The day before Cousin Francis came down here.'

'Now that I just don't believe! Appointment? Meeting in London? Why, not a soul knew Frankie was in this country. *You'd* heard nothing? – I thought not: no more had Maud and I. And, from what I've made out this morning, all the rest here today were just as much in the dark. To tell you the truth, it's been that that's hit me as hard as anything – Frankie's coming over to England and never letting me know! He and I, you know – or perhaps you don't – no, how should you? – grew up as boys together; one time, we were like brothers. Blood is thicker than water, whatever else they invent. You set store by your memories when you get to my age.' Colonel Pole, already looking unhappy, paused, frowned, and further lowered his voice. 'One or two things lately have made me ask myself whether this drawn-out wretched business about poor Nettie could have unsettled Frankie in any sort of way. Then came this Irish muddle, to top the lot – there was no braver country when I was young. Not that it does to think of the old times. Once you hand over the reins to a pack of rebels – ! But there, again, you had Frankie – obstinate as a mule. You had to allow for the fact that his roots were there: he got to be as touchy as – well, I should not care to say! For instance, last Christmas, writing my yearly letter, I couldn't resist a dig; it may have been wrong of me. I wrote: "You must be proud, these days, of your precious country." Whereupon, will you believe me, he fired a letter back fairly blowing my head off – this and that and the other, in a pretty nearly nationalistic strain. Even Maud said: "Why, Frankie's losing his sense of humour." I am bound to say that beyond agreeing with Maud, I did not make much of that at the time. It is only now – I mean, it is only since – *You* don't imagine I could have hurt him, do you? He and I have been sparring since we were so high. Still, there it stands: he came over to England this time, after all these years, without one word to me. However . . . What about more coffee?'

'No, thank you very much.'

'What you probably need, like me, is a decent lunch. Morning like this takes it out of one, makes one think. P'raps I see things out of proportion? No, whatever you say, that was *not* like Frankie. – There's another thing I should very much like to know – what's to become of the place?'

Stella raised her eyes. 'It's been left to my son.'

'Indeed? Is that so . . .?' Colonel Pole digested this slowly.

'All the more pity,' he said, 'if that's the way Frankie saw things, that that boy of yours could not be here today.' Cogitation appeared in his blue eyes; he eyed the heir's mother with unaffected concern. 'A white elephant. What will the boy do?'

'As he knows nothing yet, I have no idea.'

'The last sort of thing that *his* generation wants. Myself, I was never happier than in the old days there; I can see that place today, every stick and stone. But we've got to face it: all that's a thing of the past. It's better to me, all right, to think of Mount Morris going. At the same time,' said Colonel Pole, sternly raising his voice and squaring his shoulders, 'I advise you to advise the boy to get rid of it – sell outright, before he ties himself up. At his age, one has got to move with the times. All that timber should go for a pretty price. One thing he should do at once is take the roof off the house, or they'll be popping nuns in before you can say knife. Tell him that from me.'

'I will. But he must decide for himself.'

'Well, to think of Frankie! – D'you know, I'd no idea he'd had the pleasure of ever meeting your son?'

'They never did meet. And Roderick never has seen Mount Morris.'

'All for the best, no doubt: sentiment won't have to enter in.'

'No, I suppose not,' she agreed sadly.

'Sentiment,' said Colonel Pole, 'is the devil. Has made more mess of more men's lives, if I may speak so plainly, than drink or women. However, your young Robert –'

'– Roderick,' she impassively corrected.

'I beg your pardon: Roderick – he and his generation will have no use for that. All they will want is to travel light. After all, the future is in their hands.'

'In that case, how can they travel light?'

Colonel Pole looked baffled. 'Well, they can have the future: shall not myself be here to see what they make of it – Let's see – *you* know Mount Morris, I fancy?'

'I once did. Victor and I were there for our honeymoon.'

He dared not decide whether her eyes, with their misted askance look, were those of the victim or of the *femme fatale*. He did not know the whole of that story, and did not want to. What one had heard was this – that about two years after her marriage Stella Rodney had asked her husband for a divorce. It could but be that there was someone else in her life; however, the injured Victor, up to the last quixotic, had let her divorce him. That injustice, crowned by her being given custody of the child, had left her for ever detestable to Victor's family, headed by the Maud Pole group. Victor was understood to have worshipped Stella, how wrongly! Not long before their marriage he had emerged from the 1914 war with a wound still troublesome, shaken health – a man who called to be built up, and she had cast him down. Her worthlessness had lost him wife, son, and home. Three weeks after the decree was made absolute he had died, in the place he had taken refuge, the house of a kindly middle-aged woman who had already nursed him during the war. The sole satisfaction for Maud and the family had been this – that the unknown man for whose sake Stella had sacrificed Victor's life did not attempt to claim her now she was free; therefore, there *she* was; living, one heard, with her son in a succession of little houses about the country on an income estimated by Maud Pole to amount to about nine hundred a year. Beyond one rumour that while occupying a dower house she had been having a flirtation with her landlord, little more had been heard of her, good or bad. All that, though ancient history, had been regrettably raked up by her appearance at the funeral, and today was very much in the air.

Colonel Pole, however, still could not but think it gallant of her to have come. Having never, at least so far as he knew, found himself eye to eye with a *femme fatale*, he had no means of knowing whether he now did so. Whether it was or was not under the influence of the shock of Frankie's death that he had to, could only, speak to her from the heart, he could not say. She certainly was not barefaced – no longer meeting her eyes he looked, havering, at the string of pearls round her throat showing no sign of age. She was better than gallant, she was feeling; she brought grace to this sparse ignoble burying of poor old Frankie far from his own land. It was outrageous she should have been left to Harrison. He said: 'Well, if there's ever anything I can do . . . .'

'What I am really dying for is a cigarette.'

Stella finished herself, in the view of all, by returning to London in charge of Harrison. The Poles, she found, were travelling in the opposite direction; their homeward journey would take them into the Midlands. She had gained face, for the time being, from the length of her conversation with Colonel Pole; three or four more of the family, after that, had bowed or briefly spoken to her. But none of the few who had bowed or spoken turned out, alas, to be catching the London train; it was those who persisted in doing neither who formed, at the other end of the station platform, a close group in chilly talk. As for Harrison, he had shot out of the hotel bar in time to catch up with Stella on the station approach, saying: 'Good. So we all go the same way home . . . First smoker?' he asked, as the train drew in.

She said: 'I'm travelling third.'

'Oh, come – for Frankie's sake I think we blow the expense!' In the train he paid up the difference on her ticket – and, she saw, on his own – with the air of one getting value for money. 'It's not every day,' he said, blithely shovelling into his pocket the change from a pound note, 'that one runs into someone one's been wanting to meet. I had rather hoped your son might have been on the party also – I expect he'd have made a point of that if he'd known. I'd have liked to have met him. Perhaps we might fix that up?'

'Roderick's always away now he's in the Army.'

'Lonely for you – or is it?' Harrison said.

'I cannot quite see why you want to meet him.'

'In the first place, obviously, isn't he your son?'

Seeing no reason to take this up, she busied herself with lighting one of the cigarettes Colonel Pole had transferred from his case into her own. Harrison's case, whipped out just not in time, snapped shut again like the jaws of a chagrined crocodile.

'And another thing – or would this seem funny to you? – your son, to me, seems all that's left of old Frankie.'

'Oh!' she said, far less coldly.

'That's how I see it. At the same time, there's something else. Ha-ha – now you mustn't think I'm going to be a nuisance! I really am anxious to get back that stuff of mine, which, as I told you, they've got under lock and key with the rest of the doings at his hotel. Which could be quite a lengthy not to say ticklish matter. You know what they are, those lawyers: don't give a damn. I understand that your son is residuary legatee –'

'But isn't it the executors who would have access to Cousin Francis's things? You should go to them, surely?'

'How right you are. And that's where I shall go, of course. But here's where we come up against another awkward point – there is nothing to show that the stuff *is* mine. Me just turning up to claim it out of the blue might strike those executors as a bit fishy; I wouldn't blame them; I'd think it fishy myself. Old Frankie would have vouched for me like a rajah – but then, if we got *him* with us none of this would arise. As things are, you see how I'm placed? If your son could take me along and explain he knew me –'

'But Roderick doesn't know you.'

'Yes, but he would by then. Or say you knew me –'

'I'm sorry, but that would not be true.'

'Ha-ha – but we're rapidly making it true, I hope?'

That she did not share the hope in any possible way she intimated – by leaning absently back as he leaned ardently forward (he had secured for their journey two facing corner seats), by looking sideways out at the flying landscape, by becoming too distant even to show surprise. After a curative interval she remarked: 'I'm not even clear what you left in Mr Morris's room. Goods, of some sort? Prospectuses? Samples, of any kind?'

'Good gosh, no – simply one or two papers.'

She, who was seldom as rude as this, said: 'Perhaps you've been writing poetry?'

Focusing upon Stella his not-quite squint, he replied in good faith: 'No, that's never been much my line. No, this was simply something I jotted down, with a view to entertaining the old fellow. You remember, he was a tiger for facts and figures.'

'If you carry all that in your head, why not just jot it down again?'

'Well, it was my stuff partly, partly some stuff he gave me. We swapped; then I worked the thing out to show him how two and two made four. If you'd care to hear the entire story, off we go – it was like this –'

'– No, I needn't trouble you. Keep it for the executors.'

'In that case, we're back where we started.'

It appeared that they were. Only one thing revived her: they seemed to be nearing London. Hoardings became more frequent; garden fences criss-crossed: ruins began to string out along the main line. As the suburbs thickened on either hand she felt less constricted, and bolder. Though they were not alone she had felt gated off from their fellow-travellers by Harrison's way of sticking a leg across, and, still more, by his fixing forceful manner to her. That this had not attracted attention she could not hope. Soon now, however, should come King's Cross.

'No, I can't see how I can help you,' she said firmly. 'I could only say you knew Cousin Francis, and after all, you can always say that yourself.'

'Oh, absolutely,' agreed Harrison. 'Absolutely.'

'I see it's annoying for you.'

'It could be more so.'

'Oh?'

'It's put me into the way of talking to you.'

She raised her voice a frigid half-tone, to say:

'I might write to one executor, whom I know a little. Also, could you not show them Mr Morris's letter to you, making that appointment you kept in London?'

'That's an idea, you know.' He looked at her respectfully with both eyes.

At King's Cross she succeeded, or fancied herself to have succeeded, in giving him the slip. He went ahead to try for a taxi; she made a loop through the crowd and got into the Underground. She did not expect to have to give him another thought – after consideration, she saw no reason to involve herself in his dealings with the executors. He did not know her address; her name was not in the London telephone book. When, therefore, two evenings later Harrison rang her up to say how much he hoped she had got home safely, she was not so much annoyed as point-blank astounded. Both feelings were cast into the shade by what had become, by that time, her ruling worry – Roderick *had* been genuinely put out at not having been told beforehand about the funeral: she had never had any idea he could feel so strongly. Not only in order to make this good but that she and he might have the necessary business talk, she took yet another train on her next free day to meet Roderick near where he was in camp. Meanwhile, she posted to him the copy of Cousin Francis's will; he should have time to digest this before they met.

Had he done so? The afternoon appointed found them face to face with each other across a teashop table: Roderick, with a frown, unfolded the document, which had been a good deal thumbed. His eyes ran down the typescript till they stopped at a line – 'Look, this is where I want to know what you think. When he's said about how he bequeathes

Mount Morris, the lands, the etcetera, etcetera, and so on, to his cousin Roderick Vernon Rodney, me, he goes on, *"In the hope that he may care in his own way to carry on the old tradition." – Why* must lawyers always take out commas?'

'Because what they write is meant to be clear without them.'

'Well, in this case it isn't. Which *did* Cousin Francis mean?'

'Which what, darling?'

'Did he mean, care in my own way, or, carry on the old tradition in my own way?'

Uncomprehending, Stella returned her eyes to the cropped top of Roderick's downbent head. 'In the end, I suppose,' she hazarded, 'it would come to the same thing?'

'I'm not asking what it would come to; I want to know what he meant.'

'I know. But the first thing is that you'll really have to decide –'

'What should I decide? He's decided. It's become mine.'

'We must think what you're going to do.'

'But I want to know which he meant. Does he mean, that I'm free to care in any way I like, so long as it's *the* tradition I carry on; or, that so long as I care in the same way he did, I'm free to mean by "tradition" anything I like?'

'There was another cousin of yours, Roderick, a Colonel Pole, at the funeral, who said –'

'Yes, Mother, *yes;* but never mind Colonel Pole. What we must make out is, what Cousin Francis meant. That might make all the difference to what I do.'

'One must not be too much influenced by a dead person! After all, one can only live how one can; one generally finds there is only one way one *can* live – and that often must mean disappointing the dead. They had no idea how it would be for us. If they still had to live, who knows that they might not have disappointed themselves?'

'Is there any reason to think Cousin Francis did so?'

'He seems to have seemed, to most people, a disappointed man.'

'Cousin Nettie went off her chump; Ireland refused to fight. But that's not the same as to say he let himself down. – However,' concluded Roderick, folding the will and putting it back in the envelope, 'let's leave that at that. I've really made up my mind.'

'Colonel Pole seemed to think you really ought to think twice.'

'I have.'

'Colonel Pole felt you ought not to tie yourself up.'

'Fred takes exactly the opposite view.'

'You may not be able to go there for some time – it's in Eire, you're British, besides being in the Army.'

'I can't help that: Mount Morris won't run away.'

'But meanwhile the roof may fall in, or the trees blow down.'

'I don't suppose so,' the tranquil Roderick said.

5

What the inheritance came to be for Roderick, Robert was for Stella – a habitat. The lovers had for two years possessed a hermetic world, which, like the ideal book about nothing, stayed itself on itself by its inner force. They had first met in London in September 1940, when Robert, discharged from hospital after a Dunkirk wound, came to the War Office. The damage was to a knee; it had left its trace on his walk in an inequality which could be called a limp; he was not likely again to see active service. That honourable queerness about his gait varied: at times he could control it out of existence, at others he fairly pitched along with an impatient exaggeration of lameness further exaggerated by his height. The variation, she had discovered, had like that in a stammer a psychic cause – it was a matter of whether he did or did not, that day, feel like a wounded man. Her awareness, his unawareness of that was so deep a component of their intimacy that she wondered what, had they met before 1940, would have taken the place between them of his uncertain knee. The first few times they met she had not noticed the limp – or, if, vaguely, she had, she had put it down to the general rocking of London and one's own mind.

They had met one another, at first not very often, throughout that heady autumn of the first London air raids. Never had any season been more felt; one bought the poetic sense of it with the sense of death. Out of mists of morning charred by the smoke from ruins each day rose to a height of unmisty glitter; between the last of sunset and first note of the siren the darkening glassy tenseness of evening was drawn fine. From the moment of waking you tasted the sweet autumn not less because of an acridity on the tongue and nostrils; and as the singed dust settled and smoke diluted you felt more and more called upon to observe the daytime as a pure and curious holiday from fear. All through London, the ropings-off of dangerous tracts of street made islands of exalted if stricken silence, and people crowded against the ropes to admire the sunny emptiness on the other side. The diversion of traffic out of blocked main thoroughfares into byways, the unstopping phantasmagoric streaming of lorries, buses, vans, drays, taxis past modest windows and quiet doorways set up an overpowering sense of London's organic power – somewhere here was a source from which heavy motion boiled, surged and, not to be damned up, forced for itself new channels.

The very soil of the city at this time seemed to generate more strength: in parks the outsize dahlias, velvet and wine, and the trees on which each vein in each yellow leaf stretched out perfect against the sun blazoned out the idea of the finest hour. Parks suddenly closed because of timebombs – drifts of leaves in the empty deck chairs, birds afloat on the dazzlingly silent lakes – presented, between the railings which still girt them, mirages of repose. All this was beheld each morning more light-headedly: sleeplessness disembodied the lookers-on.

In reality there were no holidays; few were free however lightheadedly to wander. The night behind and the night to come met across every noon in an arch of strain. To work or think was to ache. In offices, factories, ministries, shops, kitchens the hot yellow sands of each afternoon ran out slowly; fatigue was the one reality. You dared not envisage sleep. Apathetic, the injured and dying in the hospitals watched light change on walls which might fall tonight. Those rendered homeless sat where they had been sent; or, worse, with the obstinacy of animals retraced their steps to look for what was no longer there. Most of all the dead, from mortuaries, from under cataracts of rubble, made their anonymous presence – not as today's dead but as yesterday's living – felt through London. Uncounted, they continued to move in shoals through the city day, pervading everything to be seen or heard or felt with their torn-off senses, drawing on this tomorrow they had expected – for death cannot be so sudden as all that. Absent from the routine which had been life, they stamped upon that routine their absence – not knowing who the dead were you could not know which might be the staircase somebody for the first time was not mounting this morning, or at which street corner the newsvendor missed a face, or which trains and buses in the homegoing rush were this evening lighter by at least one passenger.

These unknown dead reproached those left living not by their own death, which might any night be shared, but by their unknownness, which could not be mended now. Who had the right to mourn them, not having cared that they had lived? So, among the crowds still eating, drinking, working, travelling, halting, there began to be an instinctive movement to break down indifference while there was still time. The wall between the living and the living became less solid as the wall between the living and the dead thinned. In that September transparency people became transparent, only to be located by the just darker flicker of their hearts. Strangers saying 'Good night, good luck', to each other at street corners, as the sky first blanched then faded with evening, each hoped not to die that night, still more not to die unknown.

That autumn of 1940 was to appear, by two autumns later, apocryphal, more far away than peace. No planetary round was to bring again that particular conjunction of life and death; that particular psychic London was to be gone for ever; more bombs would fall, but not on the same city. War moved from the horizon to the map. And it was now, when you no longer saw, heard, smelled war, that a deadening acclimatization to it began to set in. The first generation of ruins, cleaned up, shored up, began to weather – in daylight they took their places as a norm of the scene; the dangerless nights of September two years later blotted them out. It was from this new insidious echoless propriety of ruins that you breathed in all that was most malarial. Reverses, losses, deadlocks now almost unnoticed bred one another; every day the news hammered one more nail into a consciousness which no longer resounded. Everywhere hung the heaviness of the even worse you could not be told and could not desire to hear. This was the lightless middle of the tunnel. Faith came down to a slogan, desperately reworded to catch the eye, requiring to be pasted each time more strikingly on to hoardings and bases of monuments . . . No, no virtue was to be found in the outward order of theirs: happy those who could draw from some inner source.

For Stella, her early knowing of Robert was associated with the icelike tinkle of broken glass being swept up among the crisping leaves, and with the charred freshness of every morning. She could recapture that 1940 autumn only in sensations; thoughts, if there had been any, could not be found again. She remembered the lightness, after her son had left, of loving no particular person now left in London – till one morning she woke to discover that lightness gone. That was the morning when, in the instant before opening her eyes, she saw Robert's face with a despairing hallucinatory clearness. When she did open her eyes, it had been to stare round her room in sunshine certain that he was dead. *Something* final had happened, in any case. That autumn, she was living in lodgings in a house in a square: raising the sash of her bedroom window – which, glassless since two or three nights ago, ran up with a phantom absence of weight – she leaned out and called to the square's gardener, impassively at work just inside the railings with rake and barrow. Had he, had the old man, any idea where the bombs had fallen last night? He said, some said Kilburn, some King's Cross. She shouted, 'Then, not Westminster?' but he shrugged his shoulders, once again turned his back. The sun stood so high over the opposite roof-line that Stella looked at her watch – yes, the sun was right; she had over-slept. So far, nothing had happened to anybody she knew, or even to anyone she knew knew – today, however, tingled all over from some shock which could be the breaking down of immunity. The non-existence of her window, the churchyard hush of the square, the grit which had drifted on to her dressing-table all became ominous for the first time. More than once she reached for the telephone which was out of order. Trying to dress in haste in the blinding sunshine, she threw away any time she had gained by standing still while something inside her head, never quite a thought, made felt a sort of imprisoned humming. Could this nervousness be really nothing more than fatigue?

More loss had not seemed possible after that fall of France. On through the rest of that summer in which she had not rallied from that psychological blow, and forward into this autumn of the attack on London, she had been the onlooker with nothing more to lose – out of feeling as one can be out of breath. She had had the sensation of being on furlough from her own life. Throughout these September raids she had been awed, exhilarated, cast at the very most into a sort of abstract of compassion – only what had been very small indeed, a torn scrap of finery, for instance, could draw tears. To be at work built her up, and when not at work she was being gay in company whose mood was at the pitch of her own – society became lovable; it had the temperament of the stayers-on in London. The existence, surrounded by one another, of these people she nightly saw was fluid, easy, holding inside itself a sort of ideality of pleasure. These were campers in rooms of draughty dismantled houses or corners of fled-from flats – it could be established, roughly, that the wicked had stayed and the good had gone. This was the new society of one kind of wealth, resilience, living how it liked – people whom the climate of danger suited, who began, even, all to look a little alike, as they might in the sun, snows, and altitude of the same sports station, or browning along the same beach in the south of France. The very temper of pleasures lay in their chanciness, in the canvas-like impermanence of their settings, in their being off-time – to and fro between bars and grills, clubs and each other's places moved the little shoal through the noisy nights. Faces came and went. There was a diffused gallantry in the atmosphere, an unmarriedness: it came to be rumoured about the country, among the self-banished, the uneasy, the put-upon and the safe, that everybody in London was in love – which was true, if not in the sense the country meant. There was plenty of everything in London – attention, drink, time, taxis, most of all space.

Into that intimate and loose little society of the garrison Stella and Robert both gravitated, and having done so could hardly fail to meet. They for the first time found themselves face to face in a bar or club – afterwards they could never remember which. Both were in their element, to which to have met instantaneously added more. It was a character-istic of that life in the moment and for the moment's sake that one knew people well without knowing much about them: vacuum as to future was offset by vacuum as to past; life-stories were shed as so much superfluous weight – this for different reasons suited both her and him. (Information, that he had before the war lived, worked abroad, in a branch of his father's or a friend of his father's business accumulated gradually, later on.) At the first glance they saw in each other's faces a flash of promise, a background of mystery. While his eyes, in which mirror-refracted lighting intensified a curious blue, followed the one white lock slowly back from her fore-head, she found herself not so much beginning to study as in the middle of studying this person – communicative, excit-able – from whom she only turned away to wave good-bye to the friend who had brought her across the room.

That gesture of good-bye, so perfunctory, was a finalness not to appear till later. It comprehended the room and every-body, everything in it which had up to now counted as her life: it was an unconscious announcement of the departure she was about to take – a first and last wave, across widen-ing water, from a liner. Remembered, her fleeting sketch of a gesture came to look prophetic; for ever she was to see, pho-tographed as though it had been someone else's, her hand up. The bracelet slipping down and sleeve falling back, against a dissolving background of lights and faces, were vestiges, and the last, of her solidity. She returned to Robert – both having caught a breath, they fixed their eyes expectantly on each other's lips. Both waited, both spoke at once, unheard.

Overhead, an enemy plane had been dragging, drumming slowly round in the pool of night, drawing up bursts of gunfire – nosing, pausing, turning, fascinated by the point for its intent. The barrage banged, coughed, retched; in here the lights in the mirrors rocked. Now down a shaft of anticipating silence the bomb swung whistling. With the shock of detonation, still to be heard, four walls of in here yawped in then bellied out; bottles danced on glass; a distortion ran through the view. The detonation dulled off into the cataracting roar of a split building: direct hit, somewhere else.

It was the demolition of an entire moment: he and she stood at attention till the glissade stopped. What they *had* both been saying, or been on the point of saying, neither of them ever now were to know. Most first words have the nature of being trifling; theirs from having been lost began to have the significance of a lost clue. What they next said, what they said instead, they forgot: there are questions which if not asked at the start are not asked later; so those they never did ask. The top had been knocked off their first meeting – perhaps later they exonerated themselves a little because of that. Nothing but the rising exhilaration of kindred spirits was, after all, to immortalize for them those first hours: and even forward into the time when meetings came to count for too much to be any more left to chance, they were still liking each other for their alikeness' sake. Into their attraction to one another entered their joy *in* attraction, in everything that was flattering and uncertain. There existed between them the complicity of brother and sister twins, counterpart flowerings of a temperament identical at least with regard to love. That unprecedented autumn, in which in everything round them feeling stood at full tide, made the movement of their own hearts imperceptible: in their first weeks of knowing each other they did not know how much might be the time, how much themselves. The extraordinary battle in the sky transfixed them; they might have stayed for ever on the eve of being in love.

This had lasted up to the October morning when Stella woke to the apprehension of loss, to what seemed the meaning glare of a day. Some submerged dream had accomplished work in the night; some experience, under the cloak of sleep, had had its conclusion in that supernatural nearness to her of Robert's face. Those were a series of nights in which one slept, if at all, with an abandonment in itself exhausting; but no kind of sleep accounted for the distance she felt between herself and yesterday – and, indeed, between herself and today. Nothing she saw or touched gave token of even its own reality: her wrist watch seemed to belie time; she fancied it had lost hours during the night, that this might be midday, the afternoon – her first act, as she hurried into the street, was to look about in vain for a public clock. So arrested seemed the movement of everything as she went to work that she asked herself whether the war itself might not have somehow stopped – she had spoken to nobody, since she woke, but the old mum gardener. Nothing was impossible – even so, she was late. She halted a taxi and stepped in.

Ten minutes after she sat down at her table, Robert rang up: they agreed to lunch together. The restaurant at which they met most often was this morning, he was sorry to tell her, closed – the street roped off: some nonsense about a time-bomb. They would have to try how they liked it somewhere else. To the place he suggested she, it happened, had never been: its name from being familiar in so many of friends' many stories, had come to seem to be over the borderline of fiction – so much so that, making her way thither, she felt herself to be going to a rendezvous inside the pages of a book. And was, indeed, Robert himself fictitious? She looked back, on her way to the restaurant, at their short unweighty past. The commissionaire set her spinning inside the revolving door; Robert, inside the foyer, started forward to meet her. She was struck by his limp – a limp so pronounced today that, till he spoke, he seemed like some other man.

In a dazzling blend of sun and electric light they sat side by side on velvet, backing on the wall. The pushing in upon them of the table by the waiter had been like the closing of a gate; behind this there was something a little forced about their repeated, fleeting turnings to one another, till the coming of the martinis permitted Robert to frown at, finger his misted glass. He then broke out: 'I'm very glad you are here. I was certain something had happened to you.'

'Why should it?'

'Because that would be exactly the sort of thing that would happen to me.'

She did not know, for a second, if he meant her to laugh at this unusual travesty of a glum boy's manner. She stayed with a cigarette – which before he spoke he had been on the point of lighting – held to her lips, looking tentatively at him. He kept his thumb on his lighter. So in the cinema some break-down of projection leaves one shot frozen, absurdly, on to the screen.

Here was the face of before she opened her eyes. Its fairness, not quite pallor, had a sort of undertone of exhausted sunburn.

To this impressionistic look of alightness, hair, eyebrows gave almost nothing darker, and there was no moustache; the face had only accents of shadow. The effect of his being in uniform was that the claylike khaki threw his features into transparent relief, behind which they were at the moment possessed by tension. The most curious of the qualities he should have, candescence, was at the moment less from his eyes being turned away – their flame-thin blueness was missing. The prolonging of the refusal to look at her became more of an avowal than any look; the fact, for him, of there being nothing more to be said set his mouth in a stone line which itself spoke.

To miss from his eyes, mouth, forehead the knowable unguarded play of his nature was for her, for the first time, to be made feel its force. In the unfamiliar the familiar persisted like a ghost – his attitude, the long narrow cast of his head and hands, his youthfulness – something moody, hardy, and lyrical which his being some way into his thirties had no more than brought to a finer point. He was younger than Stella by five or six years.

The gilt-faced clock in the sunburst on the restaurant's wall had, like others in London, been shock-stopped. When she began to feel about for her gloves and he began to push out the table, their two wrist watches – which, in the time to come, were to come at some kind of relationship of their own by never perfectly synchronizing – found it, respectively, to be a minute before and a minute after half past two. Half past two of a day which, having begun late for her, finished late for them both.

Habit, of which passion must be wary, may all the same be the sweetest part of love. In the two years following 1940 he and she had grown into living together in every way but that of sharing a roof. Soon they could both conjecture the ins and outs of each other's days, and of evenings which had to be spent apart they knitted together the stories when they met. Counted, the hours of any week which were their own completely were not many, but those magnetic hours drew from the rest so much that nothing was quite lost, little had gone to waste. His experiences and hers became harder and harder to tell apart; everything gathered behind them into a common memory – though singly each of them might, must, exist, decide, act; all things done alone came to be no more than simulacra of behaviour: they waited to live again till they were together, then took living up from where they had left it off. Then their doubled awareness, their interlocking feeling acted on, intensified what was round them – nothing they saw, knew, or told one another remained trifling; everything came to be woven into the continuous narrative of love; which, just as much, kept gaining substance, shadow, consistency from the imperfectly known and the not said. For naturally they did not tell one another everything. Every love has a poetic relevance of its own; each love brings to light only what is to it relevant. Outside lies the junk-yard of what does not matter.

It had been in the course of that first winter that Stella left her lodgings in the square and moved across into the Weymouth Street flat. There, the annoyance of the neo-Regency fallals was cancelled out by possessorship of the whole emptied house below them, from nightfall on: after dark the stairs went up, flight by flight, past door after door of consulting-rooms in which there was now no one to stir or listen – silence, when she and Robert came back together, stood storeys deep. Repetition gave increasing magic to those returns – to stepping over and leaving disregarded the letters on her doormat, to the hasty blacking-out of windows already black with night, to the blind course back through the dark in which Robert waited till her fingers found the switch of a lamp. At the same time, no two meetings were ever quite the same.

Roderick, at the beginning, had been the reason why the lovers did not move into the same house – the indifference of the embattled city to private lives, the exiguousness and vagueness of everybody's existence among the ruins could, but for Roderick, have made that easy. But by the time Stella's son, at the end of a phantom year at Oxford, was called up, she and Robert found themselves conscious of a submerged decision to go on as they were, for that 'time being' which war had made the very being of time. Wartime, with its makeshifts, shelvings, deferrings, could not have been kinder to romantic love. The two discussed any merging of their postal addresses not more seriously than they discussed marriage – happy to stay as they were, afloat on this tideless, hypnotic, futureless day-to-day.

It was more than a dream. More, it was a sort of growing, smiling regard, a happiness of which it seemed that the equilibrium became every day surer. The discovery together, for the first time, of life was serious, but very much more than serious, illuminating; there was an element of awe. Miraculously unhindered, the plan of love had gone on unfolding itself; the testing time, ever to be expected, had never come. There showed no sign of its coming until the Sunday when Harrison paid his evening call.

Roderick's unexpected arrival at Weymouth Street, that scarred Sunday night, had had two effects Stella had hoped it might have – that of thrusting Harrison from the immediate forefront, that of keeping her parted from Robert just long enough for the fumes of her conversation with Harrison to have had time to settle: evaporate they could not. Then, at the end of Roderick's leave, the atmosphere of the lovers' next meeting, after what had come to feel like eternity, could not but banish anything foreign to itself. It was not till two or three evenings later, back in her flat again with him, that she remarked suddenly: 'Oh, and there was not only Roderick last Sunday – that man called Harrison was here, too.'

'Which man?' said Robert unconcentratedly.

'The one who was at the funeral.'

'What, him again? What a bother. You seem to be stuck with him for life.'

'One would think so. London's got too small – wherever there's left to go, Harrison seems to be.'

'We've never run into him?'

'Never consciously; but he thinks he's seen us. He says he knows you.'

'How I wish I knew him – but no, incredible as it may sound, I don't think I know anyone of that name. Chap with a squint, you said?'

'Not a squint exactly – more, it's some way he has of using both eyes at the same time. And he has a laugh.'

'Odd. However, it can't be helped.'

'What can't be helped?'

'My still having no idea who he is. He doesn't sound like anyone very special. I know you said he wasn't a commercial traveller, but I can't remember what you said he was.'

'I think I just said he was not a commercial traveller . . . Yes, he's always about.'

'Perhaps he listens for careless talk.' Robert yanked himself out of the deep armchair to stand scrutinizing some part of his reflection in the mirror over the fireplace. 'Don't you agree,' he asked, 'it's about time I scrapped this tie?'

She answered: 'Why – who's been talking carelessly?'

'Everyone, I imagine. You know how *I* talk.'

'Only know how you talk to me. I don't count.'

'Then why don't you ask Harrison, since we hear he knows me – Darling, it isn't that I'm not interested in your new friends, but I do wish you'd give your mind to this tie question.' He untied the tie, pulled it off and, having sat down again, examined it closely under a lamp. 'A bit off,' he said, 'honestly, don't you think?'

He passed it to her. She said: 'Yes, perhaps a bit off.'

'What are Harrison's ties – nice?'

'Don't be perfunctory, Robert.'

'I am anything but. For all I know, he may be perfectly fascinating. That way of using both eyes at the same time – anybody would think, from the way you talk, you'd always lived with a cyclops, or Lord Nelson.'

Frowning over the tie she said: 'Let me look at this properly . . .'

'Yes; because this does matter.'

'The thing is,' she cried, kneeling by him with the tie in her hands, 'that really I cannot judge any tie you wear. Just as I cannot judge . . . How should I feel, for instance, if somebody tried to tell me something preposterous about you?'

'Or you wouldn't simply tell them to go to hell – no?'

'How should I even know if it were preposterous?'

'Then you simply cannot tell me about this tie?'

'Yes, I suppose you're right; I suppose it must go,' she said, blindly playing it through her fingers. 'That is, when you can remember to buy another – unless you have another?'

'You look sad,' said Robert, looking down at her face. 'What are you thinking – "One tie nearer the grave"? Or has anybody been telling you I'm two-timing?'

'No. Are you?'

'No. For one thing, where would I get the time?'

'Oh, Robert, talking of time, when can we do what we've said we might do – go down and spend a day at your mother's?'

'My heavens,' he cried, 'when I'm only just back from there! Next time I go, we both might – if you still want to. But on the other hand, why?'

'Because, why shouldn't we?'

'There's no objection; it's simply that there's no point. The only possible point could have been my father, if he hadn't been dead. However, there the other two are, as you know, if you want to see them – if you don't mind there being rather a fuss.'

'Would they not like me?'

He reflected: 'I don't see why they shouldn't, except that they never like anybody. No, I just mean fuss at my bringing *anyone* down. You would not be you. You and I are accustomed to make impressions: unless you can rid yourself of the least expectation of doing that, the day will be rather a flop. – What have you in view down there – research? My case-history?'

'Naturally,' said she.

He reached out for the tie, took it back from her, but at the same time said: 'Though, is there much point in my putting this on again.'

6

The visit to Robert's mother took place some weeks later. It was an early October Saturday afternoon when he and she stepped out of the train at a Home County station – while Robert, in a sort of rapid somnambulism, steered her towards a footbridge over the line, Stella kept glancing about at the other platforms, the shabby initialled seats, rusting enamelled advertisements which must have been here ever since Robert's boyhood, and the new posters up to discourage travel. Laudably little travel was on her conscience: since last May's expedition to the funeral she had left London not more than once or twice. This railway station made her think of the one at which she had waited with Harrison for the London train. The alikeness was less a matter of architecture (today's being that of a different company, running more decidedly to the Gothic and realizing itself in yellow rather than plum brick) than of position: in both cases a high embankment, on which the station stood, intersected a sunk concentration of roofs and roads and trees; in which, looking down from the platforms, you saw one kind of pattern of English life at its most incoherent and reassuring. The platforms themselves seemed to bear the mark of breadwinners' contented evening returns – *here* no one did anything but keep house. The two stations also, in Stella's mind, became epitomes of the two most poignant seasons – in spring, in autumn everything telegraphs its mystery to your senses; nothing is trite. And more: in these years the idea of war made you see any peaceful scene as it were through glass.

Only, while that day in May had been moody and overcast, this in October was elatingly sunny – and she was here with Robert, not Harrison.

They stepped into a taxi, which if not bespoken for Robert showed no surprise, and slid off down the station hill, passing fronts of shops which also seemed to link up with the Tringsby country. Holme Dene, Mrs Kelway's house, was apparently three miles from the station. Stella, her arm through Robert's, exclaimed: 'I forgot to ask you – what have you told them?'

'That we are coming down to go for a country walk.'

'If I had known, I would have worn other shoes. Not that I couldn't walk in these, but they look silly.'

Robert glanced without worry at her extended foot, saying: 'Ernestine's not so subtle as all that.'

'But anyway, who will she think I am?'

'I think I have got it firmly into her head that you are someone working in a government office, and that we go for tramps on Saturday afternoons.'

'So, what did she say?'

'She said, "You mean hikes." What my mother thinks I have no idea: we shall see.'

'Does that mean we shall have to go for a walk?'

'We may be glad to – remember, there will be hours before our train.'

The first intimation one had of approaching Holme Dene was a notice saying CAUTION: CONCEALED DRIVE: this projected from a ribbon of evergreens, above which rose some fine deciduous trees. The trees, to be seen going back and back, gave a ground of depths of interesting shadow to the otherwise bald white gates, and also provided the only reason why a house should occur at just *this* point along the otherwise empty road. There was no lodge but there was a letter-box on a white stake, which seemed hardly less an accessory of the Kelways' gateway, and whose slight grin still reflected Holme Dene's triumph at wresting this amenity out of the G.P.O. Here Robert stopped the taxi and they got out; Stella having agreed that, as they had no luggage, there was no point in their chuffing up to the door.

A break in the evergreens of the drive allowed the first view of Holme Dene, across the paddock and lawns. The house, which must have been built about 1900, was of the size of a considerable manor, rose with gables to the height of three ample storeys, and combined half-timbering with bow and french windows and two or three balconies. The façade was partially draped with Virginia creeper, now blood red. In the fancy-shaped flower-beds under the windows and round the sweep the eye instinctively sought begonias – one or two beds, it was true, still showed late roses; in the others, vegetables of the politer kind packed the curves of crescents and points of stars. Immediately round the beds the lawns had been mown in wavering stripes; one might guess by Ern-estine or the children. A backdrop of trees threw into relief a tennis pavilion, a pergola, a sundial, a rock garden, a dovecote, some gnomes, a seesaw, a grouping of rusticated seats, and a bird bath. Stella, who could not stop looking, could think of nothing to say, and Robert saw no reason to say anything: they thus were not interrupted, though she was startled, by somebody's shooting out round a corner of laurustinus to stand in the drive ahead of them, laughing heartily.

'Why, hullo, Ernie,' said Robert, 'where are *you* off to now?'

Ernestine answered: 'What's become of the taxi?'

'We sent it back.'

'Of course, you have come to walk,' said Ernestine, looking still better pleased by her instantaneous grasp of the situation. She had swooped upon Stella's hand rapidly, as though securing a bargain, before Robert was under way with the introduction. 'Well, I must say,' she said, 'you've hit on topping weather. Not that there's anything picturesque round here.'

Stella knew Ernestine to be her brother Robert's senior by about twelve years: widowed, she was Mrs Gibb. Between her and Robert came Amabelle, who, having married into the I.C.S., was now confined by the war to India. Amabelle's children were safe at Holme Dene, in the keeping of their grandmother and aunt – these children, the Joliffes, a girl and boy, would presumably play some part in the afternoon. Ernestine's own son, Christopher Robin, was at Woolwich this autumn, quite liking it. His being Roderick's age, in the Army and also an only son, might, Stella had hoped on the way down, furnish some point of contact between the two mothers: face to face with Ernestine, she now saw why Robert had been less optimistic. Ernestine's features, which taken one by one might not have been so very unlike Robert's, were so arranged as to make her look rather like a dog. Her face was long, her body short: both were lean. Though standing still for the moment, she vibrated with energy, seeming to be almost audibly ticking over. Her being clad in the uniform of the W.V.S. added to her air of having been torn, or having on their account torn herself, from some vital war-time activity; but Stella guessed she would look like that at any time. That she should have ever loved, married, and borne a child seemed fantastic; she certainly gave the impression of being far from sorry to have got all that over. In the look Ernestine turned from Stella to Robert the absence of human awareness was quite startling; she might have been scanning a public notice to see if anything further ought to be done.

'Well, Robert,' she said, 'you'll find Muttikins in the lounge; though of course she's been expecting to hear the taxi.' Picking her laugh up where she had left it off, she took it a few more notes up the scale; then, to Stella, remarked: 'We were only saying this morning, it took being shot in the leg to make Robert walk! – Well, I have got to rush. See you both at tea.' Disengaging herself from their company with unnecessary force, Ernestine shot onwards towards the gate, leaving them to pursue their way to the house.

Stella said: 'What was Ernestine laughing at?'

'Oh, she was just laughing.'

'But she seemed to be laughing before we met her.'

'Then I suppose she must have seen us first.'

Stella reflected, then asked: '"Muttikins"?'

'My mother: we call her that.'

The lounge of Holme Dene could be seen into from the entrance porch, through an arch. It had three sizeable windows; but was so blackly furnished with antique oak, papered art brown and curtained with copper chenille as to consume, with little to show, their light. Some mahogany pieces, such as a dining-table, a dumb-waiter and an upright piano, could be marked as evacuees out of other rooms; the grandfather clock, on the other hand, must have stood here always – time had clogged its ticking. The concentrated indoorness of the lounge was made somehow greater rather than less by the number of exits, archways, and outdoor views; the staircase, lit from the top and built with as many complications as space allowed, descended into the middle of everything with a plump. In the evident hope of preventing draughts, screens of varying heights had been placed about. Stella, keyed up to meet Robert's mother, did not know in which direction to look first: a small bowl of large orange dahlias drew her attention, like an arranged decoy. A silence, more than a sound, made her turn round quickly – Mrs Kelway, in one hand holding her knitting, had already risen out of her chair.

Small, sizes smaller than Ernestine, the mother reached up her free hand to her tall son's shoulder; Robert bowed his head, and her lips just paused on his cheek, as though to endorse the kiss placed there many times already. She said: 'Robert . . .'

'Muttikins . . .' he a shade more lightly returned. Then added: 'Muttikins, this is Mrs Rodney.'

'Mrs Rodney?' said Mrs Kelway, turning to look sceptically at Stella, after which they shook hands. 'But what became of the taxi?' she said to Robert.

'We sent it back from the gate.'

'Ernestine had been listening for the taxi; I hope she did not miss you on her way down the drive?'

'No; we ran into Ernestine – just a little *détraquée*,' he said – as though struck by this for the first time.

'It is Saturday afternoon,' Mrs Kelway said. She sat down again, in the armchair Stella should not have failed to see, for it was posted midway across the floor. Was this position strategic? – from it she commanded all three windows, also the leaded squints in the inglenook. Her crystal knitting needles went on flying along – smoothly, lightly, apparently under their own volition. 'If I had not seen you come up the drive,' she said, 'I should have begun to wonder if you had missed the train.'

'Mrs Rodney,' said Robert, 'likes to walk in the country.'

Mrs Kelway glanced for a moment at Stella's feet.

'It is so nice to be out of London,' said Stella. 'And I am so fond of autumn.' Seeing no reason not to, she sat down.

'Yes, today it is quite autumnal. I seldom go to London during the war, as I hear we are asked not to travel for no reason. Though I do not care for walking, I have always been a knitter. And now, in addition, my grandson is in the Army.'

'Oh, and so is my son!'

'I sometimes ask myself how long it will last.'

'Oh, come,' exclaimed Robert, 'the Army may not be much, but it should surely take more than Roderick and Christopher Robin to do it in!'

Mrs Kelway, without change of expression, said: 'I did not mean the Army: I meant the war.' Having watched her needles fly along half a row, she added: 'What do you mean by "Roderick"?'

'Mrs Rodney's son.'

'Oh,' said Mrs Kelway, if anything less genially than before.

Comedy, Stella understood, was to have no place in any kind of relation with Robert's mother. She was now confronting, with a submerged tremor, with a momentary break in her sense of her own existence, the miniature daunting beauty of that face. Mrs Kelway's dark hair, no more than touched with grey, was of a softness throwing into relief the diamond-cut of her features. The brows, the nose, the lips could not have been more relentlessly delicate, more shadowlessly distinct. If Ernie's regard had held unawareness, her mother's showed the mute presence of an obsession. For, why *should* she speak? – she had all she needed: the self-contained mystery of herself. Her lack of wish for communication showed in her contemptuous use of words. The lounge became what it was from being the repository of her nature; it was the indoors she selected, she consecrated – indeed, she had no reason to go out. By sitting here where she sat, and by sometimes looking, by sometimes even not looking, across the furnished lawn, she projected Holme Dene: this was a bewitched wood. If her power came to an end at the white gate, so did the world.

She wore a grey woven two-piece, pre-war in quality as in style, softened off at the throat by a fold of net.

Robert remained standing between his mother and Stella – who, looking up, saw his fair head against the glossy dark of a picture. From his attitude, back to the fireless fireplace, and the easy turns of his interest between woman and woman, you could have taken this meeting to be of the most everyday. Height, nonchalance, fairness he must have got from his father – how much, that was saving, else? He said: 'Well, should we be going out?'

Mrs Kelway said: 'Tea will be coming in.'

'Then perhaps a stroll before tea and a walk later?'

When they were out of sight, or of all but psychic sight, of the windows, he said: 'She's not really rude, more unconscious.'

Stella wondered.

'Or don't you agree?' he asked.

'Well, principally, darling, she struck me as being wicked. But you might not see that.'

'Oh, I see it constantly.'

'In London, you said she would make a fuss. I do not see any signs of that so far.'

'No, what I said was that *they* would make a fuss: so far, you've been seeing them one by one, and neither my mother nor Ernestine can make a fuss singly. As a matter of fact, my mother did make a demonstration; she told you a good deal about herself.'

'Is that not usual?'

'How can I say, really? Almost no strangers come here, and Ernie and I and the children have already been told.'

'So chiefly I was a stranger?'

'Yes, you were largely that.'

Stella, glancing across to the paddock occupied by a pony which took no notice of her, said: 'But where are the children?'

'Saturday afternoon – but we ought to see them at tea.'

The children, Mrs Kelway, Robert, and Stella were seated round the mahogany table – whose bareness had been relieved by some mats, some plates, a japanned tray of tea things opposite Mrs Kelway, buns, a loaf, an uncut cake which had the look of being of long standing, and an inviting pot of damson jam – when Ernestine dashed in and began to saw at the loaf. She then sent round the slices on the flat of the knife. 'Dear me,' said Robert, having received his, 'Mrs Rodney and I forgot about bringing our own butter.' This served to draw Stella's attention to the butter arrangements: each one of the family had his or her own ration placed before his or her own plate in a differently coloured china shell. Today was the delusive opening of the rationing week; the results of intemperance, as the week drew on, would be to be judged. Stella's solitary Londoner's footloose habits of living, in and out of restaurants, had kept from her many of the realities of the home front: for some reason, the sight of the coloured shells did more than anything so far to make her feel seedy, shady; though she could not but admire the arrangement as being at once fanciful, frank, and fair. She said hurriedly that she did not eat tea.

'I would offer you some of my butter,' said Ernestine, 'but that would only make you feel uncomfy.'

Robert helped himself to a bun, which he split open in order to spread thickly with damson jam. 'Oh I *say*!' expostulated his nephew, Peter, speaking for the first time. The girl, Anne, remarked: 'Do you do that in London? You must use a lot of jam, a most awful lot.'

'Black market,' said Robert, out of the side of his mouth.

Ernestine's laughing off of this held a warning note: 'Remember,' she said, 'that we swallow everything whole. I'm afraid we are rather a case of hero-worship.' Anne, with her eyes down, angrily suffered a slow red blush. The Joliffe children, aged about nine and seven, wore jerseys knitted when they were smaller: both looked downright and self-sufficient. A pink plastic brooch representing a dog was pinned to Anne's chest; Peter sported an armlet with cryptic letters. Anne said: 'Uncle Robert, suppose you end up in prison!'

'In that case, you'll have to come and see me.'

This was going too far; Anne's excruciating reaction strained the mesh of her jersey. 'We shall be having tears in a minute,' said Ernestine. Mrs Kelway looked at the child reflectively, but did not find anything to say other than: 'If it's not too much trouble, Grannie would like some bread.' – 'Oh, *Muttikins*, but didn't I *give* you any?' – 'Not this time, Ernestine: first I was pouring out; afterwards you were talking about the butter.' Stella turned to Peter. 'Do tell me what those letters on your armlet stand for?'

'Nothing you would have heard of,' said Peter shortly, not giving up his attempt to catch Robert's eye. 'Uncle Robert, you didn't save your taxi much petrol by getting out of it at the gate; it had to go on more than a mile down the road before it could turn; when it drives up to here it can quite easily turn in front of the door.'

'I've already decided,' said Robert, 'to never do that again'.

'We have eyes like gimlets,' said Ernestine. 'Peter, old man, you weren't wearing your armlet *outside* the gate?'

'We remained under cover.'

'Under cover or not, you know what I've always said. A game is a game, but this war's really rather serious.'

'Yes, Aunt Ernie.'

'And ask Mrs Rodney if she would like some more tea. If she says "Yes", pass her cup, and don't drop the spoon.'

'Mrs Rodney,' observed Mrs Kelway, 'does not care about afternoon tea.'

'Oh, but I *drink* a great deal – of tea, I mean: it's a bad office habit.'

Mrs Kelway stared, in evident wonder whether bad office habits could be confined to this. She then said: 'We now drink tea only once a day; otherwise we might not have enough for guests. During the week it frequently happens that my daughter has hers at the W.V.S., in which case, if it were not for the children, I should be tempted to do without mine. Afternoon tea at this table does not seem the same to me, but the gate-leg at which we used to have afternoon tea had to be taken away into the drawing-room to make place for the piano out of the drawing-room when it was moved in here: we could not have Anne practising in the cold; she is like her grandfather. Since we were told of the fuel shortage we have made a point of keeping to this room, as the most central. My daughter does not feel the cold, from moving about so much that she seldom takes off her hat. My son tells me that in London you would not notice the war; I am afraid it is far from the same here. Previously, of course, he went through so much. More than we care to speak of,' she added, looking at Robert.

Not looking at Robert, Stella said: 'I suppose so.'

'Mum is the word here,' added Ernestine. 'Isn't that so, children?'

Anne said: 'Uncle Robert is never so very particularly mum.'

Robert, trying to knife the cake, said: 'No, no one can say I don't come across. The thing with you, Ernie, is that you never listen. There's nothing I could not tell you about the great retreats. – You wouldn't think it was time we bought a new cake?'

'But that one has not been eaten,' objected Ernestine. 'I'm sure Mrs Rodney will take us as she finds us.'

'Happily for Mrs Rodney, she does not eat cake.'

'Goodness, why?' exclaimed Anne, turning to study Stella. 'Or are you always afraid it would make you fat?'

'Don't say "goodness" to someone older than you, dear. Mrs Rodney is free not to eat cake if she doesn't want to: that is just what I mean by the difference between England and Germany.'

Peter, wriggling inside his jersey, said: 'The Nazis would *force* her to eat cake.'

Mrs Kelway, whose distant ice-clear gaze had not left her son's face since his last remark, said: 'But retreats are now a thing of the past.'

The sun had been going down while tea had been going on, its chemically yellowing light intensifying the boundary trees. Reflections, cast across the lawn into the lounge, gave the glossy thinness of celluloid to indoor shadow. Stella pressed her thumb against the edge of the table to assure herself this was a moment *she* was living through – as in the moment before a faint she seemed to be looking at everything down a darkening telescope. Having brought the scene back again into focus by staring at window-reflections in the glaze of the teapot, she dared look again at Robert, seated across the table, opposite her, between his nephew and niece. Late afternoon striking into the blue of his eyes made him look like a young man in Technicolor. That the current between him and her should be cut off, she had expected; dullness, numbness, even grotesquerie she had foreseen. But what could be this unexpected qualm as to the propriety of their having come to Holme Dene? The escapade, bad enough in its tastelessness and bravado, had a more deep impropriety with regard to themselves. Nothing more psychic than Mrs Kelway's tea table, with its china and eatables, interposed between them: the tea table, however, was in itself enough. The English, she could only tell herself, were extraordinary – for if this were not England she did not know what it was. You could not account for this family headed by Mrs Kelway by simply saying that it was middle class, because that left you asking, middle of what? She saw the Kelways suspended .

in the middle of nothing. She could envisage them so suspended when there was nothing more. Always without a quiver as to their state. Their economy could not be plumbed: their effect was moral.

Apart from the ambiguities of her tie with Robert, Stella at Holme Dene felt every one of the anxieties, the uncertainties of the hybrid. She, like he, had come loose from her moorings; but while what she had left behind her dissolved behind her, what he had left behind him was not to be denied. Life had supplied to her so far nothing so positive as the abandoned past. Her own extraction was from a class that has taken an unexpected number of generations to die out – gentry till lately owning, still recollecting, land. A handsome derelict gateway opening on to grass and repeated memorials round the walls of a church still gave some sort of locale, however distant, to what had been her unmarried name. Having been born to some idea of position, she seldom asked herself what her own was now – still less, what position was in itself. Mrs Kelway and Ernestine, on the other hand, occupied a self-evident position of their own.

Further reflections were cut short by Ernestine's uttering one of her louder laughs. This was her reaction to Robert's having said that he knew Stella wanted to see the house. But ought they not to be starting out immediately on their walk? No doubt, he replied, but why not the house first? But by later, Ernestine pointed out, the sun might have set, or at least gone in. The sun was in no such hurry, maintained Robert. But *did* Mrs Rodney understand – at this point Ernestine turned to Stella – that the house, though antique in appearance, was not actually old? The oak beams, to be perfectly honest, were imitations. And moreover – in case this hope should be running through Stella's mind – Holme Dene was not, and never would be, to let. Stella replied, she had not dared hope that it was. In that case, continued Ernestine – not, of course, that *she* minded – why waste a fine afternoon? Robert, apparently made mad, said Stella was interested in interior decoration. Upon which Mrs Kelway at once said: 'I'm afraid there is nothing of that sort here. Your father always liked everything plain but good. In addition, due to the war the better rooms are shut up.'

'Then I shall show her my cricket groups.'

'Dear me,' tittered Ernie, 'won't Mrs Rodney think you are very vain?'

'Can we come too?' cried the children.

'No,' said their uncle. 'Why don't you operate on the lawn?'

'But you might not see us.'

'I might look out of the window.'

On the stairs on their way up to Robert's top-floor room, Stella said: 'You have made them think me frightfully nosy.'

'Aren't you? However, do stop thinking you're making a bad impression; I assure you you're making no impression at all.'

Robert's room decidedly gained by being an attic: its windows occupied ample gables; the slants of the ceiling reared round one's head romantic tentlike half-lights. Against such walls as offered vertical space, imposing mahogany furniture had been planted; the unblemished veneer of all these pieces showed them to be testimonials to his maturity. His reluctance to move downstairs from his boyhood's den had evidently been seen indulgently: first-floor manly comforts had moved upstairs to him. They interspersed fictions of boyishness. A 'varsity' chair was padded in fadeless butcher blue; a swivel lamp stood attentively at the chair's elbow; a hot-looking, new-looking square of turkey carpet garnished the linoed floor. Glass cases of coins, birds' eggs, fossils, and butterflies that he must once have fancied or been supposed to fancy stayed riveted where they must meet the eye; silver and other trophies, on hooks or brackets, rose in a pyramid over the chimneypiece. And something was yet more striking – sixty or seventy photographs, upward from snapshots to crowded groups, had been done in passe-partout or framed, according to size and weight, and hung in close formations on two walls. All the photographs featured Robert. By himself or with friends, acquaintances or relations he was depicted at every age.

'My dear Robert . . .' said Stella, after a minute's silence. 'I know . . .'

'You never told me – *You* didn't hang all these up?'

'No – Though, as you see, I haven't taken them down.'

'Then your mother? – Ernie?' With compunction she added: 'They must really be very fond of you.'

'Then you'd have thought,' he said, 'that they'd have wanted these downstairs. No, they expect me to be very fond of myself.'

'All the same . . .' She began to move round the exhibition which, whatever it meant to him, was a feast for her. Reflecting on his last remark, she said: 'Yet I don't think you are.' She came to a stop in front of an enlarged snapshot of Robert, in tennis flannels, arm-in-arm with a tall pretty girl in a summer frock. 'Is this Decima?' (It was to Decima that he had for a short time been engaged.)

'Yes,' said Robert, glancing over his shoulder.

Stella, unhooking Decima, carried her nearer to the light. 'I must say, I don't see anything wrong with her.'

'There wasn't; she simply came up against what was wrong with me.'

'I'm surprised, in a way,' she remarked, 'that they never took this down.'

'There may be no other of me in flannels.'

She put the picture back on its nail, and again looked round – this time at the narrow glacial bed, which, ends and all, had been draped in a starched white cover: in the neo-Sheraton book trough beside the bed the books gave the impression of being gummed together in some sort of secretion from their disuse. On the high dressing-chest, monogrammed backs of brushes stood high on their parching bristles. Everything was dustless; new air with all its perils came in now – he had opened a window. She exclaimed: 'Robert, this room feels empty!'

'It could not feel emptier than it is. Each time I come back again into it I'm hit in the face by the feeling that I don't exist – that I not only am not but never have been. So much so that it's extraordinary coming in here with you.'

'But what were you doing *then* – and *then* – and *then?*' she asked, pointing from photograph to photograph. 'Or at any rate, who was doing what you seem to have done?'

'You may ask. I not only have no idea now but must have had even less idea at the time. Me clawing at that fur rug as a decently arranged naked baby seems no more senseless, now, than me smirking over that tournament cup, or in shorts on the top of a rock with Thompson, or outside the church as an usher at Amabelle's wedding, or collaring Ernie's labrador, or at Kitzbuhl or with Decima or that picnic hamper or Desmond's horse. . . .'

'– Still, those must once have been moments.'

'Imitation ones. If to have gone through motions ever since one was born is, as I think now, criminal, here's my criminal record. Can you think of a better way of sending a person mad than nailing that pack of his own lies all round the room where he has to sleep?'

'Nonsense,' she said, 'they are only on two walls.'

'What do you think they are up to, all the same?'

Comfortably slipping her arm through his, she said, 'No, they've only made this room as though you were dead.'

'Well, damn it Stella, isn't that bad enough?'

She disengaged herself to go to the dressing-chest and pull open, by its firm knobs, one drawer: she smelled moth-balls and admired paper folded over the top. 'Socks,' she said, looking under the paper, 'beautifully put away. Roder-ick could do with a little of Ernestine.' She slid the drawer to, sighed, and sat down on the window seat, cushioned to match the chair. One elbow on the sill of the open window, she looked thoughtfully back down the room at Robert.

'What are you really wondering?' he said.

'Whether I made you go on like that at tea, or whether here you are always the *enfant terrible*; what Ernie did with her labrador; and particularly, what your father was like. In the photographs with you how nice he looks.'

'He was – Ernie's labrador? It died half-way through Munich week. Those big dogs must be sensitive; what they don't know they feel – the same was true of my father; in fact so much so that *his* dying was a cracking relief. To me, that is. Yes, look at all those pictures of me and him! We were an attractive embarrassment to each other – and, of course, in this house we were thrown very much together. Something

140

was expected: very often I did not know which way to look, and looking back I can see that he didn't either; in fact I think I realized that at the time.'

'So where did you look?'

'No option: on his insistence we were perpetually looking each other in the eye. There used to be convulsions of awkwardness when we literally couldn't unlock our looks. I suppose I could draw you a map today of every vein in his iris. The jelly of an eye, not to speak of whatever else there may be in it, has been unseemly to me ever since – haven't you seen how seldom I look in your eyes? – *at* them's an entirely different thing. Your mothy way of blinking and laziness about keeping your eyelids open didn't even so much attract me when we first met as reassure me – I felt we had the same sort of prudery without your knowing. In my father it was impossible not to see the broken spring; or at least impossible for me not to. Can you wonder I ask myself what did that to him. – What's the matter?'

'Nothing.'

'The less you say, the more you think,' he said, walking round the room, stopping to stare at the cases of moths and coins. 'However, I think you'd have liked my father. There were his looks, and he could often take refuge from his humiliations in a sort of dignity. Yes, if you, anybody like you had loved him – but no, I cannot imagine any time when that could have been in time; at any time I remember it would have been too late – and I can't imagine from his point of view a more exposing thing to have happened: that would have been the pay-off. In all but one sense he was impotent; that was what came out in his relationship to me. What I think must have happened to him I cannot while we're in this house, say. He let himself be buckled into his marriage like Ernie's labrador used to let itself be buckled into its collar. However . . .'

'*Is* Anne like him?'

'Anne?' he said blankly. 'Why?'

'Your mother seemed to suggest she had had the piano for Anne to practise on moved into the lounge because Anne was like your father.'

'Oh, yes, he was always trying to pick out tunes; whereas Anne is learning to play the piano properly but badly. My mother's *non sequiturs* do of course establish connexions one mightn't see. What else about him? He had business capacity, or we should not be where we are; yes, he could afford to retire comparatively young – in hopes of what? He gave me the start he owed me, and put good round sums into settlement for both the girls when they married. Later the slump hit him through some investments but that not even badly. He left mother enough to go on with as she always had.'

'How much did he leave you?'

'Ten thousand down; what my mother has remains at her disposition, apart from this house, which if it should still be in the family at her death comes to Ernestine and me.'

'Why should it not still be in the family?'

'Oh, it's for sale, you know. It practically always has been. He put it back again on the agent's books a year or two after we moved in. Not that he had anything against it, he merely foresaw that he would be wanting another change; in fact he had his heart set on a house called Fair Leigh outside Reigate, but nobody else bought this one, and meanwhile somebody else bought Fair Leigh. I was born in a house called Elmsfield near Chislehurst; and between that and this we lived in another house called Meadowcrest, outside Hemel Hempstead. To your eye I expect they would all look very much the same, including, I imagine, Fair Leigh – though I never saw that; it remained a dream.'

'One would have thought that somebody moving out of Fair Leigh would have been glad to acquire Holme Dene.'

'Something broke down somewhere; we got caught short. Either people no longer knew what was good for them or we were asking too much money for too few bathrooms. We would rather die than not sell for more than we gave. It's a slight, all the same, as you can imagine.'

'But Ernie made such a point, just now, of saying Holme Dene was not to let.'

'She was perfectly right; it's not to let, it's for sale. An infinite difference in prestige. We suffer no annoyance, people stopped coming to see it years before the war; at the same time, we never speak of the matter even among ourselves because we feel so sore; this has been simply one more of my father's mistakes, Or rather, that was how we used to feel: now, fortunately the war has saved our faces. We always have lived uncomfortably in this house; *now* it is possible for us to make a point of doing so.'

'All the same, how sad,' she said, 'how unsettling – surely? – I should have thought.' She looked out of the window, down at the betrayed garden, in which the gnomes, bird-bath, and rustic seats now seemed to hover indeterminately. From this attic height you looked through the tops of trees; their illusion of forestlike density was lost; their thinning foliage stood out tattered against the sky. There were no rooks. Seen through transparent dusk the pattern of flowerbeds in the lawn looked impermanent, and those pallid roses seemed to have lingered on only because they were not only for this year but for this *place*, ever, the final ones. 'How can they live, anyone live,' she asked, 'in a place that has for years been asking to be brought to an end?'

'Oh, but there will always be somewhere else,' he said easily. 'Everything can be shifted, lock, stock, and barrel. After all, everything was brought here from somewhere else, with the intention of being moved again – like touring scenery from theatre to theatre. Reassemble it anywhere: you get the same illusion.'

'You'd say this was an illusion?'

'What else but an illusion could have such power?' He made a movement of bitter carelessness – then, as though to narrow a breach between them, threw himself down by her on the window seat and picked her hand up. A movement under the window made Stella turn again and look down: the two children marched briskly into view on the lawn, looked up, then began to perform exercises. 'Oh, there they are,' she cried, 'and you promised to look at them.'

Anne's and Peter's knowing the promise was being kept betrayed itself only by sterner effort, reddening foreheads, set jaws, a fixed-eyed refusal to so much as glance at their uncle's window again. From above they looked like gal-vanized starfish. Stella, holding Robert's hand below the level of the window sill as they watched the performance, passed from wishing he and she had children to wondering what such children would have been like – 'Don't hold your breath!' shouted Robert suddenly; at which Anne's mouth flew open – she deflated, staggered, collapsed on the lawn gasping. Peter, however, went on and on till Robert said: 'That will do.' Stella, feeling something to be owing, clapped hysterically, till it became evident from everybody's manner, including Robert's, that this was uncalled for. 'Oh, dear,' she said. Robert said: 'Never mind.'

'Hot, hot!' puffed Anne, lying plucking her jersey away from her heaving chest. 'We were afraid you might have started out for your walk.'

'But we would have done this anyhow,' added Peter. 'We'd said we would.'

'We'd have done this before, only Grannie wanted us.'

'Nobody can find the half-ounce weight off the weighing machine.'

'She wanted to weigh the parcel for you to post in London.'

'You'll have now to have it weighed *in* London, she says.'

'She can't weigh it, now she can't find that weight.'

At the beginning, both children had been hampered by lack of breath; but by now, Anne having picked herself up, both had somehow got back to form and were standing bellowing under Robert's window, lusty as carol-singers. They seemed better fitted for this than for merely speaking: both had been glum at tea. There seemed so little reason why this should ever stop that Robert and Stella found themselves constrained to imitate the smilingly gradual disappearance of royalty from a balcony; or, better still, perhaps, that of Cheshire cats, leaving grins behind them on the air in the window. Intent on bringing this off, Stella was badly startled by Ernestine's bursting into the room behind them, exclaiming: 'Yes, here you are!'

'Yes, indeed, Ernie,' said Robert, 'Why?'

'I thought you must have started out for your walk, till I heard the children shouting, so put two and two together. I must say I'm very glad to have caught you – Muttikins has a parcel for you to post in London.'

'What on earth's the matter with the post office here?'

'Nothing,' said Ernestine loyally. 'But of course it's never open on Sunday, whereas in London they are.'

'That is the first I've heard of that.'

'Well, Muttikins knows *some* are. And as you know, these days every moment counts. I'm sure Mrs Rodney won't mind.'

'I'd love to post it,' said Stella.

'But can all this not wait,' said Robert, 'till we're actually starting?'

'A.,' explained Ernestine, 'there is almost always a rush at the last moment, in which one has no time to explain, and B., I always may have to dash off myself. So I thought I had better tell you there's been a small complication – we have been hunting high and low, but alas in vain, for that little half-ounce weight of Muttikins's little weighing machine; and owing to that she is far from sure that she may not have understamped the parcel: it is always so difficult to know. As you know how she hates to be in anyone's debt she is arranging to leave three pennies *with* the parcel, just in case, on the oak chest at the foot of the stairs. If you find when the post office weighs the parcel that she has not, after all, understamped it, you can always give her back the pennies next time. That is quite clear, isn't it? – everything will be on the oak chest at the foot of the stairs; in fact, I am just going down to arrange about that now. Now, Robert, can I be certain you won't forget, or how would it be if I told the children to remind you?' She sped to the window and looked out. 'No, that settles that,' she said, 'they seem to have gone – however, they are probably somewhere else: *you* can always tell them to remind you. If you do so, be sure and let Muttikins know, on your way out, that you *have* told the children to remind you, or else she may be wondering. She is in the lounge. She will of course in any case be there to see you off, but one does not want her to have anything further on her mind. – I don't know of course *where* you're planning to walk to, Robert, but if you want to get anywhere you should have started sooner; as it is you ought to start at once, or you will have brought poor Mrs Rodney down here on quite false pretences.'

Stella said: 'It's my fault; I've been looking at all these photographs.'

'Yes, quite a galaxy, aren't they?' said Ernestine. 'Robert has always photographed well; whereas my own boy Christopher Robin, unlike his uncle, flees from a camera at sight. However, these in their own way recall the past – Crooked again!' she cried, dashing to straighten several. 'Whatever have you been doing to them, Robert? – Did Robert tell you,' she added, turning to Stella, 'that this is my sister Amabelle, the children's mother, just off to golf with Robert before her marriage? She has lost a good deal of weight since she's been in India . . . And that is our father shortly before his illness: he used to radiate energy and fun, although in some ways Robert takes after him . . . And that, poor fellow, was my dog.'

'Yes, so Robert said.'

'He had wonderful faith in human nature,' said Ernestine, for the first time colouring with emotion. 'Of course, he came to us as a pup, and I am glad to think none of us ever let him down. I often think that if Hitler could have looked into that dog's eyes, the story might have been very different – Hark, though: there goes the telephone! Someone else after me!'

Robert and Stella, having allowed Ernestine a considerable start, went downstairs: Mrs Kelway looked up from her knitting in the middle of the lounge. 'You will not have time to go very far,' she said. Stella, picking up her scarf and gloves from the oak chest, saw the parcel with the pennies on it and held her breath: however, nothing further was said. As she and Robert stepped out of the porch, the children came zigzagging round the corner of the house, trying to look nonchalant. 'Can we come with you?' they asked.

'No,' said Robert.

'Oh – Are you meaning to walk through the wood?'

'We might.'

'The thing is, we are pretending that we have mined that.'

'Then you can pretend we've been blown up.'

'Oh,' they said doubtfully.

The grown-up couple made off across the garden, Stella feeling guilty about the children, at whose faces she had not the heart to look back, and Robert limping.

7

Robert was due back on duty at nine o'clock: they dined early in Soho, on their way from the station, then said good night at a street corner. Stella walked back to her flat alone. The country seemed to have followed her back into London and to be on her tracks like a disaffecting ghost, undoing the reality of the city; around her the unsubstantial darkness was quickened by a not quite wind. Shreds of leaves from the woods deadened the impact of her heels on the pavement; up out of basements came an autumnal mould smell; a loose gutter high on a damaged building now and then creaked overhead like a bough. All this, with the amputation of their 'good night' as lovers, keyed up her susceptibilities to a pitch. In the sky there was a slow, stealthy massing of clouds: she walked hatless, and once or twice a drop – single, sinister, warmish – splashed on her forehead. She was walking west, towards the torn pale late night – this troubled lingering of a day that had been troubling oppressed her, as did the long perspective of the extinct street that so few people frequented and none crossed. Never never would the peace-time lighted windows and lamps of city autumn late evening have been more comforting. Muteness was falling on London with the uneasy dark; here and there stood a figure watchfully in a doorway; or lovers, blotted together, drained up into their kisses all there was left of vitality in this Saturday's end.

She began to feel it was not the country but occupied Europe that was occupying London – suspicious listening, surreptitious movement, and leaden hearts. The weather-quarter tonight was the conquered lands. The physical nearness of the Enemy – how few were the miles between the capital and the coast, between coast and coast! – became palpable. Tonight, the safety-curtain between the here and the there had lifted; the breath of danger and sorrow travelled over freely from shore to shore. The very tension overhead of the clouds nervously connected London with Paris – even, as at this same moment might a woman in that other city, she found some sort of comfort in asking herself how one could have expected to be happy?

Carrying the hat she had worn all day, she had a finger of the same hand crooked through and cut by the string of Mrs Kelway's parcel Her finger-joint dug into the tight-bound softness of what could only be knitted wool. She had charged herself with the parcel: it was addressed, as they had seen in the train, not once but three times over to Christopher Robin. 'I may *just* remember to post it, on my way to work tomorrow: you wouldn't, I know. Anyhow, the whole thing only came up at all because I'm a woman.' 'And a mother.' 'I don't think they noticed that.' 'Well, I warned you, didn't I?' 'Yes, I really will try and post it – only do for heaven's sake keep those pennies.' 'How you do hate pennies,' observed Robert, neutrally jingling them with his other change. 'All the same, there would have been much less fuss if you hadn't tried to skid them. What a fuss, anyway – *do* London post offices stay open on Sundays?' 'I'm sure if your mother says so they must.'

She was by this time footsore. She crossed Langham Place into her own street: here her step picked up as her eye ran ahead, through the now less anonymous dark, to where her own door should be. That she should seem to perceive a figure posted, waiting, that she should instantaneously know herself to be on the return to a watched house, *could* be only another deception of the nerves. She had so dissolved herself, during the walk home, into the thousands of beings of oppressed people that the idea of the Someone was, at its first flash, no more than frightful fulfilment of expectation. Now her approaching footsteps were being numbered; no instinctive check or pause in them went unmarked. *Her* part – listening for the listener, watching for the watcher – must be the keeping on walking on, as though imperviously: the actual nerved-up briskness of her step, the tingle up from her heels as they struck the pavement, brought back what seemed to be common sense. But, her very decision that there could not be anyone synchronized with the evidence that there was – a match struck, sheltered, then thrown away. This – for how could it not be a watcher's object to stay obliterated up to the last moment? – was bravado, gratuitous. This was a sheer advertisement of impunity; this could not but be Harrison – for who else, by his prodigality with matches, in these days when there were to all intents and purposes none, gave such ostentatious proof of 'inside' power?

Having come into inside range of the door and watcher, Stella shifted her bag to take out her key. Half-way up the steps she said over her shoulder, flatly: 'Been waiting long?'

'I fancied you should be about due back.'

'You want to see me?'

'I should rather like a word.'

He was up the steps, respectfully at her elbow, before her key had turned in the latch; he had slipped round the door behind into the hall with the unobtrusive celerity of a normally outdoor dog. Automatically she started up the familiar stairs in the dark then turned round to wonder what he was doing. Of course he would have a torch – the spotlight butterflied over the doctor's letters on the table, poised itself, admiring, on a mask in the plaster arch, then began to come after her, gain on her, up the stairs. 'At least *one* in the party ought to have one of these things, I must say I think,' said Harrison. He played the beam on her fingers while she unlocked her flat. As they entered, he picked up, inside her door, the letters she always left lying when she returned with Robert. Nothing could have been worse than coming home alone; even this, with its grotesque series of variations on her returns not alone, was better. Whistling away to herself as she quickly blacked-out the windows, she thought – inconceivable, this being the same flat! Still feeling nothing whatever, she switched on the lamps and fire. She turned to find that Harrison had meanwhile sat down. He said: 'You know, this is very nice. I so often think of this place that, if you won't mind my saying so, now I feel quite at home.'

'In that case, I should like to change my shoes.' As she came back again through the door from her bedroom, now wearing green mules, she resumed: 'I've been in the country, as I expect you know.'

'Making the most of the last of the fine weather?'

'What do you mean by that?'

'I say, making the most of the last of the fine weather?' repeated Harison with patience.

'Oh. You think it will rain?'

'While I was out there just now, there were two or three drops.'

152

'I felt one, as I was coming along.'

'Yes, tonight one feels some sort of change coming on. Well, the rain falls on the just and the unjust, as they say, doesn't it? Ha-ha.'

Stella leaning exhaustedly back in her armchair, feet up on a gilt-legged stool, rolled round her head on the cushions, unable to help remarking: 'That's been the first time you've laughed tonight.'

'I always rasp you a bit when I laugh, do I? Possibly I chiefly laugh when I'm nervous – this evening I can't help feeling we understand each other. You do, for one thing, somehow seem more relaxed.'

'What I *am* is, extremely tired.'

'Must have been quite a day,' he said, nicely. 'How did it go?'

'I have no idea. Why?'

'Look, if you feel done in, you don't have to talk. I'd be always happy simply sitting around.'

'Do you often do that?'

'I am so seldom here.'

'One thing – is this your evening off?'

'I don't quite –'

'Is this business or pleasure?'

Harrison, with the extreme tip of his tongue, touched his upper lip under the short moustache. He sat planted well forward in his armchair – which, like so many third armchairs in a room in which normally only two intimate people sit, was a stranded outpost some way away down the carpet, and was turned towards hers (which faced towards Robert's, empty) at a tentative angle which he had not changed. So placed, he viewed nothing but Stella's profile, unless he could provoke her to turn her head.

It had been while in profile, and even more negligently and parenthetically than usual, that she had put the question – however, a moment later she did look round at him, as though all the same waiting for some reply. He exposed to her nothing but his forehead; frowning down at the carpet between his knees he began pushing one fist, dubiously, at no very great pressure, into the palm of the other hand. By continuing never to raise his eyes he conveyed the impression of being as much embarrassed, on her behalf, as saddened by her awkwardness. It was regretfully that he at last said: 'I should have thought, you know, that *you* ought to know.'

'Then I must be stupid this evening. You'd better talk to me. Tell me what else I have been doing.'

Harrison's grin at that was so unequivocal that she could only like him. Swiftly he ruined that – 'One thing one can see you've been doing, Stella: you've thought things over.'

She put up a hand between a lamp and her eyes.

He added: 'Don't mind me calling you by your Christian name?'

'Thought what over?'

'Your and my talk.'

She flashed out: 'When and if I ever do think of that, it's to be all the more certain I must have dreamed it!'

'Still, there are dreams one checks up on, even so, don't you think? I mean, if I'd seemed to dream I saw a chap at the foot of my bed going through my pockets, I'd take a look through my pockets first thing next morning. Who wouldn't? You would. The devil, of course, would be, what exactly *had* I had in my pockets the night before? It's queer how a thing comes popping back and back to one's mind – *something* gone, but one cannot be sure what.'

'I never have dreams like that.'

'No, exactly – you and I both know darn well there are no dreams like that. If a thing looks to have happened, twenty to one it did. It's sheer stalling to say a thing's "unlikely"; it's either downright impossible or it's a fact, to prove. Alternatively, what may look and smell like a fact still stands to be proved impossible; of course that could happen. That's the way you're determined this thing is to work out – or isn't it? For you, it's a case of my word against your – er, ideas. How about those ideas of yours, all the same? If you want to know how I know you've been thinking things over, all I say is, look at the way you've been checking up! It's funny, you know: in reverse you work just the way I would. If it bores you to go back over the last month, just take today, for instance. Today you did exactly what I should have done in your place.'

'You flatter me; but still I don't understand.'

'Went to look at the first place where rot could start. Mind, I wouldn't dream of asking you what you found.'

'You could see for yourself – or perhaps you already have? It's not a long run by train.'

'Oh, it's not the time,' said Harrison simply. 'Nor is it purely the fact that I've got all I want already; in general, I'm all for one final look round. No, it's more, to put the thing in a nutshell, that I'm not a woman. *You* would naturally bark up that tree; I bark up others. One can assume in most cases, and most of all of course, in a case like this, that there's something up more than one tree: the question is, which tree to bark up first? That depends on what type one is oneself. All trees being equal, my choice wouldn't be yours. No, all I say is, you've done what I'd have done in your place.'

'Spied round a home?'

'Your being a woman,' said Harrison somewhat regretfully, 'cuts both ways. I can't tell you anything you don't know already, and you don't like me to tell you what you don't like knowing. Whether you want to or not, you don't miss a thing – except, if I may say so, what's right under your nose. The other evening, that Sunday, last time I dropped in here, I put it up to you that such-and-such was the situation: you virtually told me to go to hell, but not absolutely. I rather took it you'd rather leave the thing in the air. Absolutely it's been the same to me to leave the thing in the air for the time being, though not of course indefinitely. If your idea was that the thing would cool off, that has not been the case.'

'I was not hoping not to see you again. I mean, I expected you would be coming round.'

'Quite so. And as you see, here I am.'

'Yes.'

'I however have made a point of not crashing in.'

'I have not said anything to Robert – apart from asking whether he knew you.'

'I'd have been very much surprised if he'd said he did: in point of actual fact I don't think he does . . . No, I may tell you it's been evident nobody's put the wind up him so far – everything's gone on taking its normal course. Only, *you're* not as natural on the telephone at nights as you used to be. Anybody would think you thought his line was tapped.'

'Would they? So that is what you do in the evenings?'

'And how have you got along with that other check-up – on me?'

'Not very far, as you may have guessed.'

'Quite an amount of people, as I did warn you, have genuinely no idea who I am – what,' he asked following her with his eyes, 'are you looking for? Can I get you anything?'

'Yes: will you bring me a glass of milk? The bottle's in the refrigerator in the kitchen.' As he sprang from the chair with an alacrity which sent it careering back on its castors, she threw in: 'You don't drink milk, I expect?'

'Well, I'm not keen. In fact, if you ever felt any kind of shortage I could drop you a bottle round every other day –. To the right, out here?'

'Second door: the first is the bathroom.'

Left like this in the room with the empty chairs, she took the opportunity to breathe. Harrison became nothing more than a person she had for the moment succeeded in getting rid of. She looked from the armchair proper to Robert to the armchair commandeered by Harrison, but found herself thinking of neither of these – of, rather, Victor, her vanished husband. Why of Victor now? One could only suppose that the apparently forgotten beginning of any story was unforgettable; perpetually one was subject to the sense of there having had to be a beginning *somewhere*. Like the lost first sheet of a letter or missing first pages of a book, the beginning kept on suggesting what must have been its nature. One never was out of reach of the power of what had been written first. Call it what you liked, call it a miscarried love, it imparted, or was always ready and liable to impart, the nature of an alternative, attempted recovery or enforced second start to whatever followed. The beginning, in which was conceived the end, could not but continue to shape the middle part of the story, so that none of the realizations along that course were what had been expected, quite whole, quite final. That first path, taken to be a false start – who was to know, after all, where it might not have led? She saw, for an instant, Roderick's father's face, its look suspended and non-committal. In this room, in which love in the person of Robert had been so living, this former face had not shown itself till tonight – now, she was penetrated not only by as it were first awareness of Victor's death but by worse, by the knowledge of his having been corrupted before death by undoings and denials of all love. She had had it in her to have been an honest woman and borne more children; she had been capable of more virtue than the succeeding years had left her able to show. Her young marriage had not been an experiment; it is the young who cannot afford to experiment – everything is at stake. The time of her marriage had been a time after war; her own desire to find herself in some embrace from life had been universal, at work in the world, the time whose creature she was. For a deception, she could no more blame the world than one can blame any fellow-sufferer: in these last twenty of its and her own years she had to watch in it what she felt in her – a clear-sightedly helpless progress towards disaster. The fateful course of her fatalistic century seemed more and more her own: together had she and it arrived at the testing extremities of their noonday. Neither had lived before. . . . The reappearance of Harrison with the glass of milk reminded her that her own extremity was in this being bargained for. The situation was such-and-such, as he indeed said.

To make room for the glass on the little table beside her, he had to shift Mrs Kelway's parcel – 'Neat little affair, your kitchen,' he remarked absently, meanwhile stooping to read the three-times-written address.

She volunteered: 'Yes, that is for a nephew of Robert's. His grandmother, I mean to say Robert's mother, wants it posted from here, from London, tomorrow, Sunday. She says we have post offices which keep open.'

'It's amazing what these old women know.'

'Yes.'

'Would you like me to take charge of this?'

'Post it? – oh, thank you; that *would* be one thing less. But it is really important: you won't forget it?'

'Practically everything is important,' replied Harrison, going to put the parcel beside his hat. Stepping between or over the smaller furniture, he made her think of that first day at the funeral, when she had turned to see him so far behind her stepping over the graves.

'*You* must have had a mother?' she said suddenly, looking at him over the glass of milk.

He seemed nonplussed but gratified. 'More or less.'

'Oh? – who was she?'

He thought. 'She was a South African.'

'What became of her?'

'She cleared out.'

'Were you sorry?'

'I was in Sydney.'

'What were you doing there? – You're not an Australian, are you?'

'That would be a long story,' said Harrison, sitting down with the evident intention of not telling it. 'Milk all right?' he said ardently, eyes upon her.

'Perfectly: why?' she said. 'Did you put anything in it?'

'Oh, I say – come!'

'By the way, *did* you get those papers back?'

'Which?'

'Those papers of yours that got locked up with Cousin Francis's things. You told me they were important.'

'Oh, those. Oh *yes;* that was all fixed up.'

'Yes, I imagine you knew it would be – if, indeed, there ever were any papers. You wanted to get to know me for quite a different reason.'

Harrison took this well. 'Look, let's,' he winningly said, 'just say I was killing two birds with the same stone. Though, I wouldn't want you to take me up wrong in one way; I had quite a genuine feeling for old Frankie. I might not, I admit, have crashed that party just for that reason; I've got too much to do.'

Stella now put down the empty milk glass, brought a mirror out and dabbed her mouth with a handkerchief. 'Odd,' she said, 'that I should have turned up in two different stories. Didn't you think that odd?'

'Yes, it did rather strike me as a coincidence. But it's amazing how often that sort of thing does happen.'

'Must be convenient, too.'

'But then as against that, there's so often a catch in things. One has got to allow for that. The trouble can be, how to allow enough – in this case, what's thrown me out was your turning out to be *you.*'

'I was bound to be someone.'

'Ha-ha, yes. But you didn't have to be someone to that extent. You had, of course, originally come in under the regulation check-up – woman or money? – in getting the layout of this whole affair. And in view of whom you are most often around *with,* I of course had often seen you around. Frankly, after the showings of the check-up, I wrote you off, crossed out *"cherchez la femme"* and switched to money. I'd made the switch, I may tell you, some weeks before we buried the old boy. In fact, I had made that switch long enough ago to have found that there wasn't anything along *that* line, either. No, I appeared to be up against sheer kink.'

'What kink?'

'There I'd thought you might help me.'

'Why should you want to know why a thing is done? You, I mean – you in your line of business? The "what" and "how" I can see; but where does the "why" come in?'

'Early on,' said Harrison keenly, 'quite near the start. There's a stage where it can be useful to get your "why". The "why" may just tip the likely up to the certain. Not to speak of the fact that I have known cases where the "why" and "how" interlock – if a chap's doing what he does for a particular reason, he's likely to do what he does in a particular way. In this case we have a chap, and a nice chap, selling his country. Now a nice chap's not likely to do that for no reason –'

'– Why would you, for instance?'

'That would rather depend.' He reflected, lighting a cigarette. 'Anyhow, I am not such a nice chap. But mind you, I've been speaking of ancient history, of last May, around that time of the funeral. *Then*, I was still rather beating about the bush: having eliminated women and money, the psychological angle looked like my only hope. Frankly, at that time it *was* my object to meet you, date up, have a drink or two, chat . . .'

'As indeed we did.'

'As we did do during the summer – and see whether you might not throw some light on him. Once at ease, the majority of women are far from cagey on the subject of any chap they're keen on; and they've no idea what's important in what they say. So, therefore, that was my first idea.'

'Did it not work?'

'Point was, that it ceased to matter whether it worked or not. Things, as they can do, took an unforeseen turn. Go right out on one thing, I've often found, and immediately something else opens up. I should say that this was a case of that. I more or less stumbled on to something that gave me all *I* wanted, as to our friend, conclusive. That was, therefore, that. I cannot say I was sorry to scrap psychology.'

'The "why" is no longer the question?'

He made a pat little gesture of wiping out. 'Unless, of course,' he added, 'you feel that's over to you?'

Stella moved; she switched on one more bar of the electric fire. She checked or attempted to hide a shiver by wrapping her arms closely across her breast: having reflected a moment in this attitude, she asked: 'Then, if you had not contrived to meet me when you did, it would not still have been necessary for you to meet me now?'

'Actually,' he had to admit, 'not.'

'What a pity, then.'

'What's a pity?'

'Why, that we ever did meet.'

He deliberated. 'I would not call it that; though there have been times when I've called it the very hell.'

'*You* have called it that?' In her chair an image of amazement pivoted round to face him. For a moment Harrison eyed the image – its sculpted erectness, breastplate of arms, eyes from which the pupils stood out as though painted. Then, pressing down his palms on the arms of *his* chair, he propelled himself out of it; to stand up harshly. No more, for him, those insidious pink springy depths – he repudiated the pretty dream of the room. No longer a person to be becalmed or side-tracked, he comprehended Stella in his outsider's glance at the lit up or shadowy trifles round him. They might not be hers, but she had, still, employed them. He burst right out of the picture – 'Yes, it has been the hell for me: what do you suppose?'

She had her own kind of violence. 'You did not have to! You did not have to dog me – to gnaw and nibble round the edge of summer, to loom and gloom! It has been detestable, because it has been unnatural, ever since last May. You forced that meeting: now you complain that it had, after all, no point. It is nothing to you that I've been annoyed for nothing? Now you come round and waste my time by telling me I waste yours. That's your affair. You did not have to – ever.'

'The not having to, but the all the same having to – that's what *has* been the hell!'

'There was no compulsion.'

This time, *he* stared. 'Then what do you think there was? You've never calculated, or you would know. Know what it feels like when anything slips up. Haywire. *I* calculate – that's my life. It's not what I've done I've liked – it's all one to me what I do – it's doing it; that's what has been the thing. You can't have any idea how you've split that up. *Your* summer – what about mine? Month after month of charging up, ticking over, getting no place – stuck. I'm not made for that sort of thing; I've got no time for it.'

'You've got no time for me, then.'

'I said I'd got no time for *this*.'

'But a woman takes time. I could take twice the time you've got.'

'In that case I should be twice the man.'

'That would still be nothing to me.'

'You have never tried. It's funny, you don't listen to what I say, yet in spite of that I can feel us getting to know each other. You and I are not so unlike – yes, it's funny.'

'Why? Below one level, everybody's horribly alike. You succeed in making a spy of me.'

Harrison jibbed, or else winced. He touched his tie, made a jerky involuntary movement of the head. She thought, prudery – but it could have passed for feeling. What had she said? It did not seem to her worse, more excruciating, than anything else he had forced her to say so far, yet here he was all at once behaving with the defençelessness of a stricken person. She had gone too far, too far; what she had said had had the effect, even, of driving him from her physically. He walked away, broke away, to one of the windows. He stood by the window headed into the curtain like an animal blindly wanting to get out of a room.

She recrossed her feet on the stool, leaned further back, closed her eyes, in the attitude of a woman so tired out as no longer to be responsible for anything.

'What's happened?' she finally lightly asked.

He mumbled: 'Think it's begun to rain.'

'Oh? See.'

Harrison parted the curtains with his thumb and edged between them; they swung into place behind him. The window embrasure was deep; nothing showed there was a person in there at all: it occurred to Stella that any night anybody could have stood hidden in there, listening. She heard him run the blind up, throw up the sash as far as it would go: an outdoor breath swelled the curtains, sifting round them damply into the room. She raised her head to listen, but heard no rain – heard nothing: the silence could not have been more complete if Harrison had walked straight on out of the window.

She got up and went after him through the curtains. Rain was to be seen glinting in the light she let through behind her; behind the fine fall was the sighing darkness. 'Mind,' he said sharply, 'careful! Either come through or go back.'

She stayed where she was, letting go the curtains, glad to be walled away by them from that haunted room. Assuaging blankness out of the open window began to enter her through the eyes. The embrasure felt like a balcony, one stood projected, high up, into the unseen unsounding sentient world of rain. Nothing more than an intimation was in the dark air; the fall's softness vicariously was to be felt on the roofs around, in the streets below. Only by the smell of refreshed stone was one to know that this rain fell on a city. The night was neither warm nor cold; it belonged to no season; it was a night of rain.

Since how long – how long had it been raining? An hour ago, perhaps, what had been being said had become not necessary; the rasping wordy battle might have been quieted before now. London itself gave out the feeling of having been alleviated for some time; nothing went on out there but that lulling fall and that sighing silence, under the breast of which late-night traffic only gave out a stifled deeper sigh. The total dark of the city became tonight as unprecautionary, natural as that of rocks, woods, and hills on which elsewhere rain fell. The peacefulness of this outcome of the late evening's tense massed warlike clouds was the one thing astonishing: now in effect the war became as unmeaning as the quarrel; two persons speechlessly at a window became as anonymous as the city they overlooked. These two, though fated to speak again, could be felt to be depersonalized speakers in a drama which should best of all have remained as silent as it essentially was.

The darkness by force of being so long looked into resolved itself into particles, some lighter; air and solids just lifted apart; rooflines took on an uncertain form. But inside here, in the embrasure, between the window-frame and the curtains, both persons still stayed blotted out: it was at an unestablishable distance from Stella that Harrison said: 'Yes, I should say this had settled in wet.' She got the impression he had put his hand outdoors, that that had been the act which had made him speak.

'Not much good,' he continued, 'waiting for this to stop.'

'Have you far to go?'

'Depends where I go to next.'

'Where exactly do you live? I have no idea.'

'There are always two or three places where I can turn in.'

'But for instance, where do you keep your razor?'

'I have two or three razors,' he said in an absent tone.

That, of course, was the core of their absolute inhumanity together. His concentration on her was made more oppressive by his failure to have or let her give him any possible place in the human scene. By the rules of fiction, with which life to be credible must comply, he was as a character 'impossible' – each time they met, for instance, he showed no shred or trace of having been continuous since they last met. His civilian clothes, though one could be remotely conscious of alternation in suit or shirt or tie, *seemed* to vary much less than Robert's uniform; the uninterestingly right state of what he wore seemed less to argue care – brushing, pressing, changes of linen – than a physical going into abeyance, just as he was, with everything he had on him, between appearances.

166

'Appearance', in the sense used for a ghost or actor, had, indeed, been each of these times the word. Coming out of that vacuum, the reiterated unrelated story of his desire could but be unmeaning. Just now, for an instant, in the darkness in which she could not even remember the colour of his coat, he had been for the first time palpably *someone* near her: a being – continuous, secretive, dense, weighty, locked in himself and face to face, beside her, with the unbounded night in which no clock struck.

'No, I have not heard a clock strike all the evening,' she said aloud. 'It might be any hour.'

He had recourse to the luminous dial of his watch. Either because she had not directly asked or out of habit, he kept what the watch had told him to himself; but said, as though in reference to the fact that time had gone by, so that any earlier movement by him or her was now history: 'I rather needed a breather. You didn't mind?'

She took this, as it could of course be taken, as a hint that though making use of her window it had been his intention to breathe at it alone. 'No, do,' she said, 'breathe as long as you like,' and turned to grope in the folds behind her for her way back between the curtains into the room. The movement of stuff and the chinks of lamplight knocked through by her touch roused him – 'You can't stay?' he said. 'Breathe too? I've been liking that. This air now – at least we have that in common. Nothing more, since you say.'

'I was sorry for what I said.'

'Did you know you said "horrible"?' He picked up the word with some hesitation, uncertain whether it would or would not sting twice. 'No, what you said was "horribly alike" – that simply made no contact with what I meant.'

'I'm sorry – I thought you meant something more. Yes, we both have natures; but what I can't bear is what you do to mine, what you make mine do. If it only were that you loved me, I could do no worse than not love you back; but there has been something worse – somehow you've distorted love. You may not feel what it feels like to be a spy; I do – ever since you came to me with that story. You've banked on my not having the courage to ask one question, and you've been right, so far. However, don't let us talk again.'

'I must say, I liked it this evening when you were tired. You let me fetch you that glass of milk.'

'And I never offer you anything to eat or drink.'

'While you still don't think you want me here, that seems fair enough. Though this evening when we came in and you changed your shoes everything began to be something like what it could be. But then suddenly, somehow, I went and put a foot wrong – got you right up again against what I do. To *me*, tonight, whatever I do's outside.'

To her, tonight, 'outside' meant the harmless world: the mischief was in her own and in other rooms. The grind and scream of battles, mechanized advances excoriating flesh and country, tearing through nerves and tearing up trees, were indoor-plotted; this was a war of dry cerebration inside windowless walls. No act was not part of some calculation; spontaneity was in tatters; from the point of view of nothing more than the heart any action was enemy action now . . . Also, letting the curtain drop, returning to lean her forehead against the pushed up sash of the window, already clammy, she understood, with regard to Harrison, the hopeless disparity between belief and truth. He was sincere in everything he said; probably she might never hear again words like these of his, concentrations of an entire being. At the same time, he mis-stated at every turn; there was monstrous heresy some-where in his love; to as much as dispute with him was to injure honour. To be in his embrace would be to accept, for ever, that strength was left in nothing but obsession. She was not to know, even, whether, in keeping her by him by the window, he might not be banking on the effect of the dark, on the senses' harmony when there is one sense missing, some sort of harmony of the blind. Indeed his psychic, his moral blindness was most nearly acceptable on unseeing terms; and his abstention from touching her, always marked and careful, was becoming, in this constriction of the embrasure, powerful as a touch. He had been acute in liking her tired: something, an involuntary overflow from her nerves, *had* begun to fill up the space between them. Only he, though, could have christened *that* misunderstanding – he, only, thus could have marked the enormous breach, the desert between understanding and where they really stood.

With a jerk, she raised her head from the sash. 'Will you go now? I think I must go to bed.'

'Right,' he said, expressionlessly and promptly.

She made her way back into the empty room; he followed. 'Your parcel,' he said, 'my hat . . .'

'I'm sorry about the rain. I still don't know where you live.'

'Might want to get in touch with me?'

'I only –'

'Don't worry; I shall look in again.'

8

Louie kept a look-out for Harrison in the park, but, as she had feared was probable, failed to see him. Evidently he only could have been there, that one Sunday, for some special purpose; she wondered what his other purposes might be. She continued to ponder, from time to time, over his and her disheartening farewell, which any other girl might have called a smack in the face. 'You never know, these days,' she would say to anyone who would listen. 'You do have to watch – you never know for instance who you might find yourself sitting next to. Anyone might be funny, for all you know. I met a man who was funny the other day.'

'What, a scream, you mean?' asked her friend Connie, when this was tried on her.

'No, I don't mean.' When anyone took her up wrong, a look of animal trouble passed over Louie's face. To talk, which she had to do, was to tender what words she had; to be forced to search for anything further, better, was as persecuting as having to dip for escaped coppers into the depths of her handbag – yes, and that on top of a pitching blacked-out bus – with the conductor standing over her snorting. 'No I didn't. I meant, a bit off.'

'You surprise me,' said Connie. 'You mean to tell me you never met but that one man in that state? To me these days a man who wasn't a bit off in one way if not another would be remarkable.'

'Ah, but you meet all sorts,' Louie said respectfully.

'I've got my head screwed on, which is more than you have.'

'*He* said that – he said I ought to take care!'

It had begun to appear to her, looking back, that Harrison had fathered and understood her.

'It's not even as if,' said Connie, 'you were a London girl.'

Louie nodded – yes, there was that, again: she was a Kentish sea-coast orphan. 'It's in a way unsettling,' she told Connie, 'not being able to get back again to where I come from.' It was that, exactly. Tom gone, she had lately felt in London like a day tripper who has missed the last night train home.

Obliteration of everything by winter was to be dreaded. Already the late-autumnal closing in of the evenings was setting a term to new adventures; their scene was vanishing – some sort of mindless hope had gone on haunting her for just so long as daylight had gone on haunting streets. Through the summer her husband's step, still only just out of hearing, could be imagined turning and coming back; while summer lasted she therefore still need not shut up shop. Within the narrowing of autumn, the impulses of incredulous loneliness died down in her; among them that readiness to quicken which had made her look for her husband in other faces. True, she felt nearer Tom with any man than she did with no man – true love is to be recognized by its aberrations; so shocking can these be, so inexplicable to any other person, that true love is seldom to be recognised at all.

Now when she came out from the factory even dusk was over; under the tattered dark of the skies everyone in the streets on the way home looked as purposeful as Harrison;

Louie was swept along in one shoal of indifferent shadows against another. Momentarily, dimmed-down blue light from inside a bus or some flash from an opened-then-shut door brought her own eyes into being – vacant, asking, ignorant, and askance. Anything else she had with which to draw a second glance from the world – wide Jutish features, big thin-skinned lips – was cancelled: the darkness did not love her. To be seen was for her not to be. It was a phenomenon of war-time city night that it brought out something provocative in the step of most modest women; Nature tapped out with the heels on the pavement an illicit semaphore. Alone was Louie in being almost never accosted; whatever it *was* was missing from her step; she walked, she strode, she bulked ahead through the dark with the sexless flat-footed nonchalance of a ten-year-old, only more heavily. No, this was no season for her to be starting anything out of doors. Neither did Sundays, her only daylight at liberty, any more bring return; from the Sunday park the illusory sensuous veil was stripped – one saw clean through the thickets into empty distance; the ilexy love mound rode in a waste of lawn like a ship abandoned; strangers gave one another unmeeting looks. Habituated lovers made the park tour briskly and arm-in-arm; along black paths and round more sheltered seats she overheard chatter of that existence which was the secret of everybody except her – even the refugees could embrace their memories and their injury. Yes, it was in the disenchanted park that London's indifference to Louie stood out most stark and bare.

There still was, however, some negative virtue in being outdoors. Indoors meant Chilcombe Street; here resided the fact of her being of meaning only to an absent person, absent most appallingly from this double room. Tom seldom had looked at Louie; he was not one to look again at anything he had once seen. He had been accustomed to spend his home evenings frowning at some technical book, or frowning because he was thinking something technical out. It had been Louie who – chair tilted back, tongue exploring her palate, mind blank of anything in particular – had hourlong passively gazed at Tom. Why now, therefore, should it be his chair that gazed at her? It directed something at her whichever way she pushed, pulled or turned it, in whatever direction she turned herself. The discountenancing of the chair by filling it had been her object in bringing strangers she met in the park back here. Now she came to think over it, this autumn, none of her visitors had been seen again: in some cases they had been no more than crossing London with perhaps an hour or two to spend. If any of them ever by chance had come back to look for her, owing to not knowing anybody else in London either, the probability was they had knocked on the wrong door; which from the point of view of her reputation was just as well – soldiers or airmen coming round asking for Louie would have looked wrong. Her wireless, by the way, was by this time dead out, finished, after all their tinkering at it; she had been sorry, each time, that she had ever said anything about her wireless in the first place – its having seemed since Tom left to be a bit off had most likely only been her imagination ... These October evenings, the silence left by the wireless was filled in by the coughing of the gas fire, which now also had some complaint. In order to delay her return home, she had formed the habit of dropping into a café in Tottenham Court Road to eat supper: the place was mirrored – she had the satisfaction of seeing, in bright steaminess, herself, Louie, walk in, look round, and sit down.

The café habit however came to be interrupted, for as against autumn deficits there was now Connie, and no evening when Connie was off duty was to be thrown away. It was true Connie did have dates, but you never knew. Connie, an A.R.P. warden, had lately moved into one of the two top floor rooms of the Chilcombe Street house. She was a year or two the other side of thirty, tough, cross, kind, with bags under her eyes under the powder, a bull fringe, and a brick-red postbox mouth. At the first glance, Louie had been alarmed by the notion that this uniformed newcomer must be something to do with the police, and even when this appeared less likely there still was something alarming about that scissor-like stride in the dark blue official slacks. It could but look as though Connie, in her braced-in tunic, must somehow be one more person empowered to tick one off. It turned out not only that Chilcombe Street was outside the area of the particular wardens' post Connie adorned, and therefore outside her official sphere, but that her ideas of off duty were stringent. She paid rent here in order to have some place to put her feet up without threat of interruption – in fact, it would always be out of order for Connie to tamper with another post's bomb. Therefore, should No. 10 Chilcombe Street chance to become an incident while she was reposing under its roof, they need not, she gave out, come coming round after her – unless, naturally, she should require to be dug out. There was not, as it happened, anything doing in Connie's line of business this London autumn of 1942; at the post throughout long hours of duty she dislocated her jaw yawning, or swapping cracks with other posts on the official telephone. To top all, as if watching the hands of the post clock go round and round, night in, day out, above

Mr Churchill's picture were not bad enough, outside persons at sight of her uniform were becoming nasty about the pay she drew, which *she* knew to be shockingly insufficient. No one who held you were paid too high for doing damn all by the hour could themselves have tried doing damn all by the hour. Not, as she pointed out, that she was by any means doing damn all; Headquarters were everlastingly thinking up something new in order to keep Connie upon the hop. But that was the civilian public for you all over; the minute they stopped being pasted they become fresh – another slight doing-over, if she ought not to say so, would once again show them where they got off. A slight doing-over of London, just now, would in fact have been to her interest: with everything going on being slack it began to look as though they might come round trying to winkle Connie out of Civil Defence. If she could have got out back to the tobacco kiosk where she used to reign, that of course would have been quite another matter, but a Mobile Woman dared not look sideways these days – you might find yourself in Wolverhampton (a friend of hers had), or at the bottom of a mine, or in the A.T.S. with some bitch blowing a bugle at you till you got up in the morning. It was well, she remarked, for Louie being a soldier's wife, though if she had half a head on her shoulders she should have started a kid also. After two or three of their Chilcombe Street evening talks, Louie's awe of Connie did not so much evaporate as shift its ground. Decidedly Connie qualified by her nerve to be a saviour of the human race; at the same time she had a tongue like a file, so that you could not take her to be the race's lover. She had walked out of the kiosk, thereby for feiting a week's pay, on 1 September 1939 because, being funny that way, she had had an intuition that something was really going to happen this time. She was bossy, if she had to say so herself; prey, since childhood, to a repressed wish to issue orders, blow whistles, direct traffic. This had always made trouble for her in previous jobs; in Civil Defence, she had been in the first place given to understand, initiative would be what was wanted. Before she knew better she had signed on. You live and learn.

Tom wrote back, he was glad to hear Louie had made a girl friend, particularly one in their own house: she sounded to him as though she should be company. Formerly Tom had not been in favour of being in any way free with other tenants, which could lead first to chattering on the stairs, next to dropping in and borrowing. It was different however now with Louie left on her own – always provided Connie *was* all she said. In fact, before Connie entered the picture, he had once or twice asked if there were no girl, of the quiet sort, Louie could cotton on to at the factory? She had written back that the trouble was that at the factory there were all sorts. She was right, of course, he returned, in being particular. The actual trouble at the factory was, that you had to have something to say, tell, swop, and Louie was unable to think of anything. She felt she did not make sense, and still worse felt that the others knew it. Women seemed to feel she had not graduated; where *had* she been all her life, they wanted to know – and, oh, where had she? It is advantageous being among all sorts if you are some sort, any sort; you gravitate to your type. It is daunting if you discover you are still no sort – the last hope gone. The one real privilege of the sheltered class is, status for the original: there was none for Louie. With Connie everything was, on the other hand, all right – Connie less spotted the vacuum in her friend than was drawn to it: she was a constitutional rusher in to fill . . . The two became introduced and intimate within the same two minutes, the night Connie happened to fall upstairs. At the sound of pound after pound of hard vegetables and an electric torch bouncing down step after step of flight after flight or dropping plumb through the banisters into the hall below, Louie could but rush out of her door. Having switched the mean landing light on she looked up, to see above her the soles of doughty shoes, in one of which was embedded a drawing-pin, fiercely scrabbling for hold on the lino treads: next Connie heaved up her spare dark behind – it was not till she was upright that she started swearing as though the house were hers: in that line she was royal. She came down three steps nearer the light in order to brush off the knees of her slacks, in the course of which she gave Louie a dirty look. 'Anything further I can do for you?' she said.

The stair and landing lighting in No. 10 was of the kind which puts itself out automatically after two minutes: it not only now did so but continued to do so throughout the search – Louie, galumphing up and down in her pink nightie, helped Connie gather up the potatoes, turnips, carrots, and it was she who finally found the torch. It was a wonderful evening. The stairs which usually smelled of null cleaned airlessness soon reeked of anger-heated government-blue serge – moreover Connie, though not redheaded, was at almost any time of the foxy type. When they were really through it was, by Connie's reckoning, 23.25; consequently there were complaints that night and more next day. Never before had Louie, with her first-floor prestige to which was added that of soldier's wife, been in this or any kind of trouble with the rest of the house. She and Connie finished by drinking tea.

There was almost nothing Connie liked better than a newspaper; she had almost always been reading one just recently. She was a collector of newspapers of almost any age, either to look at again or to wrap up things in – she acquired them by every means but purchase, keeping an eye open, wherever she might be, for one which might have been put down even for a moment. Knowing how quick people could be to serve you a dirty turn, she habitually seated herself on any paper or papers she had collected; at the post, to be forced off her papers by any duty made her as *distraite* as a mother bird. They arrived home with her limp and without a crackle. Compelled to sacrifice one in order to light a fire in the doll-sized grate of her attic at No. 10, she would, squatting, having applied the match, peer forward into the acrid smoke to read the last of the print till a flame ate it – you never knew what you might not just happen to miss. This addiction of Connie's could be and was imitated by Louie: having begun by impressing Connie, newspapers went on to infatuate Louie out-and-out. If you could not keep track of what was happening you could at least take notice of what was said – in the beginning was the word; and to that it came back in the long run. This went for anything written down.

Once Louie had taken to newspapers she found peace – so much so that she wondered why they had seemed to unsettle Tom. With the news itself she was at some disadvantage owing to having begun in the middle; she never quite had the courage to ask anyone, even Connie, how it had all begun – evidently one thing must have led to another, as in life; and whose the mistake had been in the first place, or how long ago, you would not care to say. Left to herself she had considered that anything so dreadful as this last year could only in some way have been her own fault – Singapore falling the week Tom went away; the Australians right off even where they were getting that bad fright from the Japs; us getting pushed right on top of the Egyptians in spite of everything; the Russians keeping nagging at us to do something; the Duke of Kent killed who had been so happy; even those harmless ancient cathedrals not to speak of Canterbury getting bombed also; and us running right out of soap and sweets till *they* had to go on coupons – one more headache . . . But once you looked in the papers you saw where it said, nothing was so bad as it might look. What a mistake, to have gone by the look of things! The papers knew Britain had something up her sleeve – Britain could always, in default of anything else, face facts.

For the paper's sake, Louie brought herself to put up with any amount of news – the headlines got that over for you in half a second, deciding for you every event's importance by the size of the print. As far as she could make out, the same communiques were taken out and used again and again. As against this, how inspiring was the variety of the true stories, which made the war seem human, people like her important, and life altogether more like it was once. But it was from the articles in the papers that the real build-up, the alimentation came – Louie, after a week or two on the diet, discovered that she *had* got a point of view, and not only *a* point of view but the right one. Not only did she bask in warmth and inclusion but every morning and evening she was praised. Even the Russians were apparently not as dissatisfied with her as she had feared; there was Stalingrad going on holding out, but here was she in the forefront of the industrial war drive. As for the Americans now in London, they were stupefied by admiration for her character. Dark and rare were the days when she failed to find on the inside page of her paper an address to or else account of herself. Was she not a worker, a soldier's lonely wife, a war orphan, a pedestrian, a Londoner, a home- and animal-lover, a thinking democrat, a movie-goer, a woman of Britain, a letter writer, a fuel-saver, and a housewife? She was only not a mother, a knitter, a gardener, a foot-sufferer, or a sweetheart – at least not rightly. Louie now felt bad only about any part of herself which in any way did not fit into the papers' picture; she could not have survived their disapproval. They did not, for instance, leave flighty wives or good-time girls a leg to stand on; and how rightly – she had romped through a dozen pieces on that subject with if anything rather special zest, and was midway through just one more when the blast struck cold. Could it be that the papers were out with *Louie!* – she came over gooseflesh, confronted by God and Tom. She did not begin to rally till next evening, when her paper came out strongly in favour of non-standoffishness – it appeared that we were becoming less standoffish; the Americans had been agree-ably surprised. War now made us one big family . . . She was reinstated; once again round her were the everlasting arms. Yes, she rallied – for, wife or not, she could see she was not of the flighty build, and girl or not, she rarely had ended by having what she could consider a good time. Neither did she go out with men; she was out to start with.

It had been one of those reconcilliations after which feeling enters a deeper phase. Louie came to love newspapers phys-ically; she felt a solicitude for their gallant increasing thinness and longed to feed them; she longed to fondle a copy still warm from the press, and, in default of that, formed the habit of reading crouching over her fire so as to draw out the smell of print. While deferring to Connie's *droit du seigneur* over any newspaper entering the house, Louie hated to see her use it with that sensual roughness. She was unable to watch a portion of fish being wrapped up in newspaper without a complex sensation in which envy and vicarious bliss merged. At the factory, she was drawn to girls and women in whom the same fermentation was to be felt at work – also, thanks to her daily build-up, she felt and therefore appeared, less odd. Something floated her. She was now, even, in a fair way to make those friends of whom, having Connie, she was no longer in need.

Connie's reading of papers was for the most part suspicious; nothing was to get by unobserved by her. Her re-reading of everything was the more impressive because the second time, you were given to understand, what she was doing was reading between the lines. So few having this gift, she felt it devolved on her to use it, and was therefore a tiger for information. As to the ideas (as Louie now called the articles), Connie was a tooth-sucker, a keeper of open mind – they were welcome to sell her anything that they could.

Conversations at No. 10, when Connie's off-duty fell in the evenings, had by now come to groove for themselves a course. Connie conferred herself often upon the first floor, in order to save lighting her own fire.

'You saw,' Louie had occasion to ask, 'where it says how war in some ways makes our characters better?'

'Cannot say I had noticed. Where did it say?'

'Oh, you took where it says away to your room – the one with that land girl pulling that great horse.'

'Oh, *her* – former mannequin, that was the point of her. It's not what you do that gets you into a picture, if you notice, it's what you did do formerly. She can have the horse as far as I am concerned; but I must say I could derive with some of that fresh air she says she's deriving benefit from. Down underground where I am, in our post, always upon the watch, it might be any time of year or of day or night either. – See about all those birds?'

'No, where?'

'Off to Africa once again.'

'Migratory birds those would be then: father told me. He liked birds best; ever so many springs he used to be the first to hear the cuckoo; it was chiefly a matter of paying attention, he said. Oh, he used to show me *those* birds, all along the wires! They always do do – why did it put them in?'

'Because they do keep on doing what they always did do, I should imagine. They go to show how Nature pursues her course under any circumstances. Birds like that wouldn't notice there was a war – you might say they were lucky to have no sense. Airman complained how he got in among a pack of birds flying only the other day; decapitated, he said he shouldn't wonder if many of them were. But who's to say *I* don't get decapitated any of these fine nights; and I do have sense and I do have to worry, so where does that get me?'

'Still, you'd surely not rather be like the Germans, Connie? I was told how they swallow anything they are told. I know I saw where it said how they do have papers, but not like our ones with ideas. It said how to get *them* through the war they have to kid them along, but how the war makes us think.'

'Being prone to that, I did not require war. I always would as soon think as anything else; but what gets you anywhere is character.'

'The Yanks are struck by our character now they're here.'

'You ever seen a Yank struck?'

'Well, but I saw where it said –'

'They're struck on our pubs all right: my friend and I couldn't get in anywhere edgeways the other evening. You might think this was their war *they'd* started, they and the Russians –'

'Oh, but the Russians – oh Connie, how you *can*! When you have to think of Stalingrad at every minute . . .'

Both glanced at the clock.

'They are much more different,' said Louie, 'than all of us.'

'Oh, I grant you – *they're* completely titanic. No, if it was Russians we had all over the place here, I should be the first not to complain, I assure you – fighting away like that, if it *is* chiefly in defence of their own country, they should be entitled to air their views. All I do point out is how we get overlooked, between the Yanks and Russians, when there would have been no war for either of them in the first place had it not been for us.'

'But I thought Hitler –'

'Well, who exhausted his patience? No, one thing I do agree – where it says how character's getting us there. Getting us *where*, of course don't ask me. We must live and learn. I foresee having my hands kept full doing the former.'

'But isn't much to be learned from the lessons of history, Connie?'

'What – Napoleon came to no good, nor did the Kaiser, neither will Hitler do. What we are not told is, who derived the benefit? – and if posterity's half sharp that's what they'll want to know, too. What satisfaction is it to have someone else coming along learning a lesson of history off me? Also in my experience one thing you don't learn from is anything anyway set up to be a lesson; what you *are* to know you pick up as you go along. Posterity'll only be human nature, taken up with itself. No, what credit you and I don't get now I doubt that we'll get in the hitherto.'

Louie clapped her hand to her mouth, as though to forbid it ever to speak like Connie's. Behind her fingers she said: 'No, you are unkind!'

'Who is?'

'Talking to me like this.'

'What, do you want to be like those senseless birds?'

'Oh, leave those birds be – I used to see them really. That's what I'd sooner not have about the whole war – them getting mixed up with that airman when they'd set off so gaily.'

Louie began to turn her head heavily this way, that way, under some oppression she might or might not elude. She was sitting on the hearthrug, by way of leaning against a chair, but the chair kept skidding away behind her, so also she had to support herself on her hands. Her long strong legs, stretched out in front of her, had by the latening of autumn been forced into stockings; already these were covered with lumpy darns. Connie, feet planted apart, stood up facing the mirror removing bobby-pins from her fringe: she was due on duty at 23.00, which would be only too shortly. She tucked the pins one by one under Louie's clock, but dropped the last on the rug. She paused, looked down for Louie to pick it up, then clicked her tongue in a fury. Her friend's full eyes, always of an unsafe liquidity in their shallow sockets, had this time overrun. The consequence: glaze on this idiot's cheekbones, a matted dampness – tears need volition to form and fall.

'Listen, as if I had not enough without you creating, and about birds, too! If you'd had half what I have to do with the genuine dead! To begin with, whoever saw a bird gay? When they sing it's sex. It's peculiar to me your saying you saw such real birds, or else I wonder your dad never told you that – Escaped your notice I dropped a bobby?'

'Where did you?'

'Where? – *there*, by your great feet!'

Louie plucked about blindly, all round her feet, in the tufts of rug – losing anything *was* something, now you could buy nothing. She blurted out: 'I did not intend to take on, honestly, Connie; but the birds led to father. It came to seem unnatural him being gone like that, and mum, and where we used to be nothing but thin air.'

'Oh, if that's what it was, never mind the pin. I feel bad now after what I said; but however was I to know what was on your mind? Blow your nose, though, because how you ought to look at it is this way – being elderly your dad was bound to have gone soon in the course of nature; you can't say death's so unnatural; it's just the manner. Also you've got to think how your mum and dad were united at the last, haven't you – and how they were able to take their nice home and all their things they set store by with them into the other world? Why, I have seen elderly people left behind here with nothing, everything gone ahead – so pitiful you hardly know what to say. And look at the luck you had, being married and out of it: it would have served no purpose your perishing with them. Not that I'm so sure in my own case I should not sooner be killed than die; I should sooner the less time for morbid thoughts, and what I should wish myself I should wish my dear ones, had I any.'

'Well, thank you, Connie, I'm sure.'

'Still, it *was* wicked.'

Connie, in uniform slacks and a lace blouse, looked about unwillingly for her tunic. She took off one pearl ear-ring, rubbed at the inflamed lobe of the ear, clipped the ear-ring on again with a pronounced wince. Going on night duty you had all the same to keep up a certain style, and why not? If there were no alerts just at present, not so much as a yellow, you still were not to know who might not at any moment come stumbling in down the post steps out of the black-out, lost – asking where they were and how the hell in that case they were to get to somewhere else. Was the Underground running? which way to the West End? where was Waterloo? where were they to get a put up? what was the matter with staying here with Connie? It was being locked out of every mortal place that got boys down: the post's all-night sign attracted them in like moths.

No outsider had any right in the post – a civilian ought to know better; by now even foreigners ought to have more sense, but with members of the Forces you stretched a point. For Connie it would have been against nature not to transform the post, in whose front room she watched alone, into an advice bureau: coming in from the anonymity of the darkness anyone was glad to be asked his name. Her post nights were not unlike her kiosk days – soundly as Connie might slumber beside the telephone, she could at any moment pop open a forceful eye. If the nocturnal swelling of her ears constrained her again to remove her ear-rings, not once had she failed to snap these back into place before whoever it might be was round the door. Let 'em all come, from the D.W. down – she was not to be had at a disadvantage.

'Well, you'll be all right for the night, dear,' she now stated – pigeon-breasting herself as she buttoned her tunic, tweaked at the basque of it, tautly buckled the belt. Transferring a packet of cigarettes from Louie's chimneypiece to her pocket, she directed a look at Tom's photograph, as though handing over to him. She returned for a second look, always saying nothing. That habit of Connie's of so silently and in that pert experienced manner quizzing Tom had from the first got on Louie's nerves: Connie often elected *not* to say something particular when she was on the very point of leaving the room – well she knew, marching out, shutting the door behind her, that she left you wondering what it could have been. As to the remark she had not made this time, Louie gave it up – the more hastily since it could but seem to relate to Tom. She could have suspected a touch of reproof or malice in Connie's repetitive, ostentatious drawing of attention to the photograph at which she herself rarely or never looked. She avoided it. She had seen ever so many times where it said how a photograph comforts you; but the reverse was true. She exposed the photograph out of respect for convention, under which heading came what indubitably would have been Tom's feeling. More, she wrote to him: 'I look at your picture daily.' One more misrepresentation of love's unamenable truth. Not a point-blank lie: whatever else she forgot she piously daily dusted the chimneypiece, which involved lifting the photo-frame, and what you handle you must in some way see. To see, however, is not to look.

He had provided her with the photograph, which he had had taken just before going away: he had not considered the one she already had, the enlarged snap of him in a Byron collar on Seale strand, adequately serious. His going off on

187

his own initiative to the studio had been one among the last of his farewell acts – consequently, what the camera had recorded had been the face of a man already gone. The open moodless cast of his features stood out infinitely remote against the photographer's curdled back-drop, the eyes looking straight, measuringly, unexpectantly at nothing. To attempt to enter or intercept that look at no one was to become no one – after which, how was anything to be the same again, ever? The frame with the regimental crest held a picture of what was at the best abeyance – at the worst, there came out of it a warning to the bottom of her heart, that no return can ever make restitution for the going away. You may imitate but cannot renew safety.

9

'To unload the past on a boy like that – fantastic! And now *you* mix yourself up in it. No, it's too silly, Stella!'

'But now you're talking like Colonel Pole – I thought you thought Roderick's legacy was a good thing?'

'Roderick's inheritance?'

'Sorry, Roderick's inheritance.'

'Anything's better than nothing,' admitted Robert, with a touch of the impatience he often showed when one truth got in the way of another. 'What I cannot see is, why you should have to go there.'

'Only for the inside of a week.'

'It's not how long you are going to be away, it's how much away you are going to be – there, you will be away completely.'

'Nonsense, darling.'

'Of course, what I don't like is your going away at all,' he said, though in the tone of one slighting his own feeling. He let his hand fall from the arm of the low chair and trailed his fingertips idly on the floor. In a minute, however, he was eyeing her more sturdily, as though to say, make what you like of that, and his mouth remained in a simmering unset line, till he again burst out: 'The whole thing's a racket of that old lunatic's. To get you back.'

'After all, he's dead – if you mean Cousin Francis?'

'A little thing like that wouldn't bother him.'

That called up such a speaking picture that Stella laughed. 'You might have known him,' she said.

He went on: 'But it's not simply what he wanted, it's what you really want.'

'*I* don't want to go back there.'

Robert raised his eyebrows.

'In fact,' she said, 'I dread it.'

'I'm not so sure.'

'Well, I do. But this journey's business; it's not a matter of feeling.'

'But you say you dread it – isn't dread a feeling? If it meant nothing to you I shouldn't so much mind.'

'I'd no idea,' she said, 'you were going to feel like this. Because what does it amount to? Simply a business journey – Roderick's Mount Morris affairs. You know how they have been worrying me lately, all those letters from or about that place, asking for decisions I can't make because I can't grasp, from this distance, exactly what they're about or what they'd entail. The roof, the farm, the extra planting, the cutting of the trees. Heaven knows, I wish Roderick were free enough and old enough to cope! But as it is, you can't leave a place for ever with no master. Somebody's got to get over there: he can't, I must. *As* I must, the sooner the better; better get it over – surely? Really, Robert, I've been through more than enough convincing the Passport Office that this *is* urgent – do I have to go through it all over again with you? They were perfectly satisfied.'

'They are not in love with you.'

'Weeks ago, you agreed I would have to go.'

'Did I? Yes, I suppose I did.'

She cried: 'Has anything changed since then?'

It was seven o'clock in the evening, in her flat. Early tomorrow she must be catching the Irish Mail. Robert had had an unfortunate glimpse of a half-packed suitcase in her bedroom – just not in time she had closed the door: in front of the fire in the other room he had seemed to be busy unwrapping the bottle he had brought.

However, now, with one of his turns of mood, he at once contrived to give the impression that it was she, not he, who had been making a scene – he could not help reaching out for the piece of string, which he drew out to its length, admired, then started coiling into a hank with a slow, irresistibly soothing motion. 'Here's a piece of string for you, anyway,' he remarked, having done.

'Where on earth, these days, do they still *tie* up parcels?'

'Where I get my whisky – What I do hope is that your journey won't be horribly cold.'

She thought, could any journey away from you not be a cold journey? – but said: 'It's not so late in the year. I chiefly wish I'd gone earlier because then by now I'd be back.'

'What shall I do while you're away?'

'Don't make me more unhappy!'

'You never know,' he said, spinning the circular hank of string round on his finger – 'What time of year was it when you were there before?'

'Just about this time: autumn.'

'Twenty years ago?'

'Twenty-one years.'

'What a lot of water,' said Robert vaguely, 'has flowed under the bridges since then, or hasn't it? Floods enough to have washed most bridges away.'

There was no bridge for a mile up or down the river from Mount Morris. Down its valley the river swept smoothly towards the house, then was turned aside, lost to view, round the high rocky projection on which the house stood. On the far side, unequal cliffs of limestone dropped their whitish reflections into the water; trees topped and in some places steeply clad the cliffs. The river traced the boundary of the lands: at the Mount Morris side it had a margin of water-meadow into which the demesne woods, dark at their base with laurels, ran down in a series of promontories. This valley cleavage into a distance seemed like an offering to the front windows: in return, the house devoted the whole muted fervour of its being to a long gaze. Elsewhere rising woods or swelling uplands closed Mount Morris in.

By anyone standing down by the river looking up, sky was to be seen reflected in row upon row of vast glass panes. The façade, dun stucco, seemed to vary in tone, but never altered in colour except at sunset – which, striking down the valley, gave the stucco an oriental pink and enflamed the windows.

At the hour when the master's mother arrived, reflections up from the river prolonged daylight: a smoulder of yellow from the woods entered the house. She had forgotten that by travelling west you enter longer days: this hour, as she stood looking down the length of a room at a fire distantly burning inside white marble, seemed to be outside time – an eternal luminousness of dusk in which nothing but the fire's flutter and the clock's ticking out there in the hall were to be heard.

Or, in her fatigue she could have imagined this was another time, rather than another country, that she had come to. The indoor air of the library held something outdoor; the windows could have been only lately shut on new-raked gravel of which earth had become a component part. Light lived in the particles of the air only, for the walls and soaring curtains were of a deadening red. Something more than an ancient smell reached the senses from the books cased back into the walls – possibly, these hundreds of books' indifference to the passing thought. The chief other focus of darkness here was an oil painting rising over the the fire: horsemen grouped apprehensively at midnight. The room was without poetry if this could not be felt in the arrested energy of its nature – it was in here that Cousin Francis had had his being.

On every side remained the meticulous preparations made for his departure. Inconceivably many magazines, pamphlets, prospectuses, circulars, their edges showing every age and stage of brownness, had been corded up into bales, ticketed, stacked on and underneath sideboards, sofas, tables. Balanced upon the bales, a tribe of tray-shaped baskets invited Stella's inspection of their contents so carefully sorted out – colourless billiard balls, padlocks, thermometers, a dog collar, keyless key-rings, a lily bulb, an ivory puzzle, a Shakespeare calendar for 1927, the cured but unmounted claw of a greater eagle, a Lincoln Imp knocker, an odd spur, lumps of quartz, a tangle of tipless tiny pencils on frayed silk cords. . . .

So much for the past: he had thought ahead. Stuck round inside the frame of the dark picture cards stood out white, still fresh, peremptory to the eye. Injunctions, admonitions, and warnings, unevenly block-printed by Cousin

Francis, here underlined, there enringed in urgent red. *Clocks,* when and how to wind . . . *Fire Extinguishers,* when and how to employ . . . *Locks and Hinges,* my method of oiling . . . *Live Mice* caught in traps, to be drowned *Not* dropped into kitchen fire . . . *Tim O'Keefe, Mason,* not to work here again unless he does better than last time. *Beggars,* bona fide 6d., *Old Soldiers* 1s. . . . *Hysteria, Puppies,* in case of . . . In case of *Blocked Gutters* . . . In case of *Parachutists* . . . *Birds in Chimney,* in case of . . . In case of *Telegrams* . . . In case of *River* entering *Lower Lodge* . . . In case of *My Death* . . . In case of *Emergency Message from Lady C.* . . .

She stood for some time drawn up to read the cards, then looked this way, that way along the chimneypiece – but except for another, inaudible, clock, empty branched candlesticks, and embossed bronze vases holding charred spills, there was nothing further. Resting both hands on the marble she looked down into the fire, regretting she had not any such clear directions as to her own life – which, at this moment more distant than London, would not be less problematic when returned to. Oh to stay here for ever, playing this ghostly part! Unwillingly she looked behind her – her gloves, shaped by her hands, her bag, containing every damning proof of her identity, were still, always, there on the centre table where she had put them down.

It was on that same table that Donovan, a few minutes later, put down the oil lamp. As he, stooping, turned the two wicks higher the globe welled up strongly with yellow light, throwing the caretaker's Danteësque features into masklike relief against the bookcases. 'Every other place,' he remarked, 'is terribly clumbered up; we have been distracted with the instructions to touch nothing. Latterly this has been a bare sort of time for us, with neither master – this is a poor welcome for you, ma'am, but indeed you're welcome. The daughters went to some lengths preparing the drawing-room for you, but nothing we could do to it would drive out the chill, so that in the end we gave up heart. That room is fine enough, but it has been retired altogether too long.'

Mary Donovan bore in the second lamp more breathlessly than her father: evidently she had not played this part before. She glanced at Donovan for a cue, got none, so stood her lamp down by the first. The ceremony was concluded. No one making a movement to draw the curtains, the two globes, the Donovans, Stella remained reflected in what had become jet-black panes.

'Thank you, Mary,' said Stella, looking across at the small girl inside the sheath of great white apron.

In reply, Mary's lips moved; as though she had broken down in the very, first line of a recitation she knocked back with her wrist a heavy forelock of hair. Donovan explained: 'She is over anxious – she knows there's something further she ought to be doing, but not what. Could you imagine, ma'am, what you might be wanting next?'

Stella had had to agree months ago, from a distance, to the paying off of Cousin Francis's servants: there must be no unnecessary charges on the estate. She knew now there was no one left in Mount Morris but the ageless, wifeless Donovan and his two surprisingly young daughters. She did not remember Donovan (who probably at the time of her honeymoon worked in the yard or somewhere out on the place), but did not betray this, as he remembered her.

'For the supper,' he added, 'we killed a little chicken.'

Stella said, 'How nice.' After what could have seemed a complicated moment of hesitation she asked: 'Mary, which is my room?'

'Candles!' cried Donovan wildly. 'Have you the candles, Mary?' A look flashed between father and daughter. The child, in an unexpectedly deep firm voice, declared: 'The two of them are above.'

'Jesus!' said Donovan. 'Then there'll be none to carry.'

'There'll still be light on the stairs,' Stella interposed. 'And I know my way.'

Indeed the familiarity of the house was startling: as a whole it rose to the surface in her, as though something weighting it to the bottom had let go. Expectancy rather than memory from now on guided her – she could not tell at which moment of her return journey the sensory train had started itself alight. Now she seemed to perceive on all sides round her, and with a phantasmogoric clearness, everything that for the eye the darkness hid. The declivities in the treads of the staircase, the rounded glimmer of its venetian window (ever wholly extinguished only by blackest night), the creak of the lobby flooring under the foot, and the sifted near-and-farness of smells of plaster, pelts, wax, smoke, weathered woodwork, oiled locks and outdoor trees preceded themselves in her as she followed Mary. Knowledge of all this must have been carried in her throughout the years which in these minutes fell away.

At midday, even, this lobby of many doors at the head of the windowed staircase had been always shadowy: now the doors round her were to be only felt. The suspense, a suspense so long anticipated, in which she waited to hear which handle the child would turn was, now it came to the moment, more than half fictitious, after all neither real nor deep. It was with indifference, almost, that she came to know, Donovan's choice for her *had* pitched on a room with no history. Mary, marching ahead, quenched herself in an absolute of darkness from which there was no tremor of memory to fear. Inside here, curtains and shutters did double work; Mary's position could be detected only by her striking and breaking of match after match on a damp box; meanwhile nothing guided Stella between the padded head of a sofa and knobbed foot of a bed. Care had raised the temperature of this long-empty room to the tepidity of a normal summer; a smouldering crimson fire was to be seen again in what must be a cheval glass. Then, upon Mary's succeeding in making the candles burn, bedhangings and presses, their shadows and those again of a woman standing, a girl turning eagerly round to her, staggered up into being, into that minute's meaning, but nothing more.

Innocent in its resemblance to no other, the minute merged itself in the immortality of the house.

'It was a pity for you the way you bumped yourself,' said Mary. 'I think I ran on too fast for you? – Will I leave the matches? They're a wicked box.' Having addressed herself to the fire, into which she directed an adept kick, she made haste to the washstand, unwrapped a turban of towel, and with both palms tested the heat of a brass can. 'It would still scald you!' she could but confide, triumphantly, to Stella – who, with hardly less naïvety, cried: '*Oh*, it's nice, being waited on!'

'I'm new to it, too; we'll have to see how we'll shape.'

Mary gone, Stella remembered Robert's injunction to drink – for them both, as it were, at this hour. She brought to the dressing-table water bottle and tumbler, and unscrewed

197

the top of the flask he had filled for her in London, this time two days ago. Holding up the tumbler between the candles, while she measured water into the whisky, she observed that the candles were not virgin: both had been burned already, and to unequal lengths. This surprised and puzzled her – so great so far had been the Donovans' perfectionism and good grace – it linked up with the confederate look between father and child downstairs, also, with that odd air of abstention from saying or thinking something with which Donovan had stood watching the second lamp in. Stella had assumed there to be no shortages of any kind in Eire. The exciting sensation of being outside war had concentrated itself round those fearless lights – though actually, yesterday night as her ship drew in, the most strong impression had been of prodigality: around the harbour water, uphill above it, the windows had not only showed and shone but blazed, seemed to blaze out phenomenally; while later, dazzling reflections in damp streets made Dublin seem to be in the throes of a carnival. Here, tonight, downstairs, those three yellow oblongs cast unspoilt on the gravel by the uncurtained windows had spelled ease, yes; but still more had set up a barbaric joy, as might wine let run soaking into the ground. *Now*, for a moment to have to ask oneself whether after all there might not be at Mount Morris unbroached packets of candles, drum on drum of oil, became a setback, a small but deep shock. Could the house be short, the Donovans rationed – or had they simply neglected to lay in stores? She must ask, tonight – or perhaps tomorrow. The inquiry, with its just possible hint of a fault found, should be put off, or at least ideally timed. In the end she never remembered to ask the question – what she had not cared to suspect was in fact true. Up here in her bedroom, down there in the library, she was burning up light supplies for months ahead. Well on into the winter after Stella's departure the Donovan family went to bed in the dark.

After supper she twiddled perfunctorily the knobs of the wireless beside Cousin Francis's chair – it had pleased him to have the war at his elbow; she was pleased to have only one more and more significant degree of silence added to the library: evidently the battery was dead. There never had been a telephone at Mount Morris – assurance of being utterly out of reach added annullingness to her deep sleep that night. In the morning, dressing at her window, she watched three swans come down the river to pause in midstream looking up at the house with her in it. Unimaginable early sunshine lay on everything – the grassy slopes, the rocks, the last hysterical glory of the trees; it was with the energy of lightness that she embarked on the business of this first day. The beginning, even, took her so far afield, involved so much viewing of things to be looked at many times more and wove itself into so many lengthy standing talks – apart from everything else, the Mount Morris people had not yet had their due, a full and feeling account of Cousin Francis's end and funeral – that it was not till evening, after a very late tea, that she could sit down to her letter to Roderick.

She wrote at Cousin Francis's outsize kneehole table with the worn leather top. Sorry, on Roderick's account, to have been able to find no headed Mount Morris paper, she covered sheet after sheet of her own block. Once, tearing off and casting a finished sheet on to others to the left of the inkstand, she knocked against a brass letter-weighing machine – setting the scales in motion, loosening weights in their grooves and releasing, somewhere inside herself, some repugnant troubling association . . . Mrs Kelway's parcel – *had* Harrison posted it? . . . She took up her pen again, reconsidered, let the pen roll away, made the revolving chair twirl and sped from the room to the head of the basement stairs.

'Oh, Donovan?'

'Ma'am?' He took form at the foot of them.

'One thing the master specially wants to know – is there a boat?'

He rubbed his wrist back slowly over his stiff white hair. 'He wants to know, is there a boat at present?'

'Is there a boat at all?'

'That would be, any class of a boat?'

She became distracted – 'Simply, a boat.'

'Well, there was a flat boat, and she used to hold not badly till the master sank her. He had no great satisfaction out of her at the best of times, and he said to us you were not to know these times what might happen presently, so he had the boys out one morning loading rock into her until she went down. "Well, there *she* goes," he said, the poor man, standing between myself and the gentleman on the bank . . . She should be there in the river yet – will we raise her and see if she's not too much rotted?'

'If that could be done, it could be no harm.'

'It might be,' said Donovan, warming to the project, 'that all we would have to do would be to give her a lick of pitch.'

Stella went down a step, Donovan came up two. 'It would be a pity,' he added, 'to disappoint him – So is the master a boatman?'

'Not so much that – I must show you his photograph.'

'Ah, his picture – but wasn't it queer them not letting him over to us himself? I never heard of the Army impeding a gentleman like that. However, I should imagine his heart's in it, and the war should be a great interest in that case – who knows but he might be coming out of it a general?'

'Oh no; I'm afraid he's too young for that!'

'Yet by every appearance,' said Donovan, not discouraged, 'this should be a long ambitious war – Are you writing a letter to the master?'

'Indeed, I am – When *was* the boat sunk?'

'The last time the gentleman was here.'

'Which gentleman? – oh, the one on the bank?'

'We hadn't so many visitors since the war came – chiefly only this one, and he was fleeting. He came from over. It seemed a marvel these times to see anybody travelling around the way he did – it could be he had some kind of advantage; though whether he was a Mister or Captain we never made out. In any event he was a distraction for the master; the two of them would be gabbing up to any hour into the night. This was a chap or gentleman with a very narrow look, added to which he had a sort of a discord between his two eyes. . . .'

It was her heart that now sank; going back to her letter she did not regain speed or the first concentration: she wound up inconclusively, promising more tomorrow, recollecting, as she addressed the envelope, that she had no stamp. She then pushed back her chair and began to examine the many drawers of the table, with unusual stealthiness trying each in turn: all were as locked as they looked. Walking foolishly round the room she searched for the keys, opening boxes and cabinets, shifting objects at random, even attempting once to look in the drawers themselves. She came to the point of denouncing Cousin Francis as a conspiratorial, mischievous, too-old man; when anger ran out she was left alone with uneasiness – liking the library less and less. Now primarily it was the scene, for her, of those conversations late into the nights – what *had* they been up to in here? what had they been cooking? Evidently Harrison was not a man to have come back and back for nothing. Whatever it was, he had considered it worth while to give his host the impression that he, too, Francis Morris, was in it up to the hilt – therefore, that last London meeting between the two must have been a continuation of *some* actual story, however cock-and-bull. The old fanatical Irish-man's first day back in London, last whole day on earth . . . Yes, Harrison claimed they had met, and it now looked likely. More than that now looked likely, or at any rate possible. Even the story of papers inaccessibly locked away with the dead man's luggage came up again for review – though who (as she had repeatedly asked herself, and did ask herself, if more faintly and for the last time, now) *would* hand over anything vital to Cousin Francis? Famous for honour, yes, for discretion no; above all, famous loser of all he touched? As to the existence ever, or at any rate the importance, of those papers she had kept a valuable scepticism – valuable because it could be extended to everything else that Harrison said he had or was or did. Harrison, she took it, had simply thought that one up in hopes of involving her; he had not struck lucky . . . But, what now? The conceivability of there being a grain of truth in anything he had ever, in any context, said shook her. What was her defence but this – that he lied, must lie, could not not lie, had lied from the very start?

He *had*, then, in spite of his having said he had, really been there? This book-dark darkening room, through which imperceptibly the current of time flowed, held truth sunk somewhere in it, as the river held the boat. The very possibility might not allow her to rest again – but what, now she was forcing herself to think of it, was the possibility? Cousin Francis might have, indeed must have (for if, as Robert said, he was mad, he was still no fool) taken a closeish look at Harrison's credentials and been satisfied. As against that, Cousin Francis was safely dead, so could not be asked – or rather, *could* be asked, as often as Stella chose, and could be relied upon not to answer. She understood, with a shock, that here was a question she would be prepared to put to the dead only – why? Because the answer could mean too much. She had not yet, in London, made one move towards checking up on Harrison. *Was* he what he had made himself out to be? Was he in the position to know what he said he knew, to act as he had told her he could? She could have come at all three answers: what evasion to tell herself she could not! She was not, as she had indeed told Harrison, a woman who did not know where to go; these late years she had lived at the edge of a clique of war, knowing who should know what, commanding a sort of language in which nothing need be ever exactly said. Now she looked back at that Sunday – how many weeks ago? – when Harrison had come to her with the story. 'Who are you, to know?' she had in so many words said. Had he more than discreetly shifted his eyes? – she could or dared not be certain; she remembered only what she had felt. As a whole her memory of that evening was distorted, a thing of blurs, inconsistencies, bruises and blanks and queries, such as can but be left by any internally dreadfully violent scene. Since then, it might have shifted further out of the true. She did, however, somewhere keep one impression – that Harrison had not so much defied as invited her to check up.

What had he expected her to do? Or had he expected her to do nothing? – in that case, he had been right. She had asked nobody anything about Harrison – why, yes, but of course she had: had she not asked Robert? She had asked Robert nothing about himself – but, again, what but a question about himself had been, really, the question about Harrison? On that occasion – flippancy, boredom, love: how sweet, how grateful had the diversion been! Diversion, not answer; not end, only beginning – beginning of her watch on Robert's doors and windows, her dogging of the step of his thoughts, her search for the interstices of his mind. Her espionage – but, apparently, better that. Better that than what? Than the saying of 'I am told you are selling our country: are you?' She should by now, Robert might well reply, be able to judge for herself whether that could be possible. And he would be right, she *should* know – her having ever asked must end all equability between them. A demonstration of innocence, as from him to her, could be nothing but icy cold – the more final it were, the more it must be final to everything. Volatility was a great part of Robert, but not the whole of him – laugh he might, but as a man he would not forgive her . . . Or, he could lie; or rather, lie once again – the first lie spoken not being, in most cases, the first lie acted – 'Is he,' Harrison had wanted to know, 'anything of an actor?' – *If* actor, to her and for her so very good an actor, then why not actor also of love? Incalculably calculating, secretly adverse, knowing, withheld had Robert been, all this time, from the start? No, no, no, she thought: better anything! Better what, then? Better to hear him say: 'Since you *have* chosen to ask me – yes.' That would be love; that would be the consummation. What in effect were they but one another's accomplices

already; deep into, and involving everything else in, the con-
federacy of love? Stop – stop him? It would be stopped when
Harrison closed the trap.

The lamp, borne by Mary, came to the open door.

'Mary, will you put the lamp in the drawing-room?'

'Oh, there's no fire lit there, ma'am!'

'I shan't be long.'

It was not so cold in there; the shuttered drawing-room
had conserved a temperature of its own. Evidently Donovan
and the girls, in finding anything at fault in the tranquil chill,
had finer senses than Stella; indeed, it was most of all with
the sense of some sense in herself missing that she looked,
from mirror to mirror, into misted extensions of the room.
She was proof against it. Constrained to touch things, to
make certain that they were not their own reflection, she
explored veneers and mouldings, corded edges, taut fluted
silk with the nerves of her fingers; she made a lustre tinkle,
breathed on the dome over a spray of birds, opened the piano
and struck a note, knowing all the time she was doing nothing more than amuse herself, if she *could* amuse herself, and
was outside the society of ghosts. Was it not sad, though, that
a drawing-room should have so little power over a woman? –
wondering why, she carried the lamp to meet one of its own
reflections in a mirror, and, lifting it, studied the romantic
face that was still hers. She became for the moment immor-
tal as a portrait. Momentarily she was the lady of the house,
with a smile moulded against the drapery of darkness. She
wore the look of everything she had lost the secret of being.

There was something inexorable in the judgement: she
turned away from it. After all, was it not chiefly here in this
room and under this illusion that Cousin Nettie Morris – and

who now knew how many more before her? – had been pressed back, hour by hour, by the hours themselves, into cloudland? Ladies had gone not quite mad, not quite even that, from in vain listening for meaning in the loudening ticking of the clock. (She listened, looking back over her shoulder at the chimneypiece: in the marble centre, silence – the gilt nymphs' arms upheld only a faceless hollow.) Virtue with nothing more to spend, honour saying nothing, but both present Both, also, rising and following the listener when she left the drawing-room; she had been unaccompanied by them along no path she took. Therefore, her kind knew no choices, made no decisions – or, did they not? Everything spoke to them – the design in and out of which they drew their needles; the bird with its little claws drawn to its piteously smooth breast, dead; away in the woods the quickening strokes of the axes, then the fall of the tree; or the child upstairs crying out terrified in its sleep. No, knowledge was not to be kept from them; it sifted through to them, stole up behind them, reached them by intimations – they suspected what they refused to prove. That had been their decision. So, there had been the cases of the enactment of ignorance having become too much, insupportable inside those sheltered heads. Also in this room they had reached the climax of their elation at showing nothing – hearing their dresses rustle, fearlessly intercepting flashes from their bracelets, rings, and from the brooches nested on their bosoms in the lace, they had looked about them at the lights, flowers, figures of gentlemen, flower-painted cups on the silver tray. Victory of society – but not followed, for the victors, by peace – for remaining waiting in here for them had been those unfinishable hours in which they could only reflect again. And though seated together, hems of their skirts touching, each one of the ladies had not ceased in herself to reflect alone; their however candid and clear looks in each others' eyes were interchanged warnings; their conversation was a twinkling surface over their deep silence. Virtually they were never to speak at all – unless to the little bird lying big with death on the path, the child being comforted out of the nightmare without waking, the leaf plucked still quivering from the felled tree.

The crossbars of the shutters stood out against the panels horizontally black, the one iron note in the room. She put down the heavy lamp again on a table. That was that – or, could there still be something more? That her own life could be a chapter missing from this book need not mean that the story was at an end; at a pause it was, but perhaps a pause for the turning-point? There was still to be seen what came of Cousin Francis's egotistic creative boldness with regard to the future, of his requisitioning for that purpose of Roderick. A man of faith has always a son somewhere.

For her part, she never would agree that Roderick had been victimized: he had been fitted into a destiny; better, it seemed to her, than freedom in nothing. She set herself to amuse herself in a different key, by wondering what this room might say to Roderick's wife. For marriage – so far so inconceivable in the case of Roderick that she had not bestirred herself to envisage her daughter-in-law – could not but be somewhere in the directive, as Roderick chose to read it, from Cousin Francis. It was usual in this house to bring home a wife: if that had not yet occurred to him, it would. Born but not till now thought of that future creature came into being mistily – in fact, since Stella having no daughter

207

could not conjure up youthfulness other than her own, the daughter-in-law curled forming like ectoplasm out of Stella's flank. Unmistakably, however, from the bride's fluid anatomy stood out eyes – unspent and fearless.

Daylight, nothing but afternoon in here for the newcomer; out there, a summery river flowing towards the windows. The room would be to be marvelled at, nothing more than that. Of how much, of what, or by whom, the entering smiling newcomer had been disembarrassed she never would know – the fatal connexion between the past and future having been broken before her time. It had been Stella, her generation, who had broken the link – what else could this be but its broken edges that she felt grating inside her soul?

Yes, this for the bride would be a room to be first marvelled at, then changed. Required to mean what they had not, old things would be pushed into a new position; those which could not comply, which could not be made to pick up the theme of the new song, would go. For instance, here, hung in a corner so far out of day or lamplight's reach that Stella, to see, had to strike a match, was one picture to banish. Evidently, it had been torn from a magazine of years ago; it had been stuck crooked into an alien frame – a liner going down in a blaze with all lights on, decks and portholes shining, of one half already plunged in the black ocean, the other reared up against the sky. *'Nearer my God to Thee: The Titanic: 1912.'* The significance of this drawing-room picture of Cousin Nettie's would never be known.

Stella woke next morning not knowing where she was, or when. Her place in time had been lost. A certainly new day penetrated the curtains, but which day? Her watch told her the hour, but then so did instinct – what she was forced to grope for, as though for her identity, was the day of the week, the month of the year, the year. Supine, she tried to read something into the pattern of the light-yellowed curtains. Yesterday no postman had come; there had been no sign of a newspaper; ash dust had once more settled on the knobs of the wireless. She began counting back on her fingers to the last date certain, that of her leaving London, then stopped short: she remembered another morning of waking only to Robert's face. Were these deep sleeps of hers periodic trances, her spirit's passing into another season? Were they the birth-sleeps, each time, of some profound change? That would be to be proved; she got up and drew the curtains – this morning no swans were on the river.

This was a day of October size, of unearthly disassociation from everything. Her appointment to meet the steward, to go on with their business, was for eleven o'clock – after breakfast, therefore, she crossed the gravel sweep, stepped over the parapet, and made her way down the steep unshorn slope to the river. A first breath of frost had crisped and tufted the grass: here by the sunny water's edge she stood, hands in pockets, overcoat collar up, blinking and looking into the current; then she turned and began to walk up the valley. Yes, October for a few days more – how long this autumn had felt; the season might have been staying for her decision. In the valley there was something decisive about the narrowing of this path so many feet must have trodden without a swerve. Here where she paused and stood, between the sun-shafted beech trees, it was as though the answer had already provided itself and did not matter. This was the peace of the moment in which one sees the world for a moment innocent of oneself.

One cannot remain away: while she looked up at sun-pierced triumphant golden fans of leaves it began again to be she who saw them. Still, though, this was the early morning of a unique day: the very day in which – who knew? – something might intervene to save her. She was at the foot of the most advancing promontory of the Mount Morris woods, at the point where, borne forward on inside rock, they most nearly approached the river. A rapture of strength could be felt in the rising tree trunks rooted gripping the slope, and in the stretch of the boughs; and there travelled through the layered, lit, shaded, thinning and crossing foliage, and was deflected downward on to the laurels, a breathless glory. In the hush the dead could be imagined returning from all the wars; and, turning the eyes from arch to arch of boughs, from ray to ray of light, one knew some expectant sense to be tuned in to an unfinished symphony of love.

The seeming of this to be for ever was astonishing – until a leaf fell slowly, veering towards her eyes as though she had brought time with her into the wood.

There cannot be a moment in which nothing happens. She heard or imagined she heard a call from the house behind her, and turned to walk back towards it. Ahead of her and above she at once saw Donovan standing on the parapet up there, making gestures, unhearably shouting into the air between him and her. She sent back a gesture of not hearing, feeling her heart beat as she quickened her step: he steadied himself again on the parapet before shaping both hands into a megaphone. Vowels rolled down the valley: the elder taller Donovan girl stepped up and stood beside her father.

'. . . Egypt!'

'Wait, I –'

'Montgomery's through!'

'Montgomery?'

'A terrible victory!'

Sun blinded her from above the roof of the house as she stumbled up the slope, pulling at grass tufts, stopping to shade her eyes. She panted: 'A victory in a day?'

'It's the war turning.'

'How did you hear?'

'It's all through the country. – Come up with you, ma'am.'

Donovan reached out to her; their handclasp settled into a grip then a pull upward from him. He had got her alongside him on the coping the better to transfix her with impatient prophetic eyes. 'I would give much,' he said, 'to have a hat to bare my head with: the day's famous.'

'It's a beautiful day, in any event,' said Hannah, temperately, speaking for the first time.

On Donovan there came down the loneliness of a man among women. 'Mr Morris should have lived to see this,' he said. Donovan had the doom of seeing this day alone: wherever the dead may be, they are gone. Standing to attention between Stella and Hannah he was a rocky profile, gnawing at the distance with his eyes, seeing an Egyptian rolling apocalyptic battle at the end of the valley. His lips moved silently till he declared aloud: 'We bred a very fast general. Didn't I say to you he'd be a fast general? Hasn't he got them on the run?'

Stella began to feel giddy on the parapet. She said: 'But, all at once?'

Donovan turned and said: 'He has broken through.'

Hannah so far had stood with her forehead raised in docile imitation of her father. After his last words she seemed to search the view and the morning, but to find their shining calmness as unchanged as her own. The oblation to victory being taken by her to be now ended, she stepped down quietly from the parapet and began to wander towards the house. Perhaps unwilling to leave the sunshine for the chilly shadow of Mount Morris, or just hoping her father might call her back to declare that, for whatever reason, this was a holiday, she looked back once, her face a moon in daylight between divided hair. Hannah was beautiful – a year older, yet somehow further back than her sister Mary. This was Stella's first full view of her in daylight: she stayed below stairs over her cooking, or was to be heard calling her poultry in a low, wary voice, shy while a stranger was in the house. Now, to find herself standing on this great open sweep in front of the mansion seemed to amaze her: she was a flower only out today. Childish for sixteen years, she wore the gravity of her race; something was added to her beauty by her apartness from what was going on; her mountain-blue eyes had inherited the colour of trouble but not the story. Having not a thought that was not her own, she had not any thought; she was a young girl already upon her unmenaced way to Heaven. Her roughened hands hung folded loosely over her apron.

Stella, also making for the house, became becalmed in the orbit of Hannah's gaze. She smiled at the girl, but there was nothing – most of all at this moment nothing – to be said. Whenever in the future that Mount Morris mirage of utter victory came back to her, she was to see Hannah standing there in the sunshine, indifferent as a wand.

10

'We must be running late,' the passengers had been saying from time to time, uncertainly glancing at one another as though the feeling of lateness might be subjective, then at the blinded windows of the carriage. 'Whereabouts would we be now? – how far are we along?' Now and then somebody in a corner prised at a blind's edge, put an eye to the crack – but it was useless; Midland canals and hedges were long gone from view; not a hill or tower showed through the drape of night; every main-line landmark was blotted out. Only a loud catastrophic roar told them, even, when they were in a tunnel. But by now speed had begun to slacken; from the sound of the train, more and more often constricted deep in cuttings between and under walls, they must be entering London: no other city's built-up density could be so strongly felt. Now, with what felt like the timidity of an intruder, the train crept, jarred nervily, came to halts with steam up – allowing traffic over the metal bridges and shunting on wastes of lines to be heard. Passengers who had not yet reached down their bags from the racks now shot up and did so: Stella was among them. The fatigue of the long day's journey had, while it numbed her body into a trance, reduced her mind to one single thought: she was fixed upon what she meant to say. Her hope that Robert would come to meet her had become the hope that she might speak soon.

Euston. All the way down the train doors burst open while the inky ribbon of platform still slipped by. Nobody could wait for the train to stop; everybody was hurling themselves on London as though they, too, must act upon some inhuman resolution before it died down. She, now it came to the point, was to be the last to leave the carriage; she stopped to stare at herself, as though for the last time, in the mirror panel over the seat. Picking up her suitcase, stepping out on to the platform, she looked from left to right, then began to walk along the flank of the train. The few blued lights of the station just showed the vaultings up into gloom; toppling trolleys cut through the people heaving, thrusting, tripping, peering. Recognition of anybody by anybody else seemed hopeless – those hoping to be met, hoping to be claimed, thrust hats back and turned up faces drowningly. Arrival of shades in Hades, the new dead scanned dubiously by the older, she thought she could have thought; but she felt nothing – till her heart missed a beat, her being filled like an empty lock: with a shock of love she saw Robert's tall turning head.

The whole return of sensation made her suitcase, of whose heaviness she had been unconscious, tear suddenly at her arm-muscles: She put it down – '*Robert!*'

This was to be like Donovan trying to make the victory news heard. Robert, still stock still, posted under a light, went on writing off, glance by glance, the faces surging towards him, his *égaré* disassociation from other people never more marked. She dived for her suitcase to lug it forward: when again she looked he was gone from where he had been. Despair made her press her lips. Then before she knew, under her elbow was his hand.

'What a needle in a bundle of hay,' he said.

The suitcase dropped beside them: he held her by the lapels of her coat, looking unbelievingly at his thumbs on the pattern of the tweed. '*Where* have you been, Stella!'

'Anyway, here I am.'

'Yet, now – but time can be frightful. – Come on, come along – let's get out of this!' He steered her out towards the arches; the main stream was heading another way.

'Why this way?'

'Why? – because I have got a car.'

'Where from?'

'Where cars come from.'

'I never thought,' she said. 'But I must say it's wonderful – a car.'

'There's just one snag – Ernestine's in it.'

'*Ernestine!* – Robert, good heavens, why?'

'She thought she would pop up,' said Robert vaguely. 'Business or something, I think she said. She rang up this afternoon from Harrods, saying this would be a surprise for me; and was it . . . Yes, I know, darling, but I lost my head: when she rang I was just at the height of the middle of something else. She said she was stopping up overnight, and what was I doing with myself this evening? I said unfortunately I had got to meet somebody at a station. "Dear me," she said. "I didn't know anybody was as helpless as that these days, unless it is anybody important." I couldn't think of anything but the truth. "In that case," she said, "I might as well come along; we can have our chat on the way. I don't in the least mind meeting Mrs Rodney, as I've already met her. . . ." Yes, I do know, darling, but there it was – either Ernestine now or Ernestine later on. And all we do *now* is, drop her back at her friend's.'

'But she'll have to have dinner with us, won't she?'

'No, we've gone into that: she's had an early bite. She is, you know, independent if not tactful. – Stella, you love me?'

'Why?'

'Then nothing matters.'

Through a mizzle of rain Robert had been vaguely turning his torch on the number-plates of a short line of cars parked secretively under a sweating wall. Animated thumping upon a window at this point brought the search to a close: a chauffeur threw away a cigarette, jumped to attention, smartly opened the car upon a peal of laughter. 'Well,' shouted Ernestine, bundling round invisibly inside there like a ferret, 'better late than never! – How-d'you-do, Mrs Rodney? You must be dead.'

'Not quite. How nice to see you again.'

'"See" is good! – And how was the Emerald Isle? Beef steak? Plenty of eggs and bacon?'

'I'm sorry my train was so late.'

'Yes, of all ways to spend an evening in London!' said Robert. 'Still, this was Ernie's choice.'

'Never mind,' said Ernestine, 'blood is thicker than water. And I snatched the chance to relax, which I rarely can. Tomorrow I shall have quite a morning; I am due at Headquarters at nine sharp. We're organizing a regional check over.'

'Oh yes, I see.'

'Over *there*, I suppose, no one realized a war was on?'

'On the contrary, we thought there had been a victory.'

'We really don't seem to be doing too badly,' admitted Ernestine modestly. The car, having moved off, was nosing some secret route to the Euston Road – Robert sat facing the other

two on a let-down seat; there were moments when his silhou-
ette could just be seen. He had tucked the mock-fur rug over
Stella's knees, what was left of it over some outlying part of
Ernestine – who, with a hoot, observed that the age of chivalry
was not dead. 'It is new to see Robert putting himself about,'
she added, 'though I can't say I think a car of this size necessary – for all we know, just this extra amount of petrol might
have made all the difference to Montgomery; though of course
it's too late to think of that if you have really taken it for the
evening. It's Mrs Rodney I'm sorry for; I should think she must
be feeling somewhat overpowered – I know I should be if I
were her. I always think it kinder not to let people feel one has
put oneself out for them. But Robert's in some ways unlike me.'

'What did you say?' said Robert, turning round with a
start.

'I said you were in some ways unlike me. Shouldn't you
agree with me, Mrs Rodney? They say an outsider sees still
more. – Where are we now, Robert?'

'I have no idea.'

'The man understands we are going to Earls Court? . . .
Very well, if you *did* tell him, you told him; but how was I to
know? You seemed so fussed at the station . . . I should have
expected you to know your way about London like a cat.'

'Why?'

'I should have thought under the circumstances that
would be essential,' said Ernestine in a low, significant tone.
'However . . .' Reminded of something, she snapped her bag
open to check its contents by touch, which was done con-
vulsively. Stella, who had for some time been leaning back
with her eyes closed, at last said: 'I hope you have not lost
anything?'

'*I* hope so, I'm sure! – Dear me, I thought you had gone to sleep!'

'One might have thought so,' agreed her brother, whose undetected hand lightly lay on the rug over Stella's knee. 'In fact, one would hardly know she was in the car – I suppose you are thinking,' he said to Stella, 'are you?'

'I suppose I must be.'

'I'm practically certain it must be *somewhere*,' went on Ernestine. 'Oh how helpful it would be if one could only see! I remember putting it in this morning, and I have not let my handbag out of my hand since. This is the worst of having so many irons in the fire – *Ah!* here we are! I thought so! – What were we saying, Robert?'

'Nothing particular. Or, you may care to ask Stella what she's thinking.'

Robert's manner to Ernestine was always less insolent than his words; it had, rather, a sort of provocative unindifference, as though there were always something he could not leave alone. It was evident – as during that afternoon at Holme Dene – that he must trail his coat, and that he felt for his elder sister a fondness which having some element of perversity, was ineradicable. Bizarre as it might seem, Stella understood that this evening he would not really gladly have forfeited this drive, if for no other reason than that it meant gearing down. Ernestine provided a valuable outlet for his tiresomeness – a quality either damned up or circumvented in his relation with Stella. She, for her part, found herself wondering how far, and even in what direction, frustrated tiresomeness could go. All at once she felt towards Ernestine the sort of attraction jealousy can create – to the point of wondering what would happen if she were to try slipping her arm through Robert's sister's. She wondered how Ernestine's arm would feel. She wildly contemplated, even, a conversation with Ernestine about Robert before it was too late – could there be found a vocabulary for anything so scandalizing, so impossible?

Ernestine, having snapped her bag shut again, tested both clasps. 'That,' she remarked, 'ought to be a lesson to me to not worry! – What, you expect me to offer Mrs Rodney a penny for her thoughts? I should hope not, indeed. May nobody think in peace? They say it is most restful of all to make the mind a complete blank, but as *I* know that is easier said than done. In any case, ask no questions and you'll get told no lies. – Don't you, Mrs Rodney, find that to be a golden rule?'

Robert, by suddenly letting his hand fall off the rug, seemed to leave Stella alone to answer. The car braked smoothly and pulled up: opening her eyes she met the lights red against it. It was at such a moment, she recollected, that many prisoners had made the escape leap: she went so far as to attempt to look, calculatingly through the misted safety glass beside her. The impression of being in a wood gave place to one of phantasmagoric architecture improbable in London.

'I'm certain,' she lightly exclaimed aloud, 'we have never been wherever *this* is before! – No, as a matter of fact, Mrs Gibb, I am not like that: anything I did want to know I should ask, always. If I am told lies, I expect I am none the wiser. You would really feel, would you, that I ask for them? I've no idea how many I may have been told.'

'When? – why? – who by?' said Robert. 'Never I hope by me.'

Ernestine rapped out: 'There you go again! Was Mrs Rodney saying so for a moment? I suppose, Robert, you are not the only person in the world?'

The lights changed; the car moved forward. Robert self-centredly lighted a cigarette, then said: 'No, I suppose not.'

'Goodness me,' cried Ernestine, turning to Robert's friend, 'I'm afraid *I* could not take the idea so calmly! Be told a lie? – I would sooner a spider walking down my back, or even a rat dead under the boards, or defective drains! I should be sorry for anybody trying to lie to *me*. This may be due to our upbringing, but I can't say I'm sorry. I was brought up to be sensitive on that subject, and I must say I am. So was Robert brought up; we all were – I imagine few families spoke the truth more. I am still extremely particular with my sister's children; and as for my own boy, I notice he colours up if he even has to prevaricate. Our father always used to look at us straight in the eye – Robert will remember. A fib, we knew, would have quite broken his heart. As for our mother, she of course is practically able to read thoughts. No, as children we should have never dreamed of attempting to hide anything.'

'We never should have succeeded,' Robert said.

'We should have been ashamed to try.'

'What,' asked Stella abruptly, 'were you truthful about?'

'That depended,' said Ernestine, somewhat taxed. 'We may not have been talkative as a family –'

'Under the circumstances,' said Robert, 'could we have been anything but the opposite? We were consumed by a silent envy of liars – and, if you ask me, Ernie, so are you still. Just look at the way you resent them; it's neurotic.'

Ernestine could but laugh. 'That really is good!' she said. 'However, do by all means let us change the subject – whoever began it?'

'You did.'

'No, I don't think anyone did,' said Stella. 'It was *plus fort que nous;* it was in the air.'

'Possibly you, Stella, brought it back from Ireland on you, like a cold or flu? . . . Oh, all right, then, perhaps not. In that case you must mean this is a haunted car.'

'Hired cars of this type could some pretty curious tales unfold, I shouldn't wonder,' said Ernestine. 'The fact is that nobody up to any good would dream of taking one, these days, if I may be allowed to say so. Still, Robert, you and I don't so often have the chance of a talk, and if we have dwelled a little on old times I'm sure Mrs Rodney will excuse us.' She next gave her whole attention to the window on her side. 'Hi!' she suddenly cried, '*that* looks to me suspiciously like Gloucester Road Station! If so, does the man know where to go now?'

Evidently he did. A minute or two later they had deposited Ernestine at the foot of the steps of her friend's house, watched her make successful use of her latchkey; and driven off again. Robert, getting back into the car after the good night, settled into what had been Ernestine's place. The atmosphere of the cushioned darkness, however, was still uncertain; the change down from three to two persons being hardly ever simple. Across Ernestine the lovers had spoken to one another with a sort of edgy directness not used before; they had nearly burlesqued themselves – yes, looking back at the drive, it was Ernestine who in her own way had been irreproachable. Now, no other vocabulary, least of all that of silence, at once offered itself. Stella asked: 'Who's she staying with?'

'Oh, a friend left over from the last war. They were V.A.D.s together. She has never had time to show people for no reason.'

'Yes, I could imagine most of her friends would be friends of circumstances.'

'That couldn't,' he said, 'ever be true of us?'

Stella continued: 'Now she's indoors she'll be able to go through everything in that handbag properly. Considering everything, she showed great self-control. Didn't she?'

'Yes – But you ignore what I say.'

'I thought it didn't make sense. I cannot be alone with you all at once; you must let me run on. It is a shock just to be meeting again, perhaps. It was a shock seeing you there at Euston – it's inconceivable that I could have forgotten what you're like, but had I? There was something I hadn't allowed for – you? . . . love? One can quite forget how love acts.'

'You don't really like how it acts? You are not happy?'

'Lunatic! – But I am thrown out. I had seemed to myself to be coming back with such a clear mind, and you have no idea how I need one.'

'I knew you'd come back full of some thought. I know you have been all by yourself in that house, but all the same I feel jealous, as though somehow you'd been spending your time with some sort of enemy of mine, or rival. So far the best has been my touching your coat.' He put out a hand, to continue to feel and follow the herringbone of the cuff – and that contact, or its suggestion of exclusiveness, like a blind man's experience, made her in turn jealous, or at any rate lonely. 'With this,' he said, rubbing lightly on the tweed, 'I know where I am – your coat's just the same.'

'You have no enemy anywhere in me!'

He said quickly: 'Why should you have to say that?'

'Why indeed? My darling, who could like to feel less welcome back again than her own coat! Surely either we know each other absolutely or not at all – and how can we possibly wonder which? . . . You're right in one way in what you said just now: we are friends of circumstance – war, this isolation, this atmosphere in which everything goes on and nothing's said. Or we began as that: that was what we were at the start – but now, look how all this ruin's made for our perfectness! You and I are an accident, if you like – outside us neither of us when we are together ever seems to look. How much of the "you" or the "me" *is*, even, outside of the "us"? The smallest, tritest thing I could be told about you by any outside person would sound preposterous to me if *I* did not know it. So I have no measure. – What were you going to say?'

'Nothing – why? I didn't speak.'

'Then, give me a cigarette.'

Robert wound down the window in order to drop out the spent match: there came in, damp, the tired physical smell of London. 'A car like this,' he remarked, 'that as she says nobody has been up to any good in, at any rate ought to be full of ash trays: so far, I haven't come on one. – I'd be happier if I could see your face.'

'We've just as often not seen each other's faces. – Two months ago, now, nearly two months ago, somebody (to give you an example) came to me with a story about you. They said you were passing information to the enemy. . . .'

'I *what*?' he said blankly.

She repeated the statement, adding: 'I did not know what to think.'

'I don't wonder.' But he reconsidered that. 'Yes, I *do* wonder rather. At you – what an extraordinary woman you are!'

'Why, Robert? What would a not extraordinary woman have done?'

'Well, I don't know, really – no, I have no idea. What did you do?'

'Nothing: that's what I am telling you. – It's not true, is it?'

'Two months ago . . .' he marvelled. 'You say, two months ago? There's certainly nothing like thinking a thing over. Or did it simply happen to slip your memory till tonight? No, though; I don't think you mean me to take it you never thought of it twice. In that case, why not just have come and asked me? What would have been wrong with that? – but that was too simple, apparently. Why, I suppose one will never know?'

She was unable to speak.

He went on: 'That is what beats me. If it was tact, it's the funniest I've ever come across. Whatever did you think? – that I might take umbrage?' He subsided, for half a minute, into nonplussed reflection, from which he broke out again with: 'My God, what a conversation! And you tell me you never meet anybody remarkable – who *was* this?'

'Harrison.'

'Who's that? – Harrison who?'

'No, just Harrison. The man I met at the funeral.'

'Then the fewer funerals you go to the better, I should say. Of course, yes: I remember you spoke of him, but I thought you said he was such a bore? He sounds far from a bore to me.'

'But it isn't true, is it?'

Robert could be felt turning round slowly, unwinding himself from lethargy, frivolity, forbearance, whatever it had been, to stare at the place where she invisibly was. Incredulity not only shook his voice but removed it to such a distance that he and she might no longer have been in the same car. He spoke, when he began to speak, as a man who, in an emergency more fantastic, more beyond the possibilities of experience, than any man should be asked to meet, casts round him for words at random, realizes their futility before uttering them, but does all the same utter them, as the only means of casting them from him again, rejected.

'But it can't be true that you're asking me this? If it could have come to that, if you were, would it matter very much what I said – to you, I mean? If you could come to that, nothing would matter, would it? What *do* you want me to say? There's nothing *to* say – what does one say in a situation that doesn't make sense? Between you and me this is inconceivable. The whole thing's so completely unreal to me that I can't believe it isn't unreal to you: it must be.'

'Yes, it is. But it –'

'*What* you're asking isn't the point – it's immaterial, crazy, brainspun, out of a thriller. Am I passing stuff across? No, of course not: how could I be, why should I, what do you take me for? What *do* you take me for? – I've never asked myself. What do I take you for? – You. As to one thing, we know we could never deceive each other; but that is just that, apparently – where you are concerned – just that, lovely but only that. Which I didn't realize – how was I to? How well you have acted with me for the last two months – two months, you say? Someone comes to you with a story: with you, the story takes – seeds itself in some crack that you felt between us. Some crack – should I have known it was there? I, you see, simply thought we were happy. Happy? – I hardly thought that, even; I simply thought we were us. You couldn't – no? – just have come and said: "Listen, because this is what I've been told"?'

'You have sometimes said that in one particular issue which might be found, anybody is capable of anything.'

'Have I? I don't remember,' he said, bewildered.

'I lost my head. How was I to know what was true?'

'How indeed?' said Robert, with frozen irony.

'He said it would be dangerous to you to tell you.'

'What he says, with you, then, cuts a good deal of ice?'

By silence she tried to wave that aside.

He went on: 'Then you acted on the assumption that it was true?'

'How could I take any chances, when I love you?'

'How peculiar it seems that you should love me.'

'Oh my darling, for God's sake – this is breaking my heart!'

'Am I?' he asked, dully. 'Or are you saying so? How do you expect me to know what's true, now? All I can see now is, how well you hide things – you may have been having another lover all this time for all I know; and I'm not sure I wouldn't rather it had only been that. This other thing seems colder, more up against me. This thing locked up inside you, yes; yes, but always secretly being taken out and looked at – and how without going mad am I to let myself imagine at what moments? In the night, how did I not hear it ticking under the pillow like your watch? *That's* of course quite simple – I am sold to you, sold to you, as you know. So you've always been watching me while we've been together? – that can't have been difficult, considering all I show you. While I've talked, you've been adding up what I say? We have not then been really alone together for the last two months. You're two months gone with this.'

'You did not feel any change.'

'Something in me, I suppose, must be going blind.'

'No, no, no. Anything there could ever be to be felt in me you could never not feel. That's why I say – you didn't feel any change.'

226

'You keep up the appearance of love so beautifully.'

She turned away, tried to see through the window, repeating, 'This is breaking my heart. Please, Robert, please,' she repeated.

'Well. . . .'

She heard a ghostly hoot of a laugh, uttered by herself very much as though she were making use of something of Ernestine's left behind in the car. 'One thing – I owe you an apology.'

'You what?' said Robert, now more gently, as though humouring a deranged person. 'Oh, as to that? Why, yes – if you like, I suppose you do.'

'I don't think I've known what I've been saying.'

'I suppose that's possible.'

'One can live in the shadow of an idea without grasping it. Nothing *is* really unthinkable, really you do know that. But the more one thinks, the less there's any outside reality – at least, that's so with a woman: we have no scale.'

He made no reply.

'That's all I can say,' she ended up. 'How I have shocked you – but how I have shocked myself! Until I heard my own words, and heard you hear them, I really had no idea how not only horrible in itself but insulting to you, to any man, the idea was . . . Robert?'

'Yes?'

'You are still so silent.'

'I am listening to you.'

'But say something. You must say something now.'

'I was only thinking,' he said, the liquidity of a smile coming into his voice again for the first time, 'you do not seem to have shown any very great patriotic fervour.'

'No,' she assented, hardly taking this in. For her trouble at the moment was physical; she was feeling faint – the hand with which she had pushed her hat back, the hand she was trying to draw across her forehead, shook; and as for her fingers, it was as though they had blundered upon some unknown dead face in the dark. All round was silence, but something drummed in her ears. This was what they called reaction? It seemed unpermissible – it could look like appeal. Had he not full right to be as angry, as disorientated, as shaken in love for her as he was? As for her, should she hope not to suffer that shock to him? How easily she had taken him up to now; indeed what presumptuousness love was . . . After a moment or two she wound down the window on her side and drew a deep breath.

He heard the breath drawn. 'Anything more the matter?' he suddenly said in his most light rational tone.

'I think I'm weak with hunger. I had nothing but sandwiches in the train.'

'Then I'd imagine that's what it probably is. In a minute or two, I hope, we'll be having dinner.'

'Oh, shall we, still?'

'One might not think so at this rate – what on earth's the man doing? Where does he think he's got us to?' Robert leant forward, slid back the driver's panel and forcibly put a question to that effect, remarking: 'We are not just driving round London for the fun of the thing . . . Very much not,' he said to Stella as he sat back again. 'What a conversation to have had before dinner, really; not to speak of at the end of a journey! Even I have had rather a day, too, even as days go. Ernestine would not hear of our stopping to have a drink. Yes, I see it was not a good plan bringing her along: upsetting. We're both a bit lightheaded – yes?'

'Yes.'

'Yes, a drink will sober us down.'

A sort of decorum of being known encompassed their table – they were served dinner late. Themselves in the friendly restaurant, they sat down; by this hour the place was emptying; outside their orbit lights were being put out, away in the distance in the penumbra waiters ghostly drew off the other cloths. The restaurant was waning, indifferently relaxing its illusion: for the late-comers a private illusion took its place. Their table seemed to stand on their own carpet; they had a sensation of custom, sedateness, of being inside small walls, as though dining at home again after her journey. She told him about her Mount Morris solitary suppers, in the middle of the library, the rim of the tray just not touching the base of the lamp; how she had sat facing down the room to the door flitted through by Mary, the fire behind her back softly falling in on its own ash – no, it had not been possible to feel lonely among those feeling things.

She had thought of Robert, but that was another matter. She had imagined also, how, if he had been there –

– But then, that would all have been different, he interposed. And who had Mary been? And had the business been got through? – had there been time enough? *Had* the house been as she remembered it, after twenty-one years?

Impossible to say, she said, impossible. For in those twenty-one years she had thought about Mount Morris so very seldom – yes, and she supposed by tomorrow morning she would have begun not thinking of it again. It was not her story. Though, as against that, she must not allow herself to forget anything till she had seen Roderick, who must be

told so much: his affairs were the main thing, not her sensations – which were, after all, stolen by the way. The place was
his future, which was something to have.

Robert said: 'Yes, that is a thing – yes, he's lucky. I can be
reasonable now you're back. I can even see you were right
to go . . . Me? – oh, everything has been going on much the
same. I have not been anywhere; I've been working late. So
don't think I've seen or heard of anybody in particular.'

'I don't think there is anybody in particular.'

'Am I selfish,' he asked suddenly, 'letting that go too far?
When I first met you there were so many people – have I been
letting or making you isolate yourself, out of my too much
wanting that you and I should never be anything but alone?'

'Oh, I get on very nicely, I think, Robert,' she said, vaguely
beginning to pour out coffee. But then she paused in the
act, raising her eyes: he and she returned to looking at one
another at leisure, with a sort of enchanted familiarity, across
the gold-rimmed cups.

But they were not alone, nor had they been from the start,
from the start of love. Their time sat in the third place at
their table. They were the creatures of history, whose coming
together was of a nature possible in no other day – the day
was inherent in the nature. Which must have been always
true of lovers, if it had taken till now to be seen. The relation
of people to one another is subject to the relation of each
to time, to what is happening. If this has not been always
felt – and as to that who is to know? – it has begun to be
felt, irrevocably. On from now, every moment, with more
and more of what had been 'now' behind it, would be going
on adding itself to the larger story. Could these two have
loved each other better at a better time? At no other would

they have been themselves; what had carried their world to its hour was in their bloodstreams. The more imperative the love, the deeper its draft on beings, till it has taken up all that ever went to their making, and according to what it draws on its nature is. In dwelling upon the constant for our reassurance, we forget that the loves in history have been agonizingly modern loves in their day. War at present worked as a thinning of the membrane between the this and the that, it was a becoming apparent – but then what else is love?

No, there is no such thing as being alone together. Daylight moves round the walls; night rings the changes of its intensity; everything is on its way to somewhere else – there is the presence of movement, that third presence, however still, however unheeding in their trance two may try to stay. Unceasingly something is at its work. Even, each beat of the other beloved heart is one beat nearer the destination, unknowable, towards which that heart is beating its way; under what compulsion, what? – to love is to be unescapably conscious of the question. To have turned away from everything to one face is to find oneself face to face with everything.

Stella slid Robert's cup towards him slowly across the table, saying: 'Oh, and one evening I went into the drawing-room there.'

'And what was it like?'

'Just like a drawing-room – I had almost forgotten. I imagined Roderick's wife in it one day: why not, after all? But there was a picture of the *Titanic* hanging in one corner.'

'I don't imagine,' he said, bent on some other thought, 'that that would worry a girl.'

'It was more that I –'

But he cut in – 'Stella . . .'

'Yes?'

'Talking of that, why should we not marry?'

Up went her eyebrows. 'Talking of the *Titanic*?'

'No, no – talking of Roderick. If anyone is to marry, why not us?'

'You and I?'

'Put it that way,' said Robert with pardonable irony. 'Anyway, why not?'

She drew a very deep breath, as though possibly the answer lay somewhere at the bottom of her lungs. 'We have got into the way of not marrying, I suppose. It would be such a business, Robert; I can't imagine it. There doesn't seem to be much to marry for, at the moment, does there? Why not wait till we see what's going to happen next? We always have.'

'Yes, I know; but what *I* am saying –'

'– Yes, I know; but all that would have to drag up so much.'

'I can't see why; and I cannot really see what . . . You think I am being very conventional this evening?'

'Roderick would like it,' she reflected, with an elbow on the table, supporting her temple on her hand, obliquely following with her eyes a scroll in the damask pattern of the cloth. 'At least, I'd imagine so; wouldn't you? Anyhow, I realized at Mount Morris that he really could not go on and on having a disreputable mother. And he has such a feeling for family, he would like everyone to be in it, including you. Not that I've ever asked what he thinks of you, because that would be to ask what he thinks of us. By now, I hardly know what he thinks of anything; but in principle, I'm certain, he'd be all for this. So it's not *that*. . . .'

'Well, then?'

'Considering everything,' she said, narrowing her eyes at this first allusion to the unhappy talk in the car: 'this *is* very nice of you, my darling – to ask me to marry you.'

'Surely I often have?'

'No, I don't think so; not really; not so point-blank. We have only talked about it the way we've talked about everything.' She thought carefully. 'This *is* the first time, I know – in a way I wish you hadn't chosen tonight.'

'Why not? There's nothing wrong with it now. Anything one must say, one must say as soon as one can. One cannot time feeling – at least, as you know, I can't. I suppose that's where to women most men seem to blunder. No you must face it: all along the line I'm not half so clever as you seem to have thought – or half-thought. The reason I want to marry you is that I want to marry you – I can't put up anything better, if that's not enough. This came over me while you've been away, and I can't wait to bring it out now you're back. I know you're tired – but there you are. The fact is I cannot bear you out of my sight.'

'But I hardly ever am.'

'I don't know – aren't you? I'm not so sure as I used to be about that.'

'You think I run into trouble?' she hazarded, glancing at her nails.

'Well, you do seem, don't you,' he mildly said, 'to spin yourself up into rather peculiar mare's-nests?'

'Then I need looking after?'

'Your friend What's-his-name must have thought so. If he thinks you should be more careful whom you take up with, so do I.'

'"What's-his-name"?' she said edgily. 'You mean Harrison? It is an easy name to remember.'

233

'Harrison, then . . . How if I, Stella, need looking after, too? It shook me, just now in the car, when you calmly said that where I, my life, was concerned anything, for all you knew, might be possible.'

'"*Calmly*"? – Oh, never, Robert!'

'Well, at any rate *said*. After two years, what an enormity!'

'I do see it was.

'How little you have been content to know . . . Or have you and I never quite been our ages?'

She bowed her head and said: 'I thought it had all been perfect.'

He said: 'Yes, it's all seemed perfect,' – but at the same time slowly turned his head to look into one of the dusky distances of the restaurant. 'But as you,' he went on, 'must have begun to see two months ago, and as I saw when you came out with all that tonight, all the time there must have been a catch in it somewhere. We must have been about due to take this knock.' Now, with an effect of deliberation, he fixed his eyes on her face – though somehow not, it appeared, on *her*. Nor did those eyes appear to her to be his – they were black-blue, anarchical, foreign. 'I'd really rather now,' he said, 'have things a little less perfect, if necessary. All that can cost too much – lovely, yes; but there has never been any question of faith. When it was a question of that, you were paralysed. How am I to know what more reservations you may not still have in your mind? *I* see only one way of knowing. – Are you going to marry me?'

'Robert, that's simply forcing things!'

'Then you don't want to? On the whole, you think, better not?'

She replied: 'Have you given me time to think at all?'

'Oh?' he said quickly, checked – but at the same time reassured or mollified. He made a less frozen movement and blinked his eyes shut: when they reopened they were at least familiar. 'Haven't I?' he asked, in a youthful uncertain tone. 'Is that all? . . . But it's not such a new idea, or a wild one?'

'You've made it sound wild,' she said, with brimming-over reproach, 'Robert, browbeating me and contradicting yourself. I may not have been sure where I was, but now I certainly don't know where I am. First you say, you'd made up your mind while I was in Ireland to ask me to marry you, anyhow, when I came back; *then* you say, you feel forced to ask me because of something I said just now in the car – partly because it suddenly seems to you necessary to keep me under your eye, partly because you feel I really do owe some balm to your offended honour. I can't help it, darling, that's how you make it sound – that the very least I can do is marry you, to prove to you I'm convinced that anything more I might possibly hear about you can't be true. Any of my own reasons to hesitate, to be in two minds, have got to go by the board? Nothing that's ever counted counts, then? What is this – an emergency?'

He said, askance: 'What a tongue you have!'

'Have I?' said Stella, taken aback. 'It does seem odd to be talking like this to you.'

'Yes, I would rather you talked like that to Harrison.'

'Forgive me – But what did you really mean?'

He could hardly be blamed for sighing. 'It seemed to me,' he said, 'I was clear enough. I asked you to marry me. Perhaps I was incoherent – but do, though, get this straight: my having told you I wanted to marry you had not the remotest connexion with anything you've said. If it hadn't been so dreary in that car I'd have asked you then. In fact, I started out for the station so charged up that if it hadn't been for Ernie sitting there waiting for us I'd have asked you the instant I saw you on the platform. Even, it may have been some confused new feeling I'd started having about you which made me let Ernestine string along – after all, she's my sister . . . No, I don't say that what came up after we'd dropped her had no effect on me: it did have this one – to make me more certain it was time we married. The idea of anybody who likes coming along and frightening you is appalling, Stella – Yes, I was hurt, too: how could I hide that? You know you see right through me. How could I not be hurt? For a moment the whole of love seemed futile if it couldn't keep you from – from that fantastic thing.'

'I saw it was fantastic.'

'Still, you were frightened?'

'It was only that I –'

'Yes, I thought you were frightened,' said Robert, leaning back from the table as though to get the whole thing into farewell perspective. 'For me – but also of me, a little bit?'

'It was simply that I –'

'Perfect love,' he said reflectively, 'casts out fear – No, forget that, though: naturally that's impossible. – You love me?'

Eloquently she answered nothing whatever, not even looking up. 'We're keeping the waiter waiting,' she added after a moment.

'Where?' said Robert, looking at the bill, which had been for some time unobtrusively at his elbow, then putting notes on the plate.

'Although,' she said, 'you still are wrong about one thing; not just "anybody" could frighten me. – I do wish you'd find out who Harrison is.'

'Ask my spies? By all means – but is he anybody?'

11

Dearest Mother: It was a pity we had not more time the other day, though it was nice that you came at all. It was extraordinary how much about there you had managed to notice; as you may guess I have not stopped thinking about it ever since, with a few interruptions. It was almost as if I had really at last been there, though not of course quite. I have remembered various things I had meant to ask you, also I think there were one or two things I did say which perhaps you did not quite take in. I don't think, for instance, you yet quite grasp how much it is on my mind about Cousin Nettie and that I really should do something about her. She may well feel she has had rather a bad deal. From what I can make out from what you say she has not ever been more than slightly off, and after all Mount Morris was once her home. How would you feel if you suddenly wanted to go back to a place, then found it had been given to someone else?

One thing you cannot be blamed for not knowing, because I decided I would not tell you until I saw what your attitude to the whole thing was (and owing to the short time we had and there being so much to say I don't know that yet) is, that just before you went off to Ireland I wrote to the Wistaria Lodge people to inquire how Cousin Nettie was and whether she does know

Cousin Francis is dead. Their reply I must say struck me as somewhat stuffy, and Fred agreed. They wrote ambiguously about Heaven and everything now seeming beautiful to Cousin Nettie. As far as any plain statement was concerned the letter might have been written by one of their patients, though it was signed Iolanthe Tringsby. She took up a thinly veiled 'anyhow, what the hell is that to you?' attitude which I did resent. Would you or someone mind sending her a line explaining that after all I am now the head of the family? I do not see how I can explain that myself without sounding self-important, but it would be simpler if she grasped it. Fred took an if anything still more dim view than I did, and said were we certain the Tringsbys were not fishy? All I could reply to that was to quote you and say their position was delicate. The fact remains that there Cousin Nettie is, and that I hope to arrange to see her as soon as possible. About this I intend to take up a firm line, and I do hope, mother, you will support me. I shall apply for the pass I did not have the chance to apply for for Cousin Francis's funeral, saying that a close relative for whom I am responsible has now had a mental breakdown and I must cope. I can work out trains to get there and back in a day.

If you took in more than I thought you seemed to when I brought up this Cousin Nettie problem the other day, excuse me for bringing it up again. All I don't want is to take this important step without telling you. You see, the more you tell me about Mount Morris, the more I feel I have inherited Cousin Nettie with the place. It is all very well to say she hates it and would go mad completely if she had to go back, but how can one tell? I really must see her and have her goodwill. It would spoil everything if I was a usurper.

Even here we are quite impressed by the news from Egypt. How particularly gratified Donovan must be, except that I now look unlikely to be a general. But at this rate it really does look as though I might be at Mount Morris quite soon. I suppose if I were one of my uncles I should be disappointed at the idea of the war being over before I had seen fighting or even got a commission, but under the circumstances what can you expect? Though I must say I should like to be known as 'the Captain' when I live there. Fred points out that it may still be necessary to invade Europe.

Fred asks to be remembered, and says he much enjoyed his glimpse of you the other day. He congratulated me on your being so young-looking. I hope you did not get back too tired and late? I'm sorry too there was not time for me to hear more about you, apart from Mount Morris. So I am all the more looking forward to a letter next time you have time. Try not to work too hard, and avoid worries. If you don't want to embroil yourself in this Wistaria Lodge thing, don't. But I thought I ought, and of course I wanted to tell you. Much love, from

RODERICK

P.S. Exactly how many acres did you say are to go under tillage this year? Also I forgot to ask you if there is a gun room, and if so what approximately would be its contents? Or under present regulations are there none?

Some days after the dispatch of this letter, Roderick rang the front door bell of Wistaria Lodge. His air was expectant, but at the same time mild and accommodating. As he stood, house and garden vibrated: unseen a lorry went by on the road side of the high garden wall. Otherwise everything was silence; the wistaria framed the white-pillared porch and the bay windows in its hoary powerful arabesques. This powerhouse of nothingness, hive of lives in abeyance, seemed to Roderick no more peculiar than any other abode. The brass surround of the electric bell was blondely polished, and so seldom had he the pleasure of ringing bells that he was on the point of placing his thumb on the push again when the door opened: a parlourmaid looked at him. Convincingly got up as parlourmaids used to be, she completed the old-time illusion of the façade. The maid had not finished asking whom he wanted when an askance lady took form at the end of the hall. She exclaimed: 'Oh dear!' resignedly, later adding, 'Good afternoon . . .?'

'Good afternoon,' said Roderick eagerly.

'I am Mrs Tringsby. You are not Mr Rodney?'

'Oh yes I am.'

'Oh dear,' said Mrs Tringsby again. 'I had been expecting you to be rather older and not quite so early. However, do by all means come into the drawing-room.' She made a lunge at a door.

'Oh. Is my cousin in there?'

'No, oh dear no, no: she likes to be cosy up in her room. *We* love her sitting anywhere that she likes. Much absorbed in the woolwork when I peeped in just now. She knows she is going to have a treat of some kind today, but we may find she has forgotten what. I *should* like one word with you first, if you don't mind.'

'Then I can go up? – Right.' He held the door open; she loped through it ahead of him, afterwards turning round with

240

a conspiratorial sign that it must be shut. In the drawing-room, Roderick stood looking questioningly, with candour and tolerance, at Mrs Tringsby, while she, like somebody dressing in a hurry, assembled a blended expression to meet his.

'You mustn't of course think we have been making difficulties,' she said. 'But only remember what happened last time!'

'Last time?'

'Last time she had a visitor.'

'But that was not me.'

'Such a dreadful shock for us all!'

'Yes, I know; I'm sorry. In fact I'm sure Cousin Francis would want me to apologize.'

'But you see he should never, never, never have come in that state! What *were* his doctors thinking of?'

'I don't know. Cousin Nettie does know he's dead?'

'*This* dear room,' went on Mrs Tringsby, casting her eyes around and withdrawing them with repugnance from one sofa, 'will to me, I suppose, never never quite feel the same again. But of course, it was others I had to think of!'

'Well, we were all very sorry. However, that sort of thing doesn't happen twice. The Army could tell you, *I'm* as sound as a bell, or they wouldn't have been as keen as they were on having me.'

But she went on with even greater despondency: 'Yes, that's another thing – I mean, your coming down here in uniform. Here, we are so careful not to have dreadful thoughts; we quite live, you see, in a world of our own. You won't, you won't on any account,' added Mrs Tringsby, glancing shrinkingly at Roderick's battle dress, 'talk to poor Mrs Morris about the war, will you?'

'I don't know anything about it,' said Roderick, his whole impatient interest by now directed upon the door. 'Though, look here, Mrs Tringsby,' he said, on an afterthought, for an instant turning, 'I saw troops swarming all the way along from the station here. How can you stop your people spotting them out of the top windows? Not to speak of lorries.'

'Oh, but those are not relatives.'

'Oh – Well, is there anything else? I've not got much time, you see: I'm only out on a pass.'

'In any case, you must not, better not, stay too long.'

'I didn't mean to,' he said, with unconscious hauteur.

'Just a little, light chat. *Never*, of course, the past.'

'No; what I want to talk about is the future.'

'Oh *dear* . . . And lately she has been so much herself.'

Mrs Tringsby, inflated by a foreboding sigh, rose, and like something under remote control was propelled by Roderick's will power to the threshold. 'Or, you wouldn't like me to stay with you?' she said hopefully. 'She and I could chat; you could look on and, so much more easily, judge how you think she seems . . . For one thing, how if she does not know who you are?'

'Mrs Tringsby, I relied on you to tell her.'

'Oh, I *told* her; but –'

'We can see, then – Now please, can't we go up?'

Upstairs, at the end of a passage, Mrs Tringsby tattooed on a door, opened just enough of it to glide her head round, and sang out: 'Here we are!'

'Then, come in,' argued a voice.

Mrs Tringsby glanced at Roderick, to warn him not to think it would all be as simple as this. She cleared her throat and continued: 'A nice young man to see you.'

'But I was expecting Victor Rodney's son. Has he not come?'

'But of course he has, dear!'

'Then, can he not come in?'

Roderick, asking himself why he had never thought of bringing Cousin Nettie a bunch of flowers, advanced into her room. From where she sat, on a sofa drawn across the window, she sent him a look which at once established that he and she could afford to wait to speak. Returning to her needlework she executed two or three stitches more, waiting for Mrs Tringsby to go. Mrs Tringsby, picking up by its frill the cushion of an armchair facing the sofa, shook out the cushion, seemed constrained to pause to admire it – as though it once again struck her, and should not fail to strike Roderick, that every object in Wistaria Lodge was of the very best – and invited him to be seated. He remained standing. Mrs Tringsby consoled herself by indicating, in dumb-show, the position of the bell. 'I shall be just downstairs, *just* down there in the drawing-room,' she said in a significant voice.

'Thank you, Mrs Tringsby,' said Cousin Nettie.

When Mrs Tringsby *had* gone, Roderick sat down in the armchair. Reaching out, he picked up a skein of coloured wool from the floor and replaced it on the sofa by Cousin Nettie. Sideways, he studied the square of canvas on which she was at work: the design, very possibly not of her choosing, had been machine-stamped on in lines of blue; one rose and about a quarter of the background had been by now stitched in. Cousin Nettie, though she did not look up, could be felt to check the instinctive, secretive movement with which she twitched the canvas towards herself – repenting, she held it up by the corners to full view.

'I expect,' she said, 'you would never have the patience to do this?'

'No, I expect not.'

'But you must *have* patience, to have come such a journey. It's a long way to here.'

'Not so very; not from where I came from.'

'I thought it was,' she said, for the first time troubled. 'Too far for anybody to come. You are looking out of the window; you can see for yourself.'

He had been looking past her, out of the window. A distance of fields, woods and diluted November sky did indeed stretch without any other feature: sky and earth at last exhaustedly met – there was no impact, no mystery, no horizon, simply a nothing more. This was a window at the back of a house at the edge of a town; Roderick recollected that Cousin Nettie had not for years now looked out of any other. And years ago she must have ceased to look out of this, for today she sat with her back to it with finality. What she liked must be this extreme end of the room, light on her work or the unassailing sensation of having nothing but nothing behind her back. Across the sky over her head ran the bolted window-sash: this timeless col-ourless afternoon silhouetted the upper part of her figure, her rolled-up soft hair the delicate projections of her face. From a ring on the hand methodically thrusting the needle into the canvas, drawing it out again, an opal alternated its milk and fire. From her left hand the wedding ring was gone.

She marvelled: 'So you remembered me though you never met me? Are you called Victor too?'

'No, Roderick.'

'Then I shall call you Roderick, Roderick?' she said flutter-ingly. 'I heard of you as a baby, but now you are quite a man.'

'I believe I was called after some ancestor – you might know?'

'There have been too many ancestors, I'm sorry to say. We are so mixed up by this time that it's a wonder we are anything at all. I am so glad you are not called Victor – poor Victor: really that was expecting too much of anyone!'

'I shall call my son, whenever I have one, Francis.'

'Oh, he *would* be so pleased!' exclaimed Cousin Nettie for the first time looking rather than glancing at her visitor. 'What a pity he's dead.'

It was a fleeting yet dwelling look, timidly momentary in intention but then prolonged. The fading of her pale grey eyes to a paler lightness had made even the pupils seem half extinct; there could be felt, as she kept her gaze on Roderick, a tender, quivering, too deflectible ray of humanity – nothing was strange in those eyes but their apprehension of strangeness. All Cousin Nettie's life it must have been impossible for her to look at the surface only, to see nothing more than she should. These were the eyes of an often-rebuked clairvoyante, wide once more with the fear of once more divining what should remain hidden – 'And yet,' they seemed to be protesting, 'I cannot help it, so what am I to do?'

It was to happen, this afternoon, that her look met its younger, not yet unsteadied counterpart in Roderick's. 'It's because he's dead,' he said eagerly, 'that I've come. They all seemed to think that I should upset you. I hope not?'

'I hope I shan't upset *you*,' returned Cousin Nettie, lowering her ugly embroidery as though it had up to now been some sort of guard or feint. 'I believe I am very odd. And you must not,' she said with a gesture, 'tell me I'm not, or I shall begin to wonder.'

'Do you know Cousin Francis has left Mount Morris to me?'

'Mount Morris,' she said, 'poor unfortunate house, poor thing! So there it is, after all this time; and here I am! So you see I am only in half-mourning,' she added, glancing down at the breast of her mottled dress with the black pipings. 'Mourning for a cousin – he was my cousin, you know. There should have never never been any other story. I cannot blame him, and I am trying not to blame myself, and you must not blame me.'

'Cousin Nettie, he has left me Mount Morris.'

She looked at him fixedly, halted, fingers to her lips.

'I wanted to ask –'

'– No, no,' she interrupted, '*you* must not ask me, no!'

'You mind my asking you if you mind?' said Roderick, experiencing his first moment of uncertain faith.

'I thought,' she said, still in agitation, 'it had all begun again. *You* now, now that you are the master. No, I cannot come back; I told him, again and again, and I told them – now I am telling you. Everywhere is better without me, so of all places I will not go back there. You must make the best of Mount Morris as it is.'

'I don't specially want anybody to do anything,' said Roderick.

'Oh, but you brood about what they should be doing. Whenever you remember you are unforgiving.'

'But,' said Roderick, having taken thought, 'I don't really think I'm like that.'

'*I* know, because I never have been forgiven. You should be like that: what is to become of us wrong ones if there's to be nobody who is right?'

'Well,' he could only say, 'I'm not like that.'

246

'No, not like him,' she decided, lightly shaking her head. 'Oh, I wish you could have seen him when he was a young man, when he was my cousin. Head and shoulders above all the rest of them, full of schemes and life! Who knows what might not have come of a different story, if there could have been one. As it was, he had to go out looking for a son.'

Roderick, inevitably hurt, was on the point of exclaiming: 'Do you think he chose so badly?' but decided not to allow himself the remark. Cousin Nettie, in giving him her confidence, had no more than uttered, with a fatalistic uninflected lightness, the commonplaces of her thought.

It had been to be seen, all along the line, how she charged herself with keeping the conversation within bounds. Once more she picked up her woolwork, with a conventional sigh – though this time only to turn the canvas from front to back, examine her stitches closely, then hold out the whole at arm's length for a look in which showed absolute disconnexion, as though the secret or charm of the continuity had been lost now, and she for one did not care. But no, she dare not afford *that* – she at once set out, with stork's-beak scissors, sedulously to snip off straggles of wool from the rough side. But the scissors, out of some impish volition of their own, kept returning to peck, pick, hover destructively over the finished part. So she disengaged herself from them in a hurry, dropping them in her lap. Underneath the window, a hesitating step could be heard on a gravel path.

Roderick did not want there to be a pause because he did not want there to seem to have been a crisis. He looked about the room, searching for something on which to comment. On no account was he willing to change the subject, but there might be no harm in a fresh approach. Mrs Tringsby's original choice of pictures, of a rural innocuous kind, had been supplemented by quite a little gallery of Cousin Nettie's, which were in a somehow more singular key – postcards of electrically blue foreign lakes, moonlight falling livid on the Alps' gargoyles silhouetted against a streaked sky, a chamois in balance at which one caught one's breath. Also there was a bevy of tinted pictures of children; all, it seemed, engaged innocently in some act of destruction – depetalling daisies, puffing at dandelion clocks, trampling primrose woods, rioting round in fragile feathered grown-up hats, intercepting fairies in full flight, or knocking down apples from the bough. Only their neutralizing prettiness could have got these pictures past Mrs or at any rate Dr Tringsby's eye. Their unweightiness – for they were all unframed, at the most being pasted on to cardboard – permitted of their being strung on wool from different projections about the room: evidently no pins were allowed in walls. Among them, Roderick noted, appeared not one single photograph: being himself, he could not remark on this.

'I was wondering if you'd have a photograph of Mount Morris.'

'Oh, no; they are so dark-looking. And why should I want a picture of anything I have seen? Don't *you* think,' she said, 'it is a little odd that they could expect anyone to be so forgetful?'

'People do like to be reminded, don't they, though? Everybody I know in the Army carries photographs round. They show them: but I suppose they look at them too.'

'I know I had a photograph of Victor,' said Cousin Nettie, concentrating upon Roderick, eyes wide open. 'He was just a schoolboy, but he sent it himself; so I am sure I would have put it away *somewhere;* but wherever could that have been? What a pity, because you never saw him at that age. – Oh,' she exclaimed, for the first time looking critically at the space between the chair and the sofa, 'and there is no tea: I knew something was wrong!'

'I expect it will come.'

'Poor Mrs Tringsby,' Cousin Nettie explained, 'sometimes does not know what time it is unless she looks at the clock. Shall we,' she asked, looking conspiratorially at Roderick, 'ring the bell?'

'You don't think that would simply bring her rushing upstairs?'

'Yes, it would be better for her to take a nice rest. Shall we wait and see whether tea comes?'

'At any age he was, I never knew my father. I mean, I did as a baby, but they don't count. I think I hardly should know him if I saw him – saw his photograph. Did you know him well?'

'Oh, yes,' she said, so much surprised by the question that she seemed perturbed. 'Victor? I thought everybody knew that. I was the last to see him: we both had tea in a shop.'

'What, before he died?'

'Not died, exactly; before he left your mother.'

'Oh no, Cousin Nettie; I'm afraid she left him.'

'Why afraid? How can one be afraid of what *has* happened? That is one great advantage for me.'

'I mean, afraid for her sake: it was a pity because of what everybody thought. She never is unkind, I happen to know, but it did apparently look like that – her leaving him.'

'She couldn't leave someone who wasn't there.'

'Not where – my father? Where do you mean he was?'

'Unfortunately I cannot remember where his nurse lived. She had her own little house, and he said it was very nice.'

'His *old* nurse?' said Roderick, wrinkling up his forehead.

'Well, she may have been older than Victor, possibly. She had been the one who nursed him during the war. That was why he asked me to have tea in the shop. "I cannot hope to *explain* what I am doing to anybody," he said. "So I thought I would like to talk about it to you." I said, "Because I am as odd as what you are doing?" and he said: "That must be what it amounts to." I said: "Well, Victor, they will think us both very odd now." There was a plate of little pink sugar cakes, so pretty, just back again after all that war. I was so sorry to see him so upset that I thought I had better just eat toast. But then he said: "If *you* cannot eat those cakes I shall know I really am doing something terrible." So I know I ate three. And now,' finished Cousin Nettie, looking reproachfully though without a tremor at Roderick's uniform, 'again there are no more cakes like that.'

'But what could he mean by "terrible"?'

'I knew just what he meant. It did not look well. I believe,' added Cousin Nettie, lowering her voice, 'she was quite common.'

At this point, tea made an entrance seldom more inopportunely. The parlourmaid, having lodged the equipage on the bureau, raked forward a three-legged table, which she placed in exactly the vacuum at which Cousin Nettie had stared. On the table she plonked down the tray, which was small enough to have required stacking with considerable art: she steadied a toppling pyramid of china and said: 'There, dear.'

'Thank you, Hilda.'

'Sandwiches, today, for the gentleman.'

'How thoughtful – please thank Mrs Tringsby . . . Mrs Tringsby *is* thoughtful,' said Cousin Nettie, when Hilda had gone out and shut the door. 'One has to think of her feelings; but then one has to think of everyone's feelings and she is a good soul. Many people now would like to be here, but she has never made me feel she wished I was anybody else. She understands that this is my place, so she will never take away my room. So we must not upset her.'

'No, Cousin Nettie, no. – But what about my father and his nurse?'

'Oh, *that* was not nearly enough!' she exclaimed with a touch of zest. 'She had been his nurse already, but he wanted her this time to be his wife.'

'But there was my mother.'

'I know, I know,' agreed Cousin Nettie. 'No wonder he felt he was doing something odd.'

'So then, that was the reason they were divorced?' Conditioned to be unable to ignore food, Roderick had taken and bitten into a sandwich; he now looked at it as though unable to recognize the marks of his own teeth. '– I suppose?'

'I'm afraid I don't understand what happened after that,' said she, occupied in unstacking the cups and giving the spoons little arranging touches in the saucers. 'Nobody ever told me, I don't think; and as nobody ever asked me, either, I did not tell them. It was just at that time that I was becoming odder. For so long they had said: "If you keep on not going back to Mount Morris when Francis asks you to and everybody thinks you should, people will come to the conclusion that you are odd." So at last I said: "Then that must be what I am." Because once that came to be known, nothing more could be expected, could it? So they said in that case I ought not to go on living in hotels, even quietly, even in private ones. If I was well enough to be in the hotels, then I was well enough to go back to Mount Morris. So I then said: "Very well, then, perhaps I had better go into a home." There seemed to be nowhere for me but here or there – Oh, are you *not* eating the sandwiches?' she finished, looking from them to him in distress.

'You can't remember anything more my father said?'

'He said what he was doing was for the best . . . You see, if you do not finish up the sandwiches I might be like him when he thought I was not going to finish up the cakes; I might think *I* was doing something terrible.'

But she did not think so: she replaced the lid on the teapot, which she had refilled, with the contenting touch of someone practising her craft. 'Yes, I had tea with him; and now here I am having tea with you! – Am I really to call you Roderick?'

'Yes: why don't you?'

'Roderick . . .'

Roderick paused, in deference to the moment, but when it was over shifted all the more eagerly in his chair. 'He said to you what he was doing was for the best?'

'Oh, yes – all my cousins make decisions; I have been used to that all my life. First they looked at one thing, then they looked at the other. It was only for me that there was nothing to do but what I did. I expect, as you are my cousin, you make decisions?'

'Just now I'm in the Army.'

'But you decided to come and see me.'

'Because what I *have* decided is, to live at Mount Morris.'

'Oh, but my cousin decided that for you.'

'I wanted, first, to be certain you would not mind.'

'That was why Victor asked me to have tea in the shop.'

'I never,' Roderick said, with a heaviness only just modified by his youth, 'knew what you've just told me.'

Cousin Nettie, putting her cup down, glanced over her shoulder out of the window: had it occurred to her that the outlook might have changed?

'So then,' Roderick went on, 'it was my father who asked my mother if he might go? I always thought it was the other way round. At least, that seemed to be what everyone did think, though I must say if they thought so they didn't say so: nobody has ever said anything at all to me, least of all her. Not that I suppose by *this* time anyone cares – unless she does? If I had even wondered I could have asked; but of course what one takes for granted one leaves alone. In a way perhaps my mother is rather shy.'

'Or perhaps it hurt her feelings?' said Cousin Nettie.

'It may have had an influence on her life,' said Roderick, looking at Cousin Nettie a shade severely.

'It was after tea in the shop,' she went on, 'that I got so much odder, and also poor Victor died. So I shouldn't wonder if nobody knew. How strange.'

'But what about the nurse?'

'I'm afraid she was a little common.'

'Yes, but is she alive?'

'I don't know who is alive. But what story *is* true? Such a pity, I sometimes think, that there should have to be any stories. We might have been happy the way we were.'

'Something has got to become of everybody, I suppose, Cousin Nettie.'

'No, I don't see why. Nothing has become of me: here I am and you can't make any more stories out of that. That

253

is why I am only in half-mourning.' She ran a finger down black piping to rest on a black bow, then asked, without looking up: 'So why are you looking at me like that?'

By automatically holding his cup out for more tea, Roderick must have tugged at Cousin Nettie's attention; actually he had been looking at nothing *but* her for some time. His eyes had not wavered from the sky-framed face of his Cousin Francis's cousin-widow; and that she had been aware of this, with however great unconcern, had been an element in their talk. In fact, if she had shown authentic oddness, it was in being as much unmoved by Roderick as she seemed to be. For his part, he was not now wondering how to run the blockade, he was wondering how not to show he *had* run it – obviously it did not do to tax her with being a *malade imaginaire* when she had, as she had so disarmingly told him, adopted the one possible course. There had not been a touch of hysteria about this: on the contrary, it had been policy – Hamlet had got away with it; why should not she? But there had been doubts about Hamlet, Roderick understood; and, as for Cousin Nettie, could anybody who voluntarily espoused Wistaria Lodge be *quite* normal? – but then again, normal: what was that? She carried with her – in her propriety with him, in her entire manner – the lasting dignity of a world in which it was impossible to say, 'Oh, come off it!' Nor could Stella's son have ever been so direct; though Victor's son might be itching to have the matter out. The sidelong glitter of reason, the uncanny hint of sanity about this afternoon's conversation at once frenzied Roderick and seduced him.

One could argue, she had chosen well. Here in this room her own existence could be felt condensing round her in pure drops; inside this closed window was such a silence as the world would probably never hear again – for when war did stop there would be something more: drills right through the earth, planes all through the sky, voices keyed up and up. The air would sound; the summer-humming forest would be torn. *Here* was nothing to trouble her but the possibility of being within reach: seated on the sofa with her back to what she had ascertained to be nothing, Cousin Nettie was well placed.

'All the same, Cousin Nettie,' said Roderick, 'you could be fairly quiet, as far as that goes, at Mount Morris – *I* am not asking you to come back,' he threw in hastily. 'All I am saying is, I shall consider the house as much yours as mine.'

'Consider it anything you like; that is half the fun!' She moved back on the sofa, bringing tea to an end by forgetting it, and began to hunt through the coloured wools beside her. 'Look,' she said, holding up a skein, 'now I am going to begin to embroider a purple rose. What do you say to that?'

'I don't know. I should have thought, pink?'

'Ah, but there is no more pink wool, and there *are* purple roses. Nobody believes me, but I could lead you to the very place in the garden and show you the bush. There is only one; it's not my fault if there are no others in the world; there is one at Mount Morris – an old Persian rose, only ever blooming for a week, and no sooner are they open than they die. So you must look for them at the right time.'

'There are others things I should have liked to have asked you about Mount Morris.'

Cousin Nettie, leaning across the table, lightly tapped the arm of Roderick's chair. She said, as lightly; 'Let sleeping dogs lie!'

'And about my father . . . Actually,' he went on in a more resolute voice, '*I* have never been there.'

'Indeed?' she remarked, with a curious drop of interest, vaguely threading a needle for the rose. 'Then what a surprise in store for you. Not what you expect.'

'Probably nothing ever is quite that. But it is bound to be something.'

'Oh, there will be no difficulty about its being *something*; it always has been; that always has been the trouble.' Having completed her first purple stitch, she turned once more towards him her seeing eyes. 'Of course there's this to be considered – you're a man. So you may keep going, going, going and not notice – I have seen that to be almost so with one man, although not alas quite. I wonder whether you will guess whom I mean? – Francis. He did not quite succeed. Day after day for me was like sinking further down a well – it became too much for me, but how could I say so? You see I could not help seeing what was the matter – what he had wanted me to be was his wife; I tried this, that, and the other, till the result was that I fell into such a terrible melancholy that I only had to think of anything for *it* to go wrong, too. Nature hated us; that was a most dangerous position to build a house in – once the fields noticed me with him, the harvests began failing; so I took to going nowhere but up and down stairs, till I met my own ghost. Never anything to be frightened of in the garden – but that has all run wild now, I dare say.'

'Mother (who has just come back from there) didn't say so. Of course, it was not the time of year for flowers . . . She was delighted with the drawing-room.'

'Visitors were always delighted with the drawing-room – Why are you getting up, Roderick?'

'Because I must be going now, I'm afraid.'

256

'I have not called you Victor by mistake – I have not upset you?'

'No: I hope I haven't upset *you*? – It's simply that I have got to catch my train.'

'Oh, a train. To London?'

'And then another train, on – Well, Cousin Nettie,' he said, hesitatingly standing beside the sofa, 'cheer up.'

'I am sorry to say I am very cheerful, now. – Did you say your mother is still alive?'

'Oh, yes.'

'Then please remember me to her; it was only by chance that we did not meet. Good-bye Roderick. I hope you enjoyed your tea?'

'Yes, thank you, it was excellent. And I have enjoyed myself very much. Would you like me to come again?'

'Oh . . . Well, perhaps some day. We must wait and see.'

Roderick saw that now he had reminded her of else-where by his declared intention of going there, Cousin Nettie could hardly endure his presence a minute longer. From the threshold he looked back: down the length of the room she sent him a last glance which might have been the first – conspiratorial, full of things to say, in a moment, when somebody should be gone. They were back again where they had started: he might have just arrived. He shut the door behind him, crept down the stairs – no lover's exit could have been more discreet. He got himself past the drawing-room without further interference from Mrs Tringsby, whom he saw no reason to thank.

Having emerged from the cosy white-pillared porch, he threw another last look back: it seemed to him that Wistaria Lodge had weakened and faded inside the grip of the climbing plant. As against which, the indomitable surrounding wall loomed higher. Roderick heard again that same indecisive step: a man in a muffler, trailing a croquet mallet, came round the corner of the house and stood contemplating the visitor as the latter unlatched the gate to the outer world.

Roderick, in implying to Cousin Nettie that he had to leave when he did in order to catch his train had been imperfectly truthful: in fact, he had another visit to pay. On his way from the station he had located the church, and he now returned there; once inside the lych-gate he embarked on his search for Cousin Francis. His mother's account had never been very clear; he had no guide – could instinct draw him? It seemed impossible that the old man at this moment should not speak. There would be as yet no headstone. A smell of clay still came up from places too new to be his; no bird sang; here and there flowers of wreaths rotted – he would have no wreath. No, nothing was possible but a general inclination of the head to all who lay here . . . A passer-by halted, watching across the wall in November dusk the young soldier wandering bareheaded among the graves.

12

'Oh, Mother?'

'Good heavens, Roderick! – Where are you?'

'You sound rather breathless.'

'Sorry; I'm only just this moment in – Where *are* you?'

'Talking from a box; I'm on my way back, across.'

'Back? – oh no, you don't mean to say you did go! You didn't get my letter?'

'Actually I did; but by that time everything was arranged. And I am glad I went; it was a success.'

'Oh. – I do hope you haven't goaded Mrs Tringsby? She really has had a good deal to put up with from all of us.'

'Yes, she said so. The point is, I had a conversation with Cousin Nettie.'

'How was she? Ought I to have done something about her before now? Yes, I suppose I ought.'

'No, that has been quite all right, because she hadn't realized you were still alive. However, she asked to be remembered to you . . . Mother, she did tell me one extraordinary thing. . . .'

'What?'

'Well, I don't know that there is time to discuss it now, especially as the box I am talking in is in a station; but I do want to ask you all about it as soon as possible. It throws quite a different light on so much.'

'Darling, you have to remember the poor thing's off her head.'

'Oh no; I don't think so.'

'Oh, now, Roderick, you *haven't* started anything? I asked you not to. Everything's complicated enough.'

'What's complicated? – I can't quite hear you; a huge train's just coming in.'

'Everything!'

'Considering everything, I don't wonder. Why did you never tell me anything about the nurse?'

'What nurse? – Cousin Nettie's?'

'No, no; she hasn't got one. My father's. I mean, the nurse my father –'

'I don't quite know what you are talking about.'

Astounded silence at his end.

'Look here, Roderick, can't you come round?'

'No. In fact, in a minute I ought to start queueing for my train. You must know the nurse I mean.'

'Oh, that one? Yes. Very well – what?'

'Surely that throws quite a different light –?'

'Oh, so that's what she told you? – No. I don't see why. Cousin Nettie may have plenty of time to bring up ancient history; I haven't. I thought you went down there to ask her about Mount Morris? I agree, *this* doesn't seem to be a thing to discuss on the telephone.'

'Especially as I'm talking from a station. But it was my father.'

'Yes . . . Well, look, I'll come down and see you as soon as I possibly can. Sunday afternoon? . . . Sunday afternoon, then.'

'I don't want to *worry* you, Mother.'

'I quite understand.'

'It's only that it throws such a different light –'

'Yes, yes, Roderick – yes.'

'Well, now I suppose I must start queueing for my train – I'll be seeing you, then? Good night.'

'Good night,' she said. 'I'll be seeing *you*.'

Stella, having hung up the receiver, went to the threshold of the open dividing door. 'That was Roderick,' she explained to Harrison, who, posted on the hearthrug of the other room, was waiting to take her out to dinner.

'So I had rather gathered. – Boy not making trouble for you, I hope?'

'Apparently there's enough of that already?'

'Ha-ha – but no, look, we don't necessarily, yet, have to call it that.'

'Call it what you like.'

'We'll just,' he suggested, looking deferentially at her, sideways, 'have to talk.'

'Yes, *I* know, *I* know, *I* know!' She disappeared again, to rattle about among her cosmetics on their glass-topped table – she looked round once with a pang at the bedside telephone, asking herself in what state of mind Roderick really had got into the train. 'Spending tuppence on asking me *that*!' she exclaimed aloud.

'Pardon?' shouted Harrison cheerily, from the other room.

'Nothing.'

She rejoined him, looking correct, sombre, and preceded him silently down the flights of stairs: together they took the blind dive into the street and continued in motion for some time; till she, halting in her tracks, asked him *where* they were going in a tone which barely veiled a disinclination to go anywhere.

'That,' he replied, 'can be more or less as you feel.'

'These days, *you* always talk about feeling.'

'What, I do – do I?' he said, struck.

'What I don't feel is, hungry.'

'That's too bad. There are one or two little places where I had rather thought we might just drop in.'

'Are there?' she said, with indifferent mistrust.

'Or we simply could,' he suggested, 'walk for a bit?'

'We seem to be doing that.' But after a step or two she amended: 'Sorry to be so shrewish.'

'Absolutely,' he said with fervour, 'not! Though you know, I do wish I knew what's rattled you.'

'Well, really.'

'No, but I mean just now.' He slipped a hand under her elbow, prepared to steer her across a crisis as he would have been to steer her across a street. 'For instance, that boy, isn't he starting something? Or is he not?'

'Roderick – why?' But she then reversed and went into a nervous rush. 'He's been spending the afternoon at Wistaria Lodge.' (Quite a thing, she thought, quite in itself a moment, to be telling Harrison anything he did not claim to know.)

'What, our old friend the nut-house? – *What* a day that was, that day I met you! – With Frankie's old lady? Now, what was he after there?'

'Inconceivable as it may be to you, he wasn't "after" anything. People sometimes are not. He was simply being maddeningly, pig-headedly kind. Or, fair, I suppose, above board – according to his ideas. How is one to know what anyone's, *anyone's* ideas are till they've acted on them? Still, you're right in thinking he started something – in fact, if you want to know, if he had been you he could hardly have turned up more. Cousin Nettie talked – she told him I'd been the innocent party.'

'Surely,' said Harrison blankly. 'That's always rather to the good, on the whole, useful? But innocent party when?'

'Years and years ago,' she said impatiently, 'in the divorce. You know all about that; you've got my dossier. Yes, I divorced Victor; I was officially innocent. But nobody for an instant supposed I was.'

'But you really were?'

'Well, yes. But what does it matter now?'

'Absolutely,' he said calmingly, 'absolutely. But that being so, what's rattling you?'

'Having it all dragged up. The inconvenience, the idiocy. Everything disarranged. Being told three times by Roderick that everything's now in a different light. I didn't start the story about my guiltiness, it started itself. It could. I'd always been the bright one, Victor the quiet one; I'd been the flibbertigibbet, he'd been the steady; I'd been, for all the world to see, the spoilt one; he the uncomplaining. Nothing was simpler for everyone than to see things one way – that *I* had asked for my freedom, for no virtuous reason, and that Victor, too squeamish on my behalf to put me through it (in those days one still talked of the "mud" of the divorce court) was letting me divorce him; simply being quixotic – In fact, not. Victor walked out on me.'

'Must have been mad,' said Harrison, with conviction to which was added relief – here at least, at last, one point on which to fix.

'Anyhow,' she said, 'that was how it was.'

'Oho, oho,' he said, turning suddenly, 'so you took quite a knock?'

'Why, yes.'

'What, you loved him?'

'He said not. And he said he was the one to know. If I imagined I loved him, he said, that was simply proof that I had not, as he'd for some time suspected, the remotest conception what love was – could be. I said, oh hadn't I? and he said no, I hadn't. I said had he, and if so, how? He said, yes he had; he had been loved and he could not forget it. So then he told me about the nurse. I said, if there always had been the nurse, nothing perhaps was really so much my fault then, was it? He said, he was sorry but that was just his point: if I had been, ever, anything he had hoped he could have quite forgotten her – he had meant to, tried to. She had not been in any way his type – some years older than Victor, nothing special to look at. He'd expected to think no more of her: they had said good-bye. I had seemed to be the person to be his wife; and he had given me – he implied if he did not say – a very fair trial. Somehow I had not made it. Almost any other woman he could have married, other than I, he said, could have made him forget the nurse: unhappily, I and my shortcomings had had the reverse effect. The idea of what it *had* been like to be loved haunted him. He was sorry, but there, he said, it was . . . Of course what it really amounted to was, I bored him . . . Any tiresome woman telling you about anything in her past always tells you, "I was young at the time". But I *was* young at the time. I – I was taken aback. The wind knocked right out of my sails.'

'Quite a kid . . .'

'No, not even that, unfortunately. Half-baked, bottomlessly unconfident in myself as a woman, frenziedly acting up. Not having found myself, at a time when – how boring it was, how little it matters now! – it was really exceedingly difficult to find anything. Having been married by Victor, having had Roderick like anyone else, made me think I *might* know where I was. Then, this happened – so, no: apparently not.'

Harrison, having got Stella across Regent Street and several blocks further east, braked their speed down by a further hold on her elbow, cast about for their bearings, then swung her south: she took the corner under control. With extra fervour, possibly to make up for any appparent slackening of his attention, he stated: 'You must have gone through hell!'

'What I am talking about is the loss of face.'

'Loss of what?'

'Face. How do you suppose that felt? All the world to know. To be the one who was left – the boring pathetic casualty, the "injured" one . . . It was a funny day when the other, the opposite story came round to me – the story of how I had walked out on Victor. Who was I to say no to it: why should I? Who, at the age I was, would not rather sound a monster than look a fool?'

He, not having the first idea, wisely let the question by as rhetorical.

'Where, at the start, the story came from I don't know,' she went on. 'Possibly Victor's family. The point for me was, who was to contradict it? – the nurse stayed right out of the picture; Victor first went to ground, and then, as you know, died. Whoever's the story *had* been, I let it be mine. I let it ride, and more – it came to be my story, and I stuck to it. Or rather, first I stuck to it, then it went on sticking to me: it took my shape and equally I took its. So much so that I virtually haven't known, for years now, where it ends and I

begin – or cared. Who does care? – or at least, who did? . . .
But *now* look what's happened! '

   'Here,' interposed Harrison, 'we about are, I think.'

   'Roderick hears from –'

   '– Half a minute: here we go down some steps.'

She came to a stop: he pushed against a door showing a
dimmed sign, OPEN. Inside, light came up stone stairs which
he took her down; at the foot he held open another door and
she walked ahead of him into a bar or grill which had no air
of having existed before tonight. She stared first at a row of
backviews of eaters perched, packed elbow-to-elbow, along a
counter. A zip fastener all the way down one back made one
woman seem to have a tin spine. A dye-green lettuce leaf had
fallen on to the mottled rubber floor; a man in a pin-stripe
suit was enough in profile to show a smudge of face powder
on one shoulder. A dog sitting scratching itself under one
bar stool slowly, with each methodical convulsion, worked
its collar round so that the brass studs which had been under
its ear vanished one by one, being replaced in view by a brass
nameplate she could just not read. Wherever she turned her
eyes detail took on an uncanny salience – she marked the
taut grimace with which a man carrying two full glasses to a
table kept a cigarette down to its last inch between his lips.
Not a person did not betray, by one or another glaring peculiarity, the fact of being human: her intimidating sensation of
being crowded must have been due to this, for there were not
so very many people here. The phenomenon was the lighting,
more powerful even than could be accounted for by the bald
white globes screwed aching to the low white ceiling – there
survived in here not one shadow: every one had been ferreted
out and killed.

When Harrison had put his hat on a rack he came back for Stella and put her at a small table – of these there were several along a wall, their tops imitating malachite. He remarked that this place never seemed to him too bad, and was at any rate quiet. Which was true: the clatter could not be heard; mouths worked hard to put out never much more than silence – sound itself seemed flattened out by the glare. As also there was, down here, more the look than fact of overpowering heat; suggestion made Stella take off her coat – unhelped by Harison who, throughout the minute, sat in deep brief abstraction. 'Well, what about it?' he at last said.

'About what?' She withdrew her fingers from her eyelids.

'About a spot of something? . . . A cold cut and salad? Fish? Or I shouldn't wonder if they might not knock us up something a bit more special.'

'What do you eat?' said Stella, looking at Harrison with one of those renewals of curiosity.

Aware, he smoothed the top of his head with an air of – both were rare, one could not say which – either self-effacement or vanity. He considered. 'Pretty much what there is where I am, according of course a certain amount to *when.*' He then eyed her throat, at the pearl-level, with some intensity. 'But tonight, you know, is something of an occasion – that is to say, for me.'

'I am thirsty,' she said. 'I would like some lager.'

In relays everything necessary arrived, including what Harrison, after a *sotto voce* aside talk, must have decided would be most special – lobster mayonnaise on a bed of greenstuff knifed into dripping ribbons. The dish, in a glaze of synthetic yellow, was put down in a space between knives, forks and glasses to cook in light: Harrison looked at it narrowly but without expression. 'Well, we seem all set,' he said – 'You were saying?'

'That had been quite enough.'

'On the contrary, anything but. I was listening hard. We turned in here when you were at rather a point.'

'What a lie-detecting place this is,' she remarked, feeling under the china for a fork. 'You come here often?'

'No, now,' he protested, with a twitch of the forehead, 'this is bad of you! I've been so awfully touched by your telling me all you did. Aren't I right, that's a story not so many people have heard? It does seem, again, a case of this thing between you and me.'

She was forced to say: 'I'm afraid how it happened was, I happened to be rattled, you happened to be there.'

'Still, that I *should* be there, that in itself was something, wasn't it? Up there in your flat with you. After all, it was *I* who was there.'

'Yes. But also . . .'

'Well, also?'

'This table rocks,' she said.

'Sorry, I'm probably leaning on it a bit heavily – I wish you would look at me.'

'Don't I?' she asked, thereupon looking at him – for this command performance she opened her lids wider than usual, which sent her eyebrows up. Remembering how embarrassingly repugnant the human eye, in almost all cases, was found by Robert, she looked at and into these eyes with curiosity, wondering whether now, if ever at all, she was not to be overtaken by Robert's feeling. Also, this could have been the moment to establish exactly what was queer, wrong, off, out of the straight in the cast of Harrison's eyes. But she

268

failed to do so: from so close up she only saw the structure of the expression of urgency – the pupils' microcosms, black little condensations of a world too internal to know what expression was, each mapped round with red-brown lines on a green-brown iris run to rust at the rim. Veins feathered the whitish whites. Fatigue, perhaps, reddened the insides of the eyelids; and it was in examining the start and growth of the lashes – irregular, neither short nor long – that she experienced a kind of pathetic shock. It was nothing more, perhaps, than that the existence of these eyelashes was touching – or, was what was touching their generic delicacy? They were not, she saw, even thickened by singeing at the tips, in spite of constant slovenly close-up lighting of cigarettes. They were sparse on the lower lids; here and there one was missing – about the survival of all the rest something was naïve. The shock she felt had no more than an echo of intimacy about it, as though transmitted from someone else – it was enough, however, to set up resistance in her: she hardened.

'But also,' she said, 'it is, that I simply do not care what I say to you. You're right: almost no one has heard this particular story – to be quite precise, no one I care for has. Not, if you want to know, most of all Robert – I should be ashamed, for one thing, to let him know that ever, however long ago, I could have cared so much for face. There may be other reasons; if so I do not know them. And not up to now – hence that scene this evening – Roderick. Between you and me, everything has been impossible from the first – so, the more unseemly the better, it seems to me. With you from the very beginning I've had no face: there's nothing to lose. There's an underside to me that I've hated, that you almost make me like: you and I never have had anything but impossible

269

conversations: nothing else is possible. But, when I talk as I sometimes do to you, talk as I did tonight, you should *not,*' she said, looking away from him round the room, 'feel flattered.'

There was a short pause. 'Right,' said Harrison softly. He added: 'You don't much like this lobster?'

'Oh, yes,' she with compunction said, 'I do.' She twisted ribbons of lettuce round her fork, ate, then went on, in a voice which carried a smile: 'I suppose *now* I've made it impossible for myself to say anything?'

'Not necessarily.'

'You can see then, perhaps, why what Nettie Morris – and who could have thought of *her*? – told Roderick has made such a situation? – Do you go to the theatre?'

'Well, I have been.'

'Then you know how in plays when a boy discovers his mother's guilt –'

'– Ah, but then come, wait, stop! – in this case it's entirely vice versa: *your* boy should now be right up in the air . . . He might, of course,' added Harrison, studying the short, clean nail of his right thumb, 'fairly ask you what came over you, at that time, chucking away your good name.'

'Why should I care?' said she. 'Both my brothers are dead.'

'Oh, *I'm* not asking you, mind.'

'I hope not, because I thought I'd told you. – Oh, I should doubt,' she exclaimed, 'whether there's any such thing as an innocent secret! Whatever has been buried, surely, corrupts? Nothing keeps innocence innocent but daylight. A truth's just a truth, to start with, with no particular nature, good or bad – but how can any truth not *go* bad from being under-ground? Dug up again after years and laid on the mat, it's inconvenient, shocking – apart from anything else there's no place left in life for it any more. To dig up somebody else's truth for them would seem to me sheer malignancy; to dig up one's own, madness – I never would.' She looked up at one of the glaring globes, blinked, and said: 'Roderick will not like me any better, either. He has grown up to swallowing what he's thought I did; somehow he's made the person he thought did that into the person he's loved. He has grown up defending me – possibly sometimes even against his own thoughts. *Now*, he'll hardly know me.'

'What he'll think ought to be, what a bad deal you got. He'll be,' said Harrison hopefully, 'all the sorrier for you.'

'But good heavens –' cried Stella, then broke off, looking at Harrison with a restrained, musing despair. 'Why else do you imagine I put off telling him? It's come to matter too little, having mattered too much. No, no, no: I arranged things to suit myself. –' What a lot,' she said, leaning back, scribbling a pattern of confusion on the air over the table with her finger, 'what a lot I have, you know, put Roderick through for nothing.'

'You let him think his father was quite a chap.'

'I wonder . . . I simply left it. But what was the good of that? Now he'll go, quite likely, to the other extreme of thinking Victor a skunk; which is not true either. One or the other way, Victor was his father: as, indeed Roderick said tonight. That's what matters; that's what can't be helped. I? I've done him, Roderick, out of everything ordinary – a slightly blown-upon mother, that's what he's had. Now, who can be ordinary? – it's too late. All the years to have been ordinary in are gone.'

Harrison looked at her sideways, calculating the possibilities of a remark.

'Well?' she said

'He has never, er, cut up in any way about you and Robert?'

She said: 'No,' snubbingly and remotely.

'So it has not,' he suggested, 'on the whole, worked out for you too badly? If the boy had had more illusions, you might have had more trouble.'

'Yes, I see what you mean.' She paused. 'Roderick would not take my way of life now so calmly if he had not thought, from the first, that he had a mother *capable de tout*? That is certainly,' she agreed, with the affability of extreme disdain, 'rather a point.'

It was clear that he hated the way she said so.

'You mean,' she went on, 'there's been a certain advantage in my son's feeling I had nothing left to lose?'

'No, now look here —'

'Really we cannot talk if you are so squeamish.'

'We shall have to talk,' said Harrison, 'all the same. As I did rather say, if you recollect, when you and I made this date for the evening over the phone. Then, of course, it so happened that this other thing came up. And I can't say, if I may say so, that I'm sorry it did — somehow it's brought us closer. You'd say I mustn't say that? Then let's leave it this way: it's established confidence.'

'I had almost forgotten we were not here for pleasure.'

'Knowing how *I* feel, that again is too bad of you.' He turned however, with at least some equanimity to signal for more lager and the next course. The considerable remains of the lobster were taken away; crumbs of coral, dribbles of greenery, drops of transparent yellow assiduously were wiped from the dark-topped table; two double portions of a fruit flan appeared. 'Though of course, also,' Harrison said with a second failure of confidence, 'the Welsh rarebit here has been known to be far from bad . . . On the whole, right as we are, you think? . . . In that case, O.K.,' he told the white-coated boy, whose hands' red inexpert progress about the table he had not ceased to watch, as though timing work.

'Yes,' he went on when they were once more alone, 'for me this is an occasion – if I *have* got to scold you.'

'Oh,' she said, going cold to the marrow. 'Why?'

'You have done what I told you not to.'

'I cannot think what you mean.'

'You can if you want, all right. Yes, you've been naughty.'

'Really?'

'Yes, really. Also,' he said, at his softest, 'rash. One of these days you'll be getting some of us into trouble. Don't look blank – you know very well what you've done,'

She worried with her fork at the flan pastry.

'As we know, we have a mutual friend.'

'If you mean Robert,' she flashed out, 'he doesn't know you.'

'So that's what he says?' said Harrison, looking at her twice. 'Now we know where we are. So you thought you'd take a chance on it and tip Robert off?'

'No,' she said, steadying her voice, 'not that. You expect me to have taken what you told me a good deal more seriously than I did – did ever, and certainly more seriously than I could now. Naturally I asked him whether he knew you – are we making any bones about that?'

'Right,' said Harrison imperturbably. 'Let's by all means take things a bit slower. So *he* said, no, he had never set eyes on me? (Which is not unlikely – how much good should I be if he knew he had!) Whereupon, *you* took it that that was that?'

'If you mean I thought no more of it, frankly, no: no, I didn't.'

'Frankly,' retorted Harrison, 'we're not, are we, *being* particularly frank? Because, on the contrary, I should estimate you've thought of practically nothing else. Else, why not tell *me* to go to the devil?'

'Why, indeed?' she said boldly. 'Perhaps you are growing on me, as you say.'

He took this without a flicker. Then he asked: 'Do you know you're not as bright as I thought?'

'Oh?'

'No. When I told you, at the very beginning, that I should know if you tipped him off, you should have thought twice. Try thinking now. I not only know that you have, I could tell you when. I could tell you the very day, or rather the very night.'

'What makes you think you could tell me the day or night?'

'Because, from the morning after, Robert altered his course. Pulled out of old haunts, dropped several old friends cold. Behaved, in fact, exactly and to the letter the way I'd told you he would behave from the instant he knew there was anyone on his tracks. Which was not,' said Harrison, secretively fiddling with a cigarette but not lighting it, 'unnoticed. What do you think I'm for?'

Stella opened her bag, began to powder her face: not knowing whether her hand would shake she did not take the risk of applying lipstick. Before putting away the mirror she examined her eyebrows, shaping them with the tip of her little finger. 'Well? . . .' she said, as though in abstraction – but there was a deadness, into which she failed to infuse expression, about her tone.

'Well . . .' he replied. 'So now what more do you want? If you ever wanted a proof, I suppose you have one? If you want to, think back. Months ago, when I first put this up to you, didn't I din in one thing – that if you did slip the word to him, I'd know? How? you said. I said, because he would show it. Tonight, that's what I'm telling you he's done. So now you know how I know you spoke. You know I know what you told him.'

'Told him when?'

'That night you got back from Ireland.'

She looked round the room. More people had come in; no one had gone out yet; a new row of eaters' backs was along the counter; the dog, leash trailing, now sniffed about the floor. Space between the counter and the tables was by this time congested by standing groups, holding glasses, looking (it seemed to her) with stunned calculation into each others' faces. She got the impression that news unheard by her had detonated dully among these people, without causing a blink to the lights or a shock to anyone. Perhaps the fact was that the seeing of everybody by everybody else with such awful nearness and clearness was already enough. They were neither smart nor shabby, drunk nor sober, saved nor damned – born extras, if anything too many. But nobody is hired to play for nothing however small a part: she wondered what tonight's inducement could be – here and there somebody looked around, uncertain as though the inducement were breaking down. Was it possible that some major entrance could be overdue? How if Robert were to walk in?

'I don't,' she said, 'see anyone I have ever seen. Who are all these people?'

Surprised, he ran his eye over them. 'Usual crowd.'

'You would know if any of them were unusual?'

He, looking put out, said he might or might not: evidently he felt that the situation, at this point, demanded something more from her. Concentratedly working towards this climax, he had not, as his tense fidgety blankness showed, envisaged it as it was to be. He had, as though to symbolize a sort of general coming-into-the-open, lighted the cigarette; but he smoked without satisfaction, knocking ash off faster than it could form – some fell on the sticky part of the flan.

What an evening, she superficially thought, of, among everything else, waste! She returned to scrutinizing the other people between half-closed lids. 'One girl, I see,' she said, 'has got her stocking-seams crooked. Is that unusual?'

Louie, at these words – or at what must have been their vibration, for they could not have reached her end of the room – pivoted round on the stool on which she sat. Holding on with one hand to the rail of the counter, she leaned backwards to stare at Harrison's table as though it might mean something – and, as soon became evident, it did. Her face lit up; her colour enthusiastically rose. She nodded, lost some of her countenance but went on staring. Harrison did not see her. 'Oh, but the one I mean is a friend of yours!' exclaimed Stella in the light, rather high voice which had in the last few minutes become her own. She was at a desirable distance from her soul. 'Do at least,' she said to Harrison, 'look at her!'

He did so without pleasure. Very much gratified, Louie renewed the greeting: he not so much nodded as contracted his neck-muscles with a jerk – then at once looked elsewhere. 'Oh, come,' said Stella, 'one can do better than that.'

'I haven't time,' he said. 'Nor have you. *You* – you've put us all on the spot, nicely. As things are, how long do you think I am going to carry this? What do you expect me to do now?'

'I was wondering.'

'It's a question of what I *can* do. Thanks to you, our friend has pretty well dished himself. I told you, the only case for leaving him loose was, the chance he might lead us to something bigger. Now he's put wise he's out. All this time he's been costing us quite a bit: *now*, the only possible case for leaving him loose falls down. No more reason why things shouldn't take their course. That is what it's up to me to report.'

'So you do?'

'I've got myself to think of. – And, of course, the country.'

'I see. So far, who besides you knows this?'

This must have been the question he had been waiting for. 'Up to date – as a whole, as a hang-together – only *I* know. It has still to go on up . . .'

'Still . . .' She suddenly looked him in the eye. 'I see. You wouldn't be telling me this if it had *gone*?'

'*Scram!*' said Harrison violently to the dog.

Patiently knocking itself against a leg of their table, the dog had distracted Stella's attention: it pushed its muzzle up at her, pleading to be allowed to be under obligation to *someone* – there was something umbilical about its trailing leash. Harrison reaching round, pushed at the dog with his foot: a masochistic quiver ran down its spine but it stood firm, having now lodged its head upon Stella's knee. She put her hand on its collar, counting over the studs with her finger-tips as though reading braille: 'It's not doing any harm,' she said.

'It's bothering you.'

'No, only boring me. Won't bite; I wish it would . . . We were saying?'

'You know what we were saying. You know quite well.'

'I know what you are going to say, yes. That through my blunder this is your moment to foreclose? That at last, now, it really *is* up to me? That I either buy out Robert, for a bit longer? – or?'

She broke off – for, with a lightning movement, Harrison had clapped down his hand on hers. She envisaged for a split second that, past a point insulted, he could be striking her. Then she saw what had happened, what was happening – Louie was advancing on their table. 'Excuse me,' Louie panted, 'I'm just after my dog.' She stooped and clicked a finger and thumb. 'Come on, come along with you, Spot, you bad boy! Bothering people!'

Stella, retaining a very clear impression of the dog sitting scratching long before Louie entered, looked at her with surprise. Everything ungirt, artless, ardent, urgent about Louie was to the fore: all over herself she gave the impression of twisted stockings. For this evening she had abandoned her comrade get-up and was looking smart, if not as smart as she hoped, in a claret two-piece; a handbag slithered under her elbow and in one bare hand she was mauling a pair of fancy gloves. A bow clip rode its way down her pony-rough hair. Her big lips, apart, were pale inside their crusted cosmetic rim; distended by enterprise, askance at what she found herself doing, her eyes looked oyster-pale in her ruddy face in the glare.

'I've not seen *you* in our park,' she said to Harrison with galvanized boldness, 'for ever so long!'

'You don't surprise me,' he said, picking up the end of the dog's leash and handing it to her. 'I'm never there.'

'Still, you must have been when I saw you – Fancy seeing you *here*! Excuse me interrupting; it's on account of the dog – Spot,' she said to it faltering, 'you bad boy, you. Won't leave people alone.'

'You're not interrupting us,' Stella said, looking gratefully up at Louie – who, standing looming over the table, naïvely shifted her weight from foot to foot. 'Why do you call your dog Spot? He hasn't got any.'

Louie could be seen to take rapid thought. 'He's my friend's dog, more, that I am keeping an eye on,' she said, yanking half-heartedly at the leash. 'It's nice here, really, isn't it?' she went on, looking around the room and then back at Stella: she studied Stella and her bravado ebbed. 'I hardly wonder at *anyone's* coming here.'

'Anyhow, you come. Often?'

'No, I never do. What makes it funny this evening my getting here is, I don't think it's the place I meant to. I mean, I have got a date, but I think now it must really be somewhere else. They said to keep down the street, and then it was just down some steps and I couldn't miss it; but it's surprising the way you can. If it isn't here I have no idea where they did mean: everywhere has got names, but all you can read written up is, "Open". So I thought in case it was the others' mistake I'd better give them an hour. Meanwhile I had a bite. But for my girl friend saying I always look so silly, I'd just as soon.'

'That's right,' interposed Harrison, who throughout the speech had been drumming thumbs on the table-rim, 'you'd better beat it home. You'll only be landing yourself in more trouble. And mind, put that dog back where it came from.'

'Why, look, it's taking quite a fancy to *you*, now, poor thing, isn't it? They always say a dog knows. However, I should be getting along.'

'No, don't go!' cried Stella, checking a movement to catch at Louie's arm. 'For a minute – why won't you sit down?'

'Oh, I don't think I ought to,' Louie decided, after a glance at Harrison.

'For a minute . . .'

'No, I don't think I should.' She reached an empty chair from the next-door table, turned it around and sat on it. She looked from Stella to Harrison. 'For one thing, you were talking.'

'Only deciding something,' said Stella, going dead white at the sound of the words.

'Still, even that takes time.'

The anonymous crisis at this table seemed to Louie no queerer than any other. She crossed her legs, draped her skirt on her knee, pasting it into position with the palm of a hand. Here she was, sitting like an image – up to whom was it to pass the next remark? She looked at the dog and, cricking her head sideways, re-read the address of the owner on its collar: she then reflected she should have thought of that, making her look so silly. However, you had to do something or nothing happened; and, in spite of Harrison's nasty manner, neither of them had looked again at the dog. 'How I wish I knew where this was where we are,' she said at last. 'Because they have ever such a variety of snacks.'

'I have no idea where we are!' cried Stella, starting alive, 'Where are we?' she threw at Harrison, who did not answer. 'Do at any rate,' she went on, rapidly and light-headedly, to Louie, 'tell me who you are. You see,' she laughed, indifferently as though Harrison were nothing more than a stuffed figure, 'there's no chance of our being introduced, so you tell me your name and I'll tell you mine. I'm Mrs Rodney.'

Louie only was glib when she improvised: now it was after a pause in which she seemed to quell a doubt that she at last declared: 'I'm Mrs Lewis.'

'*Are* you? said Stella, again surprised – so much so that she found herself glancing for confirmation at Louie's wedding-ring finger.

'Yes,' Louie said, with a now more confident nod. 'But you know how it is – my husband rightly should be an electrician, but now they've got him in India. Or at least,' she amended shying away from Harrison, 'that's what it appears like, but you have to be careful what you say. Wherever he is, I'm quite lonely sometimes, really. Still, as it says, we women are all in the same boat.'

'Oh, I'm not: it's just that my husband's dead.'

Louie was shaken. 'You don't mean, already killed?'

'No, he died. And that was years ago.'

'All the same . . .' Louie, having turned this over, brought her gaze to bear upon Harrison, reassessing him, from the finger-nail up to the crown of the head, in a new and it could be important light. It appeared to her that Stella should do better. Unnerved by a look from him, she again attempted to please. 'To think of you remembering me,' she said. 'After only once. But I know you did remark how you seldom forgot a face. Considering what a number there are, it ought to be quite funny inside your head by this time.'

'You're right,' said Stella. 'It is quite funny inside his head.' On hearing which words Harrison fixed his eyes on her with an either equivocal or tormented expression. But she was saying to Louie: 'You're not old friends, then?'

'Why, I don't know his name! Just we fell into conversation at a park concert. They're informal on account of the open air. You notice how they seem to attract all sorts. Such classical music, in spite of which you get the band fiddling away as gaily as anything in that nice glen. Though oh the gnats, however; and then night quite falls before you know where you are. Of course by this time of year everything's discontinued, which is just the pity – there's nothing left but London once it's winter . . . How he was thinking away to himself, though!' she said, her face retrospectedly broadening. 'I shall never forget.' She waited for Harrison to enter into the story: he did not, so she went on unaided: 'I nearly had to laugh – boxing at his hand with his other hand. You never saw such brainwork. There was I on one chair, next that an empty, then him there on the next. I need not say, it was Sunday.'

'That,' said Stella to Harrison, 'was the day you were listening to the band?'

'*You* were never his date?' said Louie, illumined. 'Doesn't that go to show.'

'Why?'

'Why, it does show. Because I did just wonder if he might not be artful – so now I ought to beg his pardon.' Her pause was proffered to Harrison: no reply. 'Though it's not,' something constrained her to tell Stella, 'that in a regular way *I* should take note of a person: you meet so many. No, what led me to take account of him was a thing he said which you don't hear often. He gave me an old-fashioned look and said: "*I might be funny*, for all you know."' As ever pleased by the words, she drank in their effect on Stella.

But Stella was not enough – exaltedly hauling on the dog's leash, Louie faced round on Harrison. 'Oh yes you did – remember? You said how you might be funny. You see, you saw I was not a London girl.'

'What I saw you were, *and* are,' replied Harrison, 'is a pest. And mind – are you trying to choke that dog?' He looked at Stella and said: 'As for you, are you off your head? Do you think we have got all night?'

She said: 'Yes, I thought we had?'

The quietness of all this made its repercussion on Louie slow: she played the leash out again to its full length, meanwhile gazing down at the dog with commiseration. But then suddenly she gave the dog a warning push with her foot, as though it would be safest as far away as possible. 'No,' she cried out, 'how he can have the heart!'

The two others, surprised, watched Louie sliding her chair back in a panic over the rubber floor. They waited with something like deference for her to go on: she did. 'Oh, I wonder you go with him! I don't wonder you don't care to stay alone just with him if you can help it. People to be friendly, that's what the war's for, isn't it? *I* never had any more motive than that poor dog!'

'I am sorry,' said Stella, stooping to pick up Louie's flimsy gloves, which had fallen hopelessly to the ground: straightening their crumpled fingers she paused to look with remorse at the pattern pinked on their backs. She returned them to Louie, saying: 'You mustn't mind his manner.'

'Don't you mind his manner?'

'One cannot always choose.'

'I should have thought you should have had other chances,' said Louie lifelessly: having let go the leash she was attempting to tug a glove on. 'Though you ought not to mind me either,' she had to add, 'because I always do get upset: they say so. You see my home was wiped out, so that if anyone goes for me I suddenly don't know which way to turn. So you must excuse my saying anything I did: all it was, that up to the very last I had understood us all to be friendly – apart that is, from his rathering me not there. How was I to know he would flash out so wicked?'

'You must not blame him,' said Stella, 'it has been my fault. He's in trouble, too – I am telling her that you are in trouble,' she said to Harrison, then went back to Louie. 'Nothing ever works out the way one hoped, and to know how bitter that is one must be a worker-out – you and I are not. This evening was to have been a celebration, the first of many more evenings. It may still be the first of many more evenings, but what will they be worth? This is the truth,' she said, looking round her at all the other people apprehensively staring into each other's faces. 'He cannot bear it; let's hope he will forget it – let's hope that; it is the least we can do; we're all three human. At any time it may be your hour or mine – you or I may be learning some terrible human lesson which is to undo everything we had thought we had. It's that, not death, that we ought to live prepared for. – What shall we do?' she said to Harrison. 'What would be least impossible, do you think? Where shall we go next?'

The overpowered Louie glanced from man to woman, heaved about on her chair as though bound by ropes to it, got herself free, stood up. 'I ought to be getting home.'

'But you said your home –?'

'I ought to be getting back where I am. Tell him it's as you were,' she said. 'People must fly off sometimes.'

'Say good night to him.'

'Me? I don't know his name.'

'Harrison – You must congratulate me before you go,' said Stella, her hand still on Louie's arm. 'I've good news, I think.'

'You have?'

Stella nodded. 'A friend is out of danger.'

Harrison's unfolding of his arms, on which he had been leaning heavily, let the table restore itself to equilibrium with a bump and a flash of cutlery. He was changing his attitude, apparently, only in order to minister to a smarting eye, which a fume from his heap of stubs must at last have caught. He scrubbed at this eye, the left, with a finger-tip, raising and lowering his eyebrows. 'Why not you two both go along together?' he said, looking at the finger when it had done. 'Don't you hear what I say?' he asked in a louder, less absent voice. 'You two had better both be getting along.'

Stella, pale again with stupidity, touched a spoon in a saucer. At last she brought out: 'But . . .'

'Well, what?'

Stella looked at Louie, as though *she* might take a turn. 'But – she and I have no idea where we are.'

'Turn right, at the top of the steps; keep on; first left, keep on again. One of you ought to know when you're in Regent Street.'

'And then, I don't know where *she* lives.'

'She may.'

He rose and pulled back the table; Stella under compulsion got slowly up. 'I don't understand,' she said. 'What has been decided? What are you going to do now?'

'Get the bill. Do you think a bill pays itself?'

285

13

'I might have known,' said Connie. 'And after the lengths my friend went to providing his friend for you. So there we had him on top of us all the evening.'

'Anyhow, you're back early.'

'What else would you suppose? No, this is the last time I take you under my wing, let me tell you. Go on: resume your usual habits.'

'I didn't, Connie,' said Louie, flopping like a flat fish across her bed, shoeless. 'Oh, my feet!'

Connie scolded: 'Round in those silly shoes!'

'All right then, I'm silly all over – go on, say it. Still, it was a pity you didn't come where I was, even if it wasn't just where you said. They had ever such a variety of snacks. And another thing –'

'Well, so they had a variety of snacks where we were. – What other thing?'

'I got right in a drama.'

'Oh, I've had quite enough of that for tonight, thank you.' Connie declared, yawning. Standing in cami-knickers in front of Louie's front-room gas fire, she balanced herself as she peeled off one stocking, then the other. 'And listen: if you wish me to sleep down in your bed with you, you go on and pop in ahead and warm it. I don't see why I should be the one to get the gooseflesh.'

'You are kind, Connie.'

'Well, rather that than up two flights in the nude. It's all one to me – though, mind you, I'm never sure this is healthy. Got your clock set?'

'It never went off this morning.'

'Then I shouldn't be surprised if you never set it. Let me look – give it here.'

Connie gave the alarum clock a good shake. 'Anyhow, what do you mean?' she went on. 'Drama? If you're going to tell me you got in a fight, don't – I have had enough of all that monotony. Or if not, then whatever kept you so long?'

Louie, half-way through pulling her nightgown over her head explained in a muffled voice: 'Walked home.'

'Whatever made you do that with the trains running? No wonder you felt your feet.'

'I got asked to accompany someone back.'

'There's nothing I can see wrong with the *clock*,' said Connie, coming to put it back on the bedside chair, 'but that's the most I can say – Got that nightie for me?' A spare one of Louie's for Connie's use was nowadays kept under Tom's pillow. 'Well, shove over,' she ordered in a minute or two. 'And mind,' she added, bouncing critically once or twice on the springs on Tom's side, 'whatever you do or don't dream during the night, don't you start kicking me with your toe-nails like you did last time: that's one of the things I don't get married for. Or maybe it was as a precaution your husband seems to have hollowed himself this deep trough? You ought to get this mattress seen to once conditions show any sign of becoming normal – though of course, again, one sign of conditions becoming normal should with luck be you having your husband coming nipping back; in which case far be it from me to dictate. I'd as soon lie level, but men are more nervous – You creamed your face?'

'I don't think I'll bother, Connie – You like to use my cream, though?'

'Nn-nn, I'll let it ride. Where has the fatal gift of beauty been getting Connie lately, I should like to know? – I'll tell you what, however: *you* ought to watch your pores. It could be your not having a London skin.'

So Louie turned out the light. But, 'Oh, *there*,' she complained, 'Connie, you went and left on the fire!' – 'Well, I haven't yet known you seven years, have I? While you're at it, you'd better undo the window, just in case that clock of yours should *not* go off.' Upon Louie's getting out with a resigned flop, Connie took the chance of appropriating the extra amount of blanket wanted for her cocoon. Louie, for her part, dawdled rather on the return journey, taking some time to feel her way round the furniture. 'Buck up,' grumbled Connie, 'Lady Macbeth! So it was the drama you accompanied home, or what?'

But this evening for Louie had rung the knell of Harrison, man of mystery, as a subject: she found, with a shock, that what she now most wanted was never to speak of him again. A fog of abhorrence was already settling over his features, blotting out what he said, blanketing the cuttingly quiet edge of his tone of voice. It seemed unseemly, even, that his companion should have claimed for him the prerogative of pain: Louie simultaneously felt he could never suffer and wished he might. It was not so much that she could not forgive him as that he seemed to her born to repulse forgiveness, with indeed all things else: tonight's most strong impression had been that in all Harrison there was no place in which to receive anything. Oh, what had come over her, in talking to

Connie, thus to have baited her talk? The truth was, she very much wanted to speak of Stella – but as to that, also probably better not. Very many nights it was Connie's way to drop into sleep bang, like a devil through a trapdoor – much was it to be hoped this might happen now. But of course, not. 'Mm-mm?' persisted Connie, yanking one arm out over the bedclothes to spank at her hip-bone, making sure in the dark it was always there. 'So what?'

Louie tried a yawn like a lion's. 'Oh Con – I – am – so – tired!'

'What do you imagine I am, always upon the watch? Not to speak of this evening, dragging around that spare. What's the matter with you is, you're getting stealthy!'

'Oh no, truly. No, all that happened was, me starting by taking a fancy to a dog. It seemed so sad. Which led me into getting into conversation with its owners.'

'What were they doing, then – ill-treating it?'

'Oh no. No, they were sitting at a table. "Well," they said, "it always is something to meet a fellow dog-lover." I said: "Funny you calling your dog Spot when it hasn't got any," so they took that well and asked me to join them, making a third.'

'Then married, were they?'

'Oh no. No, her husband was dead. No, they weren't married.'

'Then in that case how could they both have the same dog? . . . No, you've mucked up two evenings, it seems to me. So along you came, you mean, with your fatal charm, and broke that up, then saw him home?'

'On the contrary, Connie. He got indisposed so remained behind with the dog, and I saw her home. I went as far as her door. She and I became friendly. She was refined.'

'She was what?'

'Refined.'

'No wonder her friend passed out.'

'That I did *not* say! No, now you are too bad – keeping on taking me up like that! If that is all you are going to do, just you leave me quiet!' Louie heaved round to facing the other way, taking with her all she could in the way of bed-clothes, thereby creating tautness with draught beneath it between her form and the unyielding Connie's. She drew her knees up and drove her profile forward, blunted, into her pillow. All this having been registered by the bed-springs, Connie muttered: 'There you go – take on, do!' Tensity, silence. Connie acted as one thinking no more of it. But then a spring uncoiled – she brought out her arm again and dealt a wallop at the behind of Louie. 'You don't have to mind me,' she said, 'you great sissy!'

'It isn't you only. It's the taking and taking up of me on the part of everyone when I have no words. Often you say the advantage I should be at if I could speak grammar; but it's not only that. Look the trouble there is when I have to only say what I *can* say, and so cannot ever say what it is really. Inside me it's like being crowded to death – more and more of it all getting into me. I could more bear it if I could only say. Now she tonight, she spoke beautifully: I needn't pity her – there it was, off her chest. If I could put it like she does I might not be stealthy: when you know you only can say what's a bit off, what does it matter how much more off it is? He was fit to strike her, but then she passed it off – if the way she did pass it off made him fit to strike her – so there was *I* left with him ugly, which I cannot forget . . . At home where I used always to be there never used to be any necessity *to* say;

neither was there with Tom, as long as they let him stop here. But look now – whatever *am* I to, now there's the necessity? From on and on like this not being able to say, I seem to get to be nothing, now there's no one. I would more understand if I was able to make myself understood; so you know how it is, how I try everything. Excuse me, Connie, after your kindness, but you keeping asking only makes me take on. I'd sooner you some ways than a strange person; and I see you're right – to have been so happy-go-lucky like I've been does not appear true to Tom. All it is is, there's always this with a man – it need not have to come up what you cannot say, I would far sooner you there if you'd only *be* there, just.'

Connie did not reply.

'What's the matter, Connie?'

'Can't I think?'

'Oh, if that's all it is.'

'All I can say is, if I was you I shouldn't worry my head. You are not so much more peculiar than many others. I cannot say what anyone ought to do, really . . . It's late, you know.'

'Why, *yes*, I suppose it is.'

'You can tell it is, from the quiet.' They lay listening to what, under analysis, was only sound at further remove: nocturnal train-sounds, shunting, clanking, and hissing, from the network of Marylebone lines. 'Hark at those marshalling-yards,' grumbled Connie, 'you might as well be in Germany.' Then a moment later, something faltered over the ceiling: searchlights out. 'Funny it would be,' Louie remarked, 'to see light like we used to see on that ceiling, standing still. We did used to have a lamp just outside there in the street, therefore you have no idea how different this room used to be all through the middle of the night. It could have kept us awake. And that tree behind the yard, for instance; when there was a window lighted behind that the pattern of that tree used to come right on this very same bed. It used to be so lifelike you saw it move; Tom remarked you could know it was a plane tree – Think the searchlights mean anything?'

'Nn-nn: they're obliged to keep fidgeting them about.'

'We ought to go to sleep, then.'

'Yes, I said.' Connie reared up for the last time to scratch inside an armpit, then settled down – so dead still that the feeling of her beside one was that of Lot's Wife horizontal. Indeed, this applying of her whole force of character to the will to sleep was disturbing, going on close beside one – Louie, back on her back again, clasped her hands under her head and stared up at nothing – it was oppressive, though, how much of nothing there was: she escaped from underneath that, in a minute more, into wondering how Stella had done her hair. But how were you to tell? – there had been the hat. Most of all, there had been the effect – the effect, it said, was what you ought all to go for. Black best of all, with accessories, if you were the type. The effect of this person? . . . Invisible powder, mutiny, shock, loss; sparkle-clip on black and clean rigid line of shoulders; terror somewhere knocking about inside her like a loose piece of ice; a not-young face of no other age; eyes, under blue-bloomed lids, turning on you an intent emptied look, youth somewhere away at the back of it like a shadow; lips shaped, but shaping what they ought not; hat of small type nothing if not put on right, put on right, exposingly; agony ironed out of the forehead; the start, where the hair ran back, of one white lock – What had been done to her? Where had she got herself? – Fine wrist-watch not to be recollected apart from the fine wrist-bone, on her reaching down to pick up the fallen gloves. Good of her – but, dwelling on them like that? You might have thought Mrs Rodney had not seen gloves before. . . .

Louie felt herself entered by what was foreign. She exclaimed in thought, 'Oh no, I wouldn't be *her*!' at the moment when she most nearly was. Think, now, what the air was charged with night and day – ununderstandable languages, music you did not care for, sickness, germs! You did not know what you might not be tuning in to, you could not say what you might not be picking up: affected, infected you were at every turn. Receiver, conductor, carrier – which was Louie, what was she doomed to be? She asked herself, but without words. She felt what she had not felt before – *was* it, even, she herself who was feeling? She wondered if she would ever find Stella's house, the steps at whose foot they had said good night in the dark, again; still more she wondered if she would want to. 'But this is not good-bye, I hope,' had been said – but what, how much, had she meant to mean? This fancy taken to Louie, this clinging on, were these some sick part of a mood? Here now was Louie sought out exactly as she had sought to be: it is in nature to want what you want so much too much that you must recoil when it comes. Lying in Chilcombe Street, grappling her fingers together under her head, Louie dwelled on Stella with mistrust and addiction, dread and desire. Out of all the communicativeness during the zigzag walk back to Weymouth Street, there had risen not one reference to Harrison: instead, the talker had been dashing patchily back through her own past – partly as though to know by the spoken sound of it if it *were* true, partly as though she could not put too great a distance between herself and what had happened half an hour ago. She had come back and back to a son she had in the Army. Anxious? – why not; this was her only son. 'He should be a comfort to you,' Louie had interposed. 'Oh, yes, *he* is a comfort to *me!*' Having been walking fast, the talker had from that point on walked faster; Louie had been put to it to keep up with her even with her own famous big flat stride. Fast? – no, it had been something more than that: Mrs Rodney walked like a soul astray.

Those three words reached Louie imperatively, as though spoken – memory up to now had been surface pictures knocked apart and together by the heavings of a submerged trouble. Now her lips seemed bidden. 'A soul astray,' they repeated with awe, aloud.

Then in alarm she listened: silence. She listened longer – unseen, Connie might have been stone dead.

'*Connie?*'

There came a hiss of breath. 'Well, what?' replied Connie in a sharp sleepless voice.

'I couldn't hear you breathe.'

'Nor I was, till you go and make me.'

'What *were* you doing, then?'

'Trying what those Indians are said to do.'

'Which Indians? – You did give me a fright.'

'Fakers.'

'Whatever don't they do that for?'

'To attain themselves to the seventh degree of consciousness.'

'Whoever told you? Tom never repeated anything like that about the Indians when he writes letters; and he is observant – Anyway, what d'*you* want to be conscious for like that?'

'I'm peculiar,' Connie said in a Delphic tone. 'If I'm not to be one thing then I'd as soon be the other one hundred per cent. I've never been so wakeful — must be something I ate: nothing's pure these days. No, I'm not in pain, nor is it fullness or wind, only the universe fevering round inside my head. — Ever got a bicarbonate? — No, I suppose not.'

'We did have, but Tom took them in the Army — However, I could always look in the drawer.'

'What's the use of looking in the drawer when they're in the Army? — No, if I've got to have the universe in my head I might as well look it in the eye. There ought to be some advantage in seeing it in proportion, which is all it requires. I should not mind if I did. You can but try; it can do no further harm.'

'You might stop your heart.'

'Look, you buzz off back to sleep!'

'I haven't been asleep.'

'What were you talking in your sleep for, then? I was right on the point of attaining when you made me jump.'

'Ever so sorry.'

'Oh well, how were you to know?'

'All the same, I do wish you wouldn't, Connie.'

'*Now* I doubt if I can . . . And where are you getting to, I'd like to know — crying out like after a stray soul?'

14

One thing was out of the question: telephoning to Robert. There needed to be no question – when, having parted from Louie, Stella was again, alone, in her flat – of eyeing the telephone, wondering whether to or not to. Robert tonight was at Holme Dene. Summoned to a family convocation, he had arranged, he that morning told her, to dash down there by the seven o'clock train.

The occasion was without precedent: what had happened was this – Mrs Kelway had had an offer for the house. By post had arrived the thunderbolt: one of the many agents upon whose books Holme Dene had reposed for so many years had, without warning, written saying he had a buyer; or, at least, a client ready to reach that point. To say that the proposition unsettled Mrs Kelway and Ernestine would be an understatement; it threw them into disarray. Simultaneously, they declared that the deciding of anything, either way, was repugnant; and equally, that it would be unsuitable for them to decide anything, with or without repugnance, without Robert. Ernestine's letter to him to this effect had been such a combination of haste and length that he could only reply that he had not the pleasure of understanding her. She had refused to telephone on the matter except in a series of groans, warning hisses, and hydrophobic laughs, interspersing what sounded to be a code. Muttikins and she, she reiterated, quite saw that of course the war and Robert's conduct of it came first; at the same time, could he not find some teeny-weeny space in which to attend to the affairs of his own family? Muttikins was being wonderful, but it seemed unfair.

Thus had they got him there: there he was. Already for an hour they had been at it: now the clock in the lounge stood at 9.15 – Ernestine, owing to the seriousness of the occasion, had decided to give the news a miss. The curtains over archways and windows were close drawn; the decorative squints in the inglenook wore what looked like eye-patches of black cotton. The tray carried in with fuss for Robert had been carried out again with just less fuss, Mrs Kelway and Ernestine having watched him eat. The children, if not asleep, were in bed – a sense of midnight already filled the lounge; the fire, having consumed its last feed for the day, burned low. Screens had been so concentrated as to form an alcove for Mrs Kelway's chair; in this she knitted with that unflickering velocity which had alarmed Stella. Ernestine, on the opposite side of the hearth, was doing nothing other than thinking hard – as, she explained, she and they all must do, in view of the shortness of Robert's time and the necessity of deciding *something*. Sitting upright on a coffin stool collected by her father at an antique shop, she wore her uniform and a hat. As for Robert, it was useless to suggest he should sit down, though they indomitably continued to do so – up and down the lounge, to and fro across it, between the original oak pieces and the visiting mahogany furniture, he paced, he paused, stared, stood. When he ever did come to a standstill on the hearthrug, it was with the effect of sighting some resolution, which again each time he abandoned without giving it words. His keeping in movement thus gave the Kelway triangle an unfixed third point: to address Robert involved a perpetual turning of the head – at least on the part of Ernestine; Mrs Kelway seemed to see no more reason to make this concession than to make any other.

The Kelways communicated with one another with difficulty, in the dead language. At intervals, the recurrence of a remark showed that yet another circle around the subject had been completed.

'It is *something*, at any rate,' Ernestine once again said to Robert, 'that you are here. The telephone is never the same. And with letters keeping crossing each other, by the end we might not be clear what we all feel.'

'Whereas,' said Robert, momentarily resting his elbow on the top of the upright piano, 'we are now?'

'We are becoming clearer than we might have been, I think. – Wouldn't you say so, Muttikins?' went on Ernestine, hopefully glancing across at the other chair. Upon Mrs Kelway's having said nothing, Ernestine had to qualify: 'If it was not so difficult.'

'Let us sum up,' said Robert. 'A., we don't know if we want to sell; B., if we do, how much more than the offer are we to hope to get? and, C., again, if we do sell, where are you and Muttikins to go next?'

At these words his mother did bestir herself. 'I am afraid,' she said, 'it is not so simple as all that.'

'It's no good rushing things, Robert,' Ernestine pointed out. 'Better take everything one by one. There are always the children. And suppose Amabelle did not like the idea?'

'Amabelle,' said Mrs Kelway contemptuously, 'cannot get out of India. But there is more in addition.'

'Muttikins,' went on Ernestine, 'cannot help feeling that there must be something behind this offer.' She glanced across again: Mrs Kelway indicated that yes, this was what she could not help feeling.

'What's *behind* the offer is someone's wanting to buy the house.'

'Oh, I dare say, Robert; but it is so sudden. It is not even as if this was a safe area.'

'Nothing has happened,' said Mrs Kelway in an offended tone.

'Oh, indeed no, Muttikins, and why ever should it!' Having sacrificed some seconds to laughing the idea off, Ernestine resumed: 'Of course it's nice being a neutral area, not evacuated into, not evacuated out of, therefore quite quiet; but even so . . . who can be after a house no one has seen?'

'Certain no one *has* seen it?'

'No one we do not know has been to the door.'

'Well, it can be seen from the road, at this time of year, or at any rate from a little way down the drive.'

'We do not care for people coming down the drive,' said Mrs Kelway.

'That,' agreed Ernestine, 'is exactly what we do not like the idea of. If they want the house, why cannot they come to the door and openly ring the bell? Creeping and spying about when we did not know, calculating the value of everything, planning how soon they could get us out . . . This is England, Robert; one expects to have privacy.'

'I'd imagine, someone is in a hurry –'

'But, why? That is what seems suspicious.'

'Well, you know how it is –'

299

'They need not think they are going to be able to rush us,' said Mrs Kelway. '*We* did not ask them to buy the house.'

'Still, we have left it "for sale" for years on the agents' books; which, one must face it,' said Robert, 'comes to the same thing.'

'They are trying to take advantage of us,' said Mrs Kelway. 'But this is our home.'

'If that's how we do feel, how simple,' hastily declared Robert. 'We turn 'em down.'

'But it is too large.'

'In that case, we jack 'em up.'

'We have many associations with it,' said Ernestine.

'In *that* case, jack 'em up still higher.'

Mrs Kelway allowed herself, over her knitting, an infinitesimal frozen pause. 'I am afraid,' she repeated, 'it is not so simple as all that.'

'Muttikins,' said Ernestine, after a feeling silence, 'is astonished. And really I don't wonder. You talk, Robert, as though everything could be valued in money. You talk as if this was just a business transaction.'

'Surely that's what you got me down to discuss?'

'We have not yet decided whether we wish to transact anything. This has been a shock. We hoped you might understand our point of view. After all, our father bought this house himself, and we all moved into it out of Meadowcrest, because it would be nicer. And so in ways it has been.'

'It always has,' said Mrs Kelway, 'been too large. And with these days it is now too larger. Especially as it seems we have no privacy. The rates are high. Your father made a mistake, but it could not be helped; we have done our best We had to install a new cistern, which was expensive; and this room and the drawing-room had to be re-decorated in 1929. All that should be taken into consideration.'

'Our father,' Robert pointed out to Ernestine, 'saw his mistake in a flash, even before there had been time to rub it in – that was done later. It was he who put down the house on the agents' books.'

'We had at one time,' Mrs Kelway agreed, 'become accustomed to the idea of selling it. But that was long ago.'

'You feel you could be happy, Muttikins, in something smaller?'

'It is not a question of happiness,' Mrs Kelway said, 'it is a question of the future. That is for you and Ernestine. I have had my life and I hope I have done my best. Your father used to say he had not much to complain of. The cistern and the improvements to the reception rooms and the improvements to the garden, including the pergola and the statues of fairies, which were ordered by Ernestine at the Ideal Home Exhibition and came to more than we expected, as they charged for delivery, will I hope be taken into consideration. The children like them. But you must not expect me to be with you long.'

'Muttikins,' shrieked out Ernestine, 'don't say such *dreadful* things!'

Mrs Kelway raised her small silvered head, which gleamed under the light of a standard lamp, to look across at Ernestine with contempt. 'You talk,' she said, 'as though you expected not to die yourself. We shall all come to that, including the children. I have no objection to taking facts as they come, but what we now have to decide about are changes. And we should be certain of the value of things: it would not do to be taken advantage of. I have the receipts for everything in my room. In addition –'

– The telephone rang, from the other side of a curtained arch. Robert, starting violently, turned in its direction: he stopped in his tracks and listened – tense, fair, gaunt, at bay. Ernestine bounded up from the coffin stool, exclaiming with the resigned air of an indispensable person: 'That will be the W.V., for me!' She shot through the archway. Robert waited; Mrs Kelway knitted – evidently Ernestine had been right. He relaxed sharply, glanced across at his mother, lighted a cigarette. He then, as Ernestine's talk protracted itself, walked to the foot of the staircase and looked up.

Above-stairs Holme Dene was silent: without a creak it sustained the stresses of its architecture and the unsureness, manifestly indifferent to it, of its fate. Upstairs, as elsewhere, it had been planned with a sort of playful circumlocution – corridors, archways, recesses, half-landings, ledges, niches, and balustrades combined to fuddle any sense of direction and check, so far as possible, progress from room to room. The plan demanded the utmost in the way of expenditure on passage carpets and woodwork paint. What could be puzzling was that now, at night, with the hearing tuned in, so much space should give out so little reverberation. These two upper floors (for another staircase, beyond a swing door, led on up to Robert's and other attics, in an extensive range) were, in fact, not hollow, being flock-packed with matter – repressions, doubts, fears, subterfuges, and fibs. Or so he felt. The many twists of the passages had always made it impossible to see down them; some other member of the family, slightly hastening the step as one's own was heard, had always got round the next corner just in time. A pause just inside, to make sure that the coast was clear, had preceded the opening of any door, the emergence of anyone from a room. The unwillingness of the Kelways to embarrass themselves or each other by inadvertent meetings had always been marked. Their private hours, it could be taken, were spent in nerving themselves for inevitable family confrontations such as meal-times, and in working on to their faces the required expression of having nothing to hide.

At the same time, the intelligence service had been good: everyone knew where everyone else was and, in time, what everyone else was up to. Failure again to be present, after an interval, always had brought a messenger to the bedroom door or a call from the garden under the window; while to be come on looking out of a window had been to be asked to specify what one was looking *at*. It had not been possible for anybody to leave the house unseen – dashing across a lawn or heading down the drive one held oneself ready to be challenged; a potter through the boundary woods could at any time be black-marked as 'hiding'; and as for slipping off to the gate post-box, that was above all deprecated – letters might be written, but must be exposed in the hall before collection for post.

Amabelle, who early had heard the call of sex, to the accompaniment of suffusing blushes and a roundness as nonplussing to her wardrobe as to herself, had been martyred for it: no one could have been merrier on the subject than Ernestine, or more repudiatingly icy than the sisters' mother. (Mrs Kelway's way of saying 'your father' still, years after that guilty creature's death, vibrated with injury; the implication was that he had become a father at her expense.) Robert in adolescence had taken to photography, which secured him an alibi, a dark room whose door he could respectably lock, and a more or less free pass out, for technical requirements, to the nearest town.

Chiefly, Holme Dene had been a man-eating house: as such it was one of a monstrous hatch-out over southern England of the 1900s. Conceived to please and appease middle-class ladies, it had been bought by a man whose only hope was this – as a home Holme Dene might seem to be an outmoded model, but it remained a prototype. Lock-shorn, without the bodily prestige of either a soldier or a manual worker, as incapable of knocking anybody about as he was of bellowing, Mr Kelway had been to be watched seeing out at Holme Dene the last two years of an existence which had become derisory. Prestige from his money-making, unspectacular but regular, had been nil; his sex had so lost caste that the very least it could do was to buy tolerance. Only in the odd reflex or revulsion which had caused him, so soon after the move here, to put Holme Dene down as for sale again on the agents' books had Robert's father been in any way out of type. What unformulated anarchical dreams he had entertained one would never know. Unstated indignities suffered by the father remained burned deeply into the son's mind – Mr Kelway, by his insistence on Robert's constantly looking him in the eye, may have meant to challenge his son to recognize any one of them. His fiction of dominance was, as he would have wished, preserved by his widow and his daughters.

Robert's hand reposed where he remembered seeing his father's – on the polished knob terminating the banisters. Nothing but a whiff of carbolic soap from the children's bathroom came down to him: upstairs life, since the war, had up there condensed itself into very few rooms – swastika-arms of passage leading to nothing, stripped of carpet, bulbs gone from the light-sockets, were flanked by doors with their keys turned. Extinct, at this night hour Stygian as an abandoned mine-working, those reaches of passage would show in day-light ghost-pale faded patches no shadow crossed, and, from end to end, an even conquest of dust. These days, the daily servants fled Holme Dene, superstitiously, long before darkness fell: sent to bed, Anne and Peter had the empty top to themselves. It was to be hoped that Amabelle's children were impermeable.

When Ernestine came back from the telephone, Mrs Kelway said to her: 'What is Robert doing?'

'What are you doing, Robert?'

'Looking upstairs.'

'Why, anything wrong?'

'No.'

'Oh – It *has* been a day!' said his sister, sitting down again as though with little hope of remaining in that attitude long. 'There has been first one thing and then another. And I shouldn't wonder if there was more to come.'

'Ernestine has not been able to take her hat off,' said Mrs Kelway.

'Still, it's different now we have something to show,' said Ernestine. 'One hardly likes to say so, but look at Montgomery! Mrs Jebb has just told me there was something further on the nine o'clock news. When we miss that something has always happened. But tonight that is not the point. – How far *had* we got?'

'Muttikins had been saying she would not be always here.'

'Muttikins was being extremely naughty! – No, the thing is: *ought* we to sell, or not?'

'Or, to put it the other way, do we want to?'

'These days one cannot always be thinking of what one wants.'

'I never have thought of what I wanted,' said Mrs Kelway. 'Perhaps it might have been better if no one else had.'

'If everybody were more like Muttikins,' observed Ernestine, 'the world would be very different from what it is.'

'Really I doubt that,' said Robert suddenly, picking up a paper-knife from a table, putting it down again. 'Many people are unsuccessful imitations of Muttikins. – No, from the practical point of view, Ernie, I'm afraid it's merely a question of whether to sell now or later on. You can hang on, on the assumption prices will go up; but, as you so rightly say, that so much depends. This is not a house that many people would want –'

His mother said: 'Yes, it is merely our home.'

'Then again, of course,' he went on, raising his voice, 'there's the question of where you two would go next. You naturally,' he said with uncontrollable coldness, 'must live somewhere.'

'We should not at all care to live just *anywhere*, either!' cried Ernestine with a good deal of spirit.

'Naturally.'

'We had both hoped, Robert, that you might think of something, instead of merely agreeing with what we say. If we did not already agree with what we say there would be no point in our saying it, would there? – What so much depends on is, after the war: one doesn't know now what will be nicest then. And by that time Amabelle may be tired of India.'

'Amabelle,' interposed their mother, 'will be in no position to say. She has no claims of any kind. Your father dealt with her suitably when she married. If she and her husband expect more they are quite mistaken. I had always quite understood they understood at the time. If they are mistaken they had better stay in India: they went of their own accord. She was anxious to marry and did not stop to think. We have taken the children when it was not convenient; one would not expect the children to understand, but that is the most Amabelle should expect. This house is to be left to you, Ernestine, and Robert, jointly. If you do not care for it, you had better say so.'

'Oh but of course we care!' wailed Ernestine, hysterically thumping backward her green felt hat, with the W.V.S. lettering, from her forehead. 'How can I ever forget this is my home?'

'And how can *I*?' chimed in Robert.

'It would not be your home if your husband had not died,' said Mrs Kelway, looking at Ernestine disparagingly.

'I never should have forgotten it, in any case,' said the widow.

'Nobody is asking you to forget it,' said her mother, feeling round in her knitting-bag for a fresh ball of wool. 'But we see that Robert is saying nothing.'

'Oh, where *I'm* concerned,' he cried merrily, '*I* say, sell!'

There ensued a resounding pause. 'That is what I expected,' said Mrs Kelway.

Ernestine spun round on the coffin stool to examine Robert as though for the first time. There escaped from her a quite new demoralized laugh: head on one side she heard it with some alarm. She then complained: 'Well, you need not put it so violently!'

Mrs Kelway said: 'Robert does not remember.'

'There you are quite wrong, Muttikins,' said her son. Mrs Kelway allowed herself one more pause – less a query than a taking of note. 'Indeed . . .' she remarked. Ernestine meanwhile raked a worried look round the lounge, as though something from outside had got into it.

'Yes, Robert, indeed.' Again he had taken up his stand – this time, it might really be, ominously – on the rug between his sister and mother. He had placed himself where it was impossible not to see him; and Mrs Kelway, admitting this, glanced his way – as unflinchingly as if he had drawn a gun. She appeared to measure his height, from the feet up. Then: 'He talks like a man,' she said, contracting her little shoulders.

But that was lost: her son had suddenly turned and was looking beyond the screens at the staircase. 'Hel-*lo*!' he exclaimed. 'Who's here?'

'Me, Uncle Robert,' said Anne, coming on down.

'*Anne*!' expostulated Ernestine.

'Oh, Auntie Ernie, *please*!' Clip-clopping in slippers across the floor, overcoat over her striped pyjamas, Anne made for Robert, holding up her face to be kissed. 'We were not allowed to stay up,' she said, 'so I came down. Why are you standing up like that? – are you just going?'

'Both of you,' scolded Ernestine, 'ought to be sound asleep!'

'Peter is,' Anne said in a righteous tone.

'Grannie does not care for people creeping about,' said Mrs Kelway.

'I know, but –'

'– Don't say "I know" to Grannie.'

'Well, I do know, but it's Uncle Robert's fault for coming so late.'

'He did not come to see you.'

'I know, but I don't see why I should not see him.'

'Because Grannie and Auntie Ernie and Uncle Robert are deciding business.'

'I know, but –'

308

'Anne, if you keep saying "I know" you will have to go back to bed immediately. As it is, you must go back to bed at once. – Robert, you encourage her!'

'No, she encourages me. *Now* this begins to look like an evening.' He bore out the statement by throwing himself into an armchair, scooping up Anne to make her sit on the arm. 'All the same, what an un-clever, un-funny little girl you are,' he told her, gripping her by the back of her coat-belt, not altogether kindly rocking her to and fro, to the peril of her not certain balance. 'Why don't you ever manage to think up anything? Why not be walking in your sleep?'

'Because I'm awake,' Anne said, struggling round to face him. But so near did that bring her eyes to her uncle's forehead that she recoiled blinking, as though a pang of the mistrust as to the reality of the moment were passing through her. She loved him with, in her respectable way, the first intensity of her life: so much so that the woman she would become stared askance at him out of her child's features. He was right, she was a dull little girl – without animal poetry, without guile, but formed for devotion: inopportune, staunch, ruddy. But within that little stout breast, as it filled out, there would from time to time heave up some choking wish – now she was offering all she had, beginning and ending with her power to stand on her head. Reddening, looking down at the toe of her uncle's shoe as though yearning to be the one who had polished it, she asked: 'Why can't you stay tonight?'

'Because I hate early starts – How are you?'

'I'm all right.'

'Nothing to tell me?'

Anne racked her brains. 'I was top at mental arithmetic.'

'You can tell Uncle Robert all about that next time. Now –'

'– Oh, Aunt *Ernie!*'

'No really, Ernie,' said Robert.

'Well then, Anne, a moment. Only a moment, mind.'

'How many moments *are* there?' said Anne to Robert 'Sixty seconds make a minute, sixty minutes make an hour; but how many moments are there?'

'That has to depend on you.'

'How long, compared to a minute, is a moment?'

'*That* depends,' he repeated, searching her face for the face of someone else.

'You are awful,' Anne said – 'Are we going to sell this house?'

'Don't ask silly questions,' interposed her aunt. 'Uncle Robert's tired, and so should you be.'

'But I thought you said he'd say.'

'Never mind what you thought.'

'What *do* you think, Anne?' said Robert, irresponsibly turning. 'Sell out? Hold on?'

Anne bit her upper lip with her lower teeth. 'Oh, I don't care; I only wondered. What would anywhere else be like? This house *is* getting too old to be lived in much longer; the handles are coming off the doors. We could try a new one. And what's the object of this being too big when we can't go into any of the other rooms? If we sold this, with the money should we be rich? Or if not, could we be very poor? I and Peter should rather like to be *something*.'

'Indeed,' said Mrs Kelway. 'And pray, why?'

Anne let her weight sag against her uncle's shoulder – as usual when he led on, she had gone too far. 'Oo, I don't know; I don't mind,' she said with an artificial yawn.

'Anne, how you rat,' said Robert.

'I don't mind,' she doggedly said again.

Why should she? Here for her it had been a pat little lifetime without moments, an existence amongst tables and chairs, without rapture or mystery, grace or danger. Never a heartbeat; never the light disregarding act, the random word or spontaneous kiss; never laughter other than those registrations of Ernestine; anger always in a smoulder, never in a flame. Though she did not know it, she had never seen anyone being happy – what better was to be hoped of a new house if they were all to go there? This was demeaning poverty. Pity the children of the poor.

Who, however, knew when the trumpet might not sound and the walls of Jericho might not come crashing down?

The telephone rang.

Robert this time started outright – so much so that Anne, as though he had thrust her from him, grabbed at the air with a little cry. She recovered herself, but she had betrayed him: his mother fixed their chair with her eye.

'The telephone is never for anybody but Ernestine,' said Mrs Kelway. 'So what is the matter, Robert? Are you expecting anything?'

'If you imagine it is for you, Robert,' said Ernestine, clamping herself to her seat with great self-control, 'do by all means answer: I should be only too glad.'

'Knocking the child off the chair,' went on Mrs Kelway, further tried by having to raise her voice above the demoniac ringing of the telephone, 'though she had no business to be sitting on the arm.'

'I simply fell off, Grannie.'

'You should not sit on your uncle when he is nervous. – Need we have all that ringing?' To her temple she raised one little hand. 'It seems so loud – might it be better if someone answered it?'

'I'll go – oh, let *me* go!' Stopping only to hitch her slippers up on her heels, Anne bounded in the direction of the arch.

'Ernestine, do you prefer Anne to answer the telephone when she ought to be in bed?'

'Sorry, sorry, sorry – certainly *not* – Anne! . . . . I was busy wondering who it could possibly be, at this hour.'

'Something may have happened,' said Mrs Kelway, faintly contracting under the blast of sound like an anemone. 'It might be best if Robert could go and see.'

'Never mind, never mind, Robert,' Ernestine rapped out, buttoning her coat as she strode into action past him. 'I will. As you know, I invariably do.' Her brother, though he had risen stood with a hesitancy exaggerated by his height; he towered there in a sheer negation of movement, head half-turned to the curtain masking the ringing telephone. Anne, stock still half way across the lounge, fixed on him, one could not say how intuitively, her eyes.

'Wait,' interposed Mrs Kelway, for an instant removing the guard from her temple, the little hand, 'there is no point in Ernestine's answering if it *is* for Robert. Is he expecting anything?'

'No one would ring up about nothing as late as *this*,' said Ernestine, distractedly halting. 'The question is, Robert, do they know where you are?'

'It does seem very late,' said Mrs Kelway.

Robert said: 'Ten past ten?'

'It does not seem very considerate,' said Mrs Kelway, 'unless of course, something has really happened.'

'If it was for you, Uncle Robert, would you let me answer?'

'Why, yes,' he said, staring back at his niece, 'why not?'

'What should I say to them?'

'That I've left here – I'm on my way back to London.'

'Not quite true, strictly,' said Ernestine.

The ringing stopped of its own accord.

Robert sat down again; Ernestine, hand on the curtain of the important arch, laughed wildly. She then said accusingly: 'Now we may never know.'

'No,' agreed Mrs Kelway.

'If it should turn out to have been anything important, I shall always blame myself. Though if it was, it seems funny they should not have kept on. Though, of course, they may always begin again. – At any rate, Anne, *you* must go to bed. I don't know what you are thinking of!'

'I wonder what anybody was thinking of,' said her mother. 'As a rule in this house we are so prompt.'

'Now, Anne, now Anne, go and run along!'

'If I do run along, may Uncle Robert come up and say good night to me?'

'No. You have had enough excitement for tonight.'

'It is not merely that,' pointed out Mrs Kelway. 'Anne has already been said good night to. I am surprised at her.'

Anne heard nothing: she had flung her arms round Robert as high up as arms could reach. He stooped; she pressed her cheek to his very cold one, feeling meanwhile, through her unimaginative body, echoes of the beating of his heart. 'You're always going,' she mumbled, 'always going away.' However uncaring, he was slow in disengaging himself from this last haven – it was she who withdrew her face from his, the better to be able to look at him; at the same time going through uncertainty as to whether it *was* better

313

to see, or touch. Nothing solved itself: having shaken all her bed-tousled hair back, she shut her eyes.

'You're giving me a crick in my back,' he said, beginning to pull away. 'You must grow taller.'

'Just once more . . .' Pulling his head down, she butted her forehead against his: their brain-cases touched – contact of absolute separations she was not to forget. She turned away and clip-clopped to the foot of the staircase and up, up into the darkness, not having looked back once.

'Anne is getting to be quite a big girl,' observed Mrs Kelway. 'It is a pity.'

'One way and another,' said Ernestine, 'there seems to be quite a fatality against our deciding anything. How if I got a pencil and paper to jot down points?'

'In addition, there will be Robert's train.'

'Yes, there'll be my train,' he agreed, looking at the clock.

15

'And if I am?' he repeated. 'If that is what I am doing?'

Not a sign, not a sound, not a movement from where she at a distance from him lay, exhausted by having given birth to the question. Her room was bathed in a red appearance of heat from the electric fire; shadows jutted out sharply; a mirror panel reflected the end of the bed on which Robert sat. As though the sensation of this red half-dark of so many nights having within the moment become infernal communicated itself from her to him, he reached across and turned off the fire – the glow from the units died out slowly: the room, absolutely unseeable at last, might now have been any room of any size. Nothing but their two silences merging filled it, and she did not know to what part of silence he had withdrawn till he said: 'Because it has been that, all the time.'

'Why?'

'You wonder – yes, I suppose you must. We should have to understand each other all over again, and it's too late now.'

'Late in the night?'

He did not answer.

Raising herself in order to be more clearly heard, she said: 'Only, why are you against this country?'

'Country?'

'This, where we are.'

'I don't see what you mean – what *do* you mean? Country? – there are no more countries left; nothing but names. What country have you and I outside this room? Exhausted shadows, dragging themselves out again to fight – and how long are they going to drag the fight out? We have come out at the far side of that.'

'We?'

'We who are ready for the next thing.'

'Can you be so arrogant? – Why have I never felt it?'

'Because it's not arrogance; it isn't something in me; it's on altogether another scale. Would you have loved me if I'd had nothing else? For the scale it is on, there's so far no measure that's any use, no word that isn't out of the true. If I said "vision", inevitably you would think me grandeur-mad: I'm not, but anyway vision is not what I mean. I mean sight in action: it's only now I act that I see – What is repulsing you is the idea of "betrayal", I suppose, isn't it? In you the hangover from the word? Don't you understand that all that language is dead currency? How they keep on playing shop with it all the same: even you do. Words, words like that, yes – what a terrific dust they can still raise in a mind, yours even: I see that. Myself, even, I have needed to immunize myself against them; I tell you I have only at last done that by saying them to myself over and over again till it became absolutely certain they mean nothing. What they once meant is gone. – This is a shock to you, Stella? Or, is it a shock to you?'

She did not answer.

'Anyway, you're against me?'

'You're the one who's against: I've known that without knowing against *what*. Not this country, you say: you say there is no country. Then what are you against?'

'This racket. It's not I who am selling out this what you call a country; how could I? – it's sold itself out already.'

'What racket?'

'Freedom. Freedom to be what? – the muddled, mediocre, damned. Good enough to die for, freedom, for the good reason that it's the very thing which has made it impossible to live, so there's no alternative. Look at your free people – mice let loose in the middle of the Sahara. It's unsupportable – what is it but a vacuum? Tell a man he's free and what does that do to him but send him trying to dive back into the womb? Look at it happening: look at your mass of "free" suckers, your democracy – kidded along from the cradle to the grave. "From the cradle to the grave, save, oh, save!" Do you suppose there's a single man of mind who doesn't realize *he* only begins where his freedom stops? One in a thousand may have what to be free takes – if so, he has what it takes to be something better, and he knows it: who could want to be free when he could be strong? Freedom – what a slaves' yammer! What do they think they are? I'd guarantee to guarantee to every man the exact degree of freedom of which he's capable – I think you'd see that wouldn't carry us very far. As it is, what? As far as what's nothing can be anything freedom's inorganic: it's owed at least to the few of us to have a part in strength. We must have something to envisage, and we must act, and there must be law. We must have law – if necessary let it break us: to have been broken is to have been something.'

'But law – that's just what you break.'

'Nothing I can break is law!'

'What a saying!'

'You think, or really you hope, I'm mad?'

She did not answer.

'At least I am not besotted.'

In something more powerful than the darkness of the room the speaker had become blotted out: there occurred in the listener one of those arrestations of memory which made it impossible to conceive not only what the look on the face might now be but what the face had been, *as* a face, ever. The direction from which the voice came seemed so set back in distance as to be polar; the voice itself was familiar only in more and more intermittent notes: it was as though some undercurrent in it, hitherto barely to be detected, all the time forbidden and inadvertent, had come to the top. He did not speak fast, but the effect was of something travelling at the rate of light between word and word. Now he first drew in an audible breath, then moved: the sounds of physical movement came as a shock, reminding her that he after all was a presence here in the room – feet, their naked soles sucking at place after place across the thick neutral carpet, could be heard walking with a hallucinated precision towards the window. He pulled the curtains back. There was a star-filled two o'clock in the morning sky. Man in outline against the panes, his communication with the order of the stars became not human: she, turning where she lay, apprehensively not raising herself on the pillows, stared also, not in subjection but in a sort of dread of subjection, at the mathematical spaces between the burning bright points. 'Yes, I know,' she said, 'but it is not all so vastly simple as all that.'

She thought or hoped she heard, somewhere between the stars and herself, the hum of a plane tracing its own course; but the sound, if it ever had been a sound, died: nothing intervened. 'Come back to me at any rate for a moment,' she cried out, 'or come nearer.'

He came back, restlessly, to the end of the bed, where he sat down again. 'I've given you any humanity that I had,' he said. 'Don't quarrel now, at the end, or it will undo everything from the beginning. You'll have to re-read me backwards, figure me out – you will have years to do that in, if you want to. You will be the one who will have to see: things may go in a way which may show I was not wrong. – But you hate this too, you hate this most, because I've been apart from you in it, you feel? I have not been: there's been you and me in everything I have done. – You can't see that?'

Tearless, she made a wailing movement of the arms above her head. He waited; she said at last: 'Still, tell me. If you had told me more – !'

'Think again: how could I have involved you? How could I? Was this a thing to put on anyone else? – It was quite a game.'

'Which you loved.'

He reflected, then said: 'Yes – What I mean, though, is that, as has been shown, it was not a safe game: you would have been anxious, I supposed. And again, which surely you ought to see, it was not only a question of myself. In a ring, once any one person begins to talk . . . No, how was I to tell you in so many words?'

'You could have told me not in so many words.'

He again reflected. 'Sometimes I thought I had.'

'When?'

'When not? Not any one moment – but there were times when it seemed impossible that being as we were you should not know. There's been no part of my disaffectedness that

319

I've hidden from you: did it never strike you I'd have been unendurable if I hadn't found some way, that didn't meet the eye, to endure myself? In accepting me, I thought, you must somehow be in your own way accepting this. Or I thought so sometimes – sometimes so much so that I found myself only waiting to speak till you spoke: when you didn't speak I thought you thought silence better. I thought, yes, silence *is* better: why risk some silly unmeaning battle between two consciences? We've seen law in each other . . . There were other times when I was less certain you knew. But I did not know you did not know till you asked me.'

'The night I came back from Ireland?'

'The night you came back from Ireland.'

'*Then*, you said "no" to everything point-blank.'

'You didn't want an answer you couldn't take. That was the night I realized you couldn't take it.'

'You were angry with me.'

'There's a difference between being suspected of being what one is and being accepted as being what one is.'

'That was the night you asked me to marry you.'

'I wanted to see if you were frightened.'

'*You* were frightened.'

'Did I show that to you?'

'You did next day, to Harrison – Why did you always tell me you didn't know him?'

'I didn't know him; I did begin to have some idea who he must be. There'd been always X – who had always had to be *someone*. So it was that funny type . . . You were trying him out on me, then, first, that night we were looking at my tie?'

That small picture, with its concourse of others, made her unknot her hands above her head and begin to weep, the more desperately because of the desperate wastefulness of tears now in face of the end of all. Now it was a question of counting the last of the minutes as they ran out into hours, the last of the hours as they ran out into tomorrow, which was already today, as they never had. All love stood still in one single piercing illusion of its peace, now peace was no more. Unlived time was not more innocent than the time lived by them. Now, by calling him back to her from the window, she had broken the last exaltation of his she might ever feel. Now they had dropped into talking in lowered hurried voices, as though already something were at the door. 'Oh, why did you?' she cried out. 'What made you have to?'

'Stella, don't,' he said sharply, 'don't: you unnerve me!'

'Such ideas to have to have – why?'

'I didn't choose them: they marked me down. They are not mine, anyhow; I am theirs. Would you want me simply to be their prey? Would you want me simply to be a case? Would you have wanted me not to fight this war?'

'No. No, but . . .'

'Then haven't I a right to my own side?' Suddenly stretching across the bed he could be felt feeling about, beside her body for her hand. She gave it, to have its tensile fingers, the jump of nerves in it or whatever the quality was that it had of life, explored by his cold foreign fingers retrospectively: then he put it away from him. 'It was enough,' he said, 'to have been in action once on the wrong side. Step after step to Dunkirk: the extremity – I could forget it if I had not known what it meant. That was the end of *that* war – army of freedom queueing up to be taken off by pleasure boats. Days and nights to think in: does nobody ever wonder what became of the thoughts thought then, or what's still to come to them? The extremity – can they not conceive that's a thing you never do come back from? How many of us do they imagine ever have come back? We're to be avoided – Dunkirk wounded men.'

'I never knew you before you were a wounded man.'

'In one way that would have been impossible – I was born wounded; my father's son. Dunkirk was waiting there in us – what a race! A class without a middle, a race without a country. Unwhole. Never earthed in – and there are thousands of thousands of us, and we're still breeding – breeding what? You may ask: I ask. Not only nothing to hold, nothing to touch. No source of anything in anything. I could have loved a country, but to love you must have – you have been my country. But you've been too much because you are not enough – are you and I to be what we've known we are for nothing, nothing outside this room?'

No answer. Robert had moved again: now he leaned on his elbow across her feet, unwillingly. All she at last said was: 'You've been doing just what Harrison said?'

'Yes. – So you can't get away from that?'

'*We* can't get away from that . . . Were you never frightened?'

'Of getting caught?'

'I meant, of what you've been doing?'

'I? – no, the opposite: it utterly undid fear. It bred my father out of me, gave me a new heredity. I went slow at first – it was stupefying to be beginning to know what confidence could be. To know what I knew, to keep my knowing unknown, unknown all the time to be acting on it – I tell you, everything fell into place around me. Something of my own? – No, no, much better than that: any neurotic can make

322

himself his corner. The way out? – no, better than that: the way on! *You* think, in me this was simply wanting to get my hand on the controls?'

'I don't think I think.'

'Well, it's not; it's not a question of that. Who wants to monkey about? To feel control is enough. It's a very much bigger thing to be under orders.'

'We are all under orders; what is there new in that?'

'Yes, can you wonder they love war. But I don't mean orders, I mean order.'

'So you are with the enemy.'

'Naturally they're the enemy; they're facing us with what has got to be the conclusion. They won't last, but it will.'

'I can't believe you.'

'You could.'

'It's not just that they're the enemy, but that they're hor-rible – specious, unthinkable, grotesque.'

'Oh, *they* – evidently! But you judge it by them. And in birth, remember, anything is grotesque.'

'They're afraid, too.'

'Of course: they have started something.' He raised him-self eagerly on his elbow, as though a thought were renewing in him its whole original power. 'You may not like it, but it's the beginning of a day. A day on our scale.'

Instinctively she glanced first at the window, then at the window's reflection in the mirror: both were paler, it seemed to her eyes of dread. All fears shrank to this cold bare irrefut-able moment: she shivered indifferently between the sheets. It had been terror of the alien, then, had it, all the the time? – and here it was, breathing its expiring minutes, *his* expiring minutes, along the foot of her bed. He might have been right in saying she could not have loved him had there been in him no capacity other than love, but his denials of everything instinctive seemed now to seal up love at the source. Rolled round with rocks and stones and trees – what else is one? – was this not felt most strongly in the quietus of the embrace? 'No, but you cannot say there is not a country!' she cried aloud, starting up. She had trodden every inch of a country with him, not perhaps least when she was alone. Of that country, she did not know how much was place, how much was time. She thought of leaves of autumn crisply being swept up, that crystal ruined London morning when she had woken to his face; she saw street after street fading into evening after evening, the sheen of spring light running on the water towards the bridges on which one stood, the vulnerable eyes of Louie stupidly carrying sky about in them, the raw earth lip of Cousin Francis's grave and the pink-stamened flowers of that day alight on the chestnuts in May gloom, the asphalt pathway near Roderick's camp thrust up and cracked by the swell of ground, mapped by seeded grass. She could remember nothing before, everything had had this poignancy – and yet they had only been in love for two years. She could not believe they had not, in those two years, drawn on the virtue of what was around them, *the* virtue peculiar to where they were – nor had this been less to be felt when she was without him, was where he was not, had not been ever, might never be: a perpetual possible illumination for her, because of him, of everything to be seen or be heard by joy. Inside the ring of war, how peaceably little they had moved – never crossed the sea together, seldom left London – so, there had come to be the nature of Nature, thousands of fluctuations in their own stone country. Impossible that the population, the other people, should at least be less to be honoured than trees walking.

All that time, all the same, the current had been against his face. The war-warmed impulse of people to be *a* people had been derisory; he had hated the bloodstream of the crowds, the curious animal psychic oneness, the human lava-flow. Even the leaden unenthusiasm, by its being so common, so deeply shared, had provoked him – and as for the impatiences, the hopes, the reiteration of unanswerable questions and the spurts of rumour, he must have been measuring them with a calculating eye. The half-sentence of the announcer's voice coming out of a window at News hour, the flopping rippling headlines of Late Night Final at the newsvendor's corner – what nerve, what nerve in reverse, had they struck on in him? Knowing what he knew, doing what he did. Idly, more idly than all the others doing the same thing, in the streets with her he had thieved the headline out of the corner of his eye, without a break in their talk, with a hiatus in his long pitching step so slight as to be registered by her only through their being arm-in-arm in the falling evening. She now saw his smile as the smile of one who has the laugh.

It seemed to her it was Robert who had been the Harrison.

'This is some malady of yours,' she said. 'How dare you say I have been in what you have done? The more I understand it the more I hate it. You're determined, then, to be on the winning side?'

'You're thinking of your brothers? Thinking what was good enough for them, honour, ought to be good enough for me? I love your laughing photographs. They were lucky to die before the illusion had broken down – *this* is not a troubadours' war, Stella. They took what they had with them:

they were the finish. But, face it – we're left to go on living in a world which where all *that's* concerned, is as dead as the moon. In you there may persist some spark of what's everywhere else gone out: who knows why else I've loved you? Through love you've lit me – don't quarrel now with which way the fire blows. There've never been such winds as there are today, or from such directions.'

'Roderick may be killed.'

He said automatically: 'I don't think so.'

'Oh, then it's to be over as soon as *that*? The end, as soon as *that*?'

He looked at the luminous dial of his watch, then said: 'I shan't have any part in it – I suppose, now?'

'Why do you ask me?' she asked.

'I was only wondering.'

'You and I met the year France fell – For us here, for everyone here, *what* – if everything goes to plan? By now not, evidently, invasion. So what worse, what instead? What end?'

'Who am I to say?'

'You say you know what you know.'

'But that's all I do know. – Where are you going?'

She had got out of bed, had drawn up her heavy quilted dressing-gown from the floor and was unsteadily binding it with the cord round her. Without answering, she was groping over the panels of the door: having as an afterthought turned the handle she followed the opening door through into the other room, in which he was not. She switched on a lamp, but then stood recoiling from it, fingers over her eyes. She had then to turn and the door shut behind her, so that lamplight from here should not travel through to the bedroom window Robert had uncurtained. In her infestation by all ideas of delinquency any offence against the black-out seemed to her punishable by death: it could be the signal moment for which Harrison had been waiting – posted as he could be, as she pictured him, by some multiplication of his personality all round the house. Since Robert *was* what Harrison had said, Harrison himself must be what he said he was – it was something to be sure, she thought, pacing about the room, chafing together the icy palms of her hands. The room had the look of no hour: she contemplated everything in it round her in an insupportable nervous blankness of mind.

It was as impossible to be away from Robert as to be with him: she came to a stop in front of the photograph. He was right: there could be no family likeness here – her brothers had left no trace. They had been made heroes while things were simple: heroes were the creatures of a simplicity now gone, he said. But had they left *no* trace – the revulsion in her against his act? The sale of the country . . . She looked at this photograph, on this chimneypiece, of the man in the other room, at the black-and-white of what was for ever dissolved for her into the features of love – at the same time, they were the mould of what? Twisted inspiration, a sort of recalcitrance in the energy, romanticism fired once too often. The face of a late-comer. He had been right: time makes the only fatal differences of birth. He was right: it was not for her brothers or their sister to judge him.

She turned the photograph to the wall, in order to try to picture life without him. At the look of that blank white back of the mount the ice broke; she had to hold on to the chimneypiece while she steadied her body against the beating of her heart – so violent that it seemed to begin again with cruel accumulated force. She tried to say 'Robert!' but had no voice. She looked at the door: it was incredible that anyone loved so much should be still behind it.

The door opened: he stood against the darkness in the dressing-gown Roderick had worn. 'Yes?' he said – then, when she did not answer: 'I thought you called me.'

They were in each other's arms.

If there were any step in the street of sleeping houses, it was impossible it should now be heard by the two blotted out. To anyone silently posted down there in the street, the ranks of windows reflecting the paling sky would have all looked the same: it was in this room that an eyelid came down over the world. Behind their heads the photograph, bent into unaccustomed reverse, at last fell forward, then fell to the floor; but it was some time before Stella started. Her hands slipped from his shoulders slowly down his arms.

'I should never have let you come here.'

'I should have come.'

'This would be the first place they –'

'I should still have come. Last night at Holme Dene I was in terror – terror of never seeing you again. That began to come over me the minute I was in the house; began to come to a head the first time the telephone rang. Till then I'd only known I was in danger: I'd never felt it. Must have been the effect of that house, them! What a place to be taken in, to be taken away from – *theirs* to be the last faces I saw! I never had pictured arrest before: then all at once I pictured it only that way – it not only seemed the one way it could happen, equally it seemed absolutely impossible it should not happen, because here the scene was, set. My mother had been waiting for this; she wished it! It would be they who had got me into

328

the trap, so that I should never see you again. It never suited them that I should be a man.'

'Then they noticed?'

'I don't know. I gave Anne the jitters.'

'Anne? But I thought it was late at night.'

'She came downstairs.'

'Poor Anne. But when you did get back to London, why didn't you come to me? It would have been no madder last night than this.'

'How could I? Look what I'd done to Anne. How could I come to you in that state? I wore it off by walking – if I *was* tailed I gave somebody quite a run, but I don't think so.'

'All night?'

'No; I thought "Oh, the hell!", got back I don't know when, slept it out, must have slept it off: because again this morning, having my bath, drinking coffee, shaving, the whole thing looked like a hallucination.'

'You knew it wasn't; you knew it couldn't be.'

Robert walked down the room and threw himself on to the sofa on which Roderick had slept. Driving one hand down into the pocket of the dressing-gown, the pocket in which Roderick had found the paper, he dropped back his head and stared at the ceiling. 'What I've been doing's not mad,' he said, 'but it may breed a madness of one kind: you feel secure. Somehow you feel encased. Quite soon danger loses the smell it had for you – you know it's there, but only because you know it must be there. You know it's its business to shift its angle, and you watch: but it does not seem to renew itself or to renew its hold on you, like love does. Before you know what's happened it's an abstraction. – And again, too, when danger's inherent in what one's doing it comes to seem an attribute of one's own – a sort of secret peculiarity one can keep in play. To be a man in secret gets to be like being a sort of celebrity in reverse: being set apart from people becomes familiar . . . Yes, of course in theory I've known there *were* other brains, brains against me – the essential of what I've done has been to have to be careful; and I have been careful. Careful? – the thing has come to be second nature with me: never let up, night or day. I've never been off my guard – have I?'

'As far as I know,' she said, sitting down on a chair in the middle of the room, 'no.'

'So I thought. And yet at the same time, all this time, it's been becoming more and more inconceivable to me that this *could* happen. – You'd say, loss of sense of reality? You could be in one way right – I could only do what I've done so intensively that outside it there came to be nothing else – it *could* be done, is being done, better in other ways; but not by me. To be done as it should, it may be this thing should be done for money – ought they to mistrust the man they don't find it necessary to buy? I acted, *I* thought I acted, in cold blood – but not, not cold enough, apparently; or it warmed. No fascination, absolute incapacity to *be* fascinated – that ought to be the test. Yes, and they ought to bar the man who's looking for an answer. Bound to be something rocky about the man who touches a thing like this for its own sake, *his* own sake. If he were only a danger to himself it wouldn't matter; but it does matter. They'll know another time . . . I wonder what I did; what I did not think of?'

'It could be some other mistake, somewhere. A mistake of one of the others – you tell me there are the others? Somebody you were seen with.'

'I ought never to have been seen – How's Harrison?'

'If I had slept with him, *could* he have kept you out of this?'

'What, did he say so? Naturally he would say so. You didn't try?'

'I thought I would, last night, but he sent me home.'

'You left it pretty late,' was his comment, abstractedly looking at her.

'I couldn't believe him.'

'Couldn't you?'

'I couldn't make up my mind to, till last night. Why *then* should I? Because last night he accused me of having done what he'd warned me not to, for your sake: spoken to you. Knowing I had, and when, I asked, what made him think so? Oh, he didn't think so, he said: he could be certain. How? From his having watched you do exactly what he had said you'd do, and do instantaneously, if I warned you – give yourself away. Apparently the day after we'd talked you made some specific change in your movements; some change you would only make from momentary loss of nerve. So, to watch you was to see you'd learned you were watched. He volunteered to tell me the night I spoke. So I took him up. He said, the night I got back from Ireland. So then I saw.'

'I see. He's not so stupid, is he? One might have thought he knew me – What's *he* like?'

'I have less and less idea.'

'And gets I wonder what money? Considering, not so much; they none of them get so much; as against which they're on the safer side. – But, again, look, considering what we know – after all, *is* he worth to them what he does get? He sounds to me crazy, riding for a fall. I mean to say, coming to

331

you like that. What a chance to take! What was to stop you turning the story in?'

'He knew me, too, I imagine.'

'Still, you conceivably might have, which would have been the end of him.'

'Yes; but he told me that would be the end of you.'

'Any cigarettes in here?' he said abruptly. 'I left mine on your bed.'

She got up to look unexpectedly in the box: usually she kept no cigarettes in it, but tonight a packet of Players was wedged inside – she could only think the Players must have been left behind by Harrison when he came to call for her, and stowed in here by the charwoman next morning. Having shaken the packet to make certain it was not a deception, she brought the spoils to the sofa: Robert lit one for her, one for himself. They inhaled, looking at one another calmly, and said nothing. Extended at full length, narrow and Byzantine in the dressing-gown, he let one hand fall on her knee as she sat on the sofa by him. Once he rolled his head round in the direction of the uncurtained window overlooking the street; however, nothing gave any sign.

'What is it you are, then,' she said at last, 'a revolutionary? No, counter-revolutionary? You think revolutions are coming down in the world? Once, they used to seem an advance, each time – you think *not* that, any more, now? After each, first the loss of what had been gained, then the loss of more? So that now revolution coming could only be the greatest convulsion so far, with the least meaning of all? Yet nobody can rid themselves of the idea that *something's* coming. What is this present state of the world, then – a false pregnancy?'

'No.'

'No, I see you couldn't think that, or you wouldn't have . . . You know, Robert, for anybody *doing* anything so definite, you talk vaguely. Wildness and images. That may have been my bringing my feeling in. But to me it's as though there still were something you'd never formulated.'

'This is the first time I've ever talked.'

'Never talked to the others – the others you're in this with?'

'You imagine we meet to swap ideas?'

'But then in that case, all the more you've thought.'

'All the more I've thought. More and more the outcome of thinking because you never can talk is never *to* talk. The thing isolating you isolates itself. It sets up a tension you hope may somehow break itself, but that you can't break. You don't know where thought began; it goes round in circles. *Talk* has got to begin – where? How am I to know how to talk, after so much thought? Any first time, is one much good? Unformulated – what was?'

'I don't know. Or perhaps, missing?'

'How am I to know what's missing in my own thought? I'm committed to it. What did you want, then – brass tacks?'

She did not seem certain, half shook her head, but then amended: 'Though they are always something.' Embarrassed by the naïvety of the question, she said: 'You are out for the enemy to win because you think they have something? What?'

'They have something. This war's just so much bloody quibbling about some thing that's predecided itself. Either side's winning would stop the war; only their side's winning would stop the quibbling. I want the cackle cut – Well, what have I still not said?'

333

'I still don't know,' she said, taking the burned-down stump of the cigarette from between his fingers. 'Never mind.'

'Never mind then, sweetheart.'

'I wish we could sleep,' she said.

'*What* is Harrison doing?' Robert suddenly said, in the tone of somebody asking something he probably did or should know but had forgotten. 'What's he meaning to do? Just now you said something: say that again. In the end, what is he out after – nothing but to make you? I can't get him.'

'He cannot see why everything should not be arranged; it seems to him a fair deal and he's obsessed by it – or was. As to what he does expect to get out of it I can't think. He says he knows what he wants; I suppose he wants what he doesn't know. He likes it here,' she added, looking round her at the extinct pretty room. 'Likes the ash trays, for instance: he's always fingering things. That may be it, really: he wants to live here.'

'Live with you?'

'Live here with me. The uneasier he is the happier he is. He cannot see any objections, or see how I can. And yes, there's more than that – he's convinced I am really doing you a mean, bad turn by saying "no" to him, or at any rate by not saying "yes". He has quite a feeling for you.'

'That could be, I suppose.'

'He has you at heart – it's inconceivable to him that a man wouldn't rather have his immunity – a clean sheet to get on with what he wants to – than any woman. How can I not sometimes ask myself if he mayn't be right? At the same time, look at the contradiction – by his showing, he's continually trading in his own safety for the purpose of getting me . . . Tonight I see, I *should* have taken a chance on it. But that that was to have to mean, outright, the end of you and me he did from the outset make quite brutally clear. If I had been certain, if I had been certain! Last night, when I was certain, I . . . But then, he turned round and sent me home.'

'I wish we knew why. What was in the wind?'

'I had hurt his feelings.'

'Nonsense. He must have had something else to do.'

She was silent.

'Sent you home from where?' he said, searchingly looking at her. 'Where had you got to with him? Where were you?'

'I don't know, Robert!' she cried, distractedly slipping down from the sofa to kneel beside it. 'I forgot to ask. It might have been anywhere; even a girl we met there thought she was somewhere else. I'd been rattled from the beginning of the evening by Roderick's suddenly ringing up; but if I'd had any idea what Harrison was going to come out with I'd have kept my head; I can keep my head. – As it was, what do you imagine I came back here to, after he'd sent me home? I lay all night wondering what he had meant to do, what he might or might not have done if I'd been different, what he'd be doing next. Not knowing whether he ever really had meant to stop things taking their course, not knowing whether that had ever, really been in his power. Wondering whether that had once been in his power, when first he put the thing up to me, but now no longer was. Asking myself what really he *had* been up to, these last two months, and whether my always keeping on hedging, stalling, had made him angrier than he'd shown. Whether his having thrown me back in my own face meant he had, all at once, out of anger, decided to let things ride. Whether what Harrison had decided or not decided did matter, ever had mattered, really? Whether, knowing last

335

night that things were taking their course, outside his control, his idea was to save his face? The fascination for him in this thing with me could have been so much less me than himself his own all-powerfulness – a one-sided love's unnatural: there must be vice in it somewhere. If so, he would see my "yes", at *that* point, only in one way: my having called his bluff. Not that he might jib at breaking a bargain – me his: a new lease of safety for you – but, what value could I have left for him once he'd watched me see he couldn't do what he'd said? Very little, odiously little, none . . . But then I went all the way back again: I *had* hurt his feelings. If you can't conceive those you can't conceive what he is. In the end that's what makes him a dangerous man.'

Twisting round on the carpet beside the sofa, doubling into the bulky quilted folds of her dressing-gown, Stella buried her face in the cushions stacked under Robert's head. He, in the gathered stillness of someone resolved to move in a moment more, lay a moment longer staring up at the ceiling. She, in a muffled voice, ended up: 'So you see, I've no idea how we left it.'

'What? – can't hear you.'

She repeated: 'I've no idea how we left it.'

The expression on those lips of hers was familiar – its many contexts, vagrant, social, so very much not mattering, had become too many for him to count. It had come as the end, or rather the fading-out, of so many stories at the end of so many days; or, as a sort of confession as to why many stories, now that she came to tell them, had no ending. So much had had to be left in the air, so often, that her manner of saying so, every time, always had the same intonation – of fatalism of fleeting but true regret. She had been given the slip once more. 'I've no idea how we left it.' Ineffectual little expression, blent of boredom and chagrin, it had become conventional; but, at the same time, a sort of convention or shorthand of lovers' talk, stamped with a temperament and endeared by use. She had said this so many times: again it was said tonight – and the monstrous, life-and-death disproportion between tonight's context and all that host of others did not, could not, stand out as it should. She did not sound, so could not seem to be feeling, very much more inadequate than she ever had felt. Which was enough to make Robert laugh.

He laughed as it would have been possible to weep, thrown round towards her on an elbow driven into glissading cushions. It was a laughter of the entire being, racking as it was irregular in its intakes upon his body, making his face a mask of shut eyes and twisting lips, convulsing the rest of him in a sort of harmony of despair at the situation and joy in her. The sofa shook – she clung to its scrolled end as though in a high gale. 'Why?' she cried, 'what is the matter – what?' Not letting go of the sofa, she put out her other hand; which he, by immediately catching at and holding by its wrist to his breast, used to establish a sort of circuit for the joke or agony. She under this compulsion began to laugh too, though rebelliously, with bewilderment and uncertainty: it was only by laying her cheek to his, as though either to extinguish the laughter by sheer weight or draw out of him into her its unholy cause, that she comprehended. She then had to laugh entirely. 'I see,' she admitted, drawing a sob of breath, 'I see how it sounded. But that was how it was.'

At once the laughter left him. 'What a position I've put you in, all the same!' He sprang up from the sofa – 'Anyway, I must dress!'

337

'Going?' she said dully. 'But there might be someone out-side the door. We must think of that.'

'I have been thinking of that. There has been a step.'

She, tracing back by touch her one white lock of hair, said: 'When has there been a step?'

'Every now and then.'

'Every now and then?' She went to the nearer window, to stand, white face to the white curtain, arguing: 'I didn't hear. And if it had been his step I should have heard it; in fact, I should have known it before I heard it. I wonder . . .'

'Stella! Don't touch the curtain!'

'I wasn't going to – was I?'

'I thought you were.'

'I wanted to. Wanted to crash the window open and blaze the lights on. To think of him makes me angry – I wanted to say: "Yes, here we are, together: what else do you suppose?"'

'If he is down there, that's why he *is* down there. Imagine it's being gay for him, with his thoughts?'

'It's we who must think,' she said, turning from the window.

'Think away,' said Robert, shrugging his shoulders. His clothes were over a chair; already he was beginning to dress quickly: she remained, arms folded, leaning against a corner of the chimneypiece, intently blindly watching him, saying: 'I could always let you out at the back, down through the basement into the yard. There would be walls round that, but would they be such high walls? There would be the care-takers, but they would be asleep.'

'If there's somebody at the front there could be somebody at the back,' he said, dressing so mechanically that he seemed indifferent.

'No; that could depend on who the somebody at the front is. Whether it's Harrison or not.'

'Why?'

'He's in love: I live here. He could have followed you here. He could be watching the house for his own reasons: people torment themselves.'

'That doesn't alter the fact that he's what he is.'

'What is anyone? Mad, divided, undoing what they do. You were mad to come here. I told you on the telephone, as plainly as I dared to word it, not to – not on any account.'

'But you expected me.'

'I was waiting for you somehow to get in touch with me, to say where else to meet. We could have met somewhere else.'

'If I *am* tailed, what matter where I go? Somewhere else – where else? Some street corner?'

'We could have talked.'

'Yes, we could have talked. But what do you suppose I thought in my mother's house? – that I'd never be in your arms again. What do you suppose I had to make sure of? That. That, then to tell you. Because yes, that too I saw, in my mother's house – you left to wonder, to hear, to not believe, to have to believe, to never know why. So, to tell you. I came here to tell you, even if you had not asked. Why not the telling first? How was I to know that might not lose me the other? Better the last of a love in ignorance than no love, no love in knowledge.'

'But there could have been that.'

'Yes? Tonight, yes. But there may be a thing that's too much to go on knowing. A thing not meant to be known – too much to live with, to love in the face of, under the everlasting weight of. How do we know we haven't both known this was that? Dared we ever have come to the point of breaking silence if we had not known this was good-bye? Better to say good-bye at the beginning of the hour we never have had, then it will have no end – best of all, Stella, if you can come to remember what never happened, to live most in the one hour we never had. – Because now I must go,' he added, dressed, looking quickly round him to make sure he had forgotten nothing. She recollected one thing, picked up his dressing-gown and gave him his lighter out of the pocket. He corrected himself – 'Or, try to go. I do want to make it, I want to make it – my ideas, you know, are too good to be merely died for: they want life. – Did you once say there was a way out on to the roofs?'

'Yes, the landing skylight; it's been trap-doored ever since I've been in the flat, but they showed me how I could get out that way if I were cut off by a fire, or to put out incendiaries. There's that ladder that lets down on a pulley. Oh Robert, you must have seen it every night!'

'Show me.'

'But –' she began unbearably.

'Very well, what?' he cried, wheeling round.

'What do we know for certain? He may have kept his mouth shut. None of this may be true.'

'Then no harm's done: what a laugh on the roof! Either this is nothing or it's the pay-off. I don't think it's nothing – you *were* right, I had no business to come: I should have thought of you. What else should it be but this? My time's run right out; I'm watched and they know I'm wise: you know that better than I do – use your reason. Think as much as you like, but for God's sake let me get out of here while it's still dark – Do *you* want me taken?'

'Then they'd think of everything we could think of?'

'Yes, that would be up to them. Why?'

'Then there could be somebody on the roof.'

'There's one great thing about a roof; there's one way off it.'

She stood for two or three seconds, then said: 'The roof's steep. I wish you hadn't got your stiff knee.'

'I wish I hadn't had my stiff knee. We've never danced, for instance. . . . If by any chance this did have to finish that way, you wouldn't have wanted anything else for me, would you? You'd know if it came to that there could only have been one other thing, the alternative?'

'Having to face it out. . . .'

'I could. Should I? Would you be ashamed of me? Not while I was not ashamed of myself. . . . But what a stink, though, Stella – think, Stella: what a stink for you all!'

'Terrible for Ernestine,' she said, turning away her face, thinking, it is the awful ones who are the little ones one must not offend.

'There may not be anyone on the roof: it's fifty-fifty. I still somehow think I'll make it. I want to go by the roof.'

'Where are you expecting to get down again?' she said, with a light sudden curious release of her natural voice.

He repeated: 'I want to go by the roof – I don't want to run out; I want you to send me off.'

'Come on, then,' she said, in no more time than it took to draw the breath, 'we'll let down the ladder.' They went hurriedly out through the little hall of the flat, turned on the landing light overhanging the shaft of staircase and began to unwind from its staple the pulley-rope of the ladder, which from its hinge under the blinded skylight came down towards them slowly. Robert looked up it: 'Now we'll soon see,' he said. He went up it at the most eager speed compatible with the unequal action of the stiff knee, then heaved with his shoulder against the skylight, which gave: he came down again far enough to kiss her. 'Take care of yourself,' he hurriedly said. 'Now turn off the light and get back into the flat and shut the door.'

She turned off the light. 'Good night,' she said in the dark. 'Good night.'

She went back into the flat and shut the door.

In the street below, not so much a step as the semi-stumble of someone after long standing shifting his position could be, for the first time by her, heard.

16

That day whose start in darkness covered Robert's fall or leap from the roof had not yet fully broken when news broke: the Allied landings in North Africa. Talk was of nothing else. Nor had the quickening subsided when Montgomery's Order of the Day to the Eighth Army – 'We have completely smashed the German and Italian armies' – became the order of yet another day for London. There came the Sunday set for victorious bell-ringing: throughout the country every steeple was to break silence. When at last it came, the bells' sound was not as strange or momentous as had been expected: after everything these were still the bells of the former time, climbing, striving, searching round in the air in vain for some still not to be found new note. All that stood out in cities were unreverberating lacunae where there were churches gone. At the beginning, the invitation to rejoice brought out a few people into the sunless November morning streets, as though the peals and crashes were a spectacle to be watched passing: eyes for a moment seemed to perceive a peculiar brightness. Soon, however, even before the bells had come to a climax, people began turning away from the illusion, either because it had already begun to fade or because they knew it must. There was a movement indoors again: doors and windows shut.

Louie had anticipated the bells in heart ever since she heard they were to be rung; but when it came to their hour they rang false – she heard them dry-eyed; she should have been hearing the bells of home, the bells from Seale hill over the open marsh and sea. Connie, early that morning, had intercepted the Sunday papers on her way out to the post, therefore no other directive for feeling was to be found – Louie sought refuge in the streets, looking in this and that direction in hopes of a crowd moving any one way. This led her to nothing better than isolation, ever more at a loss, on an island in the middle of Marylebone Road. Then it was that she decided to view in daylight the street in which she had said good night to Stella – there, she could be certain, *someone* in London lived. She bent her steps that way not knowing exactly with what in mind. But to enter Weymouth Street was to quail at the unspeakingness of its expensive length. She had had no notion that Mrs Rodney lived so far from her; and, worse, it was impossible to be certain at the foot of which of those flights of steps they had said good-bye – for good-bye and nothing but that, she now saw it was. The chattering variation of the architecture, from house to house, itself seemed to cheat and mock her – she looked at Dutch-type gables, bronze-grilled doors, leaded casement, gothic projecting bays, balconies, discrepantly high parapets, outwitted. Outwitted, but only just – for, anything ever to be remembered here would be never, never to be forgotten. One unity, this morning, the empty Sunday street had, up and down its length – the sunless toneless reverberation, from planes of distance, of the victory bells. *That* could but be being heard – from behind which window out of this host of windows? – by Mrs Rodney. Louie stood still to listen again, in company.

She stood face up, one hand instinctively grasping one of the spearheads of railings topping an area, as though to bridge, for ever, in some memory of the body's, the sound and scene. But then instantaneously she was struck, pierced, driven forward into a stumbling run by anguish – *an* anguish, striking out of the air. She looked round her vainly, blindly, for her assailant. Flee? – no, she was clutched, compelled, forbidden to leave the spot. She remained pacing to and fro, to and fro, like a last searcher for somebody said to be still alive, till the bells stopped,

The street had again been empty for some hours when Stella came out of a door and down steps not far from where Louie had stood. This was the afternoon she had promised to visit Roderick, and there appeared no reason to change the plan. She made her way across London to the right station and took the right train. It was a slow train, one-class, made up of old stock, departing from a remote platform, crowded out of the way of anything more important on to a by-line, even so halting diffidently between its many stops. Sunday short-distance travellers getting in and out, in and out of the carriage in which sat Stella found themselves being eyed with a sort of frozen attention by the woman in the corner; they shared an uneasy feeling that she was for some reason trying to learn their faces. She seemed to be someone for the first time finding herself alone among humanity. At the same time, the conveyance of that look of hers from one to another face was to be taken as the one sign of life: otherwise this person sat like an image, upright against the grime-impregnated tapestry of the compartment, dead gloved hands crossed in her lap, palms up. There were movements, between its being a look at faces, when the look became not a look at all; but then invariably, as though in recoil from its own abeyance, it

345

would turn to the window, taking the head with it. This was always so at the many unaccountable, meaninglessly fateful stops between the stations: sometimes there was to be found nothing more speaking than embankments of bleached, soiled, already wintry grass; but sometimes Stella was fortunate in being able to see through railings or over fences not only yards and gardens but right into back windows of homes. Prominent sculleries with bent-forward heads of women back at the sink again after Sunday dinner, and recessive living-rooms in which the breadwinner armchair-slumbered, legs out, hands across the eyes, displayed themselves; upstairs, at looking-glasses in windows, girls got themselves ready to go out with boys. One old unneeded woman, relegated all day to where she slept and would die, prised apart lace curtains to take a look at the train, as though calculating whether it might not be possible to escape this time. Children turned out to play went through with the mime of it, dragging objects or pushing one another up and down short paths where vegetables had not been able to be sown. It was striking how listlessly, shiftlessly and frankly life in these houses – and what else was life but this? – exposed itself to the eyes in the passing or halting trains: eyes to be taken, one could only suppose, to be blinded by other preoccupations. It was not to be taken into account that from any one train there should be looking any one pair of eyes which had no other preoccupation, no other resort, nothing: eyes themselves exposed for ever to what they saw, subjected to whatever chose to be seen.

Though she had many times made this journey, she did not seem to know how soon, at what point along the line, she should be beginning to be expecting to get out; she was therefore forced to listen intently each time the name of a station was being called. Someone in the carriage remarked that if bells could be rung again he did not see why names should not be written up – who were we hiding from now? It was a disgrace. In the end, Stella only was made to realize she was arriving by the sight of Roderick, accompanied by the still taller Fred, on the platform: her carriage ran past them slowly and they saw her. Fred, with a nod to Roderick, thereupon made off quickly. The train stopped; Stella got out and was kissed by her son.

'Where's Fred gone?' she asked.

'He only came to the station,' Roderick continued to hold her arm as they walked down the platform. 'I'm so glad you came,' he said. 'I wondered whether you would. It's very good of you, Mother.'

'Why, because Robert's dead?' she asked, showing her ticket at the barrier.

'Perhaps it is better for you having something to do. I had been wondering what you'd most rather *I* did. I decided I'd leave it and see if you came today; but then, if not, somehow to get to London to you. I was anxious about you. What I'd have liked best, when I heard, would have been to go to you there at once. *Would* you have liked that? Only not knowing what you would really like stopped me. Because a man always does get off comparatively light when he beats it off home because of some bad news; though of course what they invariably do say is, why on earth instead of losing his head and taking the law into his own hands didn't he apply for compassionate leave, which would under the circumstances almost certainly have been granted.'

'Darling Roderick . . . I don't think it would have been granted under these circumstances.'

347

'I know how I could have put it; in fact I was going to put it that way if it came to the point – I should have put it that you and Robert were engaged. Because you easily could have been, I should think. – *Would* you have liked me to?'

'No,' she said, shaking her head but wearing the smile suddenly granted her by his love. 'For one thing, I should have been out at work; one cannot stay away if one's not ill. And, no. No, there would have been nothing for you to do.'

'Was there anything for you to do, Mother?'

'No, nothing. No, as far as I remember there wasn't anything.'

'I was so afraid that . . . Nobody came and bothered you?'

She opened her handbag, took out her handkerchief, touched her lips with it. After which: 'Where shall we go?' she said.

'Yes, that's what I've been wondering.' Roderick looked about at what was outside the station, which did not so far offer any solution. 'How would it be if we simply went to the café and sat down quietly? It isn't exactly time for tea yet, but we've been there so often that I don't suppose they'd mind us just sitting down, especially as I imagine almost nobody else will be waiting to sit there till it *is* tea-time.'

'No, let's walk first,' she said. She guided Roderick's look in the direction of the asphalt field-path she had seen in her mind's eye while she was still with Robert. 'Let's walk that way.'

The path obliquely ran across exhausted grassland offered for building: the offer remained open; the board was down – that there *was* to be building here you could never doubt. This that met the eye was the merest ghostly lingering of a landscape, gone by now if it had not been for the war. The recalcitrant swell of earth which had cracked the path would present not more than a moment's difficulty to the sinkers of foundations, however shallow. Meanwhile, the path led, ahead of the walkers, in the direction of a thin line of poplars, beyond which, one seemed to remember, was a foot-bridged brook. For some reason, because she thought of the path *as* running, she envisaged all else as standing still; so it was with surprise that, from half-way across the bridge she saw motion, more fateful for being slow, in the disks of scum and the shreds of froth on the clayey water below her. Pausing to rest her hands on the rail, she wondered what the hazards of navigation would be for a paper boat, was passed through by an impulse to fold, launch one, recollected that there was now nothing for which the boat's fortune could be an augury, but all the same turned to Roderick with her lips apart, reassembling her sharing of his childhood in her glance. But for Roderick, on the bridge beside her, this moment had a quite different sense – some sort of assuagement or satisfaction at her having rested even so much of her as her hands, for however short a time, on even this bar of unknowing wood. His pity, speaking to her out of the stillness of his face, put her in awe of him, as of a greater sufferer than herself – no pity is ignorant, which is pity's cost. She perceived him as knowing in whole the sorrow of which she, still, knew less than her little part. More than Robert's death was there in Roderick's face; the world weighed down for this instant upon this single soul. She shrank from her son as might an unavailing friend – she set herself to counting the disks of foam being sucked from sight slowly under the bridge.

She asked: 'You heard the bells, here, this morning?'

'I don't think so; I don't know where bells are, here. Fred mentioned yesterday evening that there was some rumour that they'd got to be rung; he said in that case they would be something completely new to his sister's baby. – You didn't mind Fred's coming to the station? He said he would like to, as a mark of respect.'

'You and Fred haven't looked at the Sunday papers?'

'No, I don't think so. Why?'

Stella did not answer.

'I naturally,' Roderick went on, 'told Fred something, but not what it was exactly. I think he thinks there's been some-body killed in battle.'

'Well, there has been – Roderick, I said I would come today because you wanted me to tell you about your father.'

'Yes. Still, I don't think we need talk about him today, now.'

'Just as you like: but I do not mind what I talk about. If anything, I should rather like to tell you the story now that I am beginning to understand it.'

'Just as you like, Mother; anything you'd like – but today *I'd* rather not talk about my father.' He restlessly turned away his head, looking along the shabby continuation of the path; he struck the bridge rail with an authoritatively childish gesture of dismissal – making the vibration jump through her hands. '*He* really is dead,' he said. 'After all, it was Cousin Francis who's given me my house; and with you I can only connect Robert. Cousin Nettie's bringing my father out like that may have just shown how determined she is to be mad. How is one even to know he'd have wanted that? How am I even to know he was my father? He went away.'

'Very well then, Roderick; then let's leave that story.'

'Wistaria Lodge is really the only place for anybody knowing so much that does not matter. It was stupid of me to mix myself up with that. I've kicked myself,' he said sadly, 'for ringing you up like that – but how could I know what was just going to happen?'

'Very well then, Roderick.'

'Mother?' he said suddenly.

'Yes?'

'Do you really not mind what we talk about?'

'No. No.'

'What *was* Robert doing on the roof?'

Once more she touched her lips with her handkerchief – a timid widowed habit which had come out in her only that afternoon: the white cambric bore a series of little pink-red smudges, each fainter; now there was almost no more lipstick left to come off. She then put her arm through Roderick's, as a sign of agreement that, yes, it would be better to leave the bridge. They turned, by the same kind of unspoken agreement, back, retracing the first few of their steps in silence, hearing Sunday afternoon wireless coming across the wasteland from a bungalow. It would have been easy to recline, to become suffused by indifference, to be thankful that all was over – but it was not, yet; the rest was not yet ready to be silence. By delaying her answer she would be giving her answer too much weight. 'That seemed his best way out of my flat,' she said. 'He was expecting to be arrested at any minute.'

'Oh. Why was he? *Could* he have been arrested?'

'Yes, he could have been arrested as a traitor.'

Roderick, turning to her with knitted brows, pondered; then said: 'But was he going to be?'

'That night? I don't actually know. That was what he thought.'

'But why *should* they arrest him as a – as what you said?'

'Because it had all been proved,' she said, remorselessly turning to study her son's face.

'Oh,' said Roderick formally. Changing colour slowly with amazement he added: 'Yes, I see.' They walked till they were out of hearing of the wireless music, she crumpling her handkerchief absently in her hand. 'He must have been pretty brave?' he queried, looking at her for confirmation. 'The other way round, he might have got a V.C., quite likely? . . . In a way, I rather wish I had known.'

She said nothing.

'Because I never have known anybody like that . . . He was on the other side in this war?'

'Yes.'

'He never did seem to me to be living anywhere very particular,' said Roderick. 'You don't think if you had married him it would have given him more of a stake in the country?'

She uttered a sound not unlike a laugh. A party of girls and soldiers swinging in loose formation along the path towards them could but stare: Roderick, head up, cheeks red still, outfaced the party until it had divided, swerved off left and right on to the grass and been left behind. Then: 'I suppose,' he went on, 'everything I try saying must sound ridiculous – no, must be ridiculous? You see, really I haven't got anything that I *can* say. I am so sorry, Mother; because there must be something.'

'No, I don't think there is. In which case, I had no right to tell you. One has no right to tell anybody anything as to which there's nothing to be said: Robert felt that. But you did ask me why he was on the roof.'

'Perhaps I should not have asked? It was what I wanted to know.'

'No, I'm glad you asked. – Because of course there is something to be said. There must be. There's *something* to be said.'

'I know,' said Roderick, knitting his brows again. 'But by me? Why me? After all, who am I?'

'The only person I can tell.' Having come to the end of the path, back again to the point where it branched from the by-road back to the station, they halted. Stella looked across at the agglomeration of buildings which somehow made up this town or village, having no other character than that of being near Roderick's camp. 'I cannot help expecting something from you: I must.'

She left it at that, she thought, as one was free to leave any helpless remark. Roderick, however, drew a deep anxious breath, at the same time disengaging his arm from hers.

'I wish I were God,' he said. 'Instead of which I am so awfully young – that's my advantage. The only hope would have been my having happened to say some inspired thing, but now there hasn't been that I shall be no good for about another fifty years – because all I can do now is try and work this out, which could easily take my lifetime; and by that time you'd be dead. I couldn't bear to think of you waiting on and on and on for something, something that in a flash would give what Robert did and what happened enormous meaning like there is in a play of Shakespeare's – but, must you? If there's something that *is* to be said, won't it say itself? Or mayn't you come to imagine it has been said, even without your knowing what exactly it was? . . . Or are you telling me, then asking me, because I *am* young, and so ought to last on later into time? You want me to be posterity? But then, Robert's dying of what he did will not always

353

be there, won't last like a book or picture: by the time one is able to understand it it will be gone, it just won't be there to be judged. Because, I suppose art is the only thing that can go on mattering once it has stopped hurting? . . . Mother, today I would say anything to comfort you; I do wish I had enough experience – if I could even only see the thing as a whole, like God! . . . As it is, I expect really you know what is best yourself.'

'I expect I do; I know I ought to; I must. – But the thing was, you were an outside person.'

'You do really think I am a person?' asked Roderick. They walked down the by-road into the main street, turning in the direction of the café.

17

There can occur in lives a subsidence of the under soil – so that, without the surface having been visibly broken, gradients alter, uprights cant a little out of the straight. A group of persons, of souls – perhaps not conscious, till now, of so much as being in the same neighbourhood – may thus be affected by one happening. In this case, few outward changes followed on Robert's end – Stella moved across London into another flat, off Victoria Street; Harrison vanished from London; as against which Mrs Kelway and Ernestine refused the offer for Holme Dene and stayed where they were. Roderick, having bestirred himself, obtained his commission in the autumn of 1943. Always working away at the same small factory, Louie lived on at Chilcombe Street under the surveillance of Connie – who, as Civil Defence, found herself returned to the foreground by the renewal of enemy air attacks on London early in 1944.

Internally, tensions shifted. After the night climax in Weymouth Street, Harrison made no move to contact Stella, and she did not know how to contact him: their extraordinary relationship having ended in mid air, she found she missed it – Harrison became the one living person she would have given anything to see. Ultimately, it was *his* silent absence which left her with absolutely nothing. She never, then, was to know what had happened? For, with regard to Robert the silence from behind the scenes never broke: what was most to be noted about his death was its expediency – the country was spared a demoralizing story; everything now could be, and was, hushed up. His death remained, officially, what the coroner found it – misadventure, outcome of a crazy midnight escapade on a roof; to which identification, in the popular mind, of any part of London W I with 'Mayfair' gave colour, odour, scandalous likeness. From Stella, as the woman friend in the luxury flat, were extracted the cogent parts of the inquest evidence. Having replied to questions as to the position of the ladder, the skylight, etc., she answered others.

'He was determined to leave by the roof,' she stated. 'He had the idea that someone he did not name to me had followed us back and was in the street waiting to make trouble . . . I imagine that either he did not wish to give the person the satisfaction of an interview, or that he thought a quarrel outside my door might make embarrassments for me . . . Yes, I have other men friends, I suppose . . . I beg your pardon; I mean *yes,* I have other men friends . . . No, there had never been any incident of that kind . . . No, I cannot tell you whom Captain Kelway may have had in mind: I have no idea. It might have been someone who had been trying to pick a quarrel with him for some other reason . . . No, I cannot suggest any other reason, but one never knows . . . For two years. – Two years and two months: we met in September 1940 . . . Yes, we saw one another frequently . . . Yes, I have always tried to keep some drink in my flat, never to run quite out of it: one needs it . . . Yes, naturally – I beg your pardon, I mean yes . . . No, never heavily . . . I'm afraid I cannot say; I have no idea how much other people do drink . . . No, I don't think I remember any quarrels . . . No, not that night

356

more than any other . . . We were talking about the war . . .
Late? I suppose it was; I suppose we did not notice how
time was passing; the war is a very interesting subject . . .
Yes, I did notice that Captain Kelway was in an excitable
state. Possibly that was because we had been talking about
the war; he had been taken off the active service list since
Dunkirk . . . I cannot say, I'm afraid; I did not notice . . . No,
I do not remember drinking more heavily than usual . . . As
far as I know, absolutely clear: I remember everything . . . Is
it unusual? I have a good memory . . . Off and on: I should
say that the idea of there being somebody in the street outside gained on him as the evening went on . . . As the night
went on, then . . . Yes, I suggested I should go down and
see, but he would not let me . . . I cannot say. He had never
struck me as being subject to hallucinations or delusions at
any other time . . . There may or may not have been: I have
no idea. All I can say is, there was nobody in the street when
I went down later – unless you count his body . . . No, I had
not heard anything: I simply went down . . . I went down
and opened the street door . . . I say, I simply went down.
No, nothing made me: I simply thought I would go downstairs and look out of the door. I don't know why: why does
one do anything? . . . I beg your pardon . . . No, I don't
know how long after: I didn't look at the clock. Two minutes,
five minutes, ten minutes: I don't know. Before that? Simply
waiting about . . . No, not for anything in particular . . . Very
well, then I was not waiting. When he had gone I was simply
there in the room . . . Yes, of course I knew he was doing a
dangerous thing. For a man with a stiff knee it was a particularly dangerous thing to do . . . On the contrary: I made
every attempt to stop him . . . Yes; but what could I do? . . .

I've already said so – I have already described him as being in an excitable state . . . No other occasion in particular; but I suppose everybody is in an excitable state sometimes? . . . By excitable state I mean that he was not taking anything else into consideration . . . The darkness, the steepness of the roofs, the different heights of the houses, and, as I have said, his knee . . . No, I cannot remember whether he was carrying an electric torch: he did not usually . . . Yes, I'm sorry; I agree that that is important. I must withdraw my statement that I remember everything. . . .

'When I found him? What did I think had happened? What I still think – that he had lost his footing . . . Yes, I should describe myself as agitated.

'Yes, since 1940, September 1940 . . . As much as one comes to know about the circumstances of a friend's life in two years, I suppose . . . I am not clear what you mean by "matters of a confidential nature". Naturally we did not discuss his work: I did not expect that . . . Not secretive as to his personal affairs, no. He did not give me the impression of having anything to hide . . . No I should not have thought him likely to have enemies; he was not quarrelsome . . . I agree: it does seem strange. I have no idea why. No, he did not explain. He simply said there was somebody at the door . . . No, he was not exhibiting signs of fear. I imagine that where he was concerned he would have preferred to go down and settle the matter, but that he did not want to make scenes and trouble at that late hour outside my house . . . Of course; that would have been best, but it did not occur to him . . . I cannot remember whether it occurred to me. There was no reason why he should not have remained quietly in my flat until whoever it was, or whoever he thought it was, had gone. I can only say that he did not wish to . . . Possibly. Any argument is agitating . . . Only in so far as I was trying to argue him out of what he was doing. It was not a quarrel . . . Yes, I should agree in calling it the decision of a man in an excitable state . . . No, never. Captain Kelway's behaviour never at any time struck me as abnormal. That night it could have been called abnormal in being unlike itself. Normally he would have been the last person to do an ill-judged thing . . . Yes, for some months. In fact he had not long been out of hospital when I met him . . . Only for his knee. No, there had been no question of psychiatric treatment . . . I noticed nothing. I suppose one cannot say what might be the delayed effects of strain or shock . . . No, he gave me no reason to think he had money troubles . . . I've already said, he never gave me the impression of having anything of any kind on his mind . . . I don't quite understand that question – am I to take it you want to know whether I think he went out on to the roof with the intention of taking his own life? . . . I'm sorry: I thought that was what you did mean . . . I do not know what his intentions were. He may have hoped to find a fire escape down the back of one of the other houses; he may have expected to be able to open the sky-light of another house and make his way down through that house, and so out . . . I should say he regarded the whole thing as a good idea, a joke, a way of outwitting the person trying to make trouble . . . Very well: the person he imagined to be there trying to make trouble . . . No, I did not. I have already said that I did not . . . When he had gone, I remained in my flat till I went downstairs. I went downstairs, opened the door, went out into the street. I then saw he had fallen . . . I cannot remember . . . Thank you.'

She left the coroner's court with one kind of reputation, that of being a good witness.

The afternoon of the Sunday of the bell-ringing had been devoted by Louie to an exhaustive reading of the Sunday papers – tossed in, the worse for wear, at her door by Connie, on the latter's way up to the top of the house to sleep. One paper gave a short report of the inquest; two others, however, featured extensive pieces on it. Louie saw Stella's name, re-read her address, and received, in an unbearable flash the import of that street in which *she* had that morning stood. For a moment she wondered whether it might not be Harrison who had fallen, under another name. The ill-fated officer's behaviour, as emerging from the accounts here, seemed to her in its rabid suspiciousness, its unloving ruthlessness and its queerness, to have been that of Harrison exactly – so much so that Louie toured every sensation that, in her, surrounded Harrison's being dead. Its being imperative to pity the dead made her recollect his fruitless frenzy of thought, all alone at the concert that first day. Again she took up the paper – no, but Harrison had *not* a stiff knee! No, every joint of his flexed with an uninteresting smoothness: the side-slip or jerk or jamming was in his manner – which was, she saw, as hastily she returned him to life, chronic. No, he limped no more than he had ever loved. She could not forget the calculated padding un-eager evenness of his walk that evening, after he and she left the concert. It was that bodily monotony of him which, coupled with his recalcitrance, could not but get on any woman's nerves.

All the same, she could not break some connexion between the man one night sitting at the table and the man the next night falling from the roof.

For Louie, subsidence came about through her now knowing Stella not to be virtuous. Virtue became less possible now it was shown impossible by Stella, less to be desired because Stella had not desired it enough. Why Louie should have attached her own floating wish to a face watched for an hour cannot be said: there must be faces which attract aspiration just as others focus sensuous dreams – what else had happened originally in the case of Harrison? Louie had felt herself to be in a presence. For her, therefore, now it was Stella who had fallen into the street.

It was the blanks in Louie's vocabulary which operated inwardly on her soul; most strongly she felt the undertow of what she could not name. Humble and ambiguous, she was as unable to name virtue as she had been, until that sudden view of Harrison's companion, to envisage it. Two words she *had*, 'refinement', 'respectability', were for her somewhere on the periphery. In search of what should make for completeness and cast out fear she indistinctly saw virtue as the inverse of sex: at the same time, somehow, it had distress, of one kind or another, as its sublime prerogative. – Had not Louie herself felt a distress in Stella, owing to Harrison? Now she looked back she saw, yes, there *had* also been fear, nay, terror – but, the qualitative pureness of the terror had made it seem to her pure morally. During their dark walk home Stella had given the impression of being a soul astray – but how, it had seemed for the period of illusion, should she not be? What indeed, was there for her? She could not but be out of her sphere here, nonplussed, a wanderer from some better star. It had been much to find in the world one creature too good for the world.

She had not been too good. Here, and not in one paper only, was where it said about her, the bottles, the lover, the luxury West-End flat. She had had other men friends; there nearly had been a fight. It all only came to a matter of expensiveness; there was no refinement. A nicer look and a nicer voice, but there she was with someone she was not married to – who had he not run out on the roof, tight, would be still there. She had seemed so respectable – respectable as one of those lost Seale faces – but there she had stood in court, telling them all. That was that; simply that again. There was nobody to admire; there was no alternative. No unextinguished watch-light remained, after all, burning in any window, however far away. In hopes of what, then, was one led on, led on? How long, looking back on it, it had lasted – that dogged, timid, unfaithfully-followed hope!

The November Sunday faded, as it had begun, in mist – Louie came over gooseflesh, scrambled up from the rug and put on the kettle. She was nursing her teacup in her hands when Connie, still gummed up with afternoon sleep, marched in towards her over the sheets of newspaper, the Officer's Midnight Prank headlines scattered over the floor. '*Careful*,' cried Louie, hauntedly turning, 'do be!' Connie, later, twitched up one sheet to re-read it, sucking a tooth. However, nothing connected Louie's refined new friend of the other evening with the dubious heroine of this tragedy – no name had then been spoken: now no name could be. Oh, if Connie had guessed she was being held out on! . . . Nor was this first secret to be the last – for, the long-term effects on Louie of Stella's fall were kept hidden, throughout the time to follow, with unexpected care. Louie's dropping back again into vagrant habits remained unknown. No such very great degree of dissimulation turned out to be, after all, necessary; for it happened that Connie relaxed her vigilance – a friend who had been aggravating her for some time began to be more bother than he was worth. Not so much the friend as an uncharacteristic and nagging inability to decide just how much any man *was* worth seized upon Connie, throwing her into moodiness, keeping her late abroad when she was not at the post, and confining her talk, when she did as of old look in, to a dire obsessional monologue, Connie had no longer an eye to spare. Also there went on, throughout that winter, being never a word as to hopes of leave from Tom, no longer in India now owing to being required in North Africa.

1942, still with no Second Front, ran out: nothing more than a sort of grinding change of gear for the up-grade was to be felt till the next war year steadied into its course. Cryptic were new 1943 block calendars. February, the Germans capitulated at Stalingrad; March, the Eighth Army broke through the Mareth Line. North African spring teemed with pursuits and astronomic surrenders, with a victoriousness hard, still, not to associate with the enemy. July, the Sicilian landings; the Russian opening of their great leafy Orel summer drive. Mussolini out. September, Italians out, but leaving Italy to it. Landings, beach-heads, Russian tanks lurching across the screens in London; November, Italian rivers, however, being crossed by us in strength. Winter known to have come by the Germans having their winter line shattered. Mussolini back. Pictures, less to be relished than had been hoped, of Berlin learning how it had been for London. The Big Three photographed smiling at Teheran. The idea of the European Fortress. The day after Christmas we sank the *Scharnhorst*, and upon the Russians having advanced up to sixty miles in five days in the Kiev salient, at the same time widening a breach to a front of a hundred and eight miles, 1943 expired.

War's being global meant it ran off the edges of maps; it was uncontainable. What was being done, for instance, against the Japanese was heard of but never grasped in London. There were too many theatres of war.

1944 was the year in which there could not but be the Second Front. General Smuts called it the Year of Destiny; the bombers continued to carry on preparatory work. As early as January we broke the Gustav Line; the Russians announced the lifting of the blockade of Leningrad. February, in Italy we encircled ten enemy divisions, but the Germans opened up against Anzio beach-head, which held. The wiping-out of Monte Cassino caused an uncertain breath to be drawn in cinemas: all this was going to be necessary, and more. Reflections were cut short by the renewal of air attacks on London – a five-night February season to be known as the Little Blitz.

During that week, Roderick was at Mount Morris, having got permission to view for the first time, and arrange for the administration of, his property. In mufti, he had arrived in the damp of a late-winter evening, alone. Work kept his mother in London: he was sorry and not sorry, she not sorry. Donovan, who had been listening for the hackney car, had stood holding a lamp in the high doorway at the top of the steps: he preceded his master into the hall, set down the lamp on the table and made a speech. Roderick, having listened less to the words than their echo through this house of his own, replied. Later, alone in the library, his first act had been to read the instructions printed by Cousin Francis on the cards stuck round the picture over the fire. He waited for Donovan to return in order to ask him: 'Who is "Lady C."?'

'That used to be Lady Condie.'

'What, dead now, is she? – In that case,' Roderick said, 'we shan't be getting any more messages from *her*.' He plucked from the picture that particular card, tore it across and dropped it into the fire.

'– *Did* the river rise, this winter?' he went on. 'Did it get into the Lower Lodge?'

'Not so far,' admitted Donovan. 'But it could. Mr Morris always had a scheme for removing the Lodge to some place else. Wasn't it funny, sir, them taking away Montgomery from the Eighth Army?'

But Roderick was back to reading the cards. 'What's become of the dogs which used to be the puppies? My mother said nothing about them. They weren't put down, I hope?'

'No, sir; the instructions would have been a pity; they were breedy little dogs – I put them out through the country. I could get you a pup out of one of them any time. It was only the old big dog the master shot before he went off to England – Would there be any thought of bringing the master back?'

'I don't see why not,' said Roderick, struck, 'eventually. His bones ought to be there. But of course the whole thing was a muddle – I was never let know what was going on.'

Donovan stepped back and held open the door wider, to enable Mary to enter with the large supper tray. Roderick absently eyed the younger of the two girls of whom his mother had spoken. 'I wish it were not so late!' he exclaimed suddenly. 'I wish I could see – *is* it going to be a very dark night? I want to go out and get the hang of everything – so far, I hardly realize I have arrived. Not that this is not a very nice room, of course,' he added, respectfully looking up at the ceiling. 'Larger and higher, if anything, than I had imagined. But it's baffling not to know what goes on outside it. – *Is it a very dark night?*'

'I should say middling. You ought to be able to see your hand before you. Then will I not bar the door?'

'You never need bar the door: I shall see to that.'

Mary, who had been studying Roderick without speaking, gave a final touch to the tray, then left the room: Donovan, though prepared to follow his daughter, spoke once more. 'There's a more deceptive drop from here to the river than you might think,' he said, though even so with detachment. 'I even heard how once a carriage and pair of horses pitched over it in the darkness before we had the parapet – and again there's a rocky drop from the Alpine Walk, if you should be thinking of going that way. The rest of it might be slippery but it's harmless. – However, sir, from all I hear you should have come out of a wary training. They'd want you to be precise for a war of this kind.'

'Oh, I shall know where I am once I get going,' said Roderick, confidently pulling a chair up to the tray, raising lids and beginning to eat supper. 'I've been told what's there: I must just make sure that it *is*.'

Coming in late that night he bolted, barred and chained up the door behind him, piously but with an inexpert clatter – the little lamp like a holy lamp the Donovans had left burning for him on the hall chest meanwhile magnifying his shadow. He had forgotten to ask, and they had been too deeply stirred to remember to show him, in which of the rooms upstairs he was to sleep; he had therefore to investigate, opening door after door. The darkness was nothing to him but a veil between himself and tomorrow, and his nostrils sifted out nothing but an enticing newness from the plastery smells. The house, where he was concerned, might have come into being only just in time to be here tonight; he remembered his mother's saying he must have been conceived here, but only perfunctorily did he wonder in which room. Drawn into one at last by a glow of embers and the sight of his bag put down at the foot of an opened bed, he looked no further: a row of bootjacks along the top of a press, straps on a hook and a parade of liniment-bottles along the chimneypiece told him he was succeeding to Cousin Francis. The master's bedroom had crimson hangings and paper, against which what looked like mahogany temples stood. Whistling, Roderick began to throw his things out of his bag.

But he had come in full of the outdoors, which welled up in him when, having put out the lamp, he laid down his head on the old man's pillow. Forms, having made themselves known through no particular sense, forms whose existence he was not to doubt again, loomed and dwelled within him. He had felt all round him heights weighed down upon by night, mysterious declivities, the breath through the unmoving air of moving water. Something more than silence there had been to be heard, though in the trees' leafless tops there was not even the rustle of a sleepy rook, and though throughout the relaxed woods not a bough grated or twig snapped. The invisible openness of the fields gave out not less stillness than the fern-rotted hollows; he had come to the humid stoniness of the garden wall, steadied himself on the unequal metalling of the cart tracks, put his hand on gates, struck out a twang from wire, established by touch the vital differing unhumanity of rocks, corrugated iron, tree trunks. He had from all points turned and returned to trace the elusive river-glimmer below him. Dark ate the outlines of the house as it ate the outlines of the hills and drank from the broken distances of the valley. The air had been night itself, re-imprinted by every one of his movements upon his face and hands – and still, now that he was indoors and gone to bed, impregnating every part of his body it had not sensibly touched. He could not sleep during this memory of the air.

It had not been cold: the coming of winter to a stop had been most felt in the absolute nullness of tonight. It could be that Nature had withdrawn, leaving everything to be nothing but the identity of Mount Morris. The place had concentrated upon Roderick its being: this was the hour of the never-before – gone were virgin dreams with anything they had had of himself in them, anything they had had of the picturesque, sweet, easy, strident. He was left possessed, oppressed and in awe. He heard the pulse in his temple beating into the pillow; he was followed by the sound of his own footsteps over his own land. The consummation woke in him, for the first time, the concept and fearful idea of death, his. Ahead were his five days more here; ahead again was the possibility of his not coming back. He had not till tonight envisaged not coming back from war.

Striking a match, he admired the time it burned. Then he heaved himself higher in the high bed, bracing his shoulders against the sharp-scrolled bedhead, arms folded, in order to set himself to consider the idea of succession. His instinctive antipathy to any abstract thought sent him away from that to his three fathers – the defeated Victor, the determining Cousin Francis, the unadmitted stepfather Robert: there was a confluence in him, at the moment, of the unequal three. How had *they* made out? Had there not been a prematurity about each of their three deaths, not last the obstinate old man's? Or, had they each, when it had come to a point, laid down what had become impossible to finish? Accept, as against that, that nothing might *be* possible to finish – who would, indeed, aspire to be the final man? It was a matter of continuing – but what, what? As to that, there ought to be access to the mindless knowledge locked up in rocks, in the stayers-on. Meanwhile, the Fortress of Europe was waiting to be stormed by Roderick: everything, everything, everything had to turn on that – everything but the February nocturnal existence of this place, which would know other Februaries. Should Roderick not come back . . .

Recollecting that he ought to make a will, he in his own mind mildly reproached his mother for her failure to prompt him. By a written will one made subject some other person – but he saw that what worked most on the world, on him, were the unapprehendable inner wills of the dead. Death could not estimate what it left behind it. Robert's had left grief – what more, if there had been anything more, Roderick's mother had not told him. Roderick reflected that, as things were, there would be nobody but his mother to be *his* heir, either: he felt this with chagrin both for himself and her – between them, they should have come to something further than this. He began to mutiny – which took the form of striking match after match till he had succeeded in relighting the little lamp. That done, he was once more inside four walls: drawing down in the bed he immediately fell asleep.

Next day was full of things to be seen and done. 'As I've been telling O'Connell,' he said to Donovan, 'for the present all we can hope to do is, keep this place ticking over till I get back. After that, of course, it will definitely have to begin to pay: Mount Morris has got to be my living. To start with, I'll have to learn – go to one or another of those agricultural set-ups for two, three, four years. Everything's got to be done scientifically these days; one can't just go fluffing along as an amateur. And I ought to put in capital, if I'm to get returns.'

'That way, you could sink a terrible lot of money.'

'Not if one's organized. And I should never have a terrible lot of money *to* sink,' he added, looking at Donovan formidably.

'Mr Morris used to be the one for considering improvements. It was wonderful the things he was to do – he was showing me pictures of machinery, and there were fellows for ever coming and going giving us demonstrations, until latterly the war came to be the greater interest – We raised the boat for you, sir, but she isn't much; she's decayed.'

'What boat?' said Roderick, blank. He recovered himself and said: 'Oh yes, of course; *the* boat. Well, that's a pity, but never mind: thanks. What a lot of work. I can't see, I must say, why it was ever sunk.'

'Precautions. I should say Mr Robertson had that effect.'

'Who was Mr Robertson?'

'You would never know. It could be he was keeping some sort of eye on this country. Those were suspicious times, before they turned aside the Germans,' said Donovan, dispassionately feeding wood to the range – they were in the kitchen. Two chickens fled from the swinging foot of Roderick, who was seated on the edge of the table – both girls had melted out of the kitchen as he came in, leaving a candle burning beside a teapot. The face of either Hannah or Mary appeared from time to time in the darkness of the doorway, but then always footsteps were to be heard padding lightly away again down the stone passage. 'There was nothing to show in the end of it all,' said Donovan. 'However, the master had a great time with ideas.'

'From what you tell me,' said Roderick, 'this Robertson must have been a silly man – I can't say I've ever heard of him, and I don't wonder. Intelligence my eye. What did he take the German Army for? It was really rather a good thing they never landed.'

Donovan listened, impartial, to the roar in the range.

'A chap turned up at the funeral,' went on Roderick, 'but his name was Harrison.'

'It could be: it was some name of that sort – Did you hear anything from London?' Donovan asked, facing round sombrely and abruptly.

'No. Why?'

'They're bombing away again. Isn't the mistress in it?'

'Yes. Why?'

'You left her very exposed.'

'Yes, Donovan, yes. But she's always done what she's liked.'

'I should say she'd always done what she could. Whatever she went through, she's very gentle. All the same, it was a pity you couldn't prevail on her to wait here.'

'Wait here what for?'

'The better times.'

'Oh.'

Harrison, back again, stood in the middle of a street, otherwise empty, illuminated by a chandelier flare. During the pulse of silence between the overhead throbbing and the bark of the guns, the flare made the street like a mirrored drawing-room. Above where Harrison stood peering at something jotted on an envelope, white-green incandescence flowed from the lovely shapely symbol, which slowly descended as it died – the sky to the east reflected flamingo-pink nobody could have taken to be the dawn, the west was jagged with flames. Ostensibly the population of London was underground: now and then could be heard an important clanging of N.F.S. or ambulance bells; once or twice a private car shot past. Bombardment reopened upon Harrison doggedly footing it in the direction of Stella's new flat, automatically swerving clear of buildings liable at any time to be struck and fall.

The block she lived in teetered its height up into the dangerous night. Inside, no porter was in the lodge: Harrison for himself set in motion the gothic lift. The halt of the hum and the rattle of gates on her floor gave her time to wonder before her bell rang: when it did, she came to the door, though promptly, with the air of one who had already decided this must be a mistake. She wore an overcoat and was carrying a cat. They stared at one another. She exclaimed: 'Where have you been?' The cat gave a start and tried to run up her shoulder.

'I hope this is not an awkward hour to drop in?'

'Why, no,' she said, civilly if uncertainly, 'I wasn't doing anything particular – reading, listening to the guns. Come in.' She went ahead of him through another door to put the cat down; while he had, owing to the unfamiliarity of this other, no less minute, hall, a renewal of difficulty over the old business of putting down his hat. 'Yes, it's been quite a time since we met,' he agreed, eventually following her in. – 'I see,' he added, glancing about the carpet as though he'd have liked to check up on a first impression, 'you've got a cat now.'

'Why, no; it's not mine. Nothing in this flat is – either,' she said with a vagrant, echo-aroused smile. 'It belongs next door, but its people are out, away, and I think it's nervous.'

'Pussy, hey, pussy – where are you?' said Harrison, clicking his fingers. Nothing having emerged, he squinted round to read the name of her book, left open face downward on the black fur hearthrug. 'Quite like old times,' he remarked, 'quite a dirty night. Animals don't care for this sort of thing.'

'Quite like old times,' she said, kneeling down, with her back to him, by the fire. 'Before I met you, even.' She warmed her hands. '*Is* it cold in here? Perhaps not – Do sit down,' she added, over her shoulder. 'What have you been doing?'

'One thing and another. In fact, been out of this country. But that would be a long story.'

'Yes, I expect it would. You didn't lose your job, then? Once or twice I wondered whether you had.'

'What, me? Oh, you mean over *that* affair? Oh no-no-no-no-no. Still, I was sorry that slipped up. So you held that against me?'

While she still did not answer, he sat himself down quickly in one of two armchairs, taking advantage of the very last moment in which it might be possible or at any rate sensitive to do so. She registered what had gone on behind her without turning her head. He seemed glad, eager, to take this as, however negative, a reply. Anything more coming? From her, apparently not – anything further seemed to be due from him. Forward in the armchair he began frowning, pushing fist into palm. 'Yes, that was bad,' he agreed. 'In my own way I may say I took quite a knock.'

'You did?' Stella said, rising from the hearthrug as though there were something weakening in that perpetual warming

373

of the hands. She searched the chimneypiece for cigarettes to offer him, meanwhile recollecting that she and Robert still owed him what was left of a packet. A burst of close-up gunfire shook the building – whereupon she started to pace about, looking under the furniture for the cat. Harrison, silenced by the guns, seemed at the same time to feel exonerated from making any secret of the fact that he was following her with his eyes – even, when her movements took her behind his chair, turning right round to see where she was. She scooped up the cat and stood with it held against her: its fur seemed to shrink and dampen as a stick of bombs fell diagonally across the middle distance. Then it all died down. 'It's so long,' she said, 'since we've had this. Hasn't it come back different?'

Remarking the unsteadiness of her hand on the cat's flank, he said, with intimacy and insolence: 'Perhaps you were not so sorry I came, then?'

'I wish you had come before. There was a time when I had so much to say to you. There once was so much I wanted to know. After I gave up thinking I should see you again, I still went on talking and talking to you in my own mind – so I cannot really have felt you were dead, I think, because one doesn't go on talking and talking to any one of *them*: more one goes on hearing what they said, piecing and repiecing it together to try and make out something they had not time to say – possibly even had not had time to know. There still must be something that matters that one has forgotten, forgotten because at the time one did not realize how much it did matter. Yet most of all there is something one has got to forget – that is, if it is to be possible to live. The more wars there are, I suppose, the more we shall learn how to be survivors – Yes, I missed you. *Your* dropping out left me with completely nothing. What made you?'

'That would be a long –'

'– I'm not asking for stories. What happened?'

'For one thing, I was switched.'

She stared at him.

'That was how it was,' he said, with a take-it-or-leave-it shrug. 'There was quite a bit going on around that time, if you remember. That was the long and the short of it: I was switched.'

'I see,' she said, paused, and put down the cat. 'Well, here I still am,' she said in a different tone. 'Though now, as you see, *here*.'

'Here, you're still fairly snug?' he asked, looking round the room, making an obvious effort to see it all as other than sheer 'otherness' of surroundings. These walls, of an unreflecting brown, were hung round with a set of Old London prints; there was an upright piano, a locked-looking glazed bookcase. The neck of a reading-lamp had been so twisted as to direct light on to the sage-green cushions of an armchair at present empty of her. Writing paper was stacked on a folding table, on which stood a wineglass holding a bunch of snowdrops – damaged, perhaps unpinned from her coat. From the shortness of the substantial curtains it could be guessed that the windows were set in high. He knew himself to be on the seventh floor. A dull little gun-metal ash tray caught his eye – 'Funny, you know,' he confessed, 'how I still seem to be seeing that other place. That other place where you were.'

'Yes?'

'I have so often thought of our times there.'

'What *was* our quarrel?' she hesitated, after asking him this, but then sat boldly down in the sage-green chair, full in the light. 'What did I do?'

'You were wonderful. As, a matter of fact, you are tonight – whenever you are, you are. I don't know how it is!'

'Please!' she cried, holding up her hand sharply. 'I asked you a question. *What* happened? After all, you killed Robert.'

'Now how do you make out that?'

'Only you know what happened,' she went on, indifferently giving this as a fact. 'You know what I don't: the whole of the story. You chose to take that with you: you disappeared. For a long time, that's been what I've wanted to ask you. Now you're back – but *now*, why? Why ask? Possibly the time's passed.'

He shifted his feet, equivocally, on the black hearthrug.

'What, not altogether?' she said, as though in reply to the movement. 'Very well, then in that case, tell me – you knew Robert was going to be arrested that night? How much say in that had you? When had that been decided? – or was it not?'

'*I* always rather took it,' Harrison said, 'that he himself rather took it the game was up. In that case, frankly, he knew as much as I did. That was up to him, naturally – *I* was out.'

'Since when?'

'Since the night before.'

'Since the night we quarrelled?'

'Quarrel?' he said. 'When?'

She put out a hand and bent the lamp away from her. 'If you don't remember,' she said, 'perhaps it never happened. Perhaps I've thought too much.'

'I've thought, all right.' He stopped to frown at a thumb-nail, then looked across at her now in-shadow face. 'About this thing between us – but how "a quarrel"?'

The guns rested her by opening up once more: she leaned back to hear them, acquiescent, against the cushions. The bulb of the lamp in its socket and frames of the window shook – otherwise, this room remained a dark-lined kernel of silence under the flare-pale resounding sky. In the subsidence of the shocks of the guns could be heard the lofty drumming of the raider: while this lasted one kind of utter solution was in the offing – but no, it was not to be that way; nothing fell. The guns, made fools of, died out again, askance. 'No right *or* wrong to it after all, perhaps?' she at last said.

Harrison, who had sat through the minutes with a concentrated appearance of hearing nothing, went on: 'Yes, thought about you – and in some pretty queer places.'

'All this time, you've been out of England?'

'Obviously – surely?'

'Still, you knew where to find me.'

'Oh, one soon picks up threads . . . Well, here we are, back to it. Or, don't you think so?' He fixed his eyes on her with an only wavering certainty, as though, possibly, for guidance.

'No – one never goes back. One never is where one was. I see you may have been right; I see there may *have* been something between us – if there had not *been* something, how should we both, tonight, know it wasn't there any more? If you had been here immediately after – if you had not disappeared when you did – who knows? You were the last of him. – No, not that: I am the last of him. You then? Were you then, somehow, love's necessary missing part? You brought that into us, if you killed him. But now, you and I are no longer two of three. From between us some pin has been drawn out: we're apart. We're not where we were – look, not even any more in the same room. The pattern's been swept away, so where's the meaning? Think!'

He only repeated: 'But I have thought about you,' in an unrelinquishing tone.

'There was a night – yes, that last time we met – when I said: "Very well, then, yes," but you sent me home.'

'Yes: that was not what I wanted.'

'What *did* you want, then, when it came to the point?'

He fitted his thumb-nails together, did not answer.

'You did not know; you did not know what to do.'

'What, didn't I?' he said in a driven way. He got up suddenly and walked across to the table with the snow-drops; he stood over them – 'Pretty,' he stated under his breath, giving the bruised petals an automatic touch. 'If you mean,' he added, 'that evening there was the dog, I don't remember. More, there was that other evening when there was the rain. All I know is, as I say, I've thought about you. I didn't come back all this way only to say good-bye – did I?'

'You don't think there's any virtue in a good-bye? I do. I've wanted to be able to say good-bye to you; till this could be possible you've haunted me. What's unfinished haunts one; what's unhealed haunts one. – Harrison?'

'That's the first time you've called me anything, I think.'

'I don't know your other, your Christian name.'

'I don't know that you'd care for that very much,' he said, shouldering into the curtain behind the table.

'Why, what's wrong with it? – what is it?'

'Robert.'

'Oh, I see . . . . Well, I expect in any case I should have gone on thinking of you as Harrison. I'd been going to say –'

she dropped her wrist across her eyes, as though the averted lamp were still full upon her. 'I'd been going to say, good-bye any way you like. Stay tonight, if you like, if that would finish your thoughts.'

He picked up the glass of snowdrops, then put it down again.

'No, I thought not,' she said. 'What's the good of doing anything for the sake of the past?'

'No, it's more,' he said, with his back to her, 'that I never did, remember, expect you to do anything for nothing.'

'What is "nothing"?'

'As I told you, I never have been loved – No,' he added, coming briskly back from the table, taking up a position on the hearthrug to stare down, more unequivocally than he ever yet had, at the chair with her in it, 'my forte has I suppose always rather more been, plans. – What are yours, for instance, these days? You staying on here?'

'For one thing, I think I am going to be married.'

'Indeed. Is that so?' He paused, needing all he had to keep in command his features during their change, their change into the expression of a violent, fundamental relief. 'That's so, then?' But he now began to re-eye her with severe closeness, on behalf of an unknown somebody else. 'All the same, what do you mean, you "think", though? As to a thing of that kind, surely you ought to *know*?'

'Well, I do know – now.'

'Ha-ha: better – May one ask who it is?'

She told him, adding: 'He's a cousin of a cousin.'

'Rather more than that, he's a brigadier, surely?'

'Well, I know,' she said, with a touch of the old irritation. 'So you think this is an extraordinary thing for him to do?'

'No, I wouldn't –'

'– I agree, it's nice of him.'

'No, now, come Stella, what I do mean's this: if this *is* the case, this is quite a different affair. You've got yourself to take care of. What do you think you're doing, skittering round in a top-floor flat on a night like this, with this heavy stuff coming down all over the place? Far from fair on the chap: you should think of him. You might not give a damn *what* happened – I must say, you gave me that impression, first. Does that make sense, now you've got prospects?'

'Prospects have alternatives.'

'Collect that cat, if you must, but if this keeps on you ought to think of cutting down to the hall.'

'I always have left things open. – As a matter of fact, though, I think the raid's over.'

'In that case . . .' said Harrison, looking at his watch. 'Or would you rather I stayed till the All Clear?'

Towards the end of that week of nights, Louie and Connie were doing their hair and faces, side by side, in front of the long horizontal mirror of the marbled subterranean Ladies of a West-End café. This was about ten o'clock in the evening. Connie's work on herself was thorough; Louie had for some time stood in a vacuum, twiddling at her bow clip, before, turning away her head from her own reflection, she said that she was going to have a baby.

Connie continued work on her fringe.

'Oh, you never listen to what I say?'

'You're always saying something,' grumbled her friend, groping around the basin for invisible hairpins. 'What is it now?'

380

'I said – it looks as if I was going to have a baby.'

Connie hissed: 'Shut up! – Where do you think we are?' She cast a wary rapid look round the place. Louie, however, had not chosen her moment as badly as it seemed – no other ladies happened to be down here. 'The things you think of! However could –?' All the same, slowly she put her comb down. Their eyes met in the glass.

Less in despair than fatalism, Connie exclaimed: 'Well, you *have* been a silly girl . . . Haven't you?'

Louie, as though in extenuation, said: 'Well, it's been on my mind.'

'I told and told you! Nature's ever so sharp!'

Louie, not without dignity, assented: she hung her head.

Connie, in a mechanical stunned way, amassed the rest of the hairpins and pronged them back into different curls of her fringe – but then, half-way through, the very ordinariness of the action seemed to unnerve her: she stopped dead, hands up, and cried out: 'Now we *are* in the soup! – For example, what's your husband going to say?'

'That's what I wondered.' Louie frowned and turned on a hot tap: she watched the strong jet of steamy water rush round and round the basin. 'Under other circumstances, he might have been pleased. When you think of all he and I have been through together, this seems not natural, Connie, that he should not know.'

'What do you expect *me* to do?'

'Well, I don't know really. I was more wondering what I should do myself.'

'Still, you come asking me. You know you do, you come asking me. Everyone comes asking me.' Connie shot out a hand and turned off the hot tap furiously: the wasted steam died down. 'You mad?' she cried. 'When the King himself only uses five inches in his bath? Seizing this occasion to take leave of *all* your senses? What do you think this makes you? – You're only one of many.'

This Louie seized upon. 'Well, I *am*, only, aren't I – just one of many?' A sort of illumination widened over her features – slowly, but with a sureness from which one might have suspected that it was not new to them. And worse, in the view of Connie, this settled into a look of inward complacency, even sublimity. She admitted: 'I've sometimes thought that myself.'

'Oho,' lashed out Connie, 'so you feel fine? That's fine.'

Louie flinched at once. She set and unset her lips; she held on to the edge of the marble slab – meaninglessly, unless this were for support. Between her reflection, and Connie's, and Connie's actual face, no one of them longer to be confronted, she simply physically did not seem to know which way to turn. 'Don't *you* be angry: you're the first I've told! How does it seem of me, then – so awful? Half of the time this is not half real to me, Connie; more like a thing I hear of. I don't know how I should feel: I could equally laugh or cry. Whatever *is* this? – I've got to see from you. You *are* angry?'

'No, you great sissy, no: I just give you up.'

'I would not for anything have upset you – perhaps I've been wrong?'

'Such a time to choose,' Connie could not help pointing out, 'after night after night of enemy action. Still, it had to come out.' She began to pack her compact, comb, and other etceteras into her handbag; she shut this with a very decisive click, which made her think of something more to be said. 'Who was it? – You got any idea?'

Louie, in what was just not confusion, began to ramble to and fro searching for gloves – one had fallen off the marble on to the floor: she remembered Stella's grace of two years ago. These naturally were not the same pair; they were a degree more fancy, fringed at the wrists, and still more mauled-looking. She stooped to pick up the fallen. 'Must be some friend I made . . . I don't think the name would mean anything to you, Connie.'

'*Which* name wouldn't mean anything to me?'

'You and I've seen so little of each other, this last year.'

Connie, placed her bag in position under her elbow, glanced once towards Louie, down a perspective of wash-basins, with no expression at all. 'Rightie-ho, then.' Life, it was to be seen, selected its own methods of going on. 'First and foremost,' she said, 'we had better do what we had intended: eat – That's right, that's right: take one or two more looks round. What are you leaving behind you *this* time, I do wonder? – Having had our supper, how about if we thought? We shall require to.'

She guided Louie firmly towards the exit staircase, on which they passed two ladies on their way down.

The baby, it was established, would be due about the middle of July. 'No doubt we shall be having the Second Front by that time, also,' remarked Louie. Her big sturdy build made her state not, for a good time longer, evident: Connie advised her staying on at the factory for as long as could be. Her only pregnancy sickness was for home, for Seale-on-Sea – but ever more strictly, as with each month the invasion of Europe by us loomed nearer, was the ban on civilian entry into that area being enforced. However, now in London, it came to seem to her, *all* eyes were turning towards the coast, the sea. Spring days growing longer grew more momentous; there were calculations as to the moon; day and night London shook with Invasion traffic roaring through it to unknown ports. Expectation came to its height, and stood: everybody waited. Louie found herself looking constantly into that very photograph of Tom which had once forbidden her; she felt herself beckoned into that gaze of abstention and futurity – was she not in her own way also drawing abreast of what was to be? Tom himself was in the Italy fighting: it went more against the grain with her, each time she wrote a letter, to dissimulate – why should not he reach out a hand to her as she was? She was his wife. She required to tell him of her sense of no longer being alone. That this obstinate vision of what *should* be could exist side-by-side with instructed fear of being cast out by him was a miracle: not a thing supported it. Nothing, nothing was to be said for Louie. What *would* he say?

From fear of seeing where it said what he would have a right to say, she took against newspapers – whose front pages were themselves being pervaded by pregnant secrecy. When it came to the time when Connie judged that Chilcombe Street might begin to notice – in which case, who knew who might not take it upon themselves to write Tom one of those wicked letters? – Louie was moved by Connie into another room which had been found, about half a mile away: well that she had got that money to draw on, now paying two rents. Chilcombe Street remained her postal address; she headed letters to Italy as from there. In the emptied first-floor Chilcombe Street double room, Connie considered it best to install herself – otherwise, who knew who might not get their foot round that door? Tom with no place to come back to? – that would cap all. Connie, at the start, had done what seemed only right in suggesting there could, of course, be *one* way out: she always had the address. She had not really, however, expected Louie to have that much sense, or whatever else it took. 'Right,' she therefore left it. 'I somehow knew you'd be stubborn. In fact I'm beginning to suspect this is what you want.'

'It wasn't what I *wanted*.'

'So you say. But now look how it's got hold of you.'

'All things being the same, I sooner would be a mother, I now see. I can't somehow wish to be as before.'

'What you *were* in aid of,' Connie had to admit, 'often was a mystery to me.'

'There's always only this: Tom not knowing,' Louie always repeated, with that movement of her inhabited eyes. 'I do so wish Connie, you'd think of some way I could put it rightly – What should I say?'

Automatically the question repeated itself, more and more taxing Connie as Louie's passiveness biggened with her body. Left in the world of reality, at bay, Connie fell back a little on the general belief that the Second Front would, somehow, set up a moratorium as to everything. The Second Front was thought to be, like a race, fixed for a day or two after Whitsun. Whitsun went by in an irreproachable glare of racing weather: still nothing happened. Ultimately, one afternoon in Chilcombe Street, off duty, Connie took up her pen – only to stare for some minutes longer at the cloth of the table at which, evening after evening, Tom watched by Louie had studied his technical books. It could be possible that his eyes, shifting from the page as he stopped and thought, had left some key to his ego, his mentality, in the tablecloth pattern *he* must have traced not less absorbedly than did Connie now. She started slowly to write:

Dear Tom: I take up my pen as a close friend, whom you may have heard of, of your wife Louie. Am hoping you will let my intruding pass, owing to her not knowing quite what to say, as you will understand shortly. It would mean much to her to know you saw in the true light what I shall now tell you. She has been quite a curious girl in the way she has been missing and fretting for you, always straying about like a dog with no one, and also you have to take into account how completely her parents were wiped out, unsettling her. I know this is much to ask a man, but all I can say is that I have had recently to take much that might seem peculiar into account myself. It is no use for you or me to judge, you simply have to allow for how anything is going to take a person, as to which there is no saying till you see. She thinks so highly of you that it would be of assistance if you could bring yourself to understand how it all was, and therefore think of her fondly at this time, owing to all she is going through for your sake. There is no disguising that left to ourselves many of us are peculiar, one mistake leading on to others, so must trust you will see what is to blame. I fear I ought now to come to the point, letting you know that, consequently, Louie is now about –

– Connie was interrupted by an imperative ringing of the street door bell, followed by rat-tat-tat on the knocker. Stubbing her nib on her writing-pad she listened, persecutedly, lowering her head, waiting. The attack renewed itself: no step of anybody going to the door was to be heard anywhere in the afternoon house. She put her thumbs to her ears, re-read the letter as far as it had got, then all at once found herself thinking slowly: 'How if I never had to finish it?' She went down and took in the telegram – which was, indeed, for Louie.

Having opened the telegram, Connie stood in awe. 'Nearly, I *was* presumptuous,' she thought. Questions to which we find no answer find their own. She set out to walk through the torpid glary May afternoon streets to that other room, just across the railway line, where Louie was.

'So if I had worried, it would have been wrongly, for nothing,' was one of the first things Louie remarked, later. 'I should now be blaming myself for not having known better – instead of which, it was wonderful how I did. That always came, you see, from knowing him patient with me from first to last, however upright he was – What've you done with where it says? I want to have that, to keep.'

'The telegram – do you?'

'Why yes: for the kid.'

'They're *across*!'

It had happened – under a curdled windy improbable June night. The whole of the story narrowed down to Louie, still with *her* hour ahead, heavily going to her window. Voices were in the street below; multiplied, one voice from dozens of radios came lancing across and across itself out of dozens of windows standing open. Louie leaned out and shouted: 'What – is that true?' It was. There was, however, nothing for her to do but sit down again to the seven-year-old stitching – until she, uncontrollably, dropped her work, pushed up her cheeks with both knuckles, began to pray. There was at the same time being an uncoordinated movement into churches. The unexpected-expected day, with its elsewhere-ness, ran its broadcast-echoing course. You could not take back what had been done. The lucid outgoing vision, the vigil for the fighters, lasted ten days more, till the Secret Weapon started: then, it was shameful how fear wrenched thoughts home – droning *things*, mindlessly making for you, thick and fast, day and night, tore the calico of London, raising obscene dust out of the sullen bottom mind. There was no normal hour. Connie first brought Louie back to Chilcombe Street – what did it matter, any longer? – then attempted to run her out of London – but, to where? On and off, on and off sounded the sirens in the nightmare sunlessness: perpetually, Connie had to be dashing to the post.

'I should not care to go among strangers,' reiterated the sweating Louie, holding tight to the end of the big familiar bed. Then again the wail would go up the air. 'The siren, again – whatever are they thinking of?' 'That's the all bloody clear, dear – you never learn, do you?' 'Does not make much difference, though, does it, Connie?'

The boy was born a little before his time.

Christened Thomas Victor, he took no notice of anything – however, Louie agreed she should take him out of London now he was born. He and she, accordingly, departed from the very door of the hospital into abeyance in a Midland county, in which luck guided her to a still handsome second-hand pram. This pram she learned to wheel, brake, tilt, even to tow behind her as she progressed gazingly along the windows of shopping streets. The baby's intention to survive put itself across her and

388

taught her sense: the clearance, across at the other side, of the last of the enemy out of the Channel ports made it possible for her to return to Seale-on-Sea, an orderly mother.

The sea, there, glittered as though nothing had happened.

She installed herself in the lodgings. Then, that very afternoon of her return, she could not wait; she took Tom straight round to his grandparents'. The thin air which had taken the house's place was, now that she stood and breathed in it, after all full of today and sunshine; the ridges left by the foundations feathered and stirred with grass in light and shadow. It was September, dahlias and asters blooming only a garden or two away. This was, as it always had been, a very quiet road, inland, with lime trees planted along the pavement. The baby slept in his pram on the flat site of the entrance-path to the house: uphill, the church clock struck, and she looked up at the sound.

Next day, the sun was succeeded by a white quiet light. Just after six o'clock in the evening, Louie wheeled the perambulator some way out of the town, along the canal path, towards the marsh. Reeds grew out into the still water; ahead, there was distance as far as the eye could see – a thoughtless extension of her now complete life. Across the canal the hills rose, bare, above the other bank's reflected oak trees. No other soul passed; not a sheep, even, was cropping anywhere near by. A minute or two ago our homecoming bombers, invisibly high up, had droned over: the baby had not stirred – every day she saw him growing more like Tom. But now there began another sound – she turned and looked up into the air behind her. She gathered Tom quickly out of the pram and held him up, hoping he too might see, and perhaps remember. Three swans were flying a straight flight. They passed overhead, disappearing in the direction of the west.

THE HISTORY OF VINTAGE

The famous American publisher Alfred A. Knopf (1892–1984) founded Vintage Books in the United States in 1954 as a paperback home for the authors published by his company. Vintage was launched in the United Kingdom in 1990 and works independently from the American imprint although both are part of the international publishing group, Random House.

Vintage in the United Kingdom was initially created to publish paperback editions of books bought by the prestigious literary hardback imprints in the Random House Group such as Jonathan Cape, Chatto & Windus, Hutchinson and later William Heinemann, Secker & Warburg and The Harvill Press. There are many Booker and Nobel Prize-winning authors on the Vintage list and the imprint publishes a huge variety of fiction and non-fiction. Over the years Vintage has expanded and the list now includes great authors of the past – who are published under the Vintage Classics imprint – as well as many of the most influential authors of the present. In 2012 Vintage Children's Classics was launched to include the much-loved authors of our youth.

For a full list of the books Vintage publishes,
please visit our website
www.vintage-books.co.uk

For book details and other information about the classic authors we publish, please visit the Vintage Classics website
www.vintage-classics.info

Description pps 29-31

Chagrin

Conjunction

Controvertible

www.vintage-classics.info